This Is My Daughter

A NOVEL

ROXANA ROBINSON

SCRIBNER PAPERBACK FICTION
PUBLISHED BY SIMON & SCHUSTER

SCRIBNER PAPERBACK FICTION
Simon & Schuster, Inc.
Rockefeller Center
1230 Avenue of the Americas
New York, NY 10020

First Scribner Paperback Fiction edition 1999
Published by arrangement with Random House, Inc.

DESIGNED BY MERCEDES EVERETT

Manufactured in the United States of America

1   3   5   7   9   10   8   6   4   2

Library of Congress Cataloging-in-Publication Data
Robinson, Roxana.
This is my daughter : a novel / Roxana Robinson.
—1st Scribner pbk. fiction ed.
        p. cm.
        I. Title.
PS3568.O3152T47   1999
813'.54—dc21   99-27173
          CIP

ISBN 0-684-86436-3

Praise for *This Is My Daughter*

"With almost perfect pitch, Robinson captures the clash of worldviews between adults and young children."
—Susie Linfield, *Los Angeles Times*

"Robinson writes with slow-motion precision. She registers every last gesture and nuance and gets it all right."
—Adam Begley, *People* Magazine

"Robinson's impressive new novel grows on you . . . so slowly you discover how truly ambitious and tough its intentions are."
—Francine Prose, *Newsday*

"Compelling . . . after reading this exceptional novel, it may be hard to think about remarriage without this book coming to mind."
—Beth Brophy, *USA Today*

"A clear-eyed, poignant story of a family in crisis."
—Colleen Kelly Warren, *St. Louis Post-Dispatch*

"Glitters not with rich trappings, but rich with understanding of its people."
—Linnea Lannon, *San Jose Mercury News*

"An expert on the misperceptions even the most intimate have of each other, and on the human inability to yield, particularly in marriage, with its ongoing battles and momentary victories. . . . [The] message, in the end, is the possibility of redemption."
—Tricia Springstubb, *The Cleveland Plain Dealer*

"Robinson knows all her characters well and infuses them with emotional authenticity, wisely rendering their foibles and strengths."
—Veritt Ludgate-Frase, *The Christian Science Monitor*

"Lucid and graceful prose that shines with compassion and wisdom about human frailty."
—Wendy Smith, *Publishers Weekly*

"A thoughtful, tender tale by one of our finest exponents of traditional realistic fiction."
—*Kirkus Reviews*

THIS BOOK IS FOR DEAR VICTORIA
WITH MY LOVE

A C K N O W L E D G M E N T S

I would like to thank Dr. Susan Soeiro and Christine Foster for their patient responses to my inquiries. I would like to thank the National Humanities Center for giving me space and silence in which to work. I would like to thank my family for everything.

PART ONE

1

You'll like my daughter," Peter told Emma, "no matter what she does to you. If she bites you."

Emma looked at him, to see if she was meant to laugh, but Peter was driving, and did not turn. Emma considered his profile, looking for clues: the long straight nose, the sober deep-set blue eye. The line of Peter's mouth was stern, and his tone had suggested not mirth but reproval. Disturbed, Emma turned away to face the road herself.

"I'm sure I'll like her," she said politely.

But it was an alarming announcement. She wondered what Peter meant: was he warning her that his daughter was difficult? Was he reminding Emma that she had no choice? In either case, Emma didn't need to be told. She knew it was important that she like Peter's daughter. She knew his daughter was difficult. But perhaps Peter meant neither of these things, perhaps this was an awkward joke, heavy with anxiety. Emma did not quite dare ask him what he meant.

Emma and Peter had been seeing each other for four months. Often Emma felt she knew him well, but still there were moments of complete confusion for her, dark silent pools set unexpectedly in an open rolling landscape. It took so long to know someone, Emma thought, to know easily, at once, what was meant by a comment, a tone of voice. Married, you took this ease for granted. Starting all over again, learning someone new by heart, seemed so slow. To Emma, it seemed at times impossible.

Emma was always afraid that Peter would discover something about her that he had never imagined, something that would turn him utterly against her, forever. She had seen him once, taking off a pair of wet gloves, peeling them off his fingers, ridding his flesh of them and flinging them in a crumpled mass onto a chair, where they hung for a moment and then fell to the floor. This was what she imagined would happen to her if she disappointed him.

Emma looked out the window. They were driving down Park Avenue, through the seventies. The big apartment buildings rose on either side, solid and immutable, with their clean stone facades and crisp canvas awnings. Uniformed doormen, brisk and authoritative in braid-trimmed hats, stood guard at each doorway. It was a neighborhood Emma knew well: Park Avenue, with its narrow, sooty, dignified strip of green, had, until now, run down the center of her adult world. When she had first come to New York, six years ago, she had lived with friends of her parents, in a tiny maid's room in a big duplex at Park and Eighty-first. When she was married to Warren, she had lived between Park and Madison, on Ninety-second. Peter's wife and daughter—and once Peter—lived at Park and Sixty-eighth.

Peter and Emma were on their way to pick up Peter's seven-year-old daughter, Amanda. Peter had lunch with her every Sunday, but this was the first time Emma had been included. She had been pleased and flattered when Peter asked.

"You know I've met Amanda before," Emma reminded him now.

"You have? When?" Peter asked.

"When I met you. At your cocktail party."

"I didn't know that," said Peter.

"It was very brief. She won't remember me," Emma said. "But I remember her."

They had stopped for the light at Sixty-eighth Street. The avenue sloped broadly down before them, diminishing toward the handsome Beaux Arts silhouette of Grand Central Station, which was backed by the cold blunt rectangle of the Pan Am Building. The narrow beds of earth that divided Park Avenue held neat evergreen trees, regularly spaced like musical notations, green chords struck evenly between the high stone-faced buildings. It was a clean and orderly vista, and the February sky overhead was a high pale blue.

Crossing the avenue in front of their car was a middle-aged black woman in a too-long overcoat. She held the hand of a small white girl. The girl, in a bright pink parka, green corduroy pants and scarlet boots, hung sulkily back, her body jammed into a stubborn angle of resistance. She wore no hat, and her hair blew in a wild halo around her head. The woman paid no attention to her reluctance, pulling the girl steadily along behind her. In the middle of the street the woman turned and said something, her face threatening. The girl stuck out her lower lip. When they started again the girl gave up her leaning, but each step was sluggish and resentful. Her boots slid reluctantly along the pavement, her head was down. The woman plowed ahead without looking back.

Children have no choice: they are at our mercy, Emma thought. She was glad to see, at least, that the little girl had refused a hat.

"What did Amanda do? When you met her," Peter asked, turning to Emma. One eyebrow was raised, and Emma felt the full strength of his blue gaze. He was a lawyer, and there were times when Emma felt she was being cross-examined.

"Oh, not much," Emma said. "Caroline was taking her around the party to be introduced. Amanda wasn't keen on it."

"Sounds like Caroline. Sounds like Amanda," said Peter. The light changed, and he turned the car onto his street. They pulled up in front of his old door. The doorman, short, dapper, militant, in a long buff overcoat, with heavy corded epaulets, stepped at once to the door of the car.

"Hello, Sam," Peter said.

"Good morning, Mr. Chatfield," said the doorman loudly, touching his big cap. He had bright black eyes, and the stiff overcoat nearly enveloped him.

"I'll be right down," Peter said to the doorman, and closed the car door. The doorman looked at Emma and nodded, brisk but neutral.

Emma, left sitting in the car, wished that Peter had spoken to her instead of to the doorman. She watched Peter walk into the building, where he still owned an apartment. Through the heavy glass of the door she could see the elevator man step forward to greet him. All the people here knew Peter; he would meet an old neighbor in the elevator. Emma watched, pressing her forehead against the window like a child, as Peter stood before the elevator door. His figure, tall and solid in his worn corduroys and old raincoat, turned vague and began to vanish. Emma blinked, focusing, but Peter turned steadily to smoke. She pressed closer to the window, staring intently, to retrieve him. But she could not, and drew back from the pane, perplexed. She saw it was her own anxiety that had made him vanish; her breath had steamed a widening circle of mist across the windowpane, a pale film of obscurity that blotted him out. When she drew back, she watched the window dry, and clarity spread across it.

The elevator doors reappeared, but now Peter had gone. The doors had glided somberly shut behind him, and he was now inside the hushed vault of the elevator, rising deliberately toward his wife, his daughter, his apartment, his past life. For nine years he had been part of Mr. and Mrs. Chatfield on the eleventh floor. What would he do up there, what would he say? How much could you trust a man who was in the middle of divorcing his wife? Taking back all the promises he had made to her?

The doorman stood like a small belligerent statue: chin raised, legs planted wide beneath his huge coat, one gloved hand on his taxi whistle. He ignored Emma. She felt like a trespasser, illicitly parked before this building. She turned away, wondering what was happening upstairs.

Emma had been in the Chatfields' apartment only once, a year earlier, when she was still married to Warren. Warren had been on a board with Caroline, Peter's wife, and she had asked them to a cocktail party. That night, Warren and Emma had stepped off the elevator into the foyer with its black marble floors and yellow-and-white striped walls. The front door was open, and the rooms beyond were full of noise and color. The spaces were big, the ceilings high. The surfaces shimmered: the porcelain figures on the mantelpiece, the satinwood tables, the Venetian glass mirror over the fireplace. The great satin curtains were fringed with dull gold, and held back with heavy tasseled cords. On the mahogany sideboard were twisting silver candelabra.

They stood for a moment in the front hall. A white-jacketed waiter came up, holding a silver tray of goblets, filled with pale wine. Emma and Warren each took one.

"This is quite something," said Emma, looking around.

"I told you," said Warren. He sounded smug, as though he were taking credit for the apartment. He turned. "Hello, Caroline," he said, as a woman in brilliant blue came toward them. His voice was loud and jovial, his manner somewhat unctuous. Emma could see he was awed by Caroline.

"Warren, how nice to see you." Caroline Chatfield was handsome, rather tall, and somewhat fleshy. She moved with authority, kissing Warren briskly on both cheeks. She then drew back, with a professional smile, to meet Emma.

"This is my wife, Emma," Warren said. He turned to Emma and looked at her appraisingly, as Caroline did. Emma felt them both examining her.

Caroline at once held out her hand. She set her feet neatly together and gave a little comic-opera bow over the handshake. Her hair was shoulder length, blond streaked. She had very pale blue eyes and a pointed nose. She wore gold earrings, and a strand of pearls lay neatly against the yoke of her dress. The dress was patterned indigo silk, long sleeved, high necked, and full of discreet details: small neat tucks, stitched-down pleats.

"How *nice* of you to come," Caroline said energetically. "Do you have a drink? I see you do." She looked again at Warren and turned serious. "Now, you and I have to have a talk. The plans for the spring fund-raiser are foundering."

Warren raised his eyebrows, smiling, conspiratorial. "Are they?"

"Have you spoken to Cynthia?" Caroline asked.

Warren shook his head. He was enjoying this.

"I wouldn't look forward to it, if I were you," Caroline said, and shook her head forebodingly.

"I think we'll be able to deal with Cynthia," Warren said.

Caroline turned to Emma. "Do forgive us for all this business," she said charmingly. "Your husband is a treasure. We're so thrilled to have him on the board." Warren beamed. "He's really stirring things up."

Emma smiled. "I'm sure he is," she answered, refusing to enter into the listing of Warren's merits.

"But you know that about Warren, I'm sure," Caroline said, withdrawing her attention. "Now there's Serena, I want to talk to her before she leaves. It's so nice to have met you," she said to Emma. "Please excuse me, I hope I'll see you later." She moved off through the crowd, the silk pleats on her long skirt swaying briskly.

Warren watched her go. He stood visibly straighter, preening, exhilarated. "She is really something."

"She is," said Emma, noncommittal.

"She's so elegant," said Warren. "She always looks like that. Really beautifully turned out. Hair, dress, jewelry."

Emma, who understood that this was a criticism of her, said nothing. She had grown up in Cambridge, Massachusetts, where vanity was frowned upon, and attention to appearance was considered vulgar. Beauty, like jewelry, was a matter of inheritance: either it came down in the family or you did without.

Emma was wary of women like Caroline who put such energy and concentration into their own presentation, who took such obvious pleasure in it, who looked so sleek and glowing and expensive. Emma felt both disapproving and envious: Caroline made it clear just how sure of yourself it was possible to appear.

"I want you to meet Peter, too," said Warren. "He's right up your street, actually. He has a wonderful art collection. You'll love him." He sounded bossy and proprietary: he clearly felt in charge.

Emma said nothing. She did not always love people who had wonderful art collections: they often became peculiar when they discovered that she worked at an art magazine. Their voices took on a certain urgency, they leaned too close as they spoke. The acrid smell of self-promotion began to permeate the atmosphere. They insisted on showing her their whole collection, every piece of it. They mentioned prominent museum curators who had, they claimed, said glowing things about the collection. They mentioned prices they had paid; often they lied about prices they had paid. They demanded praise, recognition, respectful attention. Sometimes Emma felt that collectors were what she liked least about art.

Emma had looked vaguely at the pictures in the front hall. Without her glasses she could see only that they were drawings, in heavy European frames. Now she entered the big living room and looked around: it was full of splendor. The walls were covered with leopard-skin paper, and there were high white wooden bookcases. A bank of great French windows opened onto a terrace. Big low overstuffed sofas and curious chairs stood about on the huge Persian carpet. It looked as though the room had been there since 1890: rich shawls hung over the backs of the chairs, and small collections—old ivory objects, burnished fruitwood boxes—were spread out on the tabletops. On the walls were paintings, and Emma narrowed her eyes and moved toward the one nearest her, a still life.

The picture was, in fact, quite nice, unpretentious and handsome: an early nineteenth-century composition of vegetables, probably American. The shapes were solid, the forms precise, the colors lucid.

"That's a favorite of mine," someone said behind her, and Emma turned to see a man looking at the painting with affection. He was big and blond and very handsome, with bushy eyebrows and intense blue eyes. Emma was skeptical of him at once: he was too glamorous, too polished, too rich to be interesting. And anyone so handsome couldn't be smart. Someone must have told him these were good pictures.

"Do you like it?" he asked.

"I do, actually," Emma said.

Now he would tell her why it was so important, according to a famous scholar or a sycophantic curator. Or he would tell her where he got it. Emma hoped he wouldn't tell her how much it cost.

"I love the red," Peter said, reconsidering the painting. "It's so bold, don't you think? And I like all these interlocking curves. I like the way it all holds together." He looked now at Emma, still smiling. He seemed completely relaxed. She looked back at the painting.

"Yes," she said, "I like the red. Is it American?"

"As far as anyone can tell."

Emma paused, still waiting for important people's opinions, but none came.

"I also like the eggplant," she offered. "I don't think I've ever seen an eggplant in an American painting."

"Have you in any European ones?" Peter asked.

"Well, no," said Emma. "They just seem more likely in European painting. Americans were so genteel. They painted fruit and biscuits and teacups. Europeans were earthier. They painted vegetables and dead rabbits."

Now he would ask her how she knew about paintings.

"It's true, isn't it," said Peter. "Europeans painted kitchen food, and Americans painted dining-room food. Now, what do we conclude from that?"

"Oh, the usual, don't you think?" said Emma. "Americans were always afraid of looking provincial. It was too risky for them, painting kitchen food: they might have been taken for cooks."

"The old problem: poor self-image," said Peter. "The anxious American. Now," he said, moving firmly closer to Emma, "tell me something."

"Yes?" said Emma. She was fixed in the beam of his attention by the clear blue eyes set beneath the thick eyebrows. He didn't seem aware of his looks, he seemed to have none of the narcissist's arrogance. In fact he seemed to have no arrogance about him at all: only ease. He seemed to enjoy himself. This interested Emma; she waited for his question.

"Do you have what you want to drink?" he asked.

"Yes," said Emma. She felt let down: evidently she did not interest him. Didn't he want to know more of her opinions on art?

"Because I need a refill," he said. "Are you sure I can't get you something?"

"No, thanks," she said, and drew away. He gave her another friendly smile and turned, moving off through the crowd.

Emma felt disappointed, and chagrined by her disappointment. He was much nicer than she had expected, and amazingly wonderful looking. She watched him stepping among the people, smiling at his friends. He moved past a satinwood table, she saw the back of his head reflected in the

Venetian mirror in the front hall. He moved among the polished surfaces easily.

Warren found her then, and a moment later Caroline appeared again. Behind her was an elderly woman in a gray uniform with a white apron.

"Warren," Caroline said to him, "I want you to meet my daughter, Amanda!" In front of Caroline stood a small girl, four or five years old. She had Caroline's face, the wide cheeks, pale skin and pale blue eyes. The girl looked sulky and belligerent; her legs were slightly spread apart beneath the ruffled dress, her arms were crossed adamantly on her chest. Her shiny hair, light brown and flyaway, was cut severely. The bangs were too short, and went straight across her forehead, unbecomingly, with hard right angles at the temples—an uncompromising chop.

Amanda stared challengingly at Warren, saying nothing. Caroline put her hand behind her daughter's back and Amanda's stance shifted. She tilted slightly backward, the feet in their black patent Mary Janes braced against the carpet. Emma could see that, while Caroline was smiling at her friends, her hand was set against Amanda's spine. Amanda crossed her arms more firmly across her smocked pink chest, her straight dark eyebrows gathered in a frown.

Caroline looked down at her daughter. "Say hello to Mr. and Mrs. Goodwin, Amanda," she said, smiling, very energetic. There was a fraction more emphasis on the last word than on the others, and there was a trace of warning in her voice. Amanda looked up grimly at Warren. She did not uncross her arms. Caroline leaned over, now clasping her hands demurely behind her back, tilting her head to one side as though this were fun.

"Aman-da," Caroline said, and looked up at Warren and gave him a conspiratorial wink. The little girl tilted her own head, ducking into her neck as though something unpleasant had brushed against her. She did not speak or put out her hand. For a moment nothing happened, and the circle of grown-ups was held, mute and motionless, by the mute and motionless child.

Now, Emma could not remember what had happened afterward, but she didn't think Amanda had given in. Later Amanda, arms still crossed, had been led away by the tight-lipped nanny, who spoke to her in a low severe voice. Caroline stayed, talking with her friends, animated, the gold bracelet glinting with her gestures, the smooth pleats in her skirt swaying as she moved.

Afterward, Warren told Emma, "Amanda is famously difficult. The headmistress at Nightingale told Caroline that if Amanda is going to stay there she has to see the school shrink. She's completely intractable. And Caroline is the most perfectly ordered woman in New York. It drives her crazy, as you can imagine."

Sitting now in the car, waiting for Amanda, Emma remembered that watchful, sullen face, those tightly crossed arms. She wondered if Amanda ever actually had bitten anyone. She wished Peter had not used that phrase. She wondered unhappily why he had chosen it.

Emma looked away. A wire mesh trash container stood at the corner, and trash littered the street around it. What was the impulse, Emma wondered, that drew people to throw trash near, but not in, a trash basket?

On the sidewalk, two women walked past in mink coats, their orange hair curled, their mouths disagreeable in bright lipstick. Emma wondered if there had ever been a city without these sharp contrasts, the rich, cocooned in entitlement, stepping blindly past the squalor on the streets. Maybe New York in the fifties? That seemed now, in retrospect, to have been quiet and romantic. The urban landscape was made up then of modest brownstones, the skyline low and manageable, a small clean grocery store on every other block, optimism and politeness the common language. Now, in the mid-eighties, squalor seemed to be winning, and resentment was the reigning emotion.

A bulky balding man passed Emma, wearing an expensive camel overcoat and walking a fat self-absorbed cocker spaniel. The dog wandered in a complicated pattern, sniffing exhaustively. He found the right place on the sidewalk and stopped abruptly, squatting. He hunched his back into a high arch, flattened his ears and concentrated, staring into space, avoiding gazes. The man looked around with furtive urgency. Emma could see his criminal plan: he was not going to clean up after the dog. When the cocker was finished with his task he straightened, lifting his nose in a dignified way. He stepped briskly away, kicking powerfully backward, dissociating himself from his act. The man did the same, his manner turning supercilious. The two of them moved off together, self-satisfied, aloof, ponderous. White-collar street crime, right in front of me, thought Emma. People justified doing whatever they felt like. She wondered what the man would say, if accused. That he hadn't known the law included cocker spaniels? But his dog was so small? Were people now really more arrogant and contemptuous than in the past, or was it just more evident now?

Emma watched them walk away. She wondered what was taking Peter so long. She wondered what she would do if Peter did not come back.

Perhaps Caroline was causing a scene. She wondered what sort of scene Caroline would make. Caroline, with her smooth hair, her pearl earrings, her neat shoes: Emma could imagine her angry, but not distraught. What would she wear for passion, anguish, intemperance? Emma thought of how Caroline must feel, waiting, in the apartment they had shared, for Peter to arrive. Seeing him appear in the door, knowing he no longer wanted her.

But what if Peter changed his mind, what if he simply fell back into his old life? What if he decided just to stay? Suppose the doorman came out to her with a message: "Mr. Chatfield says for you to go on without him." What if he decided to abandon her, Emma, instead of Caroline, leaving her illegally parked at the curb? If he did not come back, Emma would simply get out of the car and walk away.

Emma had been with Peter for the weekend. Her three-year-old daughter, Tess, was with her father until Sunday night. Emma thought of going off alone, of solitary browsing in secondhand bookstores. She would buy something old-fashioned and comfortable to read, a novel by Elizabeth Taylor. She would sit with it over a bowl of soup in a small restaurant. Imagining this, the rest of her weekend, by herself, Emma gazed out the side window again, her eyes unfocused, leaning against the cold glass.

A face was looking at her through the window: the brutal chopped-off line of light brown bangs, the heavy eyelids, the closed and recalcitrant mouth. Amanda stared in at Emma through the glass, nose to nose, bullyingly close. Beyond her, Emma knew Peter must be standing, but Amanda blocked him; Amanda's blank staring face blocked everything else from Emma's view; instinctively Emma drew back. Then Peter squatted, and his face, smiling, appeared next to Amanda's. Emma rolled down the window, now smiling too.

"Hello, Amanda," she said. "How are you?" Amanda did not answer. She looked sideways, and moved her jaw back and forth without opening her mouth.

"Amanda, this is Emma," said Peter in a loud managerial voice. Standing behind her, he could not see Amanda's face. His own face looked concerned.

"Hello, Amanda," said Emma again, leaning forward, smiling energetically. She opened the door, wondering if she should kiss her. She wanted this to start off well. She thought of her own ingenuous Tess, meeting Warren's future girlfriends. Oh, please, she thought fervently to the unknown women, be nice to my darling. Emma held out her hand to Amanda to shake, but Amanda kept her hands in her pockets and looked at the ground. Without pausing, Emma altered her gesture, reaching to the car door and resting her hand on it. She hoped Peter hadn't seen. He was squatting behind Amanda, his face tense. Emma smiled at both of them. "Come and get in the car," she said to Amanda, and turned, awkwardly opening the door behind her. Peter took Amanda by the hand, but she balked.

"What is it?" he said, bending over. Emma couldn't hear what she was saying. "What's the matter?" Peter asked. "Amanda, get in."

A pause, then Emma heard him say, "What? What is it? Oh, no sweetie, not now. Another time. There isn't room now. You sit in the back."

"What is it? Would she like to sit in front? Here, Amanda, come and sit in my lap," said Emma, smoothing her skirt.

"There, Amanda," Peter said, pleased. "Would you like to sit with Emma?"

Amanda gave Emma a long stare and slowly shook her head.

Peter's mouth grew stern, but Emma smiled at them both.

"Another time, then," she said easily.

Sternly Peter handed Amanda into the backseat, and Emma twisted to smile at her again. Peter shut the door, and while he was walking back around to the driver's seat the two were alone in the silent car.

Amanda, in a dark red wool coat, slumped at once against the seat back, her head turned toward the building she had just left. Her hands beat a noisy irregular rhythm on the seat. She did not look at Emma.

She's been forced to do this, Emma thought, watching her. Why wouldn't she hate it? Emma turned again toward the front. Peter got in beside her and pulled the door shut hard, his face closed and angry.

As he started the car, he spoke, low, under cover of the engine. "There was a firestorm upstairs."

"I thought you took a while to come down."

"There was a scene. Caroline's going to call her lawyer. She says she didn't realize *this*, she didn't realize *that*."

"She didn't realize about me," said Emma.

"Well," said Peter, "yes."

"I can go home," Emma said at once.

"No, no. It had to happen sometime. She asked me if I was going to be alone today. I said no and she blew up. She says she's going to go back and see what the agreement says about visitation rights."

"She can't have thought you'd be alone forever."

"She hasn't thought, period."

It was that Caroline didn't believe her marriage was really over, thought Emma. She didn't believe Peter had really left. He had moved out in September; Caroline still thought it was temporary. She thought Peter would come to his senses, and they could return to their real life.

Emma imagined herself in Caroline's place: it would be so bewildering, as well as painful. As far as Caroline was concerned, the marriage had carried on normally, well enough, until one day Peter had announced it was over. Caroline had been just as she always was. It was Peter who had changed, who had decided that what he wanted in a wife was someone else. He had never given warning, never said they needed to change things, or work them out, he had simply told her he was leaving. If Peter hadn't given Caroline a second chance, why would he give Emma one? How could you trust a man when the very things he was telling you were the same things he was telling his wife that he had never meant?

In downtown Manhattan the streets were almost empty. People and cars moved slowly, at a weekend tempo. Peter parked in an open lot, and the three of them walked to the South Street Seaport. On the sidewalk, Amanda hung back, waiting, until Emma took one side of Peter. Then Amanda took his hand on the other side, keeping her father between them.

Peter had planned the excursion; they went first to a small marine museum. "Ship models," he explained, pleased, looking around the room. Lighted cases, each containing a tiny vessel, stood against the walls. "Aren't these neat?" he asked Amanda, full of enthusiasm.

Emma looked dubiously at a miniature ship, the intricate rigging, the tiny coiled ropes. It was ingenious, but boring. The colors were dead grays and browns, and there were no figures, no sense of life. The only energy was implied: wind and water, abstract forces. The models were like math equations, symbols of a theoretical struggle. Intellect against nature. Suddenly Emma started to yawn. Guiltily she closed her mouth, feeling the telltale flare of her nostrils.

"They are neat," she said. "Like dollhouses," she offered.

Peter looked offended. "They're not remotely like dollhouses," he said. "Dollhouses are boring."

"What do you think, Amanda?" Emma asked.

"I like them," said Amanda staunchly, allying herself with her father. But she barely glanced at the models, and kept looking restlessly around the room. She was never still. Sliding from case to case, she was constantly in movement, lifting a shoulder, tilting her head, jogging her knee up and down, jittery, unquiet.

Beside them appeared a man and a little girl, younger than Amanda. The girl lunged suddenly toward the glass case.

"Don't *touch* that, Hilary," the man said sharply, tugging her back by the hand. Sulkily, the girl subsided, without answering. The man was dark haired and heavyset, with horn-rimmed glasses. His face was locked, his mouth stiff and determined. He looked indignantly at his daughter, antagonistic. He's divorced, thought Emma. She looked around the room at the little knots of people, wondering if all the single parents here were divorced. Moving sullenly past these handsome cases, each parent, each child waiting for the other to make a wrong move, to do something that would justify the anger they felt at the separation, the resentment they would never lose, the resentment at the great failure.

They went afterward to lunch, at a nautical restaurant that seemed a cross between a sailors' tavern and the interior of a ship. Thick ropes hung in ponderous loops against the walls. Within each loop, slightly off center, hung a lifesaver. The windows had thick round panes, like bottle bottoms. The oak tables and chairs were machine carved and heavily varnished.

Peter picked up the big menu and leaned back in his chair.

"Now, Amanda," he said expansively, "what are you going to have? Your favorite onion soup?" He looked at Emma and explained, "Amanda likes the onion soup here."

Emma smiled at Amanda. "I *love* onion soup," she said. "If you say it's good I think I'll have some myself."

Amanda shifted back and forth in her chair, frowning at the menu. She would not commit herself to an alliance with Emma. There was a pause.

"Amanda?" Peter said. "What about it? Your F.O.S.? Favorite onion soup?" There was another pause, lengthy. Amanda frowned at the menu and her mouth twisted slowly, as though she were thinking hard.

"Amanda?" Peter said again, and this third time his voice held impatience.

Still she waited. When her father opened his mouth for the fourth time, she spoke.

"No," she said, her upper lip curled meditatively. She stared at the menu, not lifting her eyes.

"No, what?" Peter said. "And stop twisting your mouth around."

"No onion soup, I bet," said Emma. "Not today. Right?" She waited. Amanda raised her eyes to Peter and nodded.

"All right," said Peter. "What *would* you like, then? How about a grilled cheese sandwich? That's another favorite of yours, if I recall correctly."

Again Amanda waited. This time Emma said nothing.

"Yes," said the child, looking up at her father. She had not looked at Emma once since she had first peered in at her through the car window. She closed her eyes now and shook her head self-consciously, as though a fly had landed on it. She opened her eyes and gazed fixedly at her father. There was a silence. Peter's face looked ominous, he seemed ready to speak: Amanda slowly gave him a wide, ingratiating smile, utterly false.

She doesn't like me, thought Emma, but why would she? How could she like the woman in her mother's place? Why would Amanda ever like another woman smiling at her father? She would have the wrong face, the wrong smile, the wrong smell. There would be nothing right about this woman at all. It was bad enough for her, having her father leave, without a stranger intruding into her private life.

Emma waited until the food had come, until they had eaten, to speak again to Amanda. Then she smiled at the child. "So," she said. "Do you and your daddy come here often?" As she said the word, "daddy," it sounded wrong. She wondered if that was what Amanda called her father. Any error would produce disdain.

" 'Daddy?' " said Amanda, wrinkling her upper lip, as though this were a word in a strange and distasteful language. She looked near Emma's midriff, then away. She shook her head.

"Yes, you do," said Peter. "What do you mean, no, Amanda? We come here all the time." Now, having eaten, he was relaxed. "Who *do* you come here with often, if it's not me? I'm getting a little suspicious, here. Who is taking you around town if it's not your loving old dad?"

Amanda leaned back against the curved chairback, putting her arms along its arms and threading her fingers in and out of its rails. She buttoned her mouth firmly closed, but a smile leaked out along the edges. Against her will, her face began to soften.

"I'm going to have to look into this," said Peter, buttering a piece of his roll. He sounded firm and efficient. "I'm going to have to get my secretary onto this right away. 'Oh, Miss Jacobs,' " he said authoritatively in a gruff bass, his eyebrows knitted, " 'would you find out who is taking my daughter to the restaurant at the South Street Seaport, please?' " His voice changed to a ridiculous falsetto, and he folded his hands tightly in front of him on the table. " 'Certainly, Mr. Chatfield. Right away at once. On the double. Chop chop.' "

Amanda's face smoothed out entirely. Her smile was wide and delighted. She began to laugh out loud.

"Miss Jacobs is not what you call her," she said to her father firmly, "and she doesn't sound like that."

"She doesn't?" said Peter, lifting his eyebrows, astonished.

"Chop chop," said Amanda, and giggled uncontrollably. "She doesn't say that."

"Miss Jacobs says 'chop chop' almost without pause," said Peter solemnly. "There's hardly a sentence she completes that does not contain 'chop chop.' "

"*Daddy*," said Amanda, giggling. She flapped her hand at him once, admonitory, flirtatious.

"What?" asked Peter. "Didn't you know that about poor Miss Jacobs? It's a kind of speech impediment. 'Good morning, Mr. Chop Chop Chatfield.' That's what she says when I come in every morning. It's sad but it's true. I don't want you to mention it to her because it would be rude."

Amanda was sitting on her hands, and she rocked back and forth happily. She laughed, her body loose.

"Daddy," she repeated, shaking her head. "Mr. Chop Chop Chatfield," she said, and lapsed into giggles again, rocking deliciously in her chair, her body full of delight. Peter leaned back, smiling, easy, the tension between them suddenly gone.

Emma could see how things would be for them, driven by blame, guilt, rage. Amanda would blame her father, for leaving her, for abandoning her mother, the darling of her world, for placing this wound at the center of her life. Peter would feel guilty, he would resent Amanda's accusations. The love between them would be fierce and strangled.

There would be moments, like this one, when calm suddenly moved across them, like the eye of a hurricane. The gales and roaring would stop, and they would be blessed with silence and peace, and allowed to act out of love alone. But the storm would recommence; this would never be easy, they were embattled. Emma's heart went out to them.

2

Late on Sunday afternoon, Emma left Peter and Amanda to go home. She now lived on West Tenth Street. She had moved downtown when she left Warren; she had wanted somewhere unexplored, a place unrelated to her old life. Greenwich Village appealed to her, with its modest scale and bohemian associations. When she first considered it, she told Warren.

"It's not you, Emma," he said at once, shaking his head and smiling. "Trust me. Divorce me if you have to, but don't move downtown. You'll hate it."

That had decided her.

Emma liked the new neighborhood. It seemed like a different city: tidy brick and brownstone facades with their bright painted doors and polished brass door knockers. It had been late summer when she moved, and there were scarlet geraniums in the window boxes and great twisting pythons of wisteria clambering up the walls. The size of the buildings felt comforting, the scale human. In the mornings, the clear sunlight slanted easily over the low roofs. Walking along Tenth Street she could hear her footsteps echo against the row of houses. At that hour the sound was neat and domestic, as though she lived in a small town.

Emma's building, on the corner of Fifth, was handsome, old and slightly raffish. When she first left Warren she had thought of a clean empty space: a bare white room, a low white bed, bare walls, polished floors, light. It was appealing, but not practical. It left certain crucial gaps: books, clothes, Tess. Emma still needed three bedrooms—for herself, for Tess and for Rachel, the Jamaican girl who looked after Tess. But the new apartment was simpler and smaller than the old and the building a bit run down. The ceilings were high, and the windows big. The rooms faced south, down Fifth Avenue, and in the afternoons light filled the spaces. She painted the walls the color of heavy cream. She had brought some old rugs with her, in deep, faded tones. The apartment now felt right to her, handsome and comforting.

Emma bought groceries on her way home, and when she arrived she went into the kitchen to unpack. Rachel's radio was playing in the back bedroom.

"Hi, Rache, I'm back," she called.

Rachel appeared in the doorway. She leaned easily against the door-jamb, her arms folded, her head cocked. Rachel was tall, with a wide face and a wide nose. Her skin was very dark yellowy brown, taut and gleaming over her sharp bones. Brown skin actually shone, thought Emma, in a way white skin did not: black skin looked polished, pale skin was a pallid matte. Rachel was barefoot, in tight jeans and a wide-striped turquoise sweater. Her hair was braided all over, tiny weightless black twists that arched and twined in the air.

"Hello!" Rachel said, her teeth brilliant.

Rachel never called Emma by name to her face. On the telephone, Emma had overheard her say "Emma," but to her face Rachel said "you." Emma was uncomfortable about this: she was the employer, shouldn't she be called Mrs. Goodwin? On the other hand, she was only four years older than Rachel, so perhaps she hadn't earned "Mrs." But didn't names indicate status? Shouldn't she have some authority? Shouldn't she be able to insist on Rachel calling her Mrs. Goodwin? If she couldn't take a stand on something basic like that, what could she take a stand on?

Race, of course, complicated the issue. Would it be humiliating to Rachel if she asked her to call her Mrs. Goodwin? Demeaning? What would Emma expect Rachel to call her if Emma were black? What would Emma expect a white girl to call her? A nice white girl from Smith? An insolent white high school dropout? The whole thing was fraught with complications, and Emma had never found the nerve to address it. Rachel was a powerful young woman, full of conviction. She might easily refuse flatly to call her Mrs. Goodwin. Then what? Besides, Emma liked Rachel, for herself: Rachel was smart and reliable and funny. And Emma *loved* Rachel for loving Tess.

Still, it was difficult having anyone live with you. Rachel had been with Emma as housekeeper and baby-sitter since Tess was born, the involuntary audience to the decline and fall of the marriage. Rachel had heard the fights between Emma and Warren. She knew who had slept where afterward. She had heard Emma's terrible late-night weeping, she had picked up the living room in the morning, put away blankets and bed pillows. And there were other things that Rachel saw, smaller but telling: she knew when Emma forgot to call the plumber or to buy the detergent. Rachel saw that Emma didn't dare complain to the painter about the job he'd done on the closet. Rachel was watching when Emma was weak willed and permissive with Tess, when she lost her temper. Rachel was a witness to every aspect of Emma's life. This had always been true, but when Emma and Warren were married Emma had had an ally, someone to take her side. When Warren had been there, the two of them had outnumbered Rachel. Now it seemed that Rachel outnumbered Emma.

Alone with Rachel, Emma stood continually in the cold glare of her judgment. Rachel belonged to the Abyssinian Baptist Church, which took a strong stand against separation, divorce and adultery. Emma too disapproved of these things, in general, but as things had turned out, she was guilty of all three. She felt that in her case there were extenuating circumstances; she also thought all this was temporary. She saw herself in the future as married and faithful. But none of this was Rachel's concern. Emma did not want to discuss it with her, and she resented the silent weight of Rachel's continual disapproval.

"So," Rachel said now, smiling at her. "D'jou have a good time?"

"I did," Emma said, wondering guiltily if Rachel could tell she had been with a divorced man.

"You had two telephone calls," Rachel said. She sounded smug.

"From who?" Emma put a bottle of grapefruit juice and a pack of English muffins into the fridge.

"Your sister," said Rachel.

Emma frowned. "What did she say?" Her sister Francie lived in California, and seldom called.

"She wants you to call her," said Rachel.

"Okay," said Emma. "Who else?"

"An admirer," added Rachel.

"An admirer?" Emma turned to face her.

Rachel nodded knowingly. "*Two* admirers, as a matter of fact," she said. She smiled again and waited.

"What are you talking about?" asked Emma, but as she spoke she realized who it had been. Her face changed, and she turned away from

Rachel. The empty bag stood on the counter; briskly and noisily she began to fold it up. "Mr. Goodwin called," Emma said, answering her own question, her voice neutral.

Rachel nodded with satisfaction. "Mr. Goodwin and Tess called. Last night. Tess wanted to say good night to you." Rachel paused, watching her. "She was sad you weren't here. I think Mr. Goodwin was, too."

Emma stuffed the bag loudly into the trash. "Well, I don't know why they called. I told Mr. Goodwin I'd be out all weekend."

Rachel's eyes did not leave her face. "I guess he forgot," she said gently.

Emma shrugged her shoulders and said nothing, angry. She left the kitchen and went to her bedroom. She knew exactly what had happened.

She could picture the two of them, in Warren's awful apartment on East Fifty-seventh Street, its low ceilings and plate-glass windows. Tess, on a chair with a pillow on it, sitting at the dining-room table. Talking to herself while Warren read the paper. Warren absent, not listening, until something caught his ear. Warren closing the paper, looking at Tess.

"You want to call your mother and say good night, sweetheart?" His voice tender. "Of course you can. Let's call your mother."

Warren helping Tess with the phone, knowing perfectly well what would happen, saying the numbers slowly so she could push each button in turn. Tess holding the phone to her ear as it rang, waiting for Emma's voice. Blinking with excitement, her face alight.

Rachel, of course, would answer.

"Rachel!" Tess would say, important. "We're calling Mommy. I want to talk to my mommy."

Tess's face, falling, as Rachel explained.

"Not there? My mommy's not there?" Tess, incredulous. The face starting to crumple.

Warren would be there, waiting. "Don't cry, little sweetheart," he would say, solicitous. "It's all right. Your daddy's here. *I* haven't left you." Putting his arms around her while she cried, comforting her.

Swine, thought Emma. She closed the bedroom door behind her. Her bedroom was small and square. In the mornings it was filled with sun, but now, with the light gone, the creamy yellow walls seemed claustrophobic. Emma began pulling off her clothes. She threw her sweater and skirt on the bed and yanked on her sweatpants, tying the cord angrily at her waist. There were no referees, she thought. She pulled a T-shirt over her head, then a heavy gray sweatshirt. There was no one to call a foul, no one to tell

Warren he was being a selfish pig. She tied her shoelaces hard and strode out of the apartment, scowling. Outside, energized by her anger, she started jogging downtown, toward Washington Square.

It was beginning to turn chilly, and the light was fading. On the corner of Fifth Avenue stood a pair of gray-haired tourists. The man was thin, his face gaunt and shattered looking, the woman plump hipped, with short hair and glasses. They wore windbreakers and heavy sneakers, fanny packs at their waists. They stood huddled together, looking at a map. As Emma passed them the woman looked up, squinting in confusion at the street sign.

"We can't be here," the woman said flatly.

It was late in the year for tourists. Emma wondered what they hoped to see in February: here in quaint Greenwich Village the sidewalks were narrow and crowded, the streets full of trash, the traffic homicidal. Homeless people trudged past, pushing shopping carts, muttering. Maybe the tourists came here just to feel relieved that they lived somewhere more sensible.

The notion of being a tourist in New York was interesting, Emma thought. Tourism implied a kind of cultural superiority. A patronizing attitude toward the natives, who were viewed as exotica. Maybe people came to New York as though they were on a photographic safari, looking at the wildlife. She imagined them showing slides, in darkened living rooms. "We found this one toward dusk, down near Avenue A. I was using a Nikon."

Emma dodged around a slow-moving man, just grazing his arm.

"Sorry," she called back.

"Fuck you," he said heatedly.

On the other hand, it was hard to patronize New Yorkers. New Yorkers didn't care what tourists thought; New Yorkers felt superior to everyone, the natives of all other places. They had earned this cultural supremacy, it was their reward for living in the worst—and best—city in the world.

Before Emma, the spacious arena of Washington Square opened up. At the center of it rose the splendid arch, serene and monumental, with its grand classical rhythms, the steadily rising verticals, the sweeping resolution of the curve. Around and below it the sycamore trees spread their spidery network of bare branches above their dreamy, dappled trunks. Emma loved sycamores, the elegant shifting patterns of light and dark on the bark, the jaunty plush balls dropped on the sidewalk in the spring. She crossed the street and turned west, running now along the sidewalk beneath the poplars. She wondered if Warren would behave this way every weekend, manipulative, shameless, using Tess to make her feel guilty. She wondered what Francie wanted. Was she leaving her boyfriend? Emma tried to remember which boyfriend it was. Roger? She was pretty sure it was Roger. He was the actor, wasn't he?

Emma dodged past a tall man with long floppy hair. His black leather jacket was opened halfway down on his narrow chest. His blond hair was silky and clean. Pretty, Emma thought, admiring. But his eyes slid coolly and deliberately past her: she did not exist in his field of vision. Maybe the tourists were here to look at the gay scene, she thought. Was that patronizing? Definitely, but the flamboyant gays, the ones who dressed up, loved being stared at. Being stared at was the point. Being watched wasn't an invasion of their privacy, it was a measure of their success. Tourists and drag queens would be mutually exploitative, symbiotic.

Running along the sidewalk was like skiing a slalom course. Emma turned sideways to slip between two couples, then dropped off the curb for a quick single step, leapt back onto the sidewalk, braked suddenly and swerved, barely avoiding a woman who stopped dead to fix her shoe.

Emma thought again of Warren, but she was no longer so angry. The rhythm of her footsteps, the steady pounding of her legs, the well-being of the body began to raise her spirits. The blood thrummed through her, her arms pumped back and forth. Warren was still a jerk, but it was not now so infuriating. She did five laps around the Arch, only a mile, but all she had time for before Tess came back.

She got home just before five, when Tess was due. Emma waited in the front hall with the door open. She was still in her sweaty T-shirt and sweatpants, giving off heat. She folded her arms and walked up and down in her small hall, thinking of Tess, imagining her already home.

No one had told Emma how it would feel to be a mother, nothing had prepared her. Before she'd had her own she'd felt no interest in other people's children, she never wanted to hold their babies. When she had Tess, the rush, the torrent of emotion had amazed her. It was like falling in love: it *was* falling in love. Acquiring a beloved, always present in your consciousness. The profound longing, when apart. This could sweep over Emma like a sickness, at any time, when she and Tess were separated only by a wall, a few feet. Nearly every night Emma took Tess into bed with her.

She did this secretively; she felt it would be frowned on by experts—surely it would spoil Tess irrevocably—but she could not resist it. The presence of the warm beloved.

Warren was late. It was now ten past five. Emma paced back and forth in the hall, in her sweaty clothes. She didn't want to go and change her clothes, she wanted to take a bath with Tess. And if she decided to change, she knew the second she was naked Warren would arrive. Twelve past. It was so inconsiderate. She wondered when she should call. Whatever time she did call, he wouldn't be there. So rude. So rude. Why couldn't he be civilized about this? Why couldn't he be on time? Five-fifteen. Five-seventeen.

The elevator door slid quietly open to reveal Julio, the elevator man, and Warren, holding Tess's hand. Emma's eyes sought only Tess, as though the three-year-old were alone, and Warren and Julio were invisible.

"Tessie!" Emma said, and stooped, holding her arms out.

"Mommy!" Tess said, her voice rising in a high excited squeak. She ran to Emma, holding out her arms. Emma caught and held her.

"Hello, Emma," Warren said. He stepped, barely, into the hall. Behind him, Julio waited, uncertain if Warren were staying or not.

"Hi," Emma said to Warren. She straightened, Tess in her arms. "Thanks for bringing her back," Emma said coolly. "Did you have a good time?"

"Oh, yes, we had a great time," Warren answered politely. "We had a great time, didn't we, Tessie?" He looked at Tess, who nodded energetically. There was an awkward pause.

There are no conventions for this, Emma thought. Should they kiss each other's cheeks, like friends? Shake hands, like recent acquaintances? Should they not touch at all, and never turn their backs, like armed negotiators?

"Daddy!" Tess said, waving vigorously, flapping her hand, coquettish. She was more than coquettish, Emma saw with distaste: she was aping babyhood. "Bye, Daddy!"

Warren turned a melting gaze on her, self-consciously tender. "Bye, sweetheart," he said. "Daddy has to go now. Daddy has to leave you."

Tess copied his tone. "Don't leave me," she said piteously.

"Daddy has to leave you," Warren said. "It's sad, but he does. He doesn't want to leave you, Tessie. Your mommy wants me to leave."

Tess looked at Emma. "Mommy?" she said. "Do you not want Daddy to leave?"

Furious, Emma stroked Tess's hair. "Daddy doesn't live with us anymore, Tess. That's why he has to leave now. He has his house, and we have our house. But you can still see him, Tessie, and you can talk to him on the telephone. Ask Daddy if you can call him tonight, later." This was malicious; Emma was certain he would be out.

Tess looked up at him. "Daddy? Can I call you tonight?"

Warren did not look at Emma, and would not answer Tess. He backed rapidly toward the open elevator door. "I'll see you soon, sweetheart, and I'll call you soon," he said.

"Why did you call me last night?" Emma asked him, as he reached the door. "I told you I'd be out."

Warren frowned, as though trying to remember. "Oh, did you?" He shook his head. "I must have forgotten." He waved at Tess. "Bye-bye, darling."

"Okay, Tess," Emma said abruptly. "Daddy has to go now."

"I love you, Tessie," Warren said to Tess. "Daddy loves you." He pursed his lips and sent a saccharine kiss through the air. Behind him, Julio looked politely into the middle distance.

"Daddy!" Tess's voice was now close to a wail.

"Tell Daddy good-bye." Emma's voice was firm. "And then guess what? You and I are going to have a bath together."

"A bath!" said Tess, now dutifully responding to her mother.

Disgusting, Emma thought, the two of us tugging at her.

"I love you, darling," Warren said huskily.

"I love you too, Daddy," said Tess, mournful again. Warren backed onto the elevator and waved. Julio now allowed himself eye contact and gave Emma a nod.

"Thanks, Julio," said Emma, and gave him a real smile. The heavy metal door slid shut.

Emma closed her front door and took a deep breath. She remembered what Francie had said about Warren, years ago. "At first I thought he was a real ass," she confided. "But actually he's not as much of an ass as he seems. Actually he's kind of fun." At the time Emma had been infuriated by her sister's condescension. Now she felt that same bewildering tug: which was it that defined Warren, his asinine qualities, or the endearing ones? Of course now she wanted him to be an ass, she wanted to be right to have left him. Otherwise she was a villain for having done this.

Emma looked down: Tess was watching her soberly. She had stopped her frenetic acting and now looked tired and forlorn. Her thumb was in her mouth, and with her other hand she rubbed a lock of hair. She stared at her mother, waiting.

Emma smiled at Tess, and took her hand.

"Bath," she said firmly. In Tess's bedroom, Emma knelt on the rug to undress her. "Want bubbles? You can pour them," Emma offered, her voice soothing.

But something had altered, and now Tess ignored Emma. Restive, she stood with one knee pulsing jerkily, as though to a dance rhythm. Emma undid the straps and slid her overalls off. Tess stepped out of them, her hands resting for balance on her mother's shoulders. The two were nose to nose, and Tess met her mother's eye. Her gaze was unfriendly. Her hands drifted upward and her fingers brushed through Emma's damp hair, roughly bumping her ears, carelessly scraping against Emma's scalp. She stared at her mother.

"Your hair is wet," she said accusingly.

"I've been running," Emma said, placatory.

Tess looked restlessly around the room. Emma laid the overalls on the floor and reached for Tess's shirt, but Tess brushed her hand away. She leaned down and picked up her overalls, then, theatrically, flung them back onto the floor. Watching Emma, Tess stamped on them in a rapid staccato.

Ignoring this, Emma took Tess's jersey and began to slide it off. "Where's Tess?" she asked, as the child's head vanished inside the shirt.

"Where's Tess?" Tess repeated the question as she was meant to, but her voice was shrill, unresponsive.

"*Here* she is," said Emma. She pulled the jersey off and smiled when she saw Tess again, as she always did. If she were calm, if everything were familiar, all this would, she hoped, restore Tess's balance.

"Here she is," repeated Tess, her face reappearing. She spoke quickly, unsmiling. She looked restively again around the room.

"Where's my panda?" she asked suddenly, accusatory.

"I don't know. Around somewhere," said Emma.

"I want my panda," said Tess, her face tense.

"Well, let's find him," Emma said.

They looked: there was the painted wooden bed with its bright quilt; the bookcase, its upper shelves full of books, its lower shelves jammed with toys. A brown monkey sat in the rocking chair by the bed, but the panda was not on Tess's pillow.

"Where is he? Where is my panda?" Tess's voice was now truculent.

"Did you take Panda to your daddy's?" Emma was still calm.

Tess's face closed and darkened.

"My panda is at Daddy's! I want him!" Her voice was shrill.

Emma's mouth tightened. "Your panda is fine, Tess. If he's at your daddy's, we can get him tomorrow." She spoke firmly, trying to quell the rising tide.

"But I want him now! I want my panda now!" Tess's voice rose higher. She was determined. She ducked her head and stamped her foot, kicking with her heel at the rug. "I want him!"

"Stop it," Emma said warningly. "Stop squalling. Your panda is safe. We'll call your father, and we'll pick it up tomorrow."

Tess ignored her. Eyes closed, she shook her head wildly. Her voice was excruciating. "I want him! I want my panda!"

"Tess, stop this *at once*," said Emma.

But Tess was past reason. She squirmed wildly against Emma, her eyes closed, her head thrown back. She stamped her feet in an ecstasy of rage. "I want him! I want him! I want him!" she screamed. That note in Tess's voice, that high, fine shrillness, needled into Emma's ear like an alarm.

"Stop it, Tess," Emma said, her own voice loud.

"*I want him,*" Tess wailed, throwing her head back and forth, her eyes closed. She was in a half-trance, caught up in the current of hysteria.

"Tess, we'll get your panda. Now, stop it," Emma said again. Where was her child? What would return her? It was Warren's fault, she thought angrily, he had wound Tess up like this, confused and disturbed her. "Stop whining," she commanded.

But Tess was lost, struggling in her arms. "I want my panda-a-a," she wailed. The needling whine was suddenly intolerable. Emma felt a burst of temper flare against the tantrum, against its deep self-indulgence. The wailing maddened her, and Emma grabbed Tess's hand and smacked the small pink palm, angry at Tess for her hysteria, for her refusal to listen, for her alliance with her father, for her abandonment and betrayal of her mother. At the blow, Tess's voice rose again, wordless, impossibly shrill, desperate, as though she were being tortured.

Emma dropped the small damp hand, and Tess, crying, threw herself down, away from her mother. She wept bitterly.

"Now stop it. Just stop it," said Emma coldly. She was flushed, her heart pounding. At this moment, her own hand stinging with the blow, she felt merciless, triumphant. She felt she was upholding some stern alliance among parents, adults. Children must realize that there are limits, she thought, self-righteous. Discipline, limits: these are important. Children need them, she thought. She'd done the right thing, to put a stop to Tess's hysteria.

Tess paid no attention to Emma. She lay messily on the rug, her limbs flung out, sobbing, heartbroken. Watching her, Emma felt her anger begin to ebb at once. Her conviction turned to remorse. She felt her own chest rise with Tess's gasps. The small warm body was broken with grief, Emma's fault. How could she have hit her? Tess was only three, and upset, disturbed by the weekend. Now her mother had hit her. What was Emma thinking of? What sort of discipline was this? Whose side was she on? She had lost her temper, she had struck her child. What had she done? Would Tess ever forgive her? How did you know how to be a mother? How many mistakes were you allowed?

Emma knelt beside Tess and gently patted her small bare back. It gave off waves of heat. She rubbed it softly, waiting until the sobs had quieted.

"Come here, my little froglet," she said, and tugged at Tess's hand. "I'm sorry I smacked your hand."

Tess's face was red and puffy with misery, her body limp and unresisting. She had no choice but to be comforted by her enemy. It was the final humiliation. Her mother was her captor, her tormentor, her judge, her punisher and her last refuge.

Emma, now aching with remorse, picked Tess up and kissed her. "I love you," she said, and holding her close, carried the beloved body to bed. She lay down, Tess against her chest. Emma stroked the hard damp skull, smoothing the fine hair. Tess's breathing began to quiet, the sobs to subside. Emma, still shocked and ashamed at her own violence, began gently to sing.

> Hush, little baby, don't say a word,
> Mama's gonna buy you a mockingbird.

The song was a favorite of Emma's: a mother's promise to her child, holding fast against the disappointments of the world. And Tess, hearing the familiar words, the slow monotonous melody, began at last to respond. Her limbs turned soft and trusting against Emma's body, as though now, finally, she belonged there.

3

In the spring of Emma's senior year at Smith, Warren had invited her on a camping trip in New Hampshire. On the morning of the climb, they drove to a rough parking lot at the base of their mountain. There were the others, whom Emma was meeting for the first time: two friends of Warren's from Williams, Jack and Winston, and their girlfriends. They had all done this before, together. They wore heavy socks and scuffed leather climbing boots, and talked about distributing the load. They each had a pack. Warren loaded Emma's for her.

"Is this going to be too much for you?" he asked, when she had shrugged it into place.

"Of course not," she said.

Warren turned to the others. "This is Emma's first camping trip," he said. "She wanted to know if she could take a taxi to the top and meet us there."

The others laughed, looking at Emma. Emma laughed too, though she was hurt: she loved climbing, and had said nothing of the sort.

All day they trudged upward in a ragged cheerful line. They wore layers of clothing, which they peeled off as the temperature around them rose, as their own bodies warmed. Flannel shirts and windbreakers were tied around waists as they stripped down to T-shirts and worn jeans. The air was pure and fresh, the sky clear and blue, with a few high muscular white clouds.

They climbed the narrow trails steadily, first winding through the silent woods, past the dim ranks of gray standing trunks. There was no wind, no sound, down there, except the rustle of their footsteps through the dry leaves. They walked single file, Warren and Emma last. Early in the climb, when they were still down in the woods, Warren called out to Emma, loudly, for the others to hear, "I know you're tired, honey, but there just isn't an escalator. Maybe you shouldn't have worn high heels." Everyone laughed.

When the path broke finally out of the sheltering trees, and began to rise diagonally up the broad upper slopes, Warren said, in an encouraging tone, "Just a few more minutes and we'll be at the hotel. Then you can have a manicure. You can have two manicures, honey." Again everyone laughed, more openly now. It seemed that this was the way Emma was to be known. As Warren went on, the others began to flash brief sidelong glances at her as they laughed. She smiled back.

In the late afternoon they reached an open rocky field below the summit. This was a slanting plateau of granite, drifted with springy greenish brown moss, crumbly lichen. The ledges were scored with longitudinal seams, deep narrow cracks. The seams held pockets of moss, and in the widest ones there were low-growing blueberry bushes. Now, in the early spring, these were scraggly, nearly bare, with only a few tattered reddish brown leaves left from the year before.

They set up camp and gathered firewood. There was still time before dark to climb to the summit for the sunset. "We're going to climb up to the top, honey," Warren said, "you stay here and watch TV." When Warren said this, Winston grinned openly, straight at Emma. His girlfriend gave a stifled snort of laughter.

It felt suddenly like a slap. Emma turned to Warren. "Warren, why do you keep saying that? I'm not complaining. I don't ever complain. What are you talking about?"

At once Warren's arm swooped around her, pulling her very close and swiveling her away from the others. He walked her off with him like a doll, tucked under his arm.

"Now, Emma," he said, his voice low, warm and tender. He was nearly whispering. "Now, Emma," he said, "don't be so sensitive." He stopped and nuzzled at her. He whispered, "Don't be so sensitive. Okay? This is just teasing. These are my friends, Em. Don't get so upset." He smiled at her, and put his hand up to her cheek. "Okay?"

His gaze was deep, kind. His arm was close around her. He rubbed her cheek gently. Emma nodded.

"Okay," she whispered, ashamed. "Sorry."

Warren smiled forgivingly, and shook his head. "You just seem foolish, when you act like that. I don't want my friends to think you're foolish." He spoke quietly. His hand curved around her jaw and stroked it. He patted her kindly and waited.

Emma nodded again.

The two of them turned back to the others. Everyone avoided their eyes.

They climbed the last steep gravelly stretch to the open sloping rock at the top. There they sat on huge gray granite boulders and watched the sun melt secretly down into the inky ridges. Above them was only sky, below them only mountains. They stood silently, arms folded, looking. There was little to say, up here. They were surrounded by space, light, distance. The sky went on and on, above them and around them. I'm free, I'm in the sky now, Emma thought exuberantly.

When the sun had entirely subsided, and the light was dissolving around them into dusk, they scrambled back down, climbing into night. They reached their camp just as the light was gone, and lit the fire. For dinner they ate thick scrambled eggs, smoky toasted bread, apples. Afterwards they sat around the fire, its small flames shifting and flickering. The fire held them connected, mesmerized, by its brilliance. Jack passed around a joint, and the sweet musky smell of marijuana began to lace the clear air. Emma took it without drawing on it and gave it to Warren; he too passed it on.

"You don't want any?" she asked.

"Puts me to sleep," he said.

Emma was falling in love with Warren, and every coincidence strengthened the feeling of magical alliance she felt. They both liked Italy better than France, they both liked the Beatles better than the Stones, and they both hated sushi.

Emma looked at him, smiling, holding his attention until he said, "You too?"

She nodded.

Warren grinned, and slowly shook his head, holding her in his bright blue gaze. "Amazing," he said. "Fate."

It was another reason for their ordained couplehood, another tiny part clicking ingeniously into place. It seemed to Emma as though Warren had some secret power, some connection to large mysterious forces. She trusted him.

Warren put his arm around her. He brought out a flask, and he and

Emma took tiny flaming swallows of whiskey. This seemed more grown-up to Emma, more dignified, than grass. They sat on the sloping rock, watching the small fierce fire, surrounded by the great ocean of darkness. Around them were the black wooded mountains, rising into the huge sky. Above them were the brilliant reaches of the universe, the darkness giddy with motionless fireworks. There they were in the midst of it, incalculably fortunate. There they were with their tents, their down sleeping bags, their canteens. They could flourish here, improbably, in this wild endless dark among the mountains: it seemed to Emma that there was nothing they could not do. Sitting next to Warren, she felt that they were partners. She thought that she was experiencing one of the great moments.

Warren put his arm around her and kissed her ear. "Little Funny Face," he said. The feel of his arm around her was wonderful. She felt valuable; he held her very close. "Funny Face," he repeated, nuzzling her ear.

Later, they struggled clumsily into their tents. All day long these had seemed very large in the knapsacks, bumping against their backs, but now, unfolded, set up, they seemed impossibly small. Warren and Emma clambered inside, zipped up their tent against the night, and began awkwardly to undress. They crouched in the tiny triangular space, their elbows and knees suddenly troublesome. They inched down into the double sleeping bag and at last clasped each other. Warren put his mouth to her ear.

"Funny Face," he whispered, "I love you." He spoke deep into her inner ear. He began to move his hand along her thigh, but Emma tensed, thinking of the other tents flanking theirs.

"Won't they hear us?" she asked.

Warren pulled back from her. "Let's give them something to hear," he said, and began to grunt like a pig, a throaty, greedy, powerful thunder. Emma began to laugh, and the more she laughed the more Warren grunted, his arms locked tightly around her.

That kind of laughter was like falling, giving up, it was like sex, and throughout it she felt Warren's arms locked tightly around her. As Emma rocked, helpless, giddy at his vulgar snortings, she was aware of the mysterious vastness of the night, the feeling of surrendering into this laughter, the feeling of both giving up and being held, safe. Warren's arms were closed around her. It felt as though he would hold her like this forever, just like this, all the length of her body, locked into his embrace, forever.

The laughing stopped and their bodies quieted, but Warren's arms didn't loosen. He began to kiss her, pressing himself against her, hard, as though he were driven to this, as though she were to be punished by his passion.

"I love you," he whispered, deep into the center of her, "I love you." He said her name over and over, as though it were a secret word of his, as though it meant something to him that was unknown to her. Warren's passion seemed grand, tempestuous, authoritative. His hold around her was fierce, fanatical. She felt herself taken over by him: it was exhilarating, faintly frightening. It felt as though she had been seized by a madman, a murderer, a predator. She felt herself giving way, she felt Warren taking charge of her. She trusted him, she had no choice, she thought, that wild ferocious grip.

They were married the following year. Emma was young, only twenty-two, but she couldn't think of a reason to wait. And Warren was determined. "You need me, Funny Face," he told her. He was absolutely sure of himself, of her. It felt safe, to Emma, this giving of herself into his charge: he loved her. He knew her needs, her weaknesses, he forgave them.

For their honeymoon, Warren's parents gave them a trip to Italy. Warren had taken a course in the history of architecture, and that year he was in love with Palladio as well as Emma. They went to the Veneto to see Palladio's work. They stayed at the Cipriani, in the old part of Asolo. The hotel was on a terraced hillside, in two seventeenth-century buildings, set at right angles to each other. One building was parallel to the street behind them; the other stretched out to the hillside. In the angle between was a small exuberant garden, with tables and an awning. Beyond it the hill dropped off sharply.

Below the hotel, in descending layers, were houses, with trees and vegetable plots crammed into corners. The steepness of the slope and the closeness of the terracing made for an odd combination of privacy and congestion. Trees whose roots and trunks stood on one level spread their limbs and foliage on the next. Neighbors who could not see each other's faces heard every cough, every whisper, in each other's bedrooms.

Warren and Emma stayed in the hotel annex, parallel to the street and overlooking the garden. Their room was large, oddly shaped, and disappointingly dark. There were windows on only one side of the room, and they were small. At shoulder height, they looked out directly into the trees. The leaves gave the light an aqueous cast, and the darkness and the high windows gave the room a faintly subterranean feeling. It made Emma claustrophobic.

"This is weird," Emma said, walking to a window. "It feels as though we're underwater. We should have on diving suits."

"You're right," Warren said. "I'll call Room Service and ask for some. How do you say 'diving suits' in Italian, do you think?"

"*Robi di diva*," Emma said.

"That sounds like what an opera singer would wear," Warren said. "I'll just say it in English. I'm sure they have this request all the time."

Emma stood at the window, her arms crossed on the sill, and leaned her head out. It was early summer, and the leaves were still pale, tender and translucent. Later in the season the trees would darken the window entirely, but now the narrow leaves merely filtered the greenish light into the room. One window looked out beyond the branches, and from it the view extended through the clear air to the facing hillside. This was wilder than their own, without terraces or other buildings. The hill was very steep, and covered in long grass that shifted silkily as the winds moved across it. The grasses there were starred with flowers. A villa, shuttered, stood alone at the top of it. No road led to the house, and it looked as though it existed in a different moment, a different place.

Emma rested her chin on her arms, leaning over the sill and breathing the Italian air, fresh, mild. It was very quiet. She heard people talking in their gardens below; she heard a dog barking in a general way, announcing the end of the afternoon. Some chickens repeated themselves distractedly. These close domestic sounds were strange against the open, distant views. It was as though she were in an apartment mountain. She liked it, the feeling of dense Italian life, of connectedness. It was not what she knew at home, where everyone's lives were private.

Behind her she heard Warren moving neatly around, unpacking, laying out his shirts in piles, in their paper-and-plastic envelopes, his polished shoes in pairs. Warren took his clothes very seriously, and he had beautiful things: soft Egyptian cotton shirts, lamb's-wool sweaters, cashmere jackets. When he was finished dressing he would look at himself in the mirror. "Not bad," he would say, shooting his cuffs with satisfaction. He would smooth his hair back from his forehead with one hand, holding himself very straight. "Who is that handsome devil? Isn't that a movie star?" It made Emma laugh. He was handsome, Warren, after all: she was proud of this. He had a broad face and smooth honey-colored skin. His bright blue eyes were narrow and slanting, and his thick dark hair fell dashingly across his wide forehead.

Emma and her handsome husband spent their days driving across the flat farmlands of the Veneto, in pursuit of Palladio's genius. Emma sat in the passenger's seat, holding an untidy sheaf of maps and guidebooks, reading relevant passages. They sought out each of the great country villas. Some weren't open to the public, and at those they parked beyond the gates and peered in at the roofline, at the bold elegant outlines. At Emo they put on huge floppy slippers over their shoes, and padded across the shining stone floors, through the ornamented rooms, past the great trompe l'oeil wall paintings. In Vicenza they stood in the narrow streets, gaping up at the implacable masonry sides of the late urban buildings, gloomy and severe.

Emma fell in love with Palladio too. She fell even more in love with Warren: it was he who was introducing her to such richness, showing her a country she had not known. The comforting order of the symmetry, the absurd elegance of the statuary figures posing airily along the rooflines— all of this delight she credited to Warren, who had spread it before her.

One morning they set out after breakfast. They started off on the narrow lane that led down the hillside, from the old part of Asolo toward the main road. Before them spread the great plain of the Veneto, green, calm, fertile, and Emma sighed with contentment. "This is wonderful," she said. "This is such a wonderful trip."

Warren, at the steering wheel, cocked his chin jauntily. "Stick with me, kid," he said. "You need someone to take you in hand."

That night they had dinner outdoors in the quiet garden, surrounded by the translucent Asolo evening. They sat beneath the awning, beside towering ancient trees, lit eerily from beneath. Waiters in white jackets bent gracefully over their table, setting gold-rimmed plates in the circle of candlelight. After dinner, giddy from the wine and air and Asolo, they went back to their silent room.

The maid had turned on the bedside lights and turned down the white linen sheets. The glowing lamps on either side of it, and the bright sheets, made the bed the center of the room, the point of the long day. Warren was in bed first, naked, and he watched Emma as she took off her clothes. She picked up her short slinky nightgown, conscious of his eyes on her.

"Don't," he said, from the bed. She turned to him. She was naked, proud of it.

"Don't what?"

"Don't put anything on," Warren said. "You have a beautiful body. Just come over here."

But Emma felt powerful, in the dim room, standing nude before him. She didn't move. "Beautiful body?" she said. "What about my face? You never say anything about my face."

"Well," said Warren judiciously. "You don't have a beautiful face. I love your face," he said, as though this were an idiosyncrasy that could be expected of no one else, "but I wouldn't call it beautiful. You have a pretty face, but not a beautiful one. Your body, on the other hand, get over here."

He climbed out of bed and came after her. He took her by the wrist, holding her powerfully, leading her back to bed, pulling her down with him, folding himself over her, insistent, demanding.

On the third night, long after they had made love and gone to sleep, Emma slowly found herself awake in the dark. It felt very late; it felt like the dead center of the night. Outside, it was absolutely silent, the deep silence of the country. Emma watched the window until she was able to make out shapes, until her eyes were accustomed to the dimness. There was a full moon; she wondered if that was what had wakened her. Its powdery radiance filled the room, dimly illuminating the mysterious forms of what Emma knew to be the great armoire, and the tables, piled with their maps and guides and books; the two low, fat armchairs. Now everything seemed enlarged, altered, menacing. The furniture seemed to have shifted position slightly. Everything, in this silence, in this silvery, ambiguous light, seemed different from what Emma remembered, from what she knew to be reality. She lay very quiet. Her own reality was this: she was here, in a hotel room with her husband. This was the beginning of her life, she thought, this was how the rest of her life was going to be. She felt fortunate, grateful.

Warren lay next to her on his back, his arms at his sides. Emma raised herself on her elbow and looked down at his face. She examined him as though he were an object. She stared. She felt faintly guilty, surreptitious and excited. At the same time she felt proud: her gaze was legitimate—he was her husband. She owned him as much as he owned her. Warren loved to examine her all over, his face intent, his hands following the path of his eyes. He stared at her face appraisingly, her body, as though he would devour her, as though he would memorize her, as though she were his object. Certainly Emma had the same right to his sleeping face.

She leaned over him, the long angle of the jaw, the dim low arch of his eyebrow, the silky ruffled hair. He lay quietly, exposed to her gaze. His hands were peacefully palm-up, his chest, with its small triangle of sparse fur, was bare, his face open, calm. His trust seemed remarkable to Emma, touching, rare. Warren's chest rose, his breath drew suddenly in, he gave a long sigh. He moved his head slightly, settling deeper into the yielding pillow behind him. The gesture—instinctive, voluptuous—aroused Emma. She thought of his body seeking comfort and pleasure in other ways. She thought of his back and hips moving against her in the warmth; she thought of his body seeking her pleasure—for he took her in hand in that, as in other ways, his voice urging her to come, come—she thought of his body moving deeper and deeper into her own.

She leaned over; the bed creaked slightly. She felt daring, in the moon-filled room, with the country silence around her. She had never done this before, never been the initiator, never asked for sex. But this was her husband, she owned him as much as he owned her. Emma leaned over and kissed Warren's mouth, very lightly. The touch of his lips was strange, they felt quiet and cool. His lips did not yet move against hers, he was still asleep. She raised her head again and looked at his face: the dark line of the eyebrows, the slightly crooked nose.

Again she felt an illicit thrill. Being the leader seemed dangerous, exciting, here in the depths of the night. She thought of Beauty and the Beast, Cupid and Psyche. Women surreptitiously lighting the candle to look at the midnight forms of their lovers: it was a moment always followed by disaster. Emma felt a sense of risk, but for no reason she could understand: Warren was not a beast.

She leaned over again and put her lips on Warren's. She became aware of her skin, waiting for him to touch it. She leaned over until her breasts touched his chest, very lightly. She felt them swell against him. Again she put her lips on his mouth, pressing gently. She ran a fingertip along the side of his head, she touched his ear, brushing the warm complexity of its delicate whorls. Her own breathing began to deepen. She thought of him touching her. She was waiting for him to awake to her. She waited for him to put his arms around her, to pull her gently over to him, to strip the sheets away from their bodies, preparing them for pleasure.

Warren's eyes opened slowly. Emma saw them opening, and then, luxuriously, knowing what would happen next, she closed her own eyes. She lifted her chin above him, exposing her throat to his eyes, his mouth. She felt Warren's hands taking hold of her, seizing her upper arms. She felt him gathering himself, felt his muscles harden, felt him tighten and heave beneath her. She felt herself thrown, hurled.

She could not stop herself, her body was not in her control, she felt herself in the air, breathless and frightened, then she felt the impact: she hit the wall. She struck it with her back and hip, then fell. The floor hit her everywhere, her breasts, her chin, her knees.

The shock was tremendous. Emma lay on the cold floor. She was struck still by fear, and did not want to move. She could hear her own breathing, and opened her mouth to silence her breaths. The moonlight still filled the room. From where she lay, in the narrow well between the bed and the wall, she could see only the ceiling, dimly patterned by the window's silhouette. She blinked her eyes, which seemed unfocused, as though she were drunk. She could not seem to take hold, she could not seem to understand what had happened, what she should address. She wondered if everything in the room had suddenly and violently moved, or if it had been only her. The houses on the terrace below came to mind: had anyone heard? Could they all tell what the sound had been? It was crucial that no one know. She felt herself again hurled through the air in the dark, out of control, lost, felt it happen over and over. She closed her eyes. What she felt was shame. She never wanted to raise her eyes again, never wanted to meet another gaze. Her back hurt, and her cheek and her neck. She realized that she had stopped breathing, and took a long quiet breath, secretive.

She stayed on the floor, mute, motionless, panicky, waiting for her breathing to subside, waiting for something better to happen. She concentrated on making her breathing absolutely silent. It seemed important. She did not dare cry, she was too ashamed. Shame was everywhere.

Later, when Emma was very cold, when the room had been silent for a long time, she climbed carefully back into bed. She moved very quietly. Warren lay with his back to her, and she kept to the far side of the bed. She waited for Warren to speak, but he did not. She felt herself begin to cry and stopped breathing, holding in the ragged breaths until she had quieted herself again. She lay without moving, curled against the edge of the bed, until, much later—the moon was nearly gone from the room—she slept.

In the morning she woke to find Warren lying on top of her. His face was directly in front of hers. She could smell him. He gazed into her eyes, he ran his hand slowly up the inside of her thigh. He had been stroking her while she was asleep, and Emma found herself already aroused. Her legs were already parted, and before she remembered she closed her eyes, sinking into this.

"I love you," Warren said urgently, as though it were a command. "I love you."

Emma, moving her shoulder beneath his hand, felt a sharp pain, and remembered. She opened her eyes again. His face was brooding, intent.

"I love you," he said, and she felt relief: he had forgiven her, then. She looked steadily into his eyes.

What she remembered from the night before now seemed impossible. The morning light was clear and fresh. The dark armoire had resumed its normal size, the armchairs had returned to their places. The pale leaves moved easily outside the window, and Warren's intimate voice was in her ear.

"I love you," he said.

Emma closed her eyes. Maybe it had not happened, maybe she had dreamt it. But with her eyes closed she felt again that terrible vertigo, the helplessness of being thrown, the hard wall, the cold stone floor. Her shoulder hurt. Maybe Warren had done it in a dream, maybe he hadn't realized what he'd done.

But whatever had happened was over, past, Emma thought. Warren had forgiven her, and he still loved her. Emma gave herself up to him again, moving carefully, so as not to awaken the pain.

Later, in the bathroom, alone, Emma turned and looked at herself over her shoulder in the mirror. She took her left shoulder in her right hand and tugged it forward, craning her neck to see this remote part of herself. On her back, on what her mother called her angel wing, was a large purple bruise, deep and mottled. The bone hurt when she moved it. She raised and lowered the wing, testing the pain, watching the mysterious patch shift over the bone. The skin was not broken, and it seemed strange to Emma that such pain could have been inflicted inside, to the bone, while the clean elastic surface of the skin stayed intact.

The bruise lasted. When the honeymoon was over it was still there, fading slowly through dim layers of green and yellow before turning to a dim roseate shadow. The nightmare memory, the feeling of being powerless and naked in the air, flung away, the feeling of the wall's immovable presence against her, did not leave Emma. Nor did the sense of relief and gratitude she had felt afterward, for being forgiven.

They moved to a cramped apartment on Ninety-seventh Street. Emma got a job at an art book store; Warren went to work for a public relations firm that specialized in political clients. "These guys are brilliant," he said importantly. "I can do a lot with this group." He liked saying the names of their famous clients. He liked to say he was tired, frowning slightly, because he'd spent the whole afternoon "talking strategy with the senator." Emma was pleased that he was so successful, so content.

One evening, before Tess was born, Warren and Emma were in their bedroom, getting dressed. They were going to a dinner party given by old friends of Emma's. They were people she loved, and Emma felt lively and pretty. She leaned over her dressing table and hummed to herself as she put on her mother's pearl drop earrings.

Warren stood before the full-length mirror that was set into the closet door. He was tying his necktie, and watching himself closely.

Emma stood and slid her dress over her head. It was a favorite: rose colored, with tiers of ruffles in the back. It had a small waist and a scoop neck, and Emma felt light and happy in it.

She stood next to Warren. "Will you zip me up?" She set her hands on her hips, to make it easy. She bowed her head, waiting for his hands on her back. But Warren was absorbed by his tie and did not look up. He was making careful loops in the heavy patterned silk.

"In a minute," he said finally.

Emma waited, her head dutifully bent. Warren did not move.

"Warren," Emma said finally, smiling. "I'm waiting."

"Hold on," Warren said. "This is important."

"Well, so is this," Emma said, laughing. She thought his vanity amusing, endearing. "I can't go with my dress unzipped."

"No one would notice," Warren said, smiling at himself.

"What do you mean?" Emma asked. She raised her head and looked at him.

"I mean, we don't get invited out to dinner because of you, Funny Face," Warren said. He looped his tie around itself, slid the knot up tight. He examined it in the mirror, lifted his chin against it, gave it a little tug, then finally an approving pat. He was ready. He shot his cuffs, looking pleased. "Who is that handsome devil?" he asked his reflection.

"What do you mean?" Emma said again.

Warren turned to her, handsome, elegant, glowing. He brushed his hair off his forehead.

"I mean, Funny Face, that your husband is a hot ticket. When we go into a restaurant, people turn around and look at me. They think I'm a movie star." He smiled, and shook his head, shrugging, a tiny smile at the corners of his mouth. "I can't help it, it just happens."

Emma stared at him.

"Now, what do you need done?" he asked, indulgent. He moved over behind her.

She watched him steadily in the mirror, and he met her eyes.

At once he shook his head. "Now, Emma, don't start. You're being oversensitive again. I can see you starting up." He smiled at her, loving, forgiving. "Remember who I am. I'm the man who loves you more than anyone in the world."

There was a long pause.

"Remember?" Warren said tenderly. "I'm your husband."

Emma said nothing, watching him in the mirror.

Warren bent over and kissed her neck. "Now, what do you need done, Funny Face? I'll do anything you want. Anything."

"Zip," Emma said, and bowed her head.

She never told anyone about the things Warren said. She was ashamed to, afraid that he was right, that the things he said were true.

4

Peter stood facing the blustering stream of the shower, sluicing the loose soapy drifts from his body. The pounding water drummed hot against his chest; he turned back and forth beneath it, letting it slide him clean. Finished, he turned off the water and stepped out of the tiled stall. The chrome shower head was old, and pitted with dark flecks. The lopsided stream did not stop at once but subsided noisily into a narrow uneven thread before it dripped to a finish.

Peter stood on the bath mat. It lay, rumpled, directly on the tiled floor; there was no rug. There were no curtains at the window, no pictures on the walls. Only Peter's shaving things, on the shelf above the sink, announced his presence in this place. He pulled his towel from the rack and set his foot on the edge of the bathtub. Leaning down to dry his leg, Peter lost his reflection in the mirror.

Most of the time he remembered why he was here. Much of the time it felt normal to him, understood. But sometimes, waking up, or on the phone, caught off guard, he forgot, and found himself suddenly in an alien place. Now, naked, bent over, balancing on one foot, he was lost, in this small bare room with its split and yellow tiles. The walls were thick with white paint, and faint cracks wandered across them. The whole apartment was like this: handsome, in decline.

Peter rubbed his towel across his toes, the rounded knob of his ankle, feeling the abrasive cloth against his damp skin. Caroline came into his mind; she did often. Her image was indistinct, her outline hazy. He could no longer exactly remember her face: he held the sense of it, what it was like to look at it, but he could not conjure up the individual features, the whole.

She was no longer his wife. His marriage was over. Each time he thought that phrase, that word—*over*—something in him lowered, mourned. He had not meant this to happen. He had believed that his marriage lay before him, a vast, unknown, fertile territory stretching out ahead. It was there, he had believed, to be explored, mapped, to be understood, slowly, over the course of his life. He had abandoned the expedition. How had he done it? How had he managed to become divorced? But he had made it happen; he had insisted. He thought of Caroline, and at the thought of returning to her, taking up his life with her again, he felt his heart snap closed. No; he would do it again, he would leave.

These feelings were continual and befuddling, like simultaneous existence in two separate universes: grief at the loss of his marriage, grim determination to end it. He saw again Amanda's face as she stood by the elevator. He saw Caroline in the bedroom, weeping, enraged.

Peter stood upright and set his other foot on the bathtub. He dried the other leg, the sharp edge of his shin, barely submerged beneath the shifting surface of the skin, the long solid slope of his calf.

He could see Caroline's contorted face, her clenched fingers. That day she had screamed at him, and cursed; it was not the first time. Angry, impatient, contemptuous: this had been more and more how he had seen her. It was strange: the first thing that had struck him about Caroline was her good humor.

He had first seen her on the beach. It was early summer, the end of his first year at law school. Peter had spent the weekend with a classmate, in Nonquitt. They had taken a picnic to a nearby private beach with the wonderful name of Barney's Joy. They parked, and walked staggering through the heavy white sand, laden with towels, sandwiches, beer. As he remembered it, the smooth wide beach was endless. A flat shingle stretching out forever, rising on one side into high swooping dunes. It seemed no one was there that day except their group, exuberant, alone in that radiant, limitless vista. (Though how would he know, he thought. In your memory, your table is the only one at the restaurant.)

The day was bright but chilly, windy. Caroline wore a sweater over her bathing suit. A big hat, Peter remembered, dark sunglasses. He couldn't really see her face, concealed by the wide straw brim, the dark glamorous lenses. Still, he had a sense of her: smiling, charming. Beautiful. She acted beautiful. Then someone, pouring from a thermos, spilled on her sweater.

Caroline whooped and jumped up. Her arms and body were loosely muffled by the sweater, her long legs beautifully bare. She capered on the sand, dancing at the shock of the liquid—was it hot or cold? She was excited, hilarious. She had squealed, but with delight, it seemed, anyway without temper. Peter had been struck at how little she minded; she brushed at the stain on her sweater, then began to laugh. He could see her face now. The wind struggled with the wide brim of her hat. Strands of long streaked blond hair blew across her mouth, and she drew them away with her fingers.

Peter scrubbed the towel at his thighs, his buttocks, his back. He moved more slowly, now that most of him was dry. He put the towel over his face, enclosing himself in its damp rough darkness. He molded hard his own features, rubbing deeply into the sockets of his eyes, scouring with his toweled fingers, as though he could scrape off some late, undesirable layer, and return himself to some earlier phase. It was over, he thought. Again, at that word, he felt cast out onto a dark turbulent place. Where was he? What had he done with his life? A part of him, his lost marriage, ached, like a severed limb, still sentient.

When Peter had met Caroline he was not yet ready to marry, not looking for a wife. He had a plan, linear, orderly: after law school he'd move to New York, find a job. He would settle these things before he took on marriage. A wife should be looked after; she was a responsibility. He wasn't ready for that. In those days, what drew and held him fixed, an invisible beam commanding the landscape, was fear about money.

At night, on the edge of sleep, Peter was visited by a scene from a nightmare. He watched from outside, mute, paralyzed, while his parents, trusting, unworldly, settled slowly and unwittingly into an inexorable slide toward poverty. He saw the pair of them, sitting comfortably before the fireplace; he saw the house begin, perilously, to tilt, the floor buckling in horrible silence, the foundations giving way, the mossy shingled roof caving in. The image came often, quickening his heart with anxiety.

But that day at Barney's Joy, watching Caroline caper on the white sand, with her smooth long legs, her hat, he found himself thinking of the word *companion*. It startled him. It wasn't what he thought he wanted in a wife, a woman. *What a good companion* was the sentence that came to him.

Now, in the small bathroom, Peter remembered his frantic anxiety about money. He could not call the feeling up again, it was like remembered pain. Now what he felt was different. He had achieved what he had wanted—security—and the things Caroline wanted: the apartment on

Park Avenue, the clubs, the private school, the nanny. Now he knew what he could do, the achievement itself was not so frightening. He felt like a horse in harness, setting his shoulder against a load he knew he could pull.

Peter was a partner in his law firm, which was midtown, midsized. He had specialized in intellectual property, at a time when few people were interested in it. Now, with the rise of the electronics industry, intellectual property was hot. Young associates crowded around him like young bullocks, eager but wary, jockeying for attention. His division had expanded. His parents would elude the poorhouse.

Peter toweled his chest and stomach, liking the abrasive drag against his skin. He was dry, clean, ready for his dinner with Emma. The glowing point at the end of his day. He stuffed the towel onto the rack, where it hung in damp crumpled folds. At home, at the place he still thought of as home, the towel would be folded neatly the next time he saw it. The next time he saw this towel it would look exactly the same: drooping, slatternly. Right, he thought.

In his bedroom Peter was surrounded by familiar objects. Here they were, companions in his flight, his exile, his liberation: the worn red Persian carpet from his library, its fringe uneven and fraying. Here was his leather wing chair, his grandfather's mahogany bureau, ponderous and gleaming. The polished wood was dark reddish brown, its fine grain like a weather map, full of drifting swirls, deep subtle currents. The top drawer bellied boldly outward, then back in again, like a half-round column laid horizontally across the chest. Below, the other drawers were soberly perpendicular, starred with a double line of crystal pulls.

Caroline had been glad to get rid of the bureau. She had called it "the Victorian horror." Peter could not tell, himself, what it looked like. To him the chest was not a piece of design but a piece of his family. It spoke to him of his grandfather. Peter had never known his grandfather, but the bureau had been in Peter's bedroom as long as he could remember. In the early mornings, when Peter lay barely awake, he looked through half-closed, slowly blinking lids, and imagined that he saw his grandfather as a boy. He wore those strange stiff clothes, the high restraining white collar, the rusty black knee-length trousers. In the dim light he stood motionless, looking into an open drawer. He never turned; Peter saw him only from behind. His shadowy imagined presence was benign, comforting.

Peter's parents still lived in Marblehead, in the house where he had grown up. It had originally been the carriage house on Peter's great-

grandparents' place. All the buildings on the property had been remod-
eled. The laundry, the stables, the carriage house were all cottages now,
occupied by cousins, aunts, uncles. The big house, Axminster, was the
only one unchanged. It belonged to Peter's uncle, also a lawyer, and the
only one who could afford to keep it up.

Axminster was dark and massive. Outside, it was unpainted shingle,
with small-paned windows and huddles of narrow chimneys, in the Arts
and Crafts style. Inside, the rooms were high ceilinged, spacious and
gloomy, with vast shining oak floors and somber wood paneling. In the living and dining rooms there were enormous rustic fireplaces made of granite. The majestic staircase rose to a half landing before continuing to the
second floor. The banisters were not columns but thin flat panels, with
heart silhouettes carved out of them. There had been a springer spaniel
named Caesar who used to sit on the landing and stick his muzzle out
through a heart-shaped cutout. Peter could not now remember if he had
ever known Caesar, or only heard of him, but he could see him clearly, sitting on the landing, the small brown snout protruding, the stumpy tail
trembling.

When Peter had brought Caroline home to meet his parents, she'd
made much of the carriage house. "Oh, it's charming," she said, over and
over. "I just love it." She was effusive, Southern.

The carriage house was also dark inside, with high wainscoting and
ceilings that were, literally, lofty. Some of the floors were narrow wooden
boards and some flagstone, varnished but uneven. The house had a rustic
aura, a subtle leaning toward its past. You felt there might be a chain
cross-tie hanging against some wall, ready still to clip onto a brass halter
ring, or in some corner a nest of worn winter horseshoes, ready to be reset
with the ringing blows of the blacksmith's hammer. The Chatfields occupied the house lightly. Things were as they were, it didn't occur to them to
make changes.

That day, Peter took Caroline for a walk after lunch. It was late fall,
and the afternoon darkened early. They walked across the mossy lawn,
crunchy with early frost. Ducking around a shrubby wall of forsythia,
they met the flat gravel drive of the main house. They followed the drive
around the curve to face the great dark facade and heavy porte cochere of
Axminster.

Caroline's eyes enlarged. "Whose house is this?" she asked.

"Uncle Punch and Aunt Judy," Peter said.

"Punch and Judy?" Caroline repeated.

"Her name's Sarah, but everyone calls her Judy because of Uncle Punch."

"And his name is really Punch?"

"Hubert."

There was a pause. Caroline said, "God, it's huge."

Peter grinned and put his arm around her. "Too bad," he said. "You picked the wrong cousin."

Caroline smiled winningly and shook her head. "Don't be silly," she said, but Peter could see she was disappointed. At the time it had amused him.

Peter's family had been in Boston since the early eighteenth century. They had been comfortable, though not rich, until the late nineteenth century, when someone had turned fortunate in the textile industry. Axminster was the name of a successful carpet. But by the time Peter was born, most of the money had trickled away, at least in his own family. Like his father, Peter had gone to St. Paul's and Harvard, but unlike his father, he had gone on scholarship.

Now Peter pulled on clean boxer shorts, snapping the waist, feeling the silky ironed cotton against his damp skin. The luxury of being clean, he thought, cool stuff against your skin. Emma came into his mind, her creamy skin. Her smooth arms. Her hands, the narrow, flexible fingers, like a lemur's, some kind of clinging prehensile creature. Her pointed chin, so neat and precise, elfish. He loved her narrow greenish eyes, bright, slanted beautifully downward, in an elegiac droop. When she smiled they narrowed, turned radiant.

Peter opened a drawer of folded shirts in plastic-fronted envelopes. He chose deep blue, with narrow white stripes, and shook out its stiff folds, sliding his arms into the sleeves.

On the bureau, on the white linen scarf, were his things: his grandfather's pair of worn ivory hairbrushes; a silver tumbler which had been an usher's present at his roommate's wedding; his leather wallet—limp, dark, packed. There was also a little silver dish, its provenance now forgotten, where he kept his change. A dizzy-looking small clay bowl, unglazed, leaned hard to the left. Amanda had made this in first grade and given it to him for Christmas. Peter kept his cuff links in it.

He slipped the links through the holes in the heavy French cuffs. The links had been a present from his father; they too had belonged to Peter's grandfather. They were small brass ovals, engraved with his grandfather's initials: PSC. The surface was worn and nicked, the engraving now blurred at the edges. His grandfather's name was Paul, not Peter, but the initials were the same. Peter was an only child, and he would inherit all the family objects, no matter what the initials. By the time his parents died, that would be all there was left: the furniture and the house. His father spent capital every year, not lavishly, but steadily.

Peter would have to sell the house. The family would be outraged if he sold to outsiders, and trying to sell it inside would become a nightmare of negotiations, recriminations, sullen silences, furious letters sent by hand, family members cut dead in the street. All these things had happened when his grandmother died and the property was distributed. One uncle had moved to Santa Barbara in a rage and had never spoken to Punch again.

Peter could not keep the carriage house. He would never find himself settled in Marblehead again, his life would not take him there. He had never talked to his parents about this, about his selling the house. Peter was forty. His mother was seventy-two, his father seventy-five. His parents were both still healthy, forcefully alive.

At this moment, nearly seven o'clock, his parents would be in the kitchen. Peter's father, Jeffrey, was a pediatrician, semiretired. He had stopped working altogether on weekends, and cut back during the week. Right now he would be sitting in the rocking chair at the end of the kitchen table. In one hand would be his sole drink of the evening, Scotch and water. In the other hand would be the newspaper. He bought the paper on his way home from work, and read it at night. He was always one day behind on the news. While his wife cooked dinner he would sit beneath the standing lamp, reading out loud to her things that amused or incensed him.

Peter's father was tall and thin, balding. He wore rimless glasses over his bright blue eyes. His cheeks were deeply lined, with long furrows, and there were tufts of wild white hair in his ears. In the winter he wore a hand-knit wool vest, and heavy tweed suits that never wore out. In the summer he wore ancient linen suits, glossy with ironing, and blue sneakers. At all times Dr. Chatfield carried an old pair of metal binoculars, dark, weighty, serious, suspended from a fraying leather strap aroun ˥is neck. He was an intent and dedicated birder, and would pull over to ˍ side of any road in order to lift and focus his binoculars. His life list was lengthy and impressive.

Polly, Peter's mother, would be moving from sink to counter to stove. She wore tweed skirts and solid-color sweaters. She dressed in dull colors, browns, grays, slate blues. She was small and comfortable, with a large sloping bosom and no waist. There was a short perpendicular crease between her hazel eyes, and small flattened pouches beneath them. Her hair was bright white, short and straight, parted on one side. She made brief replies to her husband's announcements.

When Peter told his parents that he and Caroline were separating, his mother raised her eyebrows and said nothing.

Dr. Chatfield rocked silently, thinking, looking at Peter over his rimless glasses. His mouth was puckered into angry folds.

"What did you expect?" he asked finally, the chair creaking.

Peter felt a spasm of anger himself. He waited for a moment before he answered. "I made a mistake," he said. "Caroline and I want very different lives."

"Everyone does," said his father rebukingly.

Peter did not answer, and after a while Dr. Chatfield opened his newspaper, his mouth still pursed, his eyes narrowed.

Peter, sitting across from his father, took a swallow of his own drink in the silence. He leaned his head against the stiff high-backed wooden chair, feeling its perpendicular clasp. He understood he had disappointed his parents, but why did they ask him nothing more? He resented their silent judgment. He had received no credit for his efforts to make the marriage work, no credit for any of his successes, not even the material success that was for them, too. It was never discussed again.

Afterward, often, he wondered what his father had meant. If there was an unrevealed passage in his parents' lives, Peter didn't ask about it, didn't want to know it. Its presence loomed outside his vision, hidden, like a black reef known only by white surf above it, too dangerous to approach. *Everyone does.* The phrase did not leave him.

Now half-dressed, his shirt buttoned and linked, his legs bare, Peter pulled on his socks. They were cashmere. Again he felt a deep sense of luxury, of gratitude to the world. Cashmere socks. It had not been until boarding school that he had realized how odd and idiosyncratic his family was. He had assumed that everyone could find their family name in public places: graveyards, lists on church walls, libraries. He took this for granted, though with a certain sense of entitled pride. It was not until boarding school that he realized, to his surprise and shame, that his family was poor.

The winter he was an awkward, testy seventeen-year-old, he had sat in the kitchen one night before dinner. His father was reading the paper.

"Why can't we go to Vail for spring vacation?" Peter asked, challenging, clumsy.

Dr. Chatfield raised his eyes from the paper. "Do what?"

"Why can't we go skiing in Vail?" Peter asked again, at once irritated by his father's response.

The Chatfields had always skied. The family had, for decades, owned a farmhouse near Mad River. Everyone had used it—aunts, uncles, cousins—according to increasingly complicated rules of occupancy. But the house was old, and the arrangements had become impossibly snarled and entangled, and when Peter was twelve, it had finally been sold. Since then Peter had only gone skiing when he was invited by friends.

"In Vail?" his father repeated. "Vail, Colorado?"

Peter nodded defensively.

"Why not? Because we can't afford it," Dr. Chatfield said, staring at Peter with an air of bemused alarm, as though his son had suddenly leapt on top of the table. There was a long silence, during which Peter seethed resentfully. When Dr. Chatfield felt his point had been made, he returned to his newspaper.

"Besides," Peter's mother said reasonably from the sink, "we don't know anyone who goes to Vail."

"Well, I do," Peter said.

"We're still not going," Dr. Chatfield said, behind the paper.

Peter pushed back his chair, stomped out of the room.

It had been at Harvard where Peter discovered how truly poor he was. Freshman year, his roommate was a rich Argentinian. Roberto's talk of estancias, shooting parties, weekends at beach houses, balls, dances, private planes, silenced Peter. He watched Roberto's treatment of things: Roberto dropped a cashmere blazer on the floor, and left it there for five and a half weeks. Peter owned only one blazer, and it was wool. During reading period, in January, Peter finally picked up the dusty abandoned blazer and hung it on the back of a chair. Roberto said cheerfully, "Don't bother with that. It's so filthy I'm going to throw it away."

Peter stared at him for a moment. He thought of the blazer thrown into the scrap basket in their room, he thought of it out in the big trash basket on the landing. He thought of himself, sneaking it out of the trash basket. Furious at the idea, at his own imagination, he settled the blazer's shoulders on the back of the chair.

"It's just dusty," he said coldly. Roberto shrugged. Later the blazer vanished: Peter supposed Roberto had thrown it out after all. Roberto paid no attention to his possessions. He lost his lustrous custom-made shirts, his lamb's-wool sweaters. He wore his wing-tip Peal loafers without socks, roughly stuffing his heels into them until he broke down the backs. Then he threw them away. Peter watched this without comment.

At home, Peter noticed for the first time the frayed edges of his father's blue broadcloth shirts. He noticed the tired, unrenewed quality of every-thing in the house: his mother's tattered plastic address book, the faded sofa pillows, the ragged Persian rugs. It enraged him; he blamed his father for all of this. There had been money; now it was gone.

Peter put on his suit, smoothing his shirttail down inside the trousers. His suits were made for him. Not in London, he thought that was some-thing you should inherit. His grandfather had had an English tailor, but no one knew its name. Finding a London tailor on your own, Peter thought, was like making up a family coat of arms. He went instead to Morty Sills, on Fifty-third Street. Sills's was small and snobbish, like a pri-vate club. Caroline had been delighted when he told her he was going to Sills's. Her face had lit up, as though Peter had achieved something sub-stantive, instead of merely deciding to spend a lot of money on clothes.

Caroline had seen New York, as he had, as a place in which to excel, though their goals were different. She was aiming at social triumph. She was from Louisville—*Loouhville,* he had learned to pronounce it. Her fam-ily was large, with money in the background. There were cousins, houses, parties. Caroline's mother, Mrs. Pierce, was glamorous and bossy, tall and thin, with a long corded neck. She had short rough bronzed hair, brushed up and back, with furrows as though a harrow had combed it. She wore gold jewelry that looked like braided rope, and was flirtatious with Peter. "Petah," she would call, patting the sofa next to her, "you come ovah heah and sit down and tell me who's going to be the next president of the United States." She was flattering, charming. Caroline was afraid of her.

One evening Peter and Caroline came downstairs for drinks before dinner in the Pierces' big red living room. In her mother's house, Caroline spent hours dressing, painstakingly doing her hair, her makeup. That night she was wearing new earrings. She had bought them in New York and shown them to Peter. "My mother will *love* these," she had said, exul-tant. He had realized that even in New York she dressed for her mother's eye. Coming down with her that night, he had felt Caroline's eagerness, her excitement.

There were guests, and the bright room was scattered with people. Mrs. Pierce stood in front of the fireplace, white pants, a bright red sweater, gold earrings. She was at the center of a group. Caroline, in a silvery top and black pants, her hair smooth, her patent-leather slippers gleaming, paused for a moment at the top of the two broad steps that led down into the living room. Smiling, she went down to greet her mother.

Mrs. Pierce turned, stared at her and said loudly, "Caroline, whatever *possessed* you to buy those earrings? They look like little bits of intestines wrapped in tinfoil." Everyone laughed, and Mrs. Pierce turned back to her friends, smiling. "I *loathe* the earrings you see today. I wish Fulco were still alive. Do you remember him? Oh, his things were so much fun."

Caroline, next to Peter, stood still. She touched her earrings and smiled, as the others laughed at them. Peter saw that her eyes were glittering. She said something indistinct, then turned as though she'd forgotten something. She trotted back up the two steps that led to the hall, then turned toward the dining room. Peter, following, pushed through the swinging door to the butler's pantry. He found her leaning on the counter, crying, enraged. "I hate her," she said furiously when he came in. "I hate her." She put her hands over her face. Peter put his arms around her, and she wept against him.

When they went back to the living room, Mrs. Pierce was effusively friendly to Peter. She put him at her right for dinner.

Peter turned now to the mirror, sliding his tie around the neck of his shirt. The collar stood stiffly upright. That moment, when Caroline had collapsed against him, weeping, bruised, he had felt swept by tenderness, the wish to protect her. She had seemed vulnerable, he had felt strong. All this had risen up in him, urgent, turbulent. A kind of love; he had thought it the real one.

He knotted the tie, looping the flat panel of silk around itself. Odd that you have to look in a mirror to do this, he thought, even if you know how. Even if you know the mechanics precisely, you need the eye. He watched the loop, the slipknot, the silk tails fitting neatly one underneath the other, one just the right amount shorter than the other. He remembered learning to tie nautical knots, sitting inside on rainy summer days in Maine. The rabbit comes out of the hole, around the tree, back into the ground. He was ready; he buttoned his jacket. He looked up and met his own eyes in the mirror: now, Emma.

For an instant her face came to him: brilliant, radiant against deep space. Then it dissolved, and he had to blink, mentally, and turn his mind away before he tried again.

He remembered the first time he had met her, at the cocktail party. He had thought her cool, then, self-sufficient: now he knew she was shy, self-conscious. As she looked at his paintings, he had thought her judgmental and dismissive. Now he knew she was most ruthlessly judgmental toward herself. She forgave herself nothing, permitted herself no errors: it was absurd, touching.

He felt himself yearning for her. It was so different, this kind of love. How could he have mistaken the other for it? He longed for Emma's presence, the pleasure, the luxurious solace of it. He thought of the long line of the inside of her arm, the pale untouched skin.

This part was like charging headlong down a mountainside, heedless of footing, balance, boulders, gravity, feeling only the necessity of the rush. Who knew what would happen? Who cared? How good that he was in the middle of it, in the middle of this hurtle, the thundering landslide of himself, toward her.

5

This is an experiment," Peter said, holding the door open for Emma. She stepped inside. The restaurant was Mexican, gloomy and pretentious. The rooms were high ceilinged, and on the red walls hung bad nineteenth-century portraits in ornate frames. The place was nearly empty, and the headwaiter welcomed them effusively. Bald and corpulent, he walked backward before them, bowing, as he led them to their table. He placed himself behind Emma's high-backed chair.

"Señora," he said unctuously, seating her with a flourish. "Señor," he added, bowing slightly. He handed them each a large menu, with red tasseled cords. He rubbed his hands together and smiled horribly. "Something to drink?"

When he had gone Emma asked, "Why is servility so offensive?"

"It's hostile," said Peter. "A thin skin of politeness over contempt."

"That's exactly right, isn't it," Emma said. "There's rage behind the bows. But an Italian waiter can bow all evening long, and you don't feel rage. You feel charm."

"That's because Italians don't lose face by being polite," Peter said. "They don't lose face by doing anything. They're inherently dignified. Nothing they do threatens their dignity. Americans, on the other hand, are so terrified of losing face they'll make you learn their names before they'll park your car." He looked around at the funereal room. "I don't know about this place. It's pretty terrible so far."

"Maybe the food is good," Emma said.

"At least it's not noisy," Peter said. He reached under the table and took her hand. "I like being able to hear you." He looked directly at her. "I like being able to look at you, too."

"I can't look at you too long," Emma said. "It's like looking at the sun."

She could feel him beginning to relax. By now she recognized his tension, but did not yet know how to dispel it. She didn't know how Peter would normally relax—exercise? solitude? alcohol? But this was not his normal life. He had no normal life now. Divorce had set him adrift, cut him off from the mainland.

Emma remembered the great crowd of people in his apartment the night she had met him. They seemed to her to have vanished from his life. Friends move toward the wife in a divorce. Caroline had custody of the child and the apartment; she seemed to have custody of their friends as well. Caroline continued to lead their old life, but Peter had been expelled from it.

Peter opened his menu. "Mexican food."

"I love it," said Emma. "I spent a summer in Mexico."

"Did you?" Peter looked up. "Why?"

"I was in a community aid project, in a little village in the mountains. I loved it: it was so hot and dry and remote. It was complete in itself, it was its own world. The countryside was so spare and empty, so calm. At the markets, the women knelt on the ground, and set out their vegetables in little pyramids, green peppers, red tomatoes, all of them shining and clean."

"What were you doing there?"

"The boys were building a schoolhouse. We all took turns doing the cooking. We worked in pairs, and my partner was a guy called Jeff. I had an enormous crush on him, but he didn't pay any attention to me."

"Was he blind?" Peter asked.

Emma shook her head. "He was above all that. He was very highly evolved. He was a pacifist and a vegetarian. He had views on everything. I was very impressed: I had no views on anything.

"On our last night there, Jeff and I made a big feast: a huge bean and vegetable stew. There were nineteen of us to feed, and Jeff and I worked all afternoon, peeling and chopping and mixing. When we had everything in the pot, and had poured in all the water, I added two cubes of chicken bouillon, those little golden squeezy things. When I looked up I saw Jeff watching me. He asked, 'Did you put in bouillon?' I realized what I'd done. 'Oh, God,' I said, 'I'm so sorry. I'll fish it out.' Jeff shook his head. 'No,' he said, 'it doesn't matter.'" He wouldn't look at me. The stew simmered all afternoon. At dinnertime he got himself a plate, instead of a bowl, and all he ate were tortillas. He wouldn't take a single sip."

"Ah," said Peter, "stuffy and sanctimonious. That was his problem."

"I felt like a fool," Emma said.

"You weren't the fool," Peter said. "He was. He was a self-righteous ass."

"But he was principled," Emma said. "I admired that."

"He was rigid and intolerant and unkind," Peter said. "Why admire that?" He paused. "I didn't know you were in Mexico. I like finding these things out about you."

"It makes me nervous," Emma admitted. "What if you find out things you don't like?"

"What if you find out things about me you don't like?" Peter returned. "Should we quit from nerves?"

"And then what?" Emma said, laughing.

"Exactly." Peter took a swallow of his drink. "How old were you then?"

"Nineteen," said Emma.

"And were you happy? I mean, in your life?"

"I don't know," said Emma. "I've never thought of it that way. I was too young to think whether or not I was happy. When you're young you just live."

"I think you like places you've been to when you're happy, and you don't when you're not."

"But don't you think you'd always love Venice, no matter how you felt?" Emma asked.

"I can imagine hating Venice," Peter said. "Finding it cold and sinister. Damp."

"Most unusual," Emma said.

"That I wouldn't like Venice?"

"That you'd think landscape would be colored by emotion."

"Is that unusual?"

"In a man, it is," Emma said.

"Oh, I think you'll find I'm a most unusual fellow," Peter said cheerfully. The headwaiter hovered nearby, predatory. "Shall we order?"

"Señor?" The headwaiter stepped forward at once.

As Emma gave her order, she heard the man's slow stifled breathing, like a quiet snore. When he took the menus and left, Emma said, "Poor man. I feel sorry for him."

"Why?"

"This can't be what he hoped for, when he left Mexico. All his high hopes for a better life, and he ends up in this dreary place, groveling in front of rich Americans."

"You don't know," said Peter mildly. "You're being elitist. For all you know, this was his dream: to be a headwaiter in a fancy place. Gold-framed paintings. Menus with tassels. He's put a down payment on a house in Queens, his wife drives a Honda."

Emma laughed. "Maybe. But he might hate it. I think I'll still feel sorry for him, just in case."

"Good," said Peter. "I rely on you for that."

"For what?"

"Thinking of other people," said Peter.

"And what do I rely on you for?"

"Whatever you'd like." He smiled at her easily.

Emma smiled back. Warren had never told her he'd rely on her for anything, and when he told her to rely on him it had felt like a command. This felt different: an offer of partnership.

The food was good: pale steaming tortillas, a sharp ribbon of chili running through the soft simmered beans.

"Can you cook like this?" Peter asked.

"No," Emma said. "I mean I could, but I wouldn't. It's very slow, Mexican cooking. Making tortillas, simmering beans. It takes days, it's not something you start doing at five o'clock."

"Do you like cooking?" Peter asked.

"Yes," said Emma. "Sometimes," she amended, honestly. "Not all the time. Does Caroline?" The name felt strange in her mouth. She tried to say it easily.

The subject of Warren and Caroline was always imminent, forbidden but irresistible. Merely to speak their names was a potent act. They were charged and powerful, central to the myth of Peter and Emma that was now unfolding. It was Warren's and Caroline's malevolent magic that had begun this chain of events. Telling their anguished stories drew Peter and Emma into sympathetic alliance. Out of loyalty and decency they resisted complaining, laying blame, but out of grief and rage and loneliness they yielded, doing both.

"Caroline thinks cooking is demeaning," Peter said. "In fact, the moment I realized my marriage was over was one night when Caroline refused to cook dinner."

"How?" Emma asked.

"It had started weeks before," Peter said, "We were invited to a cocktail party."

That night, Peter had come home tired and cold. It had been a long day. Caroline was standing in the front hall, waiting for him. Before the door had closed behind him she held up an envelope. She was exultant.

"Guess what," she said, waving the card in front of him. "Drinks at the Spensers'."

"Great," Peter said, not looking at her. He set down his briefcase and began unbuttoning his coat.

Caroline held up the card again, so close that he had to look at it. It was Tiffany copperplate on a stiff white rectangle. The sloping black script declared that Mr. and Mrs. Edward Spenser requested the pleasure of their company.

"Peter," Caroline said, frowning slightly, "did you see this? Did you see who it's from?"

"I saw it," Peter said evenly. "And you told me who it's from. But I just walked in the door. I'd like a chance to take off my coat before invitations are waved in my face."

There was a pause. Caroline folded her arms and stared at him. "What's the matter with you?"

"There's nothing the matter with me," Peter said, taking off his coat. "I have just walked in the door."

"I think I understand that," Caroline said. "Since you've said it twice and since I was standing here when it happened. How long would you like before you're ready to receive information about social events?"

Peter hung his coat in the closet. He closed the door with emphasis and turned to Caroline. "You can start now," he said. "Bring on our social events. What piece of earthshaking news do you have for me?"

Caroline narrowed her eyes. "I've already told you, actually," she said. "And I have the feeling that you're not taking it very seriously. It's drinks at the Spensers'."

"I am taking it seriously," Peter said, irritated. "Drinks at the Spensers'. I said 'Fine.' I'll say it again. Fine."

"Actually, you *didn't* say 'Fine.' Actually, what you said was 'Great,' " Caroline said. She spoke rapidly, blinking with irritation. "Not that it matters. The point is that this invitation is a big deal. This isn't something you just say 'Great' to."

"If it doesn't matter, then don't bring it up," Peter said, his voice rising. "What difference does it make whether I said 'Great' or 'Fine'?"

Caroline put her hands on her hips.

"Peter," she said, "this is a big deal, which you know perfectly well. We've never been invited to the Spensers' before. Why do you act as though this is nothing? It's not nothing. These people are important in New York. In fact they are *crucial*. He's a Morgan. And she's on the board of the Met. I would *kill* to get her on the board at the center."

" 'They are crucial,' " Peter repeated scornfully. "Caroline, you sound like a fool. Why are you so excited about the Morgans? I went to school with Morgans, they aren't descended from God. Waddy Baxter is a Morgan. He's a complete jerk. He used to make fart noises during the headmaster's speeches. You want to meet him? I'll introduce you."

Caroline made a disgusted noise. "Don't be ridiculous," she said, furious. "You're the one who sounds like a fool. Don't pretend that an invitation from Waddy Baxter is the same as one from Edward Spenser. You're being an ass. Don't treat this—" She stopped. "You act as though this is nothing special."

"It's just a cocktail party, for Christ's sake," Peter said. "They want you to give money to something. Don't be so naive. You act as though they've asked us to marry them."

Caroline closed her eyes in irritation and took the bridge of her nose between her thumb and forefinger. After a moment she looked at him.

"Don't condescend to me, Peter," she said.

"Don't tell me what to do, Caroline," Peter said, and walked out of the room.

On the day of the party, Peter had forgotten about it. He had been in Chicago the night before, and flew back in the late afternoon. There was fog over La Guardia, and his plane circled bumpily for over an hour. Peter finally landed, took a cab home, and arrived to an apartment empty of Caroline. He heard Amanda and her nanny, Maeve, in the kitchen, but in the bedroom there was only the invitation lying on his bureau, with a note: "See you here, I hope." The word *hope* was circled viciously.

He remembered then, of course. He looked at his watch: it was eight-twenty. The invitation said six to eight, and the Spencers lived on Fifth between Ninetieth and Ninety-first. If he left that very instant, he wouldn't arrive until twenty of nine, maybe quarter of. And he didn't want to leave that instant: he felt sweaty and wrinkled. He went into the bathroom to wash.

He raised a double handful of water to his face. His eyes closed, he thought of what it would be like, arriving at the party. The big marble-floored downstairs lobby, the rack by the elevator jammed with heavy coats. The elevator rising toward the festive crowd, the dread of imminent hilarity. Upstairs, the door opening onto the end of a winter cocktail party. The voices loud, the pitch shrill, the gestures wide, the gazes unfocused. People making promises about lunches and telephone calls that they would never keep. The host would be unfindable, and in any case a stranger to Peter. The hostess would be caught in a high-voiced tangle of people in an inner room, by a marble fireplace. Her polite but mystified look as he approached through the sea of strangers. The snobbish face of the waiter, with his tray of white wine and champagne. Peter felt exhausted by the prospect.

Caroline would be with their hostess. She would be part of that circle in the inner room, by the marble fireplace. She would be leaning forward, intent, anxious not to miss anything, her eyes blinking rapidly with concentration. Her laughter high-pitched and self-conscious. When she caught sight of Peter she would smile in an inauthentic way, watching fondly as he made his way through the encumbering crowd. When he arrived at her side, she would put her hand on his shoulder, as though claiming him, and lean forward.

"Mrs. Spenser, I want you to meet my husband, Peter," she would say, proud, officious, and Peter would feel, for that moment, as though he had become her creature, under her command.

"Fuck it," Peter said to the mirror, throwing the towel down on the sink. "It's too late to go anyway." He went down the hall to find Amanda.

"So," said Emma, shocked, "you never went at all?"

Peter shook his head.

"She must have been furious."

"She was," said Peter. "I had let her down. And I did condescend to her. She was right."

The headwaiter bustled toward them, a small busboy behind him. Their huge plates were swirled importantly away, and the tasseled menus handed back for dessert. They ordered only coffee. Disapproving, the headwaiter bowed, and backed into the gloom.

"I think when you get divorced you never feel it's your fault, no matter what," Emma said. "Everyone feels they've been driven to it, by someone else, against their wills. Everyone feels they're nice people who've been wronged."

Peter raised his eyebrows, not quite agreeing. "I suppose so."

"That's how Caroline and Warren must feel: unsuspecting innocents, ambushed by villains. And so do we. We all feel wronged, and innocent."

"I know," Peter said, now giving way. "Caroline was always the same, from the beginning. I was the one who changed. I thought, in the beginning, that our differences wouldn't matter."

They were silent for a moment.

"But what about the cooking?" Emma said. "You said the last straw was about cooking."

"Oh," said Peter. "The cooking was really tangential. That night, Caroline came home after the party around nine or nine-thirty. By then I'd made myself an omelette. I was in the library, very happy, with a book and a glass of wine.

"Caroline was furious about everything, of course, but what we ended up fighting over was the fact that she had to cook dinner for herself that night. She'd expected that I'd turn up at the party and we'd go out to dinner afterwards. But now, because of my inconsiderateness, she had to make herself something to eat."

Peter shrugged his shoulders. "It was the last straw, for me. It was the terminal moment. While we were arguing, it came to me like a sort of promise that I was not going to spend the rest of my life in this kind of argument, with a woman who took these things seriously. I realized, during that argument, that we had nothing in common—no goals, no principles, no attitudes, *nothing.* We didn't even like doing the same things. Caroline would rather watch TV than read, she'd rather read a magazine than a book, and she'd rather go to a cocktail party than anything else in the world. It was a revelation. I'd known these things before, but I'd known them separately, not as part of a whole, and they'd meant nothing. I'd thought they didn't matter, individually, because there was something central that bound us together. But in that moment I realized there was no central thing, and that what I'd thought was love was actually affection and pity. This all hit me at once, and the next thing I thought was, I'm not going on with this. When that came to me, it was like a balm, a moment of overwhelming relief."

He looked at Emma ruefully. "It sounds extreme, now. It sounds unfair to Caroline: it was just another argument."

Emma shook her head. "They build up. They aren't moments, they're crescendos. And it sounds as though Caroline was really angry at you. Underneath."

Peter nodded. "She was. She resented a lot. I never took things seriously that she wanted me to. She wanted me to be much grander than I was. What she really wanted was for me to inherit Axminster; it truly irritated her that I hadn't. When she finally met my cousin Roger, as soon as she realized who he was she started flirting with him. I thought it was funny. 'She's after Axminster,' I told him. Roger's face lit up. 'She wants it?' He turned to her and said, 'It's yours. It needs a whole new roof, new wiring and new plumbing. The electricity bill is so big we're listed as an asset at Northeastern Power and Light. When would you like title?' "

Emma laughed. "What did Caroline say?"

"She knew she was being teased, but she didn't quite know how. I don't know what she said, something charming. She can be very charming."

Rebuked, Emma did not answer. Why did he suddenly have to tell me Caroline is charming she wondered. Emma lowered her gaze to her coffee cup, reminded that Peter still felt loyalty toward Caroline, affection, regret. It was painful but she admired it.

"When I met you," she said, "at your cocktail party, you seemed so sure of everything. You seemed so confident, so married."

Peter shook his head. "By the time of that party we were barely speaking. When we were alone we hardly spoke at all. We didn't have meals together, we spent the evenings apart. It was near the end." Peter looked at her. "What about you? When did you know things were over? Did you have a moment?"

Emma nodded. "It was when Tess was about six months old. I quit working when she was born, though Warren didn't want me to. He wanted to brag about how fast I'd gone back to work, but once I'd had her I didn't want to go back at all. In the beginning I didn't have a nanny, or anyone, I was alone with Tess, all the time. I was exhausted, but I loved it. I got up in the middle of the night. I'd feed her and change her and sometimes I'd climb into her crib with her and sleep there the rest of the night. I woke up when she woke up, I slept late with her in the mornings, I took naps in the afternoon. It was sort of a dreamworld, just nursing and changing and sleeping and holding her. I didn't have any other life. I was besotted.

"Warren didn't really like it: he was used to getting all my attention. He loved Tess too, but from a distance. He'd do things for her when I asked him, but he didn't really want to. I didn't care, I loved being in charge.

"One Sunday we were in the living room, reading the papers. Warren was stretched out on the sofa, and I was sitting on the rug with Tess. She was fussing, so I started walking her around, reading the paper over her shoulder. She went on whimpering, not hard, but sort of steadily. I wasn't paying much attention to her, and then Warren said, without looking up from the paper, 'That kid is a real whiner.'

"I said, automatically, 'No, she's not.'

"Still without looking up, Warren said, 'Listen to her. Never stops.'

"I said, 'She's not a whiner. She just needs a nap.'

"Warren said, 'She just got up. She's a complainer.' He shook his head, as though he were the authority.

"And I suddenly thought about what he was saying. I looked at my watch. I said, 'She did not just get up. She's been up for four hours, and she's had breakfast, and now she needs a nap. She's not a whiner, and you know nothing about it.' I took Tess and stalked out of the room.

"It was the first time I ever contradicted Warren. I was furious that he could criticize his own daughter in such a casual, contemptuous way, and that he was so completely and totally wrong, so unfair. I remember standing in the bedroom with Tess, settling her in the crib, smiling, calming her down. But my heart was pounding, and I kept thinking, That's it. That's it. I felt jubilant. I didn't know really what I meant. I wasn't thinking about a divorce, but I felt freed. I suddenly felt higher than he was, larger, as though I'd become a cloud, vast and airborne. I knew I wasn't going to go on like this, putting up with the things he said. I would have put up with them forever, for myself, but I wasn't going to for Tess. I felt freed." She looked anxiously at Peter. "This feels so disloyal. It sounds so callous."

Peter took her hand and stroked it. "It's no worse than what I've told you. We've done the same thing. I tell myself it's not callousness, it's resolution. But it's sad."

He wished he could get past this sadness, get through these layers of guilt, rage, shame. He wanted to be over all this, to be certain of his life again. He wanted everything to be decided. He wanted Amanda to be happy. He wanted Emma.

The headwaiter arrived, ponderously discreet. Eyes lowered, mouth compressed, he bent over and slid a small brown folder onto the table next to Peter. In a low rasp he whispered, "The check, Señor."

Peter put a credit card inside the folder, the headwaiter picked it up and vanished.

Emma glanced after him and shook her head, smiling. "Poor thing," she said to Peter. He smiled.

"You're kind," Peter said suddenly, fervent. "You're kind and brave."
Now he longed for her kindness. He longed to be alone in the world with
her, to close his eyes and receive her kindness. He leaned toward her.
"There's nothing you should be afraid of telling me," he said, "nothing. I
know you. Nothing you say will change that. I know who you are. I love
you, I love what you are. You can trust me."

Emma raised her eyes to meet his. Without speaking they looked
steadily at each other. Her gaze was generous and clear: it was what he
yearned for.

6

Opening her eyes into the nighttime silence, Emma saw first a high shadowy ceiling. The room around her was dark. A shaft of light slanted sideways into the dim space, through a narrowly opened door. The harsh brilliance of the light suggested a bathroom, but this door was in the wrong place. It was on the wall to the right of the bed; in Emma's bedroom the bathroom door was on the left.

Blurry eyed, half asleep, Emma tried mentally to reverse the door's position. In the murky light she blinked, struggling to place the doorway where it ought to be. It stayed immobile, glowing, lit mysteriously from beyond.

Blinking, confused, she raised her head from the pillow, half blind, half panicky. She squinted into the transparent gloom, trying to force it into focus. For a moment she could not decipher the room. She was in bed, in the dark, a man beside her. She felt a flicker of the awful Asolo panic, of being hurled through the air. Fear set a cold clamp on her, and she opened her mouth to breathe. In the next moment, as she stared into the dark, the room came suddenly clear, resolving itself into a space she knew. Peter's room, Peter's bed.

Emma dropped her head back onto the pillow and lay still, looking at the ceiling. Peter lay on his side, facing away, his bare shoulder a smooth silhouette rising from the crumpled sheet. Emma, awake, was no longer alarmed, but uneasiness lingered. Risk still coiled around her; she was still in someone else's apartment, someone else's bed.

She lay motionless, flat on her back. She drew long quiet breaths to calm herself. It was still dark, though the tall windows were slowly becoming luminous. Light spread mysteriously upward from the foot of the white shades, pulled almost down to the windowsills. The shades gave a papery rustle as they breathed gently, in, out, on the shifting early morning air. On either side of the windows, dim outlines began to appear of the heavy damask curtains, too long, which fell into soft rumpled heaps on the rug. The standing lamp in the corner dimly announced itself against the wall. The landscape was no longer strange, but unease persisted.

The clock said six-twelve, time to leave. She wanted to be home when Tess woke up, to give her breakfast before leaving again for work. Tess would be asleep now; Emma's urgency was for Rachel. She didn't tell Rachel when she spent the night out. She wanted to creep quietly back into the apartment before Rachel was up.

Each time, returning home, Emma was seized by guilt. Unlocking the door, in those last seconds before she stepped inside the apartment, Emma was struck by fear that something had happened, that her undeclared, selfish, illicit, irresponsible absence had resulted in disaster. Each time, turning the key, her heart pounding, she swore to herself that the next time she stayed out she would tell Rachel. Each time, entering the apartment, moving quickly through the hall, she found Tess sleeping peacefully in her crib, healthy, pink, undisturbed.

Emma didn't tell Rachel when she spent the night elsewhere because she didn't want to see the look on Rachel's face. Rachel would grin broadly, raise one eyebrow and say something Emma did not want to hear—something intimate, about her sex life. Or else Rachel would raise both eyebrows coldly and say nothing at all. Emma didn't mind Rachel knowing about her private life, but she didn't want to hear Rachel's opinion of it.

She would have to tell Rachel eventually. Things would change; they would either become more permanent or less so. Emma wanted to wait until she could make a real announcement. Until then, she returned surreptitiously, and fished anxiously for her keys, consumed by guilt.

Now, Emma slid quietly out of bed, tucking the sheet around Peter against a draft. Naked, barefoot, she stepped across the shadowy room, through the crepuscular silence. She felt invisible.

Her clothes lay in a careful pile, and she dressed rapidly, with distaste. Her unwashed panty hose were dry and gritty, bagging sourly at the knees. Her red silk dress, pristine and smooth the night before, now felt dank. Emma swung her long hair to one side and tugged the zipper up her back. She stepped into her high heels, her ankles wobbling: it was too early for this sexy off-balance tilt. Her nighttime self—short skirted, high heeled, mascaraed and perfumed—now seemed absurd. Last night, leaning across the table at the restaurant, in the dense glow of candlelight, dancing later at the club, Emma had wanted to look just exactly as she had looked. Now, all this seemed noisy, shameless, coy. Now she was a mother. She wanted jeans and sneakers, heels flat on the ground.

Emma was dressed, though not really up: her face unwashed, her teeth unbrushed. All she was doing here was leaving; she would address the day at home. She put on dark glasses to conceal the mascara smears below her eyes. She coiled the chain of her purse in her hand, muffling it.

Soundless, she leaned over Peter's sleeping face. He lay now on his back. His lips were barely parted, and he took a long silent breath as Emma watched. Along the top of his cheekbone was a faint ruddiness, a bloom in the pale skin. Below the clean line of closed eyelids was a dry tangle of eyelashes. It made her anxious, this silent invasion, examining his sleeping face without consent. She bent quickly to kiss him good-bye.

"Peter," she whispered.

Before she touched him his eyes opened. His gaze was clear and focused, and he put his arms around her at once, as though he had been waiting for this moment. He pulled her down, against his chest. Pulled off balance, she knelt first on the bed, then collapsed gently onto him. His body was warm, radiant, smelling like him. She breathed deeply, and closed her eyes for a moment. He kissed her lengthily, and she felt her body waken, quicken. She felt the heat from his body, felt him begin to start slowly up, like a great engine. His hands moved across her skin; she felt his tongue flicker along the inside of her lip. Her heart sank.

"Peter," she whispered, troubled.

"Mm," he whispered back. His eyes were closed. He slid his hand onto the top of her leg.

"Peter," she said, out loud.

His hand stopped, and he opened his eyes. "What?"

"I have to leave," she said, anxious.

"Why?" His hand continued moving.

"I've told you," Emma said. "I have to be there when Tess wakes up." She was still lying on top of him. She could feel his warmth through her

silky dress. His arms were still around her. His hand slid again up the back
of her thigh.

"Not just yet," he whispered. His fingers were warm, slow. He kissed
her more. The clock now said six twenty-three. After a moment she spoke.

"Peter."

"What," he said. He slid his fingers further up. His eyes were on hers,
steady, holding her still.

Emma pushed herself up, off him. "I have to go, I'm sorry."

"I don't see why." His voice was now challenging, unfriendly. "Isn't
Rachel there?"

"I still have to go." Emma stood up. She felt guilty, refusing him. But
the night was over; the thought of Tess drew her now.

Peter, relinquishing her, put his arms behind his head. He watched
her without speaking, his mouth firm with disapproval.

"I'm sorry," Emma said helplessly, but he said nothing. "I don't *want*
to leave."

"Then don't."

"I have to."

"Emma, you don't," he said. "It's ridiculous."

"Peter, I'm away all day," Emma said, pleading. "I only get to see her a
short time in the morning, and then a short time at night."

"It's six o'clock in the morning," Peter said. "You get to work at nine-
thirty."

"It's six-thirty," Emma began, but she could not go on. Chilled, disheartened, she could not explain herself, she could not say anything at all
in the face of his cold disapproval. She walked to the door.

In the doorway she turned, but Peter had rolled back over, his head
submerged again in the pillow.

"Well, good-bye," she said.

He looked up, his face set. "Good-bye."

Emma waited for a moment, hoping he would relent, smile, soften, but
he did not. She walked slowly down the long hall. She stood before the
closet, putting on her coat, pulling her hair outside the collar, shaking it
down her back, slowly drawing the belt tight. There was no sound from
the bedroom. She let herself out, shutting the door quietly behind her. She
was still listening.

The outside hall was grand and shabby; this had been an old town
house. Heavy plaster cornices edged the high ceiling, their intricate sil-

houettes picked out in precise detail by dust. The floor was a black-and-white checkerboard of stone tiles, soiled and chipped. The walls were a bleak oyster white, faint cracks trekking across them. The air in the hallway was unused, still chilled from the night.

Emma pushed the unpolished brass button for the elevator and waited. The early air drifted around her legs, cold and unfriendly. She pulled her short coat close. She felt in disgrace.

She had slept only three or four hours—Peter had wakened her over and over in the night—and her eyes now felt burnt, as though she stared out through blackened holes. She could feel the dark hollows beneath them. Her hands were deep in her pockets, her shoulders hunched. Her back was to Peter's door, but she listened for it to open. She wished he would appear in his doorway, changed, kind, himself once more, apologetic, loving.

The elevator slid silently up from below. Its window appeared, a lighted rising capsule, like a diving chamber. The door rolled open. Emma hesitated, then stepped on. She moved to the back and turned to face the front. It was Peter's last chance. She pictured him throwing open the door, lunging for the elevator button, catching it just as the metal gate scissored shut.

But his door stayed closed, the elevator door slid across the opening. The floor sank away beneath her, and Emma dropped swiftly through the darkness. At the bottom the door opened again, and she stepped out into the marble lobby. The doorman stared boldly at her.

"Good morning," Emma said briskly. She was suddenly conscious again of her sunglasses, black stockings, high heels, her dressy evening coat. It was so obvious she had spent the night, but didn't live here. The doorman held the door for her, but she didn't ask for a taxi. She wanted to leave this place.

Outside, Emma walked quickly toward Madison. The early air was still cool and fresh, and she took deep breaths, trying to restore her presence in the world. I have my own apartment, she told herself, a job, my own life. How dare Peter be so hostile? She would not put herself in this position again, she told herself. She would not stay overnight.

At the corner, Emma turned down Madison. There was no traffic now, and the avenue was wide and empty in the early light. It was clean, slick with the night's dampness. The Westbury Hotel stretched grandly southward, and Emma walked toward its entrance. The windows along the street—shops, the Polo Bar—were dark, the vitrines glossy and immaculate. Emma walked past, feeling calmer, relieved by their impersonal perfection.

Two cabs stood at the Westbury's big front doors. Engines off, taxi lights on, they waited for early fares. Emma went to the first, opened the door and began to climb in. The driver turned to her over the seat back. He was middle-aged and burly, unshaven, with black-rimmed glasses. There was baggy flesh beneath his chin, and a dark mole by the base of his nose.

"No, no," he said loudly, nodding toward the lobby. "I'm going to the airport."

"To the airport?" Emma said, confused. She looked at the dim and silent lobby. Inside the heavy glass doors the doorman watched impassively.

"Yeah," said the driver, raising his voice. "Go on, get out, get *out*." He leaned over the seat back. His tone was insulting, and he waved his hands, sweeping her out. "Go on. *Go. Go*. Get. I'm not taking you." He shook his head.

Cowed, confused, Emma backed from the cab and closed its door. She walked to the second cab. As she climbed in, its driver turned toward her, his face dark and suspicious.

"No, no," he said, flapping his hand. He was Hispanic, short, slight, black haired, with gleaming dark eyes.

But now Emma was prepared. "What do you mean, no, no?" she said. She sat down and shut the door hard.

"No, no, I no take you," said the driver, his voice loud.

"Yes, you do too take me," said Emma, angry. "Fifth Avenue and Tenth Street."

"No, no," the driver said again. He shook his index finger at her and closed his eyes, refusing to see her, but Emma settled herself firmly on the seat and leaned back.

"You take me to Fifth Avenue and Tenth Street or we'll call the police," she said. "You take me where I tell you to go. And don't you tell me no, no."

"Why he no take you?" asked the driver, suspicious, but beginning to yield.

"I don't know why, and I don't care. But you're going to or we'll call the police," said Emma, suddenly furious. *"Policia."*

She crossed her arms on her chest and turned to look out the window. The driver did not start the engine; he was staring at her in the mirror. She felt his black eyes stabbing hatefully at her. She refused to meet them.

She sat motionless, staring at the dim lobby and the statue of the doorman. At last the driver muttered to himself and pulled down the taxi flag, starting the meter. He turned on the engine, and they pulled away from the curb.

Arms folded, Emma stared out the window as the taxi rattled downtown through the empty streets. The driver drove too fast, hurtling through just-red lights, skidding around corners, shifting capriciously between lanes. Emma, who could not face another argument, sat silently on the slippery backseat, thrown sideways around corners, into the air over potholes. Angry, she puzzled over the first driver's refusal. He had lied about the airport, there was no one but the doorman in the hotel lobby. But why had he refused her? It was illegal to turn down a fare.

Emma saw herself, in her high red heels, her short skirt, her sunglasses. Her loose hair, the early hour, her solitude: the driver had thought she was a whore.

A whore. Emma looked out the window. This was a bad morning.

She leaned back against the seat, avoiding the sight of her skirt. Everyone wore these clothes: short, tight, stretchy, bright. Sexy was how you were meant to look. The magazines showed fifteen-hundred-dollar black leather dresses that barely reached the thigh. You wore them with wild hair and no bra. You wore them with slave bracelets tight around your arm, with wide chokers, tight around your neck. You wore them with stiletto heels, with leather boots that slid up over your knees. It was the way everyone dressed.

We dress like whores, thought Emma, but we're insulted to be taken for them. She stared out the window. She felt greasy, ashamed, as though she'd been caught at something. The cabdriver was watching her. His eyes flickered meanly at hers in the mirror, as though he knew something shameful about her.

When they stopped at her building Emma gave the driver the exact fare, pouring bills and coins into his hand and sliding out of the backseat at once. The driver stared suspiciously at the money in his hand, counting. He called out to her, enraged.

"Lady!" he said. "You don' give me no tip!"

Emma turned back to him.

"That's right," she said. "No tip. A tip is extra. You were rude and unpleasant. Next time when someone gets in your cab you don't tell them to get out. Then maybe you'll get a tip." She meant to sound Olympian, dignified, but her voice turned uneven. On the last words her voice broke altogether, and she slammed the taxi door like a two-year-old in a tantrum.

"You fuck youself, lady," the driver yelled, gunning the engine. He shot away from the curb in a swell of rage, leaving clouds of exhaust, quivering and blue, fouling the early air.

Emma walked into her lobby. She was furious at Peter, the cabdrivers, and herself. Why had she stooped to the driver's level? Shouting and slamming doors like a fishwife: she should have given him a meager tip and stalked away. But why give him a tip at all? Why should he be so rude and horrible, and why should she ignore it? Or reward it? "Lady" he had called her. Where were the rules here? She felt in a wonderland of impossible choices: be rude or be weak, be racist or be lectured. In the elevator she closed her eyes to rid herself of the whole thing.

Upstairs, she let herself quietly into her apartment. She eased the heavy door shut behind her, holding the doorknob so it would turn soundlessly. Inside, she listened for a moment, holding her breath.

She was home. In the silence, in the early light, standing in her own front hall, she felt calm begin to return. She hung up her coat and went in to find her daughter. Tess lay on her belly, her small rump slightly raised. Her face was turned toward Emma: the pale satiny skin, the innocent bluish hollows beneath the eyes. The swell of the cheek, the brief swoop of the nose.

Emma leaned over Tess, stroking her head. Her breathing was soundless, and Emma watched for the tiny rise and fall of respiration. The small head was warm. Her pale hair was slightly matted, the fine strands sifted into each other, damp from Tess's own heat, from the steady beat of her heart.

Emma picked the sleeping child up, and carried her into her own room. She settled Tess in bed, pulled off her clothes, and climbed into bed with her daughter. She had forty-five minutes. Listening to Tess's peaceful breathing, Emma closed her eyes. She began to drift toward sleep.

Emma found herself somewhere else—a narrow street full of talking shoes—in the beginnings of sleep. Among the gabble of shoes something intruded: the rustle of sheets. Emma felt the slight shift of weight as Tessie raised her head; she heard the delighted intake of breath as Tess realized where she was. Emma kept her eyes shut, feigning sleep, but it was no use. She felt Tess's delicate fingers on her face, her eyelids.

"Is Mommy asleep?" Tess whispered earnestly. "Mommy, are you asleep, Mommy?"

It was irresistible. Emma opened her eyes to Tess's radiant face.

"I thought you were not awake, Mommy," Tess said, "but you are."

Tess sat up with a deep sigh of pleasure. Her eyes began to roam her mother's room for things to explore. Weariness now broke over Emma like a wave. Her eyelids, unbearably heavy, resisted movement. Tess climbed cheerily down and began walking around the room, picking things up. Emma dozed, half-watching her, dazed with tiredness. At seven-thirty her alarm began to buzz.

Fifteen minutes later, showered and dressed for work, Emma carried Tess into the kitchen. Rachel, in her purple bathrobe, was already there. She looked sulky, and did not smile at Emma.

"Good morning," Emma said, determinedly cheerful.

"Good morning," Rachel said, not at all cheerful.

"Rachel! Hi, Rachel!" Tess was radiant. "Rachel! Are you not dressed, Rachel? Did you have a good dream?"

Rachel and Emma both laughed. Rachel was not sulky at Tess.

"Hi, Tess," Rachel said. "No, I'm not dressed yet. And you aren't either." Rachel smiled at Tess, but her face fell back into sullenness when she stopped talking, and she did not look at Emma.

Emma ignored Rachel's mood. She had been up for over two hours, had gotten dressed twice, traveled sixty blocks and dealt with three hostile men. Rachel had barely gotten up, she had not gotten dressed, and was already cross.

Emma lifted Tess into the high chair, buckling the cotton strap across her small belly. She got out bowls and cereal.

"Okay, Tessie," Emma said, "what do you want this morning, Mommy cereal or Tessie cereal?" Emma liked monotony in meals; she had, week in, week out, the same cereal for breakfast, the same sandwich for lunch. She ate granola, with milk and yogurt, but Tess ranged energetically back and forth across the cereal field. At the question Tess leaned forward, hunching over her clenched fists, then threw her head back, supple and elastic, like a gymnast. She closed her eyes.

"Which do I want?" she asked the air. "Which do I?"

Emma filled her own bowl and shook on a white dollop of yogurt. "Better hurry up, or I'll finish mine."

Rachel stood in the doorway, her face remote.

"So, Rachel," Emma said, placating, "What's on for today?" She did not dare look at her.

Rachel shrugged her shoulders. "Park in the morning. Nap in the afternoon. Supermarket afterwards." Her tone was heavy with indifference.

"The park!" Emma said to Tess. "Oh, Tessie. You'll have fun at the park."

Tessie sucked her breath in. "I like the park."

"When I come home," Emma promised, "you can choose two books for me to read. But right now, I have to go to work." Emma stood up, and Tess looked anxious at once.

"Do you not have to go right now, Mommy?" she coaxed.

Ah, here it was, the dread moment. Now speed was of the essence. Emma kissed the top of Tess's head.

"I have to go right now, or my boss will get angry with me, and he'll say I'm not doing a good job."

She was talking fast, brightly, but she knew it wasn't working. Nothing worked at this stage.

Tess's face began to crumple. The eyebrows pulled together, the fragile skin furrowed, the mouth drew down at the corners. Misery took over. Tess's eyes filled, but she said nothing. She dropped her chin on her chest, her small body jerking with each breath.

"I have to go, Tessie, but I love you. I'll call you on the phone as soon as I get to work. Okay?" Tess would not look at her. Emma squatted next to the high chair, trying to look up into Tess's face, but Tess twisted her face away. Now she was crying loud, anguished sobs.

Emma looked up at Rachel. This was where she was meant to step in, comforting and distracting, pulling Tess onto a different path, away from this one of despair. Instead, Rachel turned to leave the room.

"Rachel, could you come and take her please?" Emma said.

At this, Tess wailed louder. Rachel turned back without a word, and walked heavily over to Tess. She plucked her from the high chair: Tess shrieked as though bitten, twisting wildly in Rachel's arms.

"No, no!" she said, "I want Mommy! I want Mommy!"

Rachel began patting her, jiggling her against her chest, but she said nothing.

"She hasn't had her breakfast," Emma said.

Rachel gave her a look of contempt. "I thought you asked me to take her," she said.

"I did," said Emma. "I just wanted you to know she hasn't eaten."

"I know that," said Rachel.

Rachel and Emma glared at each other. Tess was crying loudly, and Rachel held her like an infant, jogging her, the long brown fingers tracing calming circles on Tess's unhappy back.

"Can I ask you something?" Rachel said. Her tone, her eyes were insolent. She stood with her legs apart, swaying back and forth with Tess.

At the sound of Rachel's voice, Emma folded her arms on her chest. "What is it?"

Rachel's short black braids were in full toss, her bathrobe was open over her droopy white nightgown. Emma was dressed for the office: turtleneck sweater, neat skirt, stockings and heels. She was already a part of her other life, the larger world, far from this domestic disorder. She was impatient, ready to walk out no matter what. But this is what husbands do, she thought suddenly, walk out on all of this—the crying child, the snarled mess of emotions. They leave all this for their carpeted, air-conditioned offices, their secretaries, as if the things here weren't real, or serious.

Rachel tilted her head to one side, her eyes narrow with resentment.

"Next time you spend the night out, will you tell me beforehand, so I don't spend all night worrying is the door double-locked, and listening for Tess from the other end of the apartment?"

Guilt froze Emma. "Yes, of course," she said, frowning, her tone distant. She turned away and took her bowl to the sink, washing it noisily. She felt mortified. How could I have been so inconsiderate, she wondered. Still, she resented Rachel's criticism. I won't apologize, she thought. I won't let Rachel dictate my behavior. Emma was afraid that if she apologized, she would be admitting to something fundamental, fatal. It would an admission from which she could never recover. It would give Rachel permanent advantage over her. It was too risky. Emma said nothing more.

Rachel waited, swaying imperiously, Tess in her arms. "If you're going out for the night, I'll take Tess in with me."

"Fine," Emma said, nodding, not looking at Rachel. "Good idea. Next time I'll let you know." She opened the dishwasher, popped in her bowl, and closed the door with a flourish. "All right, I'm off. See you later."

Tess, stilled momentarily by tension, now started a new wail, but Emma was no longer placatory.

"I'll see you later, Tessie," she said, her voice firm. "I love you."

Tess wept.

Emma kissed her, but carefully unwrapped the child's hands from around her neck, loosening the strands connecting her here, disentangling herself from her domestic world. Her mind was shifting focus. She was now only halfway here with Tess: her heart was here, but her mind was moving on to her next destination. It was now the office that drew her.

She escaped. As the door closed behind her she could hear Tess's voice rise into a despairing shriek. In the hall Emma pushed the elevator button and then closed her eyes, trying to shut out the sad wails that came through the wall. She still heard them, wincing, as she stepped into the elevator.

The elevator door scissored closed. For the second time that morning she fell away, anxious and distressed, setting off for a new place, driven by time, by obligation, hoping that what she was leaving would resolve itself, hoping that the right thing was to move on, go forward, wondering uneasily if it was. She felt stretched, taut; carried along by the momentum of her day, the momentum of momentum itself.

7

Emma's office at *Art & Culture* was a narrow rectangular box, with one window overlooking Third Avenue. Hanging on the scuffed gray walls were Emma's favorite posters: a great O'Keeffe flower, deep and luscious, and a long horizontal Winslow Homer of a young woman reading, stretched out full-length on the grass, and completely absorbed by her book. Emma liked the juxtaposition: the life of the mind, the life of the body.

The small room itself was charmless. The black metal desk was battered, the flimsy metal bookcase stuffed haphazardly with art books and exhibition catalogs. The window was ungenerous, giving onto a small square of revealed sky, cramped by walls of pollution-stained white brick. Emma's desk, dominated by the computer terminal, was piled with manuscripts. An industrial gray Rolodex sat by a box of Kleenex, a flimsy red stapler and a round Florentine box of paper clips. A pottery mug held a clutch of pencils, pens and a single emery board, worn entirely smooth.

Emma arrived late. The official hours at the magazine were nine-thirty to five-thirty, but most people came in late and stayed later. Emma didn't like to stay late because of Tess, so she tried to come in early, but that morning everything slowed her up. It's the mental transactions, not the physical ones, she thought, turning in to the cavernous lobby. It's not traveling time, it's talking time that makes me late. I only allow time for what I have to say, never for what anyone else says back. She thought again of Peter's cold voice, the cabdriver's fury, of Rachel, Tess. By the time Emma arrived on the seventh floor it was ten of ten.

Emma took off her coat and headed for the coffee machine. She could hear Robert, the editor in chief, talking in a terminatory way to the art editor, whose office was next to Emma's. "Okay," he said. "Right. Great."

But the art editor was trying to keep him. "I also want to talk to you about the June issue," he said. "The sculpture article." Emma, who wanted solitude, hoped the art editor would keep Robert with him, and out of her office.

Robert was determined. "Right," Robert promised, "we need to discuss it. I'll get back to you," he said, then Emma heard his footsteps on his way down the hall.

Robert was thin and intense, with small gray eyes, a wide Slavic face and a pointed chin. His graying hair was a springy mass of tight curls. He wore round black-rimmed glasses and bow ties. Every morning, as soon as he arrived at work he took his jacket off and rolled his shirtsleeves up, not the decorous two cuffs' length, but all the way up over the elbow, as though ready for rigorous and unpredictable tasks.

When Emma returned to her office, Robert was waiting for her.

"Oh, good," he said, "you're here."

"Come in," Emma said, though he was already in, already sitting on the uncomfortable aluminum-frame chair next to her desk. She wanted her office empty, so Peter could call.

"The Whitney Biennial," Robert said.

"Oh, God," Emma said, and sighed. This exhibition was always huge, boisterous and confrontational. "It's too early in the morning to think about the Biennial."

"Well, try. Think about who we should get to review it."

"Hm," said Emma. She sipped at her coffee, hoping he would leave. "What about Jed Perl?"

"I thought a woman. Think of a woman."

"Oh," said Emma. She lifted her mug to her mouth. "All right. Let me think."

Robert nodded and rose to leave. At the doorway he turned. "D'you think this is sexist?" he asked. "It probably is."

"No, no," said Emma. Go, she thought. She didn't look at the telephone, for fear this would make it ring.

"Margot is always talking about creeping sexism," Robert said. His wife was a lawyer, and fierce. "Toward women, obviously. I'm trying to avoid it, but doesn't this seem as though I'm being sexist toward men?"

"You're not being sexist, you're being fair," Emma said. Why didn't he leave? "This is equal time. I'll come up with some names."

"Or do you want to write it yourself?" Robert asked, turning to go.

"God, no," Emma said, shaking her head. "Whatever you say about that show, you enrage half the people in New York. I don't want all that ambient hatred."

"Really?" Robert said, interested. He leaned against the wall. "I like stirring things up. Why do you care if other people disagree with you?"

"I'm a coward," answered Emma. "I hate having people angry at me." Will you go, she thought. Go.

Robert shook his head. "Women are peculiar," he said. "I *love* controversy. It's the only way to live." Emma smiled at him, but did not answer. He smiled back, raised his chin toward the winds of conflict, and left at last.

Emma took a long sip of coffee and set her mug down. She leaned back in her chair, alone, for the first time that day. Solitude, she thought, the greatest luxury. She could now begin to address the day. She would have to think of a woman writer for Robert, though it would do nothing to combat creeping sexism. As long as men were the buyers, the art world would cater to men. She wondered when Peter would call.

She looked at her desk, avoiding the telephone from superstition. It sat beside her left hand. If it rang, she could answer it on the first ring. Her calendar was covered with notes. She scanned it: this week there was an article due, from a notoriously late writer. She would have to start her calls to him. On the first call he would tell her that the article was going very well, and he was almost finished. At the end of the week, on the second call, he would tell her that he still wasn't quite finished. By the end of the following week she would no longer be able to reach him directly. She would leave messages on his machine, and sometime during the week after that he would leave a message on her machine—in the evening, when he knew she wouldn't be there—telling her that something had come up, and that he wouldn't be able to turn the article in on time. She would need to call the gallery, too, at some point, for photographs to accompany the article. She would make none of those calls now, though: she wanted to leave the telephone free.

She thought of Peter, at his office, which she had never seen. She imagined a sleek modern corner room, with plate-glass windows, a big clean desk, a stiff armchair facing it. One wall of legal reference books, in sets, soberly bound. A big potted ficus tree in a corner, tended by a plant person. What was Peter doing, in that office? Was he thinking of her? Why did he not call?

On her desk was the untidy manuscript of an article to be edited. At *Art & Culture* they used computers themselves, but they still asked for articles in manuscript. "Hard copy," they called it, slightly self-consciously: jargon from a strange language. It made ordinary pages sound brisk and inflexible, though they were really gentle and compliant. Text on a screen was held at a cold flickering remove, an endless liquid scroll, floating in deep space. Emma wanted actual ink on rustling paper. Real pages were accessible in a way that a machine was not. The computer, with its tiny glowing lights and faint high-pitched hum, was endlessly busy with arcane internal doings. It waited to be interrupted, but it was already going, already occupied. Its indefatigable busyness, its active readiness to do *something*, in a rapid electronic manner, intruded between the reader and the text. The only action between a reader and a text ought to be the silent absorption of one by the other—the Winslow Homer woman lying on the grass, oblivious. The computer was useless here. Reading text on a computer was like reading a book while sitting in your car with the engine running.

Emma picked up the manuscript. The article was deeply respectful, about an artist who embedded bits of plates in his canvases. Emma, who liked Caravaggio and Thomas Eakins, sighed. The language of modern art was so arcane and insular: no one outside a small circle of New Yorkers would have any idea why this idea—broken crockery—was interesting. It was hard to understand, now, why the avant-garde had wanted to cut themselves off from all but the cognoscenti. Why would you not want to include everyone who was interested in art? Why would you work actively to antagonize your audience?

The telephone rang, and Emma's hand was on it at once. She let it complete its ring, for dignity, before she picked it up.

"Emma?" It was Francie; Emma braced herself. She hated talking to her sister.

Francie was three years younger than Emma. When the girls were little, Emma had looked after her. Francie had been Emma's doll. Emma had helped her sister dress in the morning. She brushed her hair, told her stories and taught her to skip and to read. Francie believed everything Emma said. The two girls had shared a bedroom until Emma was thirteen.

On the last night of their shared room, Emma had gone to a school dance. She had brought back contraband from the drugstore, and spent all afternoon getting ready. She washed her hair and cream-rinsed it. She shaved the long slopes of her legs, the awkward hollows of her armpits. She smoothed an herbal mask on her face, letting it cake and dry until her features were white and stiffened, like an African deity. She scrubbed it all off; underneath, her skin was pink and glowing. She leaned close to the mirror and struggled with mascara, dabbing ineptly at the lashes next to her alarmed and fluttering eye. She brushed a tiny drift of rosy brown blusher on her cheekbones. She dipped her finger into the pot of lip gloss and smoothed a shining layer onto her mouth. She arranged her long silky hair on her shoulders.

Francie, awed and excited, lay on her bed and watched, offering opinions. At first Emma talked and laughed, but as the dance drew closer Emma became quieter. When she began getting dressed, Emma changed her mind over and over. The bed, the chair, the rug became layered with discards. Emma felt dread begin to rise within her. She stopped laughing with Francie. Francie was a child, she knew nothing about this dance, the world of Emma's classmates. She stopped talking to Francie altogether. She settled finally on her clothes, but they were wrong, she hated them: purple striped hip-hugger bell-bottoms, which felt suddenly tight; the burgundy toes of her favorite boots, poking out beneath them, were scuffed. A white turtleneck and her favorite red tunic top, which had a stain on the shoulder. She looked in the mirror and turned away in despair. She saw how she looked: fat and hopelessly stupid, out of step with the rest of the world. Her friends would see at once that she was a fraud and impostor. When Emma turned away, anguished, Francie drew in her breath.

"You look beautiful," she said solemnly.

Emma, sick with fear, could not answer. Francie's admiration was proof of how babyish and pathetic she looked. She left, filled with gloom.

Arriving at the dance, Emma felt her throat close with anxiety. The gym was huge and dark, the music pounding. At first she could find no one. Her friends were in drifting groups that dissolved and merged. Their voices were shrill. Emma did not feel like one of them, and she could think of nothing to say. She heard herself laugh too much, and foolishly. The boy she liked, whose name she had written secretly over and over on the soles of her sneakers, did not look at her once. He danced with another girl twice, but spent most of the evening outside with his friends smoking dope.

Halfway through the endless night, Emma went into the ladies' room.

When she came in it fell suddenly silent. Three girls, combing their hair, met each other's eyes in the mirror. Emma, awkwardly, said "Hi," and there was a chorus of responses, but they looked at her only for a moment. Emma stood at the sink, letting the water run over her hands, hoping dumbly that something would change, that the world would become kind again. She heard a hissing whisper: "She's not going. Joanna didn't invite her." Emma turned off the faucet and left the room without looking back. She had to wait until the end of the dance; she was part of a car pool. For the rest of the evening the sentence burned inside her. She stood alone, at the edge of the dance floor, or in the shadows just outside the side door of the gym.

At the end of the dance she and four other girls were picked up by someone's mother. Emma sat in the front with the mother. During the drive the girls didn't speak to Emma, but when they reached her house they turned suddenly effusive. They called good night in loud bright voices as Emma got out of the car. Emma did not answer. She thanked the mother and turned away toward her house so she would not see the car drive off toward Joanna's.

When Emma let herself into the front hall she saw Francie, in her nightgown, sitting at the top of the stairs. Francie's face lit up and she clapped silently. *Emma!* she mouthed.

Emma said loudly, "You're supposed to be in bed, Francie."

"I had a nightmare," Francie said, defensively, standing up. When Francie woke in the night, Emma had always taken her into bed with her.

Now Emma made a derisive sound in her nose. "I bet," she said, still loudly. She went into the living room, where her parents were reading. They looked up as Emma came in. Her mother smiled.

"I'm back," Emma announced curtly.

"Where have you been?" her father asked.

Emma stared angrily.

"You know, Everett, she went to a dance. Did you have a good time, Emma?"

"A dance?" her father said, disapproving. "Dressed like that? You look like a court jester in those silly trousers."

Emma turned to leave.

"Everett," said Emma's mother. "Emma, come back."

Emma stepped warily into the doorway again.

"I think you look very nice," her mother said.

"She looks nice except for those silly trousers," her father said. He stared at her. "And what's that on your chin?"

Emma put her hand on her chin, scowling. "I don't know. What?" She lifted her chin. There was a silence. She looked down suspiciously, sideways, at her father. "What is it?"

"Nothing," he said, looking pleased with himself.

Emma lowered her chin. "What is it?"

"It's nothing after all," he said.

"What did you see?" Emma demanded, lowering her chin.

"It was nothing. Just a little roll of flesh, underneath your chin," he said. "Nothing. It goes away when you lift your jaw."

Emma turned and left the room. She pushed past Francie, who was hovering anxiously in the hall in her nightgown.

"*You* are supposed to be in bed," Emma said furiously to Francie. "Eavesdropper." As she pounded upstairs Emma yelled down, "I'm not sharing a room anymore with that spoiled brat. I want my own room."

When Francie came up Emma was already in bed, curled into a tight ball, the light off. Francie opened the door and came inside. She whispered Emma's name, but Emma lay still and said nothing. Her chin was sunk deep into her neck, her hands were fists. By now the other girls were all at Joanna's, whom Emma hated. Maybe the boys had gone there, too. Francie got quietly into her bed, pulled up the covers and lay down, her face toward Emma. They had lain like that in their twin beds, facing each other in the dark, night after night, for as long as Francie could remember. In the light from the window they could see faint gleams from each other's eyes.

"Emma?" Francie whispered.

Emma said nothing.

"Em?" Francie whispered again, quieter.

Emma said nothing. Her eyes were not closed, and she knew Francie could see the gleam. She lay without stirring. She had never been to Joanna's house. It was in Brookline. They would all be there by now. They would be laughing.

The next day Emma moved into a smaller room down the hall. Her alliance with Francie was over. Emma felt tainted by childhood in Francie's presence.

Emma had gone docilely to both their mother's schools: Milton and Smith. But Francie was tumultuously rebellious. She left Milton after ninth grade and went to public high school in Cambridge. Francie grew her hair, smoked a lot of dope and barely graduated. She refused to go to college. She said college was too structured. She wanted to absorb knowledge by living it. Emma told Francie she was ridiculous, and Francie told Emma she was boring. They drew apart. Francie moved to San Francisco, married, had two small children, and divorced. She came back east seldom, and only to see her parents.

"Hi, Francie," Emma now said. She was tying up the line. What was Peter doing? "You're up early."

"I always get up early," Francie said.

Emma, who doubted this, said nothing.

"Did you get a message that I called?" Francie asked.

"Oh, that's right, I did," Emma said guiltily. "On Sunday. Sorry I haven't called you back. I was going to do it today." Resenting the guilt, she said briskly, "So, what's up?"

"I just wanted to tell you about something I'm doing," said Francie.

"What's that?" Emma said.

"It's like a series of seminars," Francie said. "I'm going to be giving them back east, this summer."

"Seminars?" Emma said. She thought of European history; the politics of slavery. "On what?"

"On evolving. The success of the self. You know. Awareness. It's a whole program."

"Oh," Emma said, in a different tone.

"It's a really interesting series," Francie said. "It's really amazing."

"Great," said Emma. "Have you taken it yourself?"

"Yeah," said Francie. "At this institute out here."

"And where are you going to give it here?"

"Well, that's what I thought you might help me with," Francie said. "It's a fantastic series, an amazing bargain. The whole series, five seminars of four hours each, is only two hundred and eighty dollars."

"Amazing," said Emma.

"Yeah, isn't it? But I need a place to give them," said Francie. "The institute here doesn't really have a base in New York yet."

"I don't really know of a place," Emma said.

"I thought maybe your apartment," Francie said smoothly.

"It's tiny," Emma said. "It wouldn't be any good."

There was a pause.

"There wouldn't be very many people at one time, Emma," Francie said. "It's a very peaceful series. You know, I mean there's no arguing, or anything like that. It's self-awareness."

"My apartment is tiny," Emma repeated. "I've moved, you know. There's really no room."

There was another pause. "So, you won't help us," Francie said.

"Francie, this isn't fair," Emma said.

"It's really simple," Francie said. "You have the chance to help or not to help."

"Francie, you're asking me to give up my apartment for your business scheme."

"It's self-awareness, Emma, it's not business."

"Where am I supposed to live? Where is Rachel supposed to spend the day? Or the evenings? My apartment is where I live. Why should you ask me to turn it over to you?"

Francie sighed. "Thanks, Emma."

"Francie," said Emma.

There was a long silence.

"I knew you wouldn't be able to see this," said Francie.

"It's not a question of seeing it. You're trying to impose on me."

"People in New York are so resistant to these ideas. It's really interesting," said Francie.

"I'm not resistant to the idea of the seminar. I'm resistant to giving up my apartment."

"So, if we find a place will you take the seminar?"

Emma shut her eyes in irritation. "Francie, I have my own life. If I want to take a seminar, you have to trust me, I'll sign up for it on my own."

"It's self-awareness, Emma. Everyone needs it."

"That's your view, Francie."

"Do you think you're so evolved that you don't need it?"

Emma shook her head. "I am what I am. I'm not asking you to decide how evolved I am, okay? What about the parents?"

"What about them?"

"Why don't you give your seminars in Cambridge, at their house?"

"Are you out of your mind?"

"Well, it's not fair to ask me to give up my apartment, Francie, so don't do it."

"I'll give you the series for nothing," Francie said. "It's self-awareness, okay? If you change your mind, call me back. Just let me know."

"I'm not going to change my mind," said Emma crossly.

"You know," said Francie, now coaxingly, "you're my only sister. I feel really responsible for you."

"Francie, look. I'm not going to change my mind."

"It's okay," said Francie. "You can call any hour of the day or night. This is something you need. Trust me. This kind of knowledge is important. I know you think it isn't, I know you think only the conventional academic stuff is important, but I want you to try to open your mind. I know it will be hard for you, but I want you to try."

"Francie, how would you feel if I started telling you that you should go to college?"

Francie laughed indulgently. "Trust me, Emma," she said. "You can call any time."

Emma hung up and stared at her computer screen. What was the point, she thought, in being good, in doing what was expected of you?

One summer afternoon, when Emma was nine and Francie six, they had gone into an old-fashioned general store in Cape Cod. Their father was buying the paper. The pinewood floor was dark and oil soaked, soft beneath their bare feet. Emma held Francie's hand, showing her the things on the shelves, saying the names. "Shoe polish, Francie," she said, "Cordovan." At the counter, a stranger was buying an ice cream cone. Francie told Emma she wanted one and Emma told her no. Francie turned loud and fretful. She tugged at Emma's shorts.

"I want ice cream," Francie said over and over. She stamped her small feet, then squatted on the floor in a rage.

Emma bent over her. "Francie," she said. "Not between meals. It's not allowed." Francie wailed louder, and when their father turned, with his paper, she was howling.

"What is it?" he asked, frowning.

"She wants an ice cream cone. I told her she couldn't because it was between meals, but she's still complaining," Emma reported virtuously.

"She can have an ice cream cone." Their father looked down at them, towering, perfidious. "What kind do you want, Francie? What flavor?"

Emma still remembered the sense of outrage, vast, irredeemable. The law being so casually flouted, the ground sinking beneath her feet. On the way home Francie sat beside her in the backseat of the car, licking the melting drips of strawberry. She eyed Emma, wary but triumphant. Emma had refused her own cone, on principle. Someone had to teach Francie about the rigors of the world; clearly their parents would not.

Now Emma stared at her manuscript, angry at Francie.

The telephone on her desk rang again. It was Francie again, she knew.

"Hello?" It was Peter.

"Hello," Emma said, flustered.

"Do you have a minute?" Peter asked. His voice was gentle.

"Yes," said Emma. She leaned toward the desk, turning her back to the door.

"I'm sorry about this morning," he said. "I don't know why I got so angry."

"Oh," said Emma. "Thank you."

"I overreacted. I didn't want you to leave," he said.

"You made that clear," said Emma. "I felt so miserable. I kept hoping and hoping you'd come out and find me."

"I'm sorry," he repeated. "I don't know why I got so angry. I know you want to see Tess."

"I'm caught in the middle," Emma said. "I don't want to leave either, but when I start thinking about Tess, I get frantic. It makes me feel as though I have to take sides with one of you against the other. I hate it."

"I shouldn't have tried to make you stay. It's not fair."

"Thank you," said Emma.

"What do you think about moving in together?"

There was silence.

"I love you," Peter said.

Emma felt tears, unexpected, rise behind her lids.

She was unprepared for this. The idea seemed charged with risk. She had only just begun to feel peaceful on her own. Her habits were becoming her own; she turned the light off when she pleased. Silence was hers to break or stretch. She was wary of any male presence, demanding, intrusive, ready to impose itself. His ideas would become part of everything. He would be there in her rooms, all the time. He would have the right to her bedroom, his heavy wool suits would hang in her closet. What if Rachel quit? And would he love Tess?

"You don't have to answer now," Peter said. "But think about it. I think it would be easier for you. It'd be easier for both of us. The way it is now, you're pulled in two."

It was true that Peter was kind, and he slept all night with his arms around her. Still she said nothing.

"Is there anything else?" he asked. "I hear you hesitating. What is it?"

"Tess," said Emma.

"One thing I don't like, now," Peter said, his voice gentler still, "is that I get to see her so little."

"Really?" Emma asked, amazed.

"Really," Peter said.

"And Amanda?"

"Will be a part of it too."

Emma looked out the window. Across the street the white brick building had been cut diagonally in half by the slanting morning sun, the lower part drenched in somber shadow. The upper stories rose in a series of receding steps. These airy, outdoor stairs were fiery with sun, brilliant and angular against the deep sky.

"My sister Francie just called me," Emma said. "She wants me to give up my apartment so she can give seminars in it, on self-awareness."

"Tell her your apartment is full," said Peter. "Tell her you've moved in your own private instructor."

Emma laughed. It was a relief, talking to Peter. She felt such trust in him. And he pressed on, which she admired. Besides, he was part of her life already. She wanted to wake up with him in the mornings, drift into sleep beside him. Remembering his touch on her throat she closed her eyes for a second, slipping into that steamy bath.

She looked out again at the fiery stairs leading upward. There was always a reason to hang back, to refuse, to disengage. There would always be drawbacks, problems. Independence would blur easily into loneliness. It was brave to be independent, braver still to engage.

8

Peter moved into Emma's apartment at the beginning of March. That spring was slow, and three weeks later it was still cold and raw.

Emma was working late, and it began to rain just as she left her office. When she came out of the subway at Fourteenth Street, it was after seven, and dark. By then it was pouring, and the water pelted down on her bare head. She had no umbrella, and there were of course no cabs.

There were never any cabs when it rained. At the first drop they vanished from the streets. Emma imagined them all rushing to a secret cab-gathering arena, deep in the unknown interior of the city. Here all the cabs lined up in gleaming yellow ranks, the rain drumming on their roofs. The solitary drivers sat patiently inside their steamy glass shells, their radios playing low as they waited out the storm.

Emma turned her collar up and tucked her pocketbook closely under her arm. The sidewalks shimmered with puddles, she felt water seeping through her shoes. Tomorrow they would have faint irregular stains, outlining islands of damp on her insteps.

The sidewalks were nearly empty. The small brassy discount shops that lined Fourteenth Street, their windows full of red lettering and extreme promises, were all closed. The street seemed wider in the dark, deserted. The few cars hurtled past, hissing fans of cold water onto the sidewalk. The rain dripped through Emma's hair on her forehead, and she blinked against it. An exploratory drop started down her neck, slithered sideways and headed down her back. Her fingers were numb, and her shoulders hunched tightly against her neck. Five minutes, she promised herself, and I'll be home. Five minutes.

Opening the front door Emma heard Mozart: Peter was there. She took off her coat and went in. He was in the living room, reading. He had changed into corduroy trousers, a plaid shirt and moccasins. He looked peaceful and happy, and when he saw Emma he spread open his arms.

"Em!" he said. "You're soaked."

"Really?" said Emma, smiling. She kissed him. His neck smelled delicious, and she closed her eyes. He pulled her down to him, but at that Emma stiffened. She didn't want Rachel to find her on Peter's lap.

"Not in front of the help," she said decorously, standing up. She smoothed her rain-damp skirt. "Where's Tess?"

"Kitchen," Peter said.

"I'm going to say hello," Emma said.

Tessie and Rachel were at the table. Tess was fresh from her bath, glowing and rosy, her blond hair dark with damp at the edges. Her face lit up when she saw Emma.

"Mommy!" she said blissfully, and held out her arms.

"Tessie," Emma said, holding out hers. At the sight of her daughter something in her loosened, gave way; an answering bliss ran through her. She picked up the small heavy body, and Tess threw her arms tightly around Emma's neck.

"Mom-my, Mom-my," Tess chanted, in an urgent whisper. Emma kissed her, deep in the fold of her neck, and then turned to Rachel.

"Hi, Rache," she said, "what's up?"

Rachel leaned her chin on her hand, her face blank. "How do you mean?" she asked stonily.

If talking to Tess made Emma giddy with delight, talking to Rachel made her burdened by guilt.

"Oh, you know. Anything," Emma said, ignoring Rachel's sullenness. Tess reared back and began patting Emma, fiercely, on the shoulders, on the ears, on the head.

"The cleaners say they don't have your red dress," Rachel said.

"But they do, don't they? Don't you have the ticket?"

"You took it there," said Rachel. Her eyes were heavy lidded and her face immobile. "You have the ticket."

"Did I? I don't know where it is. But they know me. I probably just left the dress on the counter. I was in a hurry."

Rachel shrugged her shoulders ominously. Emma gave up and turned to Tess.

"Want to come in while I change?" she asked.

"She's not finished her dinner," Rachel said.

"Oh, she's not?" Emma looked at Tess's plate. "But nearly. She's had enough. Tess, have you finished your dinner?"

Tess nodded, looking attentively at her mother, then at Rachel. Rachel pursed her lips and folded her arms.

"I'll just take her with me while I change," Emma said, not looking at Rachel. Rachel stood and began clearing Tess's supper.

"You can leave that for when we come back," Emma said, but Rachel ignored her, taking the plate and scraping it into the trash.

Emma carried her daughter off under a cloud of guilt. It was not because of Tess's unfinished supper but because of Peter's presence in the apartment. Rachel had sulked since he moved in, and Emma didn't know what to say to make her stop. The thought of the discussion exhausted Emma—why should she have to explain her moral position to her housekeeper? She'd hoped that she could avoid it, and that Rachel would stop sulking by herself. When she and Peter knew what their plans were, Emma would talk to Rachel. Until then she didn't want Rachel as either her judge or her confidante.

Emma hoped she would marry again; she felt uncomfortable as a single mother. She was cheating Tess, raising her in this unnatural, asymmetrical, fatherless household. But if it was Tess that made Emma want to marry, it was also Tess that made it difficult. Tess was three, healthy, energetic and noisy. She was used to having all Emma's attention. Each time she was with both Tess and Peter, Emma felt tension rise, she felt torn between them. She was afraid that Peter would not put up with Tess's constant interruptions and demands. Why should he? His life with Caroline had been so different. She knew he was used to calm and order, to immaculate rooms, quiet servants, a carefully tended child. What must he think of Emma's household? Sullen Rachel, in her turquoise sweater and tight jeans, and boisterous Tess, running in and out of Emma's room. All this made Emma feel tense and helpless: her greatest fear was that Peter would begin to feel resentful toward Tess.

One night, when Tess was bouncing raucously on their bed, Emma had stood laughing at her antics. She'd looked at Peter, to share her delight, only to see his disapproving stare. What she saw was a beloved child, beautiful, joyful; he saw chaos, noise and lack of discipline.

"You don't love her, do you," she said, sobered.

"Not like you," he said gently.

"At all," Emma insisted.

"I'll treat her better because of that."

Chilled, she looked at him. She had brought a man into her household who did not love her daughter. At any moment he might lose patience with it all, with her, with Tess, with everything.

Since then Emma had felt she was living on a volcano. To prevent the eruption, she had shielded Peter from domestic mechanics. She never asked for his help, never asked him to look after Tess, to drop something off at the cleaners, to lend her cash for Rachel. Peter's half of the rent was his only obligation. The running of the household was her responsibility. Emma felt that anything—anything—might be the last straw, might set him against her small daughter.

In the bedroom Emma took off her wet clothes while Tess waddled cheerfully about in her footed pajamas. She carried a stuffed raccoon under her arm and talked busily to herself.

It was seven-fifteen. Emma had to make dinner for herself and Peter, read to Tess and put her to bed. Tess's bedtime was seven-thirty. If she put Tess down first, Peter would be testy at the late dinner. If she cooked dinner first, Tess would be whiny and exhausted tomorrow. Emma would have liked Rachel to cook their dinner, and let Emma put Tess to bed, but when she first arrived Rachel had declared her position. "I'll do child care and cleaning," she said. "I'm not doing dinner parties." At the time, Emma had cared only about Tess's care during the day, but now, looking back, she wished she had negotiated. She wondered if she still could. But Rachel was so angry at her now, Emma was afraid she might quit. And no matter how grumpy Rachel was toward Emma, she was tender and conscientious toward Tess, who loved her fiercely. For that, Emma would put up with almost anything.

In jeans and a sweater, Emma passed back through the living room. She would have to break her rule and ask Peter to help out a bit, if they were to eat before midnight.

"Would you mind setting the table?" she asked him timidly. "I'm going to read to Tess while I start dinner."

Peter closed his book. "What are we having?"

"Lamb chops, rice and peas," Emma said, not looking at him. She knew he'd be disappointed. Peter was an austere eater. He ate no fats, no beef. He liked sushi, grilled tuna, exotic greens and spices, curries. She knew he'd prefer something that had simmered on the back of the stove for days. This meal was bland and boring, but quick: half an hour from start to finish.

In the kitchen, Tess clambered onto a chair and spread out her book. "And now, Mommy, we'll read," she said.

"In just one second," Emma said. Rice first, then the chops, then the peas. She measured out water in one pot for the rice, and ran a brief stream into another for the peas. Inside the pot was a feathery black honeycomb, the ghostly silhouette of peas Emma had burnt in the past. She had a bad record of burning vegetables, no matter how careful she thought she was being. Tonight, though, it couldn't happen, because she would be sitting next to the stove, reading to Tess. The peas would be there under her eye.

Peter came in. "What things do you want me to use?"

"The mats are down there," Emma said. "The silverware's in the top drawer. The plates are in that cabinet, and so are the glasses." Tess gummed the edge of her book, impatient. "Just one minute," promised Emma. She began to rub the lamb chops with rosemary.

"Up here?" Peter asked, opening the wrong cabinet. He stared dimly at a stack of casseroles.

"The one next to it," Emma said, wiping her meat-slimy hands. She picked up the bottle of olive oil, but her hands were too slippery to grip the cap. Tess began to fuss, pouting and making gusty little warning whimpers. "Just one more minute, Tessie," Emma said. "I have to get the water boiling and put the rice in." Her fingers slid fruitlessly around the metal cap.

"I'm afraid I don't see them," Peter said. He had opened another wrong cabinet.

"Not there," Emma said. "Over here." She opened the right door. "Any of these plates, any of these glasses. Would you open this?"

"What?" Peter said, turning slowly.

She handed him the olive oil.

"It's covered with gook," Peter said, frowning. "What did you put on it?"

"Mom-*mee*," Tess said urgently. "Mom-*mee*." She bounced up and down in her chair.

"One second, Tess," Emma said to her. "Lamb slime," she said to Peter. "Thanks." She dribbled oil on the chops. The water in the saucepan was beginning to stir; tiny silvery bubbles sidled mysteriously up toward the surface. Not a rolling boil, but she couldn't wait. Emma poured in the rice, the translucent grains sliding heavily into an underwater pyramid. She covered the saucepan and gave the timer a ratchety twist. Seven thirty-five. "Okay, Tess," she said, and sat down.

"These?" asked Peter, behind her.

"Fine," said Emma, not looking up.

"Here," Tess said, sliding the book over. "Right here," she said, stabbing at the text. Emma began reading, her mind on dinner. Tess leaned forward, her hands cushioning her chin on the table edge. Her eyes were rapt.

"Wait," Emma read, "wait till the moon is full." She looked at Tess and widened her eyes. Tess watched her mother's face, her own eyes widening, as if they both watched the same scene: rabbits, raccoons, woodchucks, possums, all dancing in the meadow, darkened grasses and flowers beneath the dancers' feet, the vast white moon casting a magical silver light.

When Emma finished, the chops were not quite brown enough, but Emma turned them and started a low flame under the peas. She would have to leave them, but she'd take the timer. "Come on, Tessie, I'll sing you a song when you're in bed." She would just have time—to brush Tess's teeth, sing the bedtime song and say good night—before the rice was done.

The toothbrushing was endless. Tess, feeling Emma's urgency, dropped first the toothpaste, then its cap, then the toothbrush. Emma tried to keep impatience from her voice, but by the time she had gotten Tess into bed, clean, under the covers and with the right animal, Emma was wild. She felt the fate of the dinner hanging precariously over her.

"Now the song, Mommy," Tess said, settling comfortably against her pillow. The good night song was a slow lullaby. It could not be hurried.

Emma began. "Hush-a-bye," she sang, trying to sound peaceful, "don't you cry. Go to sleep, my little Tessie." Tess, her thumb deep in her mouth, watched her gravely. "When you wake, we shall take all the pretty little horses."

At the end, Tess reached up and patted Emma's cheek. "Don't go now, Mommy," she said coaxingly.

"I have to go, Tess, it's bedtime." Emma looked at the timer. She wondered if the chops were all right. The peas.

"No, Mommy," Tessie said, patting her more strongly. "Just one more song, please? I have been waiting for you all day."

Emma looked at Tess's wistful face. She had only been home for half an hour, and now she was putting Tessie out like a tiny light, extinguishing her bright consciousness, cutting her off from the steady glow of her mother. The peas were about to burn. She should have waited to turn them on.

"Tessie, I love you," Emma said. "I'm sorry I got home so late tonight. But now I have to go back and cook dinner for Peter." As she said the name she thought: a mistake.

"For Peter?" Tess repeated.

"And me," said Emma quickly. "I haven't had any dinner."

Tess slid instantly sideways and patted the sheet next to her.

"You could sit by here, Mommy, while you ate your dinner. You could sit next to me while you ate." She spoke moistly around her thumb.

Emma smiled. "Thank you, sweetie, but I can't do that."

If she had been alone, though, she would have. She would have sat on the bed, reading first out loud to Tess, then, as her daughter slid gently into sleep, getting out her own book and reading to herself. It was Peter who came between them.

"I have to leave, Tessie, before the dinner burns," Emma said. The ticking timer was speeding up, approaching its tiny one-note finale. "But I'll come back, after dinner, and give you another kiss good night. All right?"

Tess looked at her, her mouth working steadily on her thumb.

"All right, Tessie?" Emma leaned forward. The bell rang. The dinner was about to be charcoal. "I love you," she said to Tess, and kissed her soft cheek. Tessie's eyes were brilliant, liquid with tears. She said nothing. Emma's heart smote her. "I love you," she said again, and Tessie nodded. Her eyes followed her mother as she left the room.

Peter looked up as Emma hurried past. "Anything I can do?"

"Come in," Emma said. "Dinner's either ready or ashes."

It was ashes. She smelled it as she came into the kitchen: the rubbery stench of the peas, the strong charcoal of the lamb, the dry sizzle of the rice. She turned off the burners and carried the peas to the sink. She ran cold water over the pot; steam rose furiously. Rachel's door was shut. Emma wondered if she had smelled the burning dinner.

The peas were a blackened mass, but part of the rice was salvageable and she skimmed the unscorched grains off the top. The chops were acceptable, if you liked them charcoal-coated. Emma made a salad.

"Well, here it is," she said finally, handing Peter a plate. His face was unhappy. "Charcoal is good for your teeth," said Emma hopefully. "That's what my mother always said when she burnt the toast. The toast was always burnt, in our house: our toaster was an arsonist. It was years before I knew what normal toast was."

Peter smiled, but did not answer. He chewed the rice in unforgiving silence.

At the end of the wordless meal Peter stood up. "Thank you," he said gravely, "for dinner." He carried his plate into the kitchen and went back into the living room to read. Emma scraped her own plate into the trash.

She stood at the sink, watching the water run off the greasy dishes. This would never work, she thought, Peter would be gone by the weekend. She could hardly blame him.

The dishes done, Emma went back through the Mozart-filled living room. She did not look at Peter, she did not want to see his frowning face. As she passed the sofa his hand grabbed her wrist and stopped her. She looked down: his face was raised to kiss her.

"Come here," he said kindly, pulling her down. Emma thought of Tess, waiting in the bedroom, but she let herself descend.

Peter put his arms around her. "Now, look," he said. "This was a hard evening for you. I could see that."

"It wasn't great," Emma admitted.

"No. And it wasn't great for me either."

For him? Emma stiffened: this was going to be complaints, not compassion. "No, I suppose not."

"But you could see that," Peter said, smiling at her.

"Well, I'm sorry," Emma said dryly. "It must be unpleasant to smell dinner burning while you're reading. And such a nuisance to go and shut the door, to keep out the smell."

"That's not what I meant," Peter said, his face closing.

"What did you mean, then?" Emma asked.

"I didn't feel that I got much of your attention," he said.

"My attention!" Emma laughed shortly. "Well, I'm sorry for that. This can't have been what you'd expected. You thought we'd sit having drinks in the living room while the help put Tess to bed and fixed dinner."

Peter looked at her, his face serious, his mouth now tight. "That's an unfriendly thing to say," he said.

"Well, I don't think what you said was very friendly," Emma said, standing up. "I have to go back to Tess. I told her I'd go back again after dinner." Emma waited, but Peter said nothing more. He watched her, his face tight, until she turned and left the room.

Tess's room was dark. Emma pushed open the door quietly. In the dim light she could see Tess, her head turned to one side. Her arms were upraised and her hands were open against her pillow as though flung there by speed, as though acceleration into sleep had thrown her deep into the yielding softness of the pillow.

Emma leaned over the bed. "Tessie?" she said, whispering. There was no answer. Tess's eyes were closed, and her breath came quietly, almost inaudibly. Emma sat down, finally free to talk to her small daughter, ready to play with her small hands, ready to make her laugh. Emma felt her own throat tighten, looking at Tess's trustful face. The eyebrows slanted mournfully down. In her sleep she was still waiting for her mother. In the darkened room, Emma watched her daughter, listening to her soft irregular breaths.

When Emma left she went quietly into the bedroom, avoiding the living room. She closed the bedroom door behind her. The maple bureau from her parents' house, the velvet slipper chair from her grandmother's bedroom, her own double bed with the white spread all welcomed her, but the room was no longer hers. On the bureau, next to her three small china Battersea boxes, was Peter's fat leather wallet, his noisy set of keys, small change, his maroon silk handkerchief. In the closet, next to her high-necked fragile white silk blouse, hung his dark suit, dense, heavy, full of weather and business, smoke and soot. What had she done, letting him into her life?

She undressed. Her nightgown was cotton, old and soft. Awaiting Peter's anger, the nightgown seemed suddenly flimsy, poor protection. She should be wearing long underwear, ski socks, a wool hat.

Emma brushed her teeth and flossed them roughly, making her gums sting. The bathroom door was half open, and she watched for Peter. What if he came in and started packing? What if this had been the last straw? Was it over?

She brushed her hair, creamed her face and got into her side of the bed. She opened her book, then looked anxiously at the clock. It was so difficult, living with someone. What was he thinking, alone out there?

Emma remembered Peter as she had first seen him: moving through those big elegant rooms filled with friends. He had moved so smoothly, he had been so effortlessly in charge. Emma felt she could not measure up to that sort of life. She could not manage it. It was not in her to make a room like that, gold and scarlet, filled with glitter and conversation. Peter had chosen the wrong woman. It was not in her even to cook a simple dinner: she thought of the ghastly evening, the ruined meal. She could not tend to both Peter and Tess. She could not make this work.

When Peter came in Emma did not look up or speak. She stared intently at her book. Peter said nothing. From the corner of her eye Emma watched him moving about. Rereading the same sentence, she watched him undress. He stepped out of his pants and swung them smoothly upside down, twinning the cuffs neatly, aligning the legs, letting gravity create order before he hung the pants over the back of the chair.

There was nowhere else for him to hang them. Peter had no closet of his own here, no bureau. He had put a suit in the closet, and on top of the bureau in the closet was a small pile of clean things: underwear, a few shirts. He kept his dirty things in a discreet pile on the closet floor, bundling it under his arm and taking it away every week. Watching Peter's careful gestures, Emma was reminded of his neatness, his thoughtfulness, his courtesy. She shifted uncomfortably: she should have talked to Rachel when he moved in. She should have made things clear, given him a place in the household. She must do this. She would talk to Rachel tomorrow. But maybe it was too late, maybe he had already decided to leave.

Peter stood before the closet, unbuttoning his shirt. His hands moved fast, his eyes were lowered and angry.

Emma was afraid of him. Arguing with Peter made her feel shrill and insignificant. His view of things seemed ordered and real in a way hers was not. Emma felt she must keep him from discovering her incompetence, the fact that she might be worthless. She could only hope to do this by diversion, by charm or by anger: anything to keep his cold, level gaze away from her character.

Peter stepped over to the bed and lifted the covers on his side. "I think I'll spend tomorrow night at my place," he said.

"Fine," said Emma, without looking up.

Peter got into bed without touching her. He picked up his book. The room became silent. Emma could hear the street noises from outside. It was still raining, and the cars below passed with rapid swishes.

It was a good idea, Emma told herself. A night off would be a relief for her as well. She could spend the evening with Tess, she could give her all her attention, without guilt. She lifted her chin and smoothed her hair back. Peter lay beside her in charged, resentful silence.

"Peter," she said finally.

He turned, his expression cool.

"I can't do everything in the evenings," she said, "especially when I come home late. I'm sorry I burnt the dinner." Her tone was unapologetic, challenging.

Peter snorted. "The dinner is the least of it."

"What do you mean? What's the worst of it?"

Peter put his book down. "I suppose the worst is that you make me feel like an outsider."

"An outsider? What do you mean?"

"What am I doing here?" Peter said angrily, looking at the ceiling. "You make it clear that I have no place. You come in and rush around, talking to Rachel, reading to Tess, cooking dinner. I'm supposed to stay in one room, alone, all evening. I kept thinking, Why am I here? You don't want me to talk to Rachel, you don't want me to talk to Tess, and you don't want me to talk to you. You didn't even come back in to sit with me after you put Tess to bed." He turned to her.

Emma said nothing, angry at his criticism, and hurt by his plan to spend the night elsewhere. His feelings for her were waning, he was disappointed by her.

Still, she had not thought of this from his point of view: Peter alone all evening, hearing her in the kitchen with Rachel, watching her pass back and forth with Tess, her attention always elsewhere, pushing him away. The awful dinner. Unfriendly Rachel, competitive Tess. Emma felt ashamed. She stared at her book.

"Well?" said Peter. "Do you have nothing to say to me?"

Emma raised her head and looked at him. She did not know how to begin.

"Nothing?" said Peter, his voice angry, and he put his book down.

Emma closed her book and put it on the table. She reached out and put her hand on Peter's shoulder. It was tense.

"I hadn't thought of that," she said. "Of how it was for you."

"Well, try," Peter said crossly.

"I didn't want to ask you to do anything," Emma said, placatory. "I know you aren't used to it."

"What are you talking about?" Peter said. "What do you think I'm not used to? You think I'm used to carrying my dirty shirts in a bundle on the street? This is like a boardinghouse. I get bedroom privileges but no services. I pay half the rent, but Rachel acts as though I'm not here. She won't say my name, and she looks right through me. Why don't you ask her to take my things to the cleaners with yours? Am I on probation here?"

Emma now looked at him directly, abashed.

"I'm sorry," she said. "I didn't think of that. It was just that I haven't known exactly what to say to her."

"What's so hard about saying, 'Will you take Peter's clothes to the dry cleaners?' Why is that so difficult?"

"No, I mean I don't know what to say to her about why you're here. Because of her church: she's against divorce. And she won't say my name either, it's not just you."

"What do you mean she won't say your name?" Peter's voice was raised.

"Because," Emma said. "It has implications. And anyway, she doesn't work for you, she works for me. You don't help me with her salary. I mean, who are you in this household? Are you just a boarder? Are you here for good? Is this temporary?"

"How do I know? How do you know? It will certainly be temporary if I'm not allowed in half the rooms or to talk to anyone else who lives here. You tell me what you want. If you want me to pay part of Rachel's salary, that's fine," said Peter resentfully, "though I have to say I don't see why I should."

"Because Rachel cleans the rooms you live in," said Emma, "she washes the sheets you sleep in, she buys the food you eat."

"I suppose that's right. All right, fine. I'll pay half her salary. But then I goddamn want her to look me in the eye and say, 'Hello, Mr. Chatfield,' when I come into the room."

"Of course she *should*," Emma said, "but she won't do that for *me*."

"What's the matter with her? What's the matter with you? Why won't she call you by your name? Whose name does she call you by? This is like a lunatic asylum."

"She doesn't call me anything," said Emma. "I think she doesn't want to."

"Well, God forbid Rachel should have to do something she doesn't want to. You do whatever you like, but I want to be called by my own god-damned name. And I want to be treated like a member of the household. I don't want to be limited to the living room."

"It was just that I didn't want Tess to disturb you," Emma explained. "I'm just trying to keep you from being disturbed."

"Well, stop it!" Peter shouted at her, his temper lost. "Disturb me!"

"All right, fine!" Emma said. "*Fine.* I will."

They glared at each other.

Emma turned herself away from him. She leaned over to the bedside table for her book, and as she did Peter slid his arm across her chest, from behind. His touch on her was brilliant, electric. It took hours.

9

Tess, hovering alone by the front door of the apartment, was talking quietly to herself.

"Are they not here yet?" she asked earnestly. "Is Peter and Amanda not here outside the door?" She paused, motionless, in the act of listening, her ear set against the heavy door.

In the dining room, Emma was setting the table with fancy blue mats, and paper napkins printed with jungle animals. At two places she put small pink-wrapped packages: these were flowered barrettes, roses for Tess, daisies for Amanda. Emma could hear Tess's low serious voice.

"They will be here soon," Tess promised herself.

Tess had been waiting all morning. She had been waiting all week, ever since the moment Emma had told her that Peter's daughter, the mysterious grown-up Amanda, was coming to lunch.

That morning, when Emma came into Tess's bedroom, Tess awoke at once, sitting urgently upright. Her slept-in face was miraculously fresh, the pale skin smooth and translucent.

"Today is the day that Amanda comes," she said, blinking with sleep, but already full of purpose. "I would like to wear a party dress."

"It's not really a party," said Emma.

"But it's *kind* of a party," Tess pointed out. "We are having *guests* to come. I think a party dress would be a good idea."

Tess thought this every day. She yearned for lace, ribbons, petticoats, as though she had been brought up in a bordello. Emma slid the footed bottoms of Tess's pajamas down her pearly legs.

"Amanda won't be wearing a dress," Emma said. "She'll be in every-day clothes." Emma had a sudden image of Amanda: stony eyed, implacable. "You'll want to be able to play," Emma said, "How about your sweater with the ducks? And the white blouse with the ruffle?"

"My blouse with the long ruffle?" asked Tess, interested. "All the way around?"

"That's the one," said Emma.

Now Tess trotted in to report that no one had yet arrived. She wore corduroys and the duck sweater. At her neck rippled the white ruffle. Tess leaned heavily against her mother's side. She sighed loudly. "I wish they would come," she said, despondent.

"They'll come soon," Emma promised.

"I wish they would come *now*," said Tess. She put her head down on the table in despair.

Emma patted her. Waiting was dreadful for a child. There was no sense of time passing, no belief that it ever would.

"They'll come soon," Emma repeated: Peter was always on time.

Tess raised her head. "But Amanda's mommy is not coming?"

"No," said Emma.

"But where is Amanda's mommy?" Tess asked, squinting.

Emma had explained this before. "She's at home, in the house where she lives with Amanda."

"And Amanda doesn't live with her daddy?"

"No. She's like you. You don't live with your daddy," said Emma. She wondered if Tess really understood who Amanda's father was, and where he lived.

Tess stared up at her. "Mommy," she said, "how old is Amanda?"

"I've told you," Emma said. "Seven."

"Seven," Tess repeated. Awed, she said, "But, Mommy, I don't play with such old girls."

"But you will with Amanda," Emma reassured. "You'll have fun with her."

"Will I?" asked Tess, hopeful.

"You'll be friends," Emma promised. At that moment they heard the front door.

"They're here!" whispered Tess.

Peter closed the door with a jubilant slam. He wore a tweed jacket against the cool April morning, a wool scarf. He brought in with him a swirl of fresh air, and his cheeks were rose from the chill and excitement.

Smiling, he raked his wheat-colored hair back from his forehead. His gestures were swift and generous, as though he had energy and happiness to spare.

"Hello, sweet," he said to Emma.

Amanda, in jeans and a tan jacket, looked small beside her father. His hand was on her shoulder; she leaned away as though it were a tether. Her hands were deep in her pockets, her face seemed pinched.

Tess, brazen with excitement, ran headlong toward them. When she reached them she stopped, suddenly shy.

Peter, exuberant, stooped to pick her up. "Hello, you," he said, and swung her into the air for a kiss.

Tess, her eyes fixed on his, rose in his hands, in a swift spiraling arc. Peter leaned up toward her. He was a man who had left his wife and child, he was the source of grief and loss, but in this moment, lifting Emma's daughter up to a flying kiss, he declared himself again a man of family, a man who loved, who could be forgiven. The swoop was full of spirit and hope. At the peak of it Peter lifted his face to kiss Tess, his lips prepared for her small mouth, the earnest sweetness of her kiss, redemption.

But Tess, self-conscious, embarrassed in the presence of this glamorous stranger, struggled in his arms. She twisted her head sharply, away from his kiss. "Put me down," she commanded, squirming. "I want to be down." Obedient, disappointed, Peter set her down.

Tess turned to face Amanda. Amanda stared briefly, then coolly turned away. Tess shuffled a step closer and put her hands behind her back. She was waiting for it to begin, for them to start being friends. Amanda looked over her head, into the distance.

Emma stepped forward. "Hello, Amanda," she said. She leaned over to kiss her, but as she neared Amanda's face, the child jerked back. Her expression was so alarmed, then so chill, that Emma lost heart. She put her arm around Amanda's shoulder and gave her an awkward hug instead. Amanda flinched slightly as though at a blow.

Peter squatted between the two girls, putting a hand on each one's shoulder. "Amanda, I want you to meet Tess, Emma's daughter," he said. "Tessie, this is Amanda. She is *my* daughter."

Amanda looked down at Tess. "Hello," she said.

"I am Tess," Tess announced. She raised her shoulders elaborately, then dropped them.

Amanda looked around the hall, mute, her hands deep in her pockets.

She hates being here, Emma thought, her heart sinking. She hates everything: the air.

"Amanda, why don't you give me your jacket, and I'll hang it up," Emma said.

Amanda looked around without moving. There was a pause. She shifted her gaze to the top of the doorframe. She was waiting to go home.

"Amanda?" Peter said. "Give Emma your jacket."

Amanda looked at him, remote. The jacket was zipped tightly up to her chin. Emma pictured someone—Caroline?—kneeling on the rug in front of her, smiling, zipping Amanda into a warm snug cocoon.

Peter's eyes did not leave Amanda's face. "Amanda," he repeated. "What did Emma just say to you?"

Amanda's hands were rooted deep in her pockets, her arms close at her sides. She looked intently into the middle distance. Tess stood beside her, staring up at Amanda's face, respectful, fascinated, anxious. There was a pause.

"Amanda," Peter said again. His voice was firm.

"She can keep it on, it doesn't matter," Emma said. "Tess, why don't you show Amanda your room?" She wanted them to be alone together, away from the noisy thrust of their parents' expectations.

"Come on," said Tess at once. "Want to come to my room, Amanda?" She beckoned officiously and started off down the hall. Reluctant, Amanda followed. Tess turned back. "Come on," she said brightly, as though Amanda were a puppy. Amanda followed slowly. Her hands in her pockets, she gave a small contemptuous kick with each step. She stared boldly around as she walked through the rooms, like a monarch in exile.

Emma turned to Peter. "Come help me in the kitchen."

The lunch was planned for Amanda: onion soup, quiche, salad. Ice cream and cookies. Emma lifted the lid on the saucepan: steam rose warm and damp against her face. On the dark surface floated filmy strips of onion. The quiche was in the warm cave of the oven. Emma began to make the salad dressing; Peter slid the long loaf of French bread from its paper jacket.

"God," he said forcefully.

"She doesn't want to be here," said Emma.

Peter looked up. "What do you mean by that?" he asked. "This is her only chance to see her father. This is my new life."

"She doesn't want you to have a new life," said Emma.

Peter began slicing the loaf, quick, deliberate diagonal strokes. "I told her she had to be nice to Tess."

"They'll be fine," Emma said, wondering if they would. "In a while. It's hard for Amanda. She's jealous of Tess."

"Well, she'll just have to learn not to be," said Peter.

"You can't tell her how to feel," Emma said. She poured a smooth ribbon of olive oil into the glass jar. The yellow-green oil coiled swiftly, dissolving into itself.

"Yes, I can," Peter said. He began buttering, hard, the slices he had cut. "Everyone controls their feelings."

"No," said Emma. "You control your actions. You can't control the way you feel."

"Of course you can."

"No," said Emma again. She poured a dark globe of vinegar into the oil. "You can't make yourself love someone."

"Children love whoever loves them," Peter said. He began setting the slices onto a metal pan. "I love Amanda, you love her, Caroline loves her. Tess will love her. What more could a child want?"

Emma, who did not love Amanda, said nothing. She screwed on the top and shook the jar. Inside, the oil and vinegar dispersed into tiny globules. With each shake they shattered more, glistening, jostling, tiny: they would never dissolve. Each time Emma saw Amanda, the child's hostility rose up at her in great waves, chilling, repelling. What if she could never love her?

"Ready?" Peter asked.

"I'll get the girls," Emma answered.

Approaching Tess's room, silent on the carpet, Emma heard them talking and paused outside the door. First she heard Tess's high, serious piping, then a silence, then Amanda's low voice.

"It's your turn to take a card," Amanda said. After a pause she asked, "Where's your mom's room?"

"You mean my mommy's?" asked Tess, uncertain. Emma disliked the word *mom*.

"Your mom's," Amanda repeated, a thread of contempt in her voice.

"My mommy's room is in there," Tess said, conciliatory. "My mommy's and Peter's. They share that room together."

Amanda did not answer.

"This is my room," Tess said hopefully.

There was a pause.

"My room is bigger than this," Amanda said, as if to herself. There was a fluttering sound, cards being shuffled. "A lot bigger," Amanda said thoughtfully. "It's your turn."

"I have a closet," Tess offered, but Amanda did not answer.

"Want to see it?" Tess asked.

"No," Amanda said cruelly.

There was another pause; cards slid about on the rug.

Amanda said, "I won. Look."

"Why?" Tess asked.

"I have all four elephants. Look."

"But you won last time," Tess said wistfully.

"I won this time too," Amanda said.

Emma stepped into the doorway. The girls were sitting on the rug, the cards scattered in ragged lines in front of them.

"Hi, guys," Emma said. They looked up. Amanda, holding Emma's eyes with hers, made a swift guilty gesture. Certain cards slid quickly behind the curve of her hand.

"We are playing the animal game," Tess said, "and, Mommy, Amanda is the winner."

"That's how it is," Emma said. "Sometimes one person wins, sometimes the other."

"Yes, but she is *always* the winner," Tess said sadly. "And you know, Mommy, *I* like to be the winner."

Amanda stood, making a wild swirl of the cards with her foot. "We're finished now, anyway." She glanced at Emma, then away.

Emma gave her an admonitory look to let Amanda know she knew how she had won. But Amanda lifted her chin and would not meet her eye.

At the table Emma and Tess sat side by side, facing Peter and Amanda. Tess picked up the package at once.

"What is it?"

"A present," said Emma.

"Can I open it?"

"Why don't you save it for dessert? Amanda has one too."

Amanda eyed her package without speaking.

Emma ladled the soup into bowls, and Peter set into each a perfect crouton. Tess leaned over her bowl, nearly plunging her nose into the liquid. She gave a long, audible sniff. "What is this soup, Mommy, is this soup I like?"

"It's onion, Tess, I don't know if you've had it before. But Tess," Emma said, "it's not polite to lean into your bowl like that, and sniff at your food."

Stricken, Tess looked up at her mother. She said nothing, putting her hands in her lap and leaning back in her chair. Amanda looked at Tess, now interested.

Emma saw her mistake too late. "It's all right, Tessie," she said. "It's just not something you should do next time."

She had made it worse. Tess dropped her head; her chin pressed against the white ruffle. She sat motionless, head down.

"Tess," Emma said, but Tess would not look up.

Amanda now watched Tess intently, without courtesy or compassion, staring as though Tess were on display. Tess had put her spoon down; Amanda now picked hers up with meticulous care, and, fastidiously, began to eat. After every few spoonfuls, she picked up her napkin and wiped her mouth. She ignored Peter and Emma.

Emma, watching Tess, began sipping her own soup. Peter, with tactful indifference to the whole thing, was eating steadily.

"Good soup," he said. He looked at Amanda and waggled his eyebrows. She looked away.

Tess's head dropped lower and lower. Her shoulders began to jerk with little coughing sobs.

"Tessie?" Emma said, but there was no answer. It was no use. Emma put down her spoon. She picked Tess up from the chair and carried her into her room, where she sat down with her on the bed.

"Tessie, I'm sorry I said that to you, in front of other people," she said. Tess was now sobbing openly, brokenly.

"Amanda is a *big girl*," Tess said. "You shouldn't say those things to me in front of a big girl."

"I'm sorry," Emma said again, hugging the small heated body. It was her own rule, not to criticize Tess in public: why had she broken it? It was Amanda, she realized. She was trying to protect Tess from Amanda's scornful glance, the raised eyebrows, the condescending smile. She didn't want Amanda judging Tess; she was trying to correct her before Amanda noticed.

"I'm sorry," Emma said again. She would have to get better at this. She took Tess on her lap. She could feel the sobs lessening. She kissed the top of her head and held her until she was quiet.

When they returned, Peter smiled at Tess.

"Here she is," he said. Cheered, Tess climbed back in her chair and picked up her spoon.

After a moment, Emma turned to Amanda. "Amanda, where do you go to school?"

Amanda looked at her, then away. "Nightingale."

Emma nodded. "That's a very good school. And did you know, Tess, that it's the name of a bird, too? A bird with a beautiful song."

"The name of a bird? Is your school the name of a bird?" Tess had bounced suddenly back into good humor, her face full of hilarious incredulity.

But Amanda saw nothing amusing about the name of her school. She looked coldly at Tess without speaking.

"The name of a bird, and the bird with the most beautiful voice in the world," said Peter.

"A school with the name of a bird," Tess said, mirthful.

"And Amanda is in the first grade there," said Emma, trying to move on. "And what's your favorite subject? What part do you like the best?"

"Reading?" Peter prompted. "Music? Arithmetic?"

For the first time, Amanda's mouth broke out of its strict tautness into a curve. The corners slid reluctantly into a smile. "Daddy," she said, "we don't call it arithmetic."

"No?" said Peter. Everyone waited. Tess leaned forward.

"It's called *math*, Daddy," Amanda said, with exquisite condescension.

Peter shook his head. "Oh, no," he said, "I've done it again. I've said the wrong thing." He looked up at the ceiling. "Math," he whispered sternly to himself. "Not arithmetic. *Math. Math.*"

Amanda allowed herself to giggle. "Why did you say 'arithmetic'?" she asked, as though the word itself were absurd.

"Why did I?" Peter asked. He shook his head. "It's hard to say. These things just come to me. Sometimes 'arithmetic' just jumps in front of another word I'm trying to say. It gets there first. Sometimes, in the morning, I ask for a cup of hot arithmetic."

Both girls laughed out loud, and Tess looked at Amanda.

"A cup of hot arithmetic!" she said exuberantly, sharing the joke.

But at this, the notion that they were allies, Amanda quieted at once. Her face closed, and she looked down at her soup. Soberly she lifted a spoonful to her mouth.

Tess tried again. Her eyes fixed on Amanda, she laughed shrilly, hoping to recover the moment of shared hilarity.

Amanda ignored her; the moment was over, it was as though it had never been. Precisely she opened her mouth for her soup.

Tess watched her hopefully, but Amanda stared steadily in front of her, ignoring Tess, and Tess's face fell.

Peter drank from his water glass, watching the girls from the corner of his eye. "I should have known that 'arithmetic' wasn't what big girls would call it."

Emma, watching, thought, He is so brave, he tries so hard. She looked at Amanda.

Amanda ignored them all. She chewed slowly, swallowed. She licked her lips, then wiped her mouth with icy hauteur. She turned to Tess. "Where's your nanny?"

"My nanny?" asked Tess. She looked at Emma. "What is my nanny?"

"She means Rachel," said Emma.

"My baby-sitter? My baby-sitter is Rachel. She's not here. It's her day off."

Amanda stared. "Why do you call her your baby-sitter?"

"Because," Tess said, nodding for emphasis on each word, "she, is, my, baby-sitter."

Amanda raised her eyebrows and took another mouthful.

"Amanda has a nanny who looks after her," Peter said. "Her name is Maeve."

"I've always had her," Amanda said. "Since I was born."

"Maeve takes Amanda to school in the morning, and picks her up in the afternoon," said Peter.

"That is like my baby-sitter," Tess said happily. "The same which my baby-sitter does."

"They're different," said Amanda loftily. "A nanny does more than that. She's better than a baby-sitter."

Emma hoped Amanda would not tell Tess that a playgroup was different from school. She tried to remember if Rachel had gone out or not. She hoped Rachel was not in her bedroom, ten feet away.

"A nanny isn't better, Amanda," Peter said. "Just different."

Amanda shrugged her shoulders.

Tess leaned forward. "My baby-sitter is a brown. Is your nanny a brown?"

Amanda frowned. Emma, praying that Rachel was out, said, "Not a brown, Tess. Rachel is black."

Tess shook her head stubbornly. "No, she is not black. Her skin is *brown.*" Tess pushed her chair back and stood up. "Come, I'll show you."

"No," Emma said quickly, "it's Rachel's day off. We'll let her have some time to herself." She turned to Amanda, changing the subject at random. "Now, Amanda, do you have a birthday coming up soon?"

"May," Amanda said to the air.

"My birthday is in May too," Tess said, climbing back onto her chair.

"Is it?" Emma asked. "I thought your birthday was in August."

"Yes," said Tess. "Sometimes it is in June."

"Tell us what you do on your birthday," Emma said to Amanda.

"My mom takes us to the movies," Amanda said. "And then afterward we come home and have cake and presents."

"Presents?" Tess asked.

Amanda stared at her. "At birthday parties you have presents."

Abashed, Tess tilted her head and said nothing.

"Remember at Samantha's?" Emma said. "We took her a present." Tess nodded.

"How old are you?" Amanda asked her.

"More than three," Tess offered.

"Four?" asked Amanda.

Tess shook her head.

"She's three," Emma said. "Right, Tess? You'll be four on your next birthday."

"But I am more than three, because my three birthday is past," said Tess anxiously.

"True," said Emma. "You're three and a half."

"Three," Amanda murmured to herself.

Troubled, Tess watched her.

"Amanda, are you being mean to Tess?" Peter asked suddenly.

Amanda twisted her head ambiguously, shrugging her shoulders. Emma stood.

"If you girls are through, let's have the quiche." She picked up their bowls. "Peter, will you bring in the salad?"

In the kitchen she said, "Don't be too hard on her."

"What is the matter with her?" Peter asked.

"It's her first time seeing you here. It's hard for her."

"It's hard for all of us."

"She doesn't like you living with another little girl."

"Well, I do," said Peter. "She has to get used to it."

Emma pulled the tray from the oven, and without looking at him, said tentatively, "Maybe after lunch you should take her out somewhere with you. Maybe she'd like a walk in the park or something."

Peter frowned. "A walk in the park? It's about thirty degrees outside."

"Or go to a museum, or something."

"A museum. Dragging Amanda from room to room at the Whitney. That'd cheer her up, I'm sure. My God." Peter put his hands on his hips. "What's the matter with you? Don't you want her here?"

"No, no, it's not that," Emma said guiltily. "It's just that I think she'd like being alone with you."

Peter laughed unpleasantly. "Are you kicking us out?"

"Of course not," Emma said.

"Why can't we stay here? I thought the girls could play a game together after lunch."

Emma thought of Amanda's surreptitious hand among the cards. "I just think Amanda would rather be alone with you," she said, but she was retreating, she had lost.

"She has to get used to my life the way it is now," Peter said. "This is where I live. I'm not spending the afternoon dragging her through the streets like a homeless person."

Emma said nothing.

"Where do you want me to go?" Now he sounded not angry but desperate, and Emma reached out to him, smoothing his hair.

"Here," she said, "stay here."

In the dining room, the girls sat in silence. Tess gazed longingly at Amanda, who stared fixedly into the distance. Emma slid them each a neat wedge of quiche, its crusty surface crumpled and steaming.

"Now." Peter sat down. "See if you can eat it without eating the tip first." The girls looked at him. "Not the tip."

"But I want to eat the tip first," Tess said cheerfully.

"Right," Peter said. "Everyone does. Try not to."

Tess shook her head serenely. "I want to." She picked up her fork and stabbed off the point of her piece, then ate it, watching Peter. "Mm," she said. Peter and Emma laughed.

Amanda ignored her, picking up her fork and cutting the slice in half lengthwise. She took a bite from the outer portion.

"There you go," said Peter. "That's another way. Good for you, Nanna."

Tess said suddenly, "My present!"

"What is it?" asked Emma.

"It's gone!" Tess's voice was piercing. "*Where is my present?*" She put her head down on the table, then threw it back, banging it against her chairback. "It's gone!"

"Stop it, Tess," said Emma, getting up. "What are you talking about?" The package was not there.

"*My present is gone,*" wailed Tess. She squirmed in her chair. Emma squatted beside her, looking under Tess's plate, beneath her mat. She looked under the table. The package was gone. Beside her Tess keened, her voice shrill, intolerable.

"*Stop it,*" Emma said, rattled. "It's here somewhere. Stop whining."

Peter looked under the table. "Where was it?"

"By her glass," Emma said. "It's got to be here. It was here when we sat down."

"Where is my *present?*" Tess whimpered.

Amanda glanced sideways at her. She put her hands beneath her thighs and swung her legs under the table.

"We'll find it, Tess," said Emma. "Don't worry. It's here, it has to be." She looked again under the table, as though she might have over-looked a bright pink package among the chair legs. Peter stood by Tess, frowning.

Emma picked up Tess's plate, her mat. "Stand up for a second, Tess," she said, "maybe you're sitting on it."

Tess slid off her chair. The seat was empty.

"It's gone," Tess said, collapsing into sobs. "*It's gone.*"

The day, which she had so eagerly awaited, was ruined. This girl, the glamorous older girl who was to become her friend, would never be her friend. Tess had lost the card games. Amanda had been contemptuous of her age, her baby-sitter, her birthday. Amanda had mocked and ridiculed her. The day that had begun with such excitement had held nothing but disappointment, and now the one certain pleasure—the present from her mother—was gone.

"This is bizarre," Emma said to Peter. "Where is it?"

Amanda picked up her water glass and drank lengthily.

"Amanda," Peter said. He folded his arms, his mouth grim. Next to her small frame he looked suddenly very large.

"Amanda," he said again, "do you know where Tess's present is?"

There was a pause. Slowly Amanda shook her head. She did not look at him.

"Amanda," Peter said, "look at me."

After a moment she turned. She looked at him, her eyes hooded.

"Answer me," Peter said, his face bleak. "Do you know where Tess's present is?"

Amanda did not answer.

"Stand up," he said.

Amanda deliberately turned away from him. She looked straight ahead. She picked up her spoon and dropped it lightly, negligently, on her mat.

Tess, next to Emma, slid down against her mother's leg. She collapsed onto the floor and began to cry in earnest. "Ssh, Tess," Emma said. She was watching Peter.

Peter leaned over Amanda, took her by the shoulder; this time his grip was not proud, not loving. Amanda twisted away from her father's hand, her face darkening angrily.

Emma almost spoke, almost stepped forward to stop him. Peter was too angry, too powerful, to confront this small child. But Emma had her own small child, smaller, wailing with despair against her leg. She saw again Amanda's hand slipping the cards out of sight, heard her low voice spurning each of Tess's innocent offerings. Emma felt her own heart tighten, her own chest rise angrily. Her throat felt hot and swollen. Her own child lay weeping on the floor.

"Stand up," said Peter. His voice was terrible.

Nothing could save Amanda now. It will never work, thought Emma. In that long instant before Amanda reluctantly stood, it felt to Emma like the last moment on top of a ski run, when you pause, thrilled, terrified, your heart sinking inside you. You see before you the endless icy slope, descending, descending. You realize now, clearly, that it is too steep. You see that certain disaster waits below, but you are there, at the top, it is too late to change, to stop, you know that, it is just before you begin the long swoop down it, as you must.

10

Here goes," Peter said, opening the car door.

Outside in the summer evening there was silence, broken only by a quiet shore breeze. The sandy driveway ended in an open space, casually ringed by Cape Cod underbrush. A path led through it to the house, set in a stand of tall spare pines. Beyond it were the high dunes.

"You're very brave," Emma said, climbing out and opening the back door. Tess, in her car seat, squirmed to be set free.

"I am." Tess nodded, looking solemn. "Why am I?"

"Not you," said Emma, unbuckling her. "Peter."

"Had to happen sometime," said Peter, opening the trunk.

"Why is Peter brave?" asked Tess, held her arms out for release. Emma freed and lifted her without answering.

"Here we are, Tessie," Emma said. "Gonny and Grandfather will be so glad to see you."

"Yes," Tess agreed.

It was just past sunset. On the rippling dune grass, the scrub pines, the laurel and bayberry bushes, was the light open darkness that settles along the ocean. Emma led the way, moving by feel and by feet's memory, up the sandy path, brushing through the bayberry leaves with their sweet coarse tang, past the bare-trunked, rough-barked pines. The house lay along a low ridge like an ocean liner, long and mysterious, its windows radiant.

"Have I got everything?" Peter asked suddenly, from behind her. "Two suitcases and a baby bag?"

"That's it," said Emma, carrying only Tess.

He was nervous, after all, she thought: this was the first he had shown it. Answering him, she did not turn her eyes from the house. She walked toward it, holding it in her gaze as though to lose sight of it would mean stumbling.

In the quiet summer darkness, the front hall was like a stage set, vivid and brilliant against the shadows. The big front door stood open, and coming up the path Emma could see her parents waiting inside.

Emma's father, Everett Kirkland, taught economics at MIT. He was tall, with a broad barrel chest and a curved powerful nose. He had dark hair and dark eyes, and commanding eyebrows. He stood very straight, with his head tilted slightly backward and his chin slightly raised. The lift of his jaw gave a diagonal slant to his gaze; he seemed to look down on other people, even if they were exactly the same height.

Emma's mother, Aline, was also tall, but slightly stooped. She leaned anxiously forward, her shoulders hunched. Her eyes were blue, her cheeks full and pink. She had a small sweet bow-shaped mouth, and fine light straying hair. They were in their mid-sixties; both wore khaki pants, blue sneakers, sweaters.

A ship's lantern hung directly overhead, casting deep shadow on their faces. They had heard the car, and now stood side by side, motionless, poised, like actors before the curtain rises. Approaching through the darkness were their divorced daughter, her divorced lover, her daughter by another man. They disapproved of all of this.

Emma pushed open the screen door and stepped inside. "Hello there," she said.

"My Gonny! I am here to see you!" shouted Tess, holding out her arms and launching herself through the air toward her grandmother. Emma turned to her father.

"Hello, Daddy," she said. Her father put one hand lightly on her shoulder and kissed her cheek. His skin, set briefly against hers, felt dry and lined.

"Hello, Emma," her father said. "Hello, Tess." He turned courteously to Peter, who was struggling with the suitcases against the screen door's stubborn closing tug. "Here," said Emma's father, stepping forward, "let me give you a hand."

"Oh, that awful door, I'm sorry," said Emma's mother in a worried undertone. She spoke as though the door were an old enemy, a foot soldier in the army of things that continually assaulted her.

"Hello, Mr. Kirkland," Peter said, finally inside. He set the suitcases down and stepped forward to shake hands.

"Daddy, this is Peter," said Emma, anxious. "My father, Everett Kirkland." They stood face-to-face. They were the same height: it surprised her, though she didn't know whom she had thought was taller. Peter looked directly into her father's eyes.

"And this is my Gonny," said Tess, loud and excited, patting Mrs. Kirkland's shoulder hard.

"It's so nice to see you, Peter," said Mrs. Kirkland, nodding and smiling. With Tess still in her arms, she held out an awkward left hand to him.

"Hello, Mrs. Kirkland. It's so nice of you to have me here," Peter said, giving a friendly shake. He seemed entirely at ease.

"Well, we're delighted," said Mrs. Kirkland. "We've heard so much about you."

This was not true; Emma had said little about Peter to her parents.

Peter nodded politely again. "And I about you," he said, which was more truthful. "It's a great pleasure to be here."

Emma, watching them, saw that it would be all right. With Warren it had been different: Warren charmed, he didn't stand his ground. He had never stood eye to eye with her father; instead, he had slid dexterously into the role of adopted son. He had been playfully flirtatious toward Emma's mother; Gonny had been his nickname for her. He had formed a male alliance with Mr. Kirkland. Warren teased Emma outrageously in front of him, claiming that she was shamefully lazy, hopelessly antisocial, a terrible cook. Emma's father was too remote and ponderous to tease, but Warren's sallies amused him. For Emma it was reassuring to feel that the two men were allies. It meant she would never feel torn between them. It also meant she could never challenge Warren, for if she challenged her father's ally, she was also challenging her father.

Now, seeing Peter's calm eye on Everett, Emma felt things shifting. Assessments were being made, measures taken. Peter would never play the adopted son, he would never curry favor. He would never take Everett's side against Emma. This was, unexpectedly, exhilarating, and Warren's wheedling partnership seemed now adolescent. But it was also unnerving, for if Peter and her father were not allies, with whom did her allegiance lie?

Emma turned to her mother. "Will you keep Tess while we take things upstairs? Is Peter in the end room?"

"He is," her mother answered, holding Tess. "I've put Tess in with you in your room."

The house, built in the twenties, was rambling and irregular, with odd angles and unexpected gables. Emma led Peter down the upstairs hall to a small square room. Twin beds, covered with old blue cotton bedspreads, stood side by side. Under a mirror was a white painted bureau, with a frayed linen runner, an ironstone pitcher and basin. Low shelves, lined haphazardly with faded books, met the sloping eaves. The floor was painted dark blue; there was a ragged woven rug before the bureau.

The air was hot and unused. Emma heaved up the swollen, reluctant window; at once the sea's salt presence filled the room. A night breeze touched the limp white curtains, and outside, beyond the dunes, invisible waves rolled smoothly up the flat beach and sank, hissing quietly, into the porous sand.

Emma turned back inside. Peter, the suitcases beside him, stood in the middle of the room. He looked out of place, too big for this awkward space with its cramped ceiling, its narrow beds.

"Don't worry," she said.

"I'm forty years old," said Peter. "I'm not worried about your parents." He put his arms around her.

"Good," said Emma. "My mother will love you," she promised hopefully, into his chest.

"And your father?"

"How could he help himself?" asked Emma.

"I can imagine it," said Peter.

They had dinner in the kitchen. The worn pine table, with its warped leaves, was surrounded by a battered assortment of wooden chairs, which had, once, all been painted blue. The table stood in the bay window, looking out toward the ocean.

Emma's parents always ate in the kitchen, now there was no cook in it. Their last cook, Alice Sullivan, had been a local woman from South Yarmouth. She was a widow, lean and composed, with short springy gray hair. She wore metal-rimmed glasses and a blue denim apron. She had one child, a teenage son. One night when she was cooking for a dinner party, she made an announcement to the Kirklands and their guests. As she handed around the silver tray of cheese puffs, she told them that her son had received a scholarship to Exeter. She didn't say this to them, but it was the first time anyone in her family had gone to a private school. All of the

Kirklands' guests knew Exeter, of course; all of them had gone to private boarding schools, and their children as well. Everyone congratulated Alice, as they took cheese puffs from the tray. When they went back to their conversations with each other, Alice took the silver tray back to the kitchen. She set it down on the counter. The lamb was finished roasting, and the plates were in the warming oven. The vegetables were simmering on top of the stove. Alice took off her apron, hung it in the closet, and walked out the back door.

After that there were no more full-time cooks; people didn't want that kind of job anymore. Most of the summer families did without, eating in the kitchen and cooking for themselves. For dinner parties they called a caterer: each season an energetic young divorced mother set herself up as a live-out cook. She lasted a few seasons, then retired, and a new one set up shop. It was not perfect, but it was perfectly all right.

Mrs. Kirkland, who was not interested in food, didn't care whether she had a cook or not. Like her mother, she had grown up with a cook in the kitchen, and had never learned the skill herself. She took little pleasure in either cooking or eating, and saw meals as mild ordeals to be gotten through somehow. Mr. Kirkland, too, was indifferent to food: at lunchtime, here, he grabbed two slices of bread and smeared a clot of tuna fish between them. He carried this sad creation off with him, taking ragged bites on his way down to the dock. Asked later if he had eaten lunch, he would not remember.

Dinner that night was canned tomato soup, made with water, not milk, and salad of brown-edged iceberg lettuce. A chipped white plate held a cold block of pale cheddar cheese, surrounded by broken Wheat Thins. The untouched slab and the scattered shards of crackers looked like a model of an archaeological site.

As they sat down, Emma's mother said vaguely, "I thought we could have those crackers."

"But we *can*," said Tess, baffled. "We *can* have the crackers, Gonny." She looked intently from mother to mother. "Why did Gonny say that she thought that we could?" But Emma only smiled at her, she did not answer.

At her parents' house Emma fell into a mild trance. To do anything differently from the way it had always been done, to challenge her parents' ways, to alter her own, or at times to do anything at all, seemed impossible. She was taken over by the powerful silent current of her parents' wishes; she fell back, helpless, into childhood. She felt this way even though she was thirty-two, with a job and a daughter, right in the foaming middle of her own choppy life, in riotous currents that were entirely her own creation.

Emma's father ate slowly, leaning slightly forward, and slipping his spoon sideways into the watery soup. "We've been having pretty good sailing weather," he said, not looking at anyone. He set his spoon down and looked at the table in front of Peter. He folded his hands, falsely docile. "Don't know if you're a sailor," he said deprecatingly.

"A bit of one," said Peter easily.

There was a silence. Mr. Kirkland looked at him appraisingly, then picked up his spoon again.

"Is that so?" he asked finally. "Where do you sail?"

"I don't, now, but I grew up sailing, in the summers anyway," said Peter.

"And where was that?" pursued Mr. Kirkland.

"Maine," said Peter. "A place called Sorrento."

Mr. Kirkland frowned. "Sorrento," he repeated.

"East of Bar Harbor, on the mainland."

Peter needn't have said anything after "Maine," Emma thought. Maine, with its cold terrifying fogs, its ferocious tides, its threatening granite shores, was the grand master of sailing teachers. It was not possible to be dismissive of a sailor from Maine, not even for her father, who was the grand master of dismissiveness.

"Sorrento," said Mrs. Kirkland. "Isn't that where the Pattersons go? Evelyn and Roger Patterson?"

"Their house is near my parents'," Peter said.

Mrs. Kirkland smiled. "Remember, Everett? We saw them up there, one summer, when we went up with the Yacht Club cruise."

Mr. Kirkland, who did not want to talk about the Pattersons, addressed himself to his soup, and made an indeterminate noise.

"I went to school with Evelyn," Mrs. Kirkland persevered. "At Smith. She was such fun."

"She's a good friend of my mother's," Peter said.

"And who is your mother?" asked Mrs. Kirkland brightly. She took a piece of shattered cracker and began taking small bites.

"Polly Morris, she was in college," said Peter.

Mrs. Kirkland shook her head regretfully, disclaiming acquaintanceship.

"She went to Miss Hall's and then Smith." He turned to Mr. Kirkland. "My father went to Harvard, but Emma told me you were at Yale."

Mr. Kirkland nodded slowly. "Class of 'Forty-one," he said.

"My father was 'Thirty-eight," said Peter.

" 'Thirty-eight. I wonder if your father knew my cousin, Carter Lawson," said Mr. Kirkland thoughtfully. "I think he was 'Thirty-eight."

"They rowed together. Carter Lawson was cox."

Mrs. Kirkland smiled at Peter.

Emma, watching the faces, thought triumphantly that they would have to like him. Not only was Peter a sailor, not only had his father rowed with Carter Lawson, but on top of everything else, Peter was nice, and it showed.

"There's more soup for everyone," Emma's mother said. She looked around the table. "Or are we ready for salad?" She touched the salad bowl.

"*I* don't want any more soup, Gonny," Tess said firmly. She took another piece of shattered cracker. "*And* I don't want any salad." She pointed at the bowl. "Because I hate that kind of salad, Gonny."

"Don't be rude," said Emma, but her mother smiled serenely. It was impossible to offend her about food.

"It *is* kind of awful, isn't it?" Mrs. Kirkland said, peering with interest at the browning lettuce.

"No more crackers, Tess," Emma added automatically but realized as she spoke that, besides the watery soup, there was little else for Tess to eat. Emma stood up, taking the plate with the lonely slab of cheese. "What if I make some grilled cheese sandwiches? Would anyone like one?"

"Oh, *what* a good idea," said Mrs. Kirkland, marveling.

Everyone wanted one.

"Francie's been here, hasn't she?" Emma asked, forcing the knife through the cheese.

"She was here for a week," her mother answered. "With the girls. And, you know. That man."

"And how was it?" asked Emma. Her parents answered at the same time.

"Fine," said her mother.

"Pretty bad," said her father.

"Is that *my* Francie?" Tess asked Gonny.

"That's *your* aunt Francie," said her grandmother, "and *your* cousins Rainie and Mallow."

"Are they all going to be here now? When I am here?" asked Tess.

"Not this time, Tess," said Emma. "Why was it pretty bad?" she asked her father.

Her father sat back and folded his arms across his chest. "She's with that terrible man," he said, lifting his chin.

"Oh, now, Everett, he's not so bad," Mrs. Kirkland protested gaily. She smiled at her water glass.

Emma's father put his spoon down. "Aline, you cannot say that and mean it," he said. "You cannot say that and mean it."

Mrs. Kirkland said nothing, and Mr. Kirkland turned to Emma. "The man is a complete fool. He has no education, and no intention, or hope either, of getting one."

"Well," offered Emma, "that's not the absolute worst—"

"Let me finish, please," said her father loudly. "This man has no education whatever, and he has no intention of getting one. He has no job, either. He keeps talking about wanting to do something outside 'the system.' " Emma's father said this phrase as though he were saying "the sewer." "Finally I asked him just what he thought 'the system' was." He shook his head. "He had no coherent answer, of course. I said to him, 'If you want to know, "the system" is the means by which salaries are earned, and by which goods and moneys are transferred from one person to another.' " Emma's father looked triumphantly around the table. "Now, how are you going to get a job outside 'the system'? You tell me that."

There was a pause.

"And what did Francie say?" Emma asked.

Her father gave a short unfriendly cough of laughter. "Your sister went up in smoke, naturally," he said. "She claimed I was 'attacking' him. She left in a huff and told your mother she wouldn't come here anymore."

"I think her feelings were hurt," Mrs. Kirkland told her water glass.

"Well, they needn't have been," Mr. Kirkland said loudly. He leaned back and wiped his mouth, hard, with his napkin. "I didn't say anything to hurt *her* feelings."

"Well, Daddy," Emma said, placatingly, "it doesn't sound as though you were very nice to Francie's boyfriend."

"It would be impossible to be very nice to her boyfriend, let me assure you," said Mr. Kirkland. "Impossible," he repeated, folding his arms magisterially.

Tess looked up at him. "But you are very nice to *my* mommy's boyfriend, Peter, aren't you, Grandfather? You are? Isn't Peter very nice, do you think?" She nodded urgently at her grandfather, coaxing him to nod back.

Mr. Kirkland stared at her crossly for a moment. "I hope I am nice to everyone, Tess," he said.

"But you don't seem as though you are Peter's *friend*," Tess said.

Mr. Kirkland frowned. "We have just *met*, Peter and I," he said, raising his chin. "We are still *acquaintances*. Friendship takes time to develop, Tess."

Before Tess could answer, Emma's mother bent toward her.

"Tessie, do you want Gonny to put you to bed tonight?" she asked.

Distracted and indignant, Tess said, "Not now! It's not time for my bedtime."

"Now, Tess," Emma began the nightly ritual of commands and compromise.

After doing the dishes, Emma and Peter were alone; the Kirklands had gone to bed. In the living room a bank of mullioned windows looked out toward the water. Beneath the windows stood a mildly battered sofa, covered in worn flowered chintz. Most of the furniture was battered; fraying threads hung along the bottoms of the slipcovers, and grayish holes spread across the chair arms.

Emma sat down next to Peter. "Why am I so tired? It's not late, and I've done nothing." She leaned her head back and closed her eyes. Peter put his arm around her, and, her eyes still shut, Emma put her hand flat on his chest. Peter covered her hand with his.

"It's being with your parents," Peter said.

Without opening her eyes Emma asked, "Are they all exhausting? Are you exhausted by yours?"

"Differently from the way you are. But my parents are sort of the reverse of yours. My father's absentminded and cheerful. He makes puns. My mother's the austere one."

Emma turned to look at him. "Is my father austere?"

"What do you think?"

"I can't tell. I think of him as the way a father is. Fatherly."

"Well, I wouldn't call him fatherly," said Peter. "I'd call him austere."

"I'd call yours charming," said Emma.

"He'd call you charming," said Peter.

"Did he think Caroline was charming?"

"Well, my father loves women, period," said Peter diplomatically.

So he had loved Caroline, thought Emma. At once she disapproved of Peter's father: his mindless chat, his silly puns.

"But they didn't really get along," Peter went on. "My parents aren't grand enough for Caroline. Their house isn't big enough. Their friends aren't fancy enough. Caroline kept hoping we'd be asked for drinks somewhere glittery."

"Really?" Emma asked, pleased. How contemptible Caroline was, she thought. She felt a surge of loyalty to Peter's father, his delightful sense of humor, his sympathy for women.

"But tell me about your sister, and her paragon of a boyfriend."

"Francie always has a boyfriend," said Emma critically, as though this were a flaw.

"Why shouldn't she?" said Peter.

"She has too many," said Emma. "They're always awful, and she never marries them."

"She married one."

"One she shouldn't have."

"And your father doesn't like any of them," said Peter.

"They're always like this one, Rex," said Emma. "They're all terrible flakes. How can he like them?"

"What do Rex and Francie live on?" Peter asked.

"Schemes. And my father gives her an allowance, and then he complains. Now it's self-awareness seminars."

"Ah, yes, the self-awareness seminars." Peter shook his head. "How do you happen to be so normal?"

"You only think I'm normal because I'm like you. I'm sure Rex thinks *Francie* is the only normal person in the family."

"Well, I'm glad I met you and not Francie," Peter said.

Emma put her head against his shoulder.

"I'm sorry they grilled you about your parents," she said. "I hate it when they do that."

"I don't mind," said Peter. "Why shouldn't they want to know who I am?"

"I hate it," Emma repeated. She lay back, her head against the sofa. "Tomorrow he'll ask you to go sailing."

"Will you come?"

"No," said Emma.

"Why not?"

"The last time I went sailing with Daddy I was thirteen. That was the year he decided I was old enough to crew for him in the races. I did it all that summer, even though I hated racing. Out on the water the wind was too hard, the sails were too heavy. The spray was freezing, I was always cold. My fingers would get numb, and I couldn't hold the lines or undo the knots. I'd fumble, and my father would yell at me, and then I'd fumble worse.

"The last time I sailed with him was the last race of the series. Daddy'd done really well that season, and we went into the last race in a three-way tie for first place. He was really excited, he'd never done that well before. We had a good wind, and we got off to a great start. We took the lead, and we held it for nearly the whole race, until right near the end, when another boat in the tie, the *Sea Witch*, started to close in on us. We were nearly at the finish line, and we could see the people on the Committee Boat watching. The *Sea Witch* got nearer, and Daddy decided to tack. As we were coming about, the jib sheet got caught on something up on the foredeck, and the jib stuck halfway round. Daddy shouted at me to go up and free the line. We were heeled way over, and I went sliding up on my knees, with the mainsail flapping over my head and the jib slamming around like a trapped lion. I crawled up onto the foredeck and found the sheet had gotten tangled up on a cleat. My wet fingers were numb with the cold, and I was trying to free it and I could see the *Sea Witch* getting nearer. I could hear my father shouting at me to hurry up. He was frantic. I was frantic. I tugged on the lines to get them loose, and right in front of the Committee Boat I uncleated the wrong line and I brought the jib down. The whole sail came crashing onto my head. The boat ploughed to a dead stop, I nearly went overboard, the *Sea Witch* won the series, and my father never asked me to go sailing again."

"What did he say about it afterwards?"

"He never mentioned it again. We never discussed it. It was too terrible."

Peter put his arm around her. "Well, I love you," he said.

Emma closed her eyes, comforted. "Thank you."

The living room was almost dark; only the standing lamp by the sofa was lit. Its shade had deepened with age to a dark ocher, and the light it shed was subdued. The rest of the room was in shadow, dusk spread across the big faded chairs. Behind Peter and Emma, through the window, beyond the dunes, the ocean whispered. Inside the house it was quiet.

In the morning Emma came down early with Tess. By the time her parents appeared, Emma was in the kitchen, wearing Alice Sullivan's denim apron.

"How would everyone like your eggs?" she asked, as her father came in.

"His eggs," said her father.

"Her eggs," said Emma. "How?"

"Oh, *eggs*," said Emma's mother, coming in behind him. She was in khaki pants and a white turtleneck, a sweater over it. The turtleneck was frayed at the cuffs, and the sweater's elbows were worn. "*What* a good idea." She rubbed her hands together, nodding admiringly.

When Mrs. Kirkland was in charge of breakfast, people milled slowly around the kitchen in a dream of disorder, getting quietly in each other's way, shuffling silently in and out of the refrigerator, all of them on private errands, all in a thick fog of early morning introspection. They spilled milk on the counter, unwittingly took each other's toast from the toaster and struggled to spread the soft surfaces with icy chunks of butter. They put down the cereal box and set off for bowls, to return and find the box gone, put down elsewhere by someone who had then set off for bowls. And always the missing carton of orange juice, gone from the refrigerator, forgotten on the counter by the stove, where it stood warming slowly.

Now Emma set the big black iron skillet on the burner, while Peter and Tess set the table. Tess, kneeling on a chair, folded each napkin into an uneven triangle. Emma made scrambled eggs, scraping a soft steaming yellow cascade onto the plates.

When Mr. Kirkland finished eating, he leaned back and looked appraisingly at Peter, who'd just walked in.

"Thought we might go out this morning. East wind."

"Sounds good," said Peter.

"I could go, too," Tess said, hopeful, diffident, but Emma smiled and shook her head.

"You're staying here with me and Gonny."

The three of them went down to say good-bye to the men. They set off in the dinghy, Mr. Kirkland rowing. Peter, in the stern, turned to wave as they moved off. Mr. Kirkland, facing them, frowned, pulling hard as the dinghy bucked over the wake of a passing motorboat. The women waved intermittently until the men reached the boat. Then the three of them walked back up the narrow clanging metal gangplank up to the high dock. On top of the dunes the wind was steady, and the flag snapped and rippled over their heads.

"They'll have fun, I think," Emma said cheerfully.

"Yes," said her mother. "It's nice he can sail."

"His name is Peter," said Emma.

Her mother squinted at the wind, and pulled her sweater across her chest. She said to Tess, "Come on in with Gonny and we'll find you some crayons."

Emma and her mother cleared up the kitchen while Tess sat at the table with a coloring book. Emma moved around the room, mopping up and putting away, while her mother stood at the sink.

"I'd forgotten these plates," said Emma, holding one. It was white, with a wreath of bright blue chicory flowers around the edge. "I always loved these."

"They've always been here," said her mother, indifferent. She was running water, and Emma could see beyond her the slow rise of a stiff white landscape: suds. Mrs. Kirkland didn't approve of the dishwasher. She turned off the water, tested it and turned it on again. The foamy landscape rose unevenly.

"I hope you know what you're doing," Mrs. Kirkland said.

Emma straightened, at once hostile. Her mother knew nothing about her life, nothing.

"I hope so too," said Emma, brisk.

There was another pause.

"I'm afraid it will be hard on her," her mother said, nodding toward Tess.

"I'm afraid it will," Emma agreed. She snapped the mouth of the open milk carton closed and put it back in the refrigerator, shutting the door hard.

Did her mother think it had never occurred to Emma that divorce would be hard on Tess? And her mother had given no advice about marrying Warren. That was what Emma should have been warned about, not this, not Peter. But her mother's experience was so different from hers. Mrs. Kirkland had married a man she respected, and with whom she had a decent life. Emma had married a man she came to despise, and with whom she had felt at moments suicidal. How could her mother give her advice?

"I'm sure it will be hard on Tess. It's hard on all of us," Emma said, her voice cold, "but it's done. It's final."

"You've never said why you did it," Emma's mother said. She turned off the tap and turned to look at her daughter. She tilted her head to one side, waiting. In the silence Emma heard the steady seesaw strokes of Tess's crayon.

Emma had not said why. She could not tell her mother about her marriage.

Mrs. Kirkland stood by the sink, looking at Emma. Her blue eyes were hooded by age. If she felt irritation at her unyielding child, who offered no hint of what her thoughts were, what her life was like, she gave no sign. Her hands hidden inside the radiant landscape, she waited.

Emma looked back without speaking. She could not tell her mother about the shame of her life with Warren. And she could offer her mother nothing instead, no rosy future. Emma didn't know if she and Peter would get married. Sometimes she thought their marriage was wonderfully certain, and sometimes she could not bear the thought of living with Peter for another hour,

The silence between them made Tess raise her head. She looked alertly from mother to mother, from face to face, trying to read them. It was Emma who turned away first, pulling open a cupboard, putting the honey inside. She closed the wooden door with a soft kitchen thud.

"Do you want to save this or throw it out?" she asked, holding up a plastic bread bag. Two skinny end slices swung forlornly in its foot. Her mother would save them, and the bread would stay in the cupboard until it was petrified.

"Throw it out," her mother said, turning back to her fragile white mountain range.

"Throw it out?"

"Yes," said her mother shortly.

Tess, anxious at the tension, sat bolt upright. "I could take it," she cried. She looked from her mother to her grandmother. "I could take it and give it to the birds."

Emma handed her the bag.

"Good idea," said her grandmother.

They both smiled at Tess, aloof to each other.

Outside on the lawn, Tess stood frowning. She tore the bread into big careless shreds and threw it angrily into the wind.

It was late in the afternoon when the men returned. Watching them cross the sandy lawn, Emma could see that the day had gone well. They walked side by side, their movements loose and companionable. They were wind whipped, red faced, salt haired and cheerful. Emma followed Peter upstairs to hear how it had been.

"It was great. He's a good sailor, your father," Peter said. He pulled off his sodden shirt and dropped it onto the floor. Emma admired the line of his bared arms, the spring of his chest. He looked very different now, standing in the little room, barefoot, shirtless, his hands low on his hips. The casual geometry of his limbs, his ease, the salt-wet shirt on the floor, all declared him at home beneath the slanting eaves.

"Did he shout at you?" asked Emma.

"All captains shout. Sailing is noisy. You have to shout to be heard. And things have to be done right away."

"So you didn't mind?"

Peter grinned at her. "Oh, I hated it. I told him"—he set his hands prissily and peeped shrilly—"if he yelled at me one more time I would lower the jib."

"Very funny," said Emma. "But why don't you mind? It's so *rude.*"

"Men *don't* mind," said Peter. "Men yell at each other all the time. I don't care if your father yells at me."

Emma shook her head. "I would care."

Dinner that night was different: Emma had taken charge of the kitchen. She had gone out and bought groceries. She stewed a chicken; she made rice, a new salad. For dessert there was ice cream.

Her mother had taken charge of the hors d'oeuvres. She had found a small group of carrots in the refrigerator, and set them out in a dish that was too large for them. They had been scraped several days earlier, and now were pale and dry, the woody streaks at their centers prominent, their ends curled up. She had found a second box of broken crackers: scarlet cartouches, pink squares. These bright scraps she put in a small glass bowl by themselves, like peanuts. They were salty as peanuts, but damp, and felt to the teeth like old root vegetables.

Sitting down to the table Mr. Kirkland rubbed his hands heartily.

"Well, that was a really good day," he said, looking around.

"Where did you go?" Emma asked. She did not care where they had gone. You never went anywhere, sailing, you just flapped back and forth on top of the water. What did it matter which bit of water it was?

"Well, we had the tide with us, all the way to the mouth of Bass River," Mr. Kirkland said with enthusiasm. He laid his fork down, the better to hold forth. "We had the tide with us, and the wind just off to starboard, so we were in pretty good shape. We only had to come about twice between here and the mouth of the river." He looked around proudly.

"Only two tacks! Oh, that's very good," said Mrs. Kirkland, nodding.

Mr. Kirkland waited, but no one else responded. "I've made it out to the mouth before, tacking only twice, but I've never done it on one. Two's my record. Steve Steadman has done it with only one tack, but I've walked the distance, and I figure his dock is about eighty feet closer to the mouth of the river than ours is. That doesn't seem like much, but that eighty feet includes the beginning of the bend in the river. Now, that makes a big difference. I told him if he could make the mouth in one tack from *our* dock, that would be something." He paused again, pleased, and looked down at his plate. "Then when we got out to the mouth, we decided to go out to the gong."

"All the way out there," murmured Mrs. Kirkland. "Goodness."

Emma remembered it: the dreadful gong buoy, swinging endlessly back and forth on the deep green waters, its hollow, mournful tones echoing across the dismal waves. Chillingly far from shore, the gray bubbles sliding aimlessly and forever around its solemn rocking form.

"We had a good breeze going out. I had planned it so we'd have the tide with us, coming home." Mr. Kirkland looked around. He had still not taken a bite of food. "Well, we would have, but the wind changed around and then dropped, and by the time we reached the mouth of Bass River, boy, that tide had started against us. We had a terrible time, beating back up that river."

"It was fun, though," said Peter, nodding.

Mr. Kirkland frowned, preferring "terrible" to "fun."

"Of course, if you're used to sailing in Maine, what we do here may not seem like much," said Mr. Kirkland, offended.

Peter shook his head. "Anyone who sails up and down a narrow tidal river is an expert, as far as I'm concerned. I don't know anywhere like that in Maine."

"Well," said Mr. Kirkland, mollified, "we manage to have some pretty good times. You should come out racing sometime. We do have a little fun with the races."

Peter said politely, "Sounds great."

"Is Peter any good at all on a sailboat, Daddy?" Emma asked. "I have the feeling that he's all talk."

But her father frowned: Emma was being frivolous. He looked down at his plate and picked up his knife and fork.

"He's not bad," said Mr. Kirkland judiciously. "Not bad at all."

"Well, you've finally done it, have you, Emmy?" said Mrs. Kirkland. She leaned back in her chair, looking at Peter. "For once."

"What," said Emma.

"Brought home a man who can sail. Neither of you girls has ever managed it before."

Mr. Kirkland frowned again. He had not finished what he wanted to say, and felt he was losing control of the conversation.

"I'm not sure that finding a sailor has been Emma's first priority," he said.

"What about my daddy?" asked Tess. "He can sail."

Everyone smiled at her; no one spoke.

"My daddy can sail," Tess said, anxious. She looked at her grandfather, then her grandmother.

"You're right that your daddy can sail. But he wasn't—sailing wasn't his *favorite* thing," Emma said. "That wasn't what he was best at."

"Yes, it was," said Tess. Her voice rose. "He was best at sailing."

"I don't think so," said Mr. Kirkland. He gave a small laugh. "I hope that's not what he was best at."

Tess looked at him, fearful. "Yes, he was," she said, her voice rising further.

Mr. Kirkland looked at her. "I think I'm a better judge of that than you are, Tess," he said. "Your father can't sail worth beans, I'll have to say." He looked smug.

Tess's face turned dark.

Emma interrupted. "Daddy, how can you say that?" she said. She looked at her mother, but Mrs. Kirkland was bent over her plate. She held a piece of chicken in both hands, delicately, with the tips of her fingers. Taking fastidious bites, she did not look up.

"It's a fact," said Emma's father, closing his mouth on the last word. "This isn't a question of being polite. It's not a matter of opinion, it's a fact. Your father couldn't sail worth beans." He smiled at Tess.

Tess pushed herself violently away from the table, the chair stuttering along the floor.

"Nothing to cry about," said Mr. Kirkland. "A fact, that's all."

"*I hate you,*" Tess said shrilly to her grandfather. She started to cry.

"Daddy," said Emma, furious. She stood, glaring, but her father shrugged his shoulders. "Come on, Tess," Emma said. She picked up the sobbing child.

"No," shrieked Tess, "no, no, no. *Don't touch me!*"

Emma carried her off, raging.

When Emma came back to the kitchen, the room was silent. As she pulled out her chair Peter smiled and gave her a friendly blink, but no one spoke as she sat down.

"Daddy, you shouldn't have said that about Tess's father."

"It was true," Mr. Kirkland said, sounding satisfied.

"I don't care if it's true," Emma said. "It's rude."

Her father drank contemptuously from his glass.

"It's rude," repeated Emma. "You can't talk like that to anyone, even a three-year-old."

"Emma," said her mother.

"What?" asked Emma.

"Don't make a scene," said her mother. She was concentrating on cutting the chicken with the side of her fork.

"*I'm* not making a scene," Emma said angrily. "Daddy's making the scene, and pretending he's not."

"I'm not pretending anything," said her father loudly. "And I don't think you are in a position to tell anyone else how to behave."

"What do you mean by that?" asked Emma.

"You know exactly what I mean," said her father.

"I have no idea what you mean."

"I mean," said her father deliberately, "that you have surrendered the right to take a moral position on things."

"Do you mean because I've gotten divorced?"

"Do you think divorce means nothing?" her father's voice rose terribly. "Do you think marriage is of no consequence? Do you think you can casually renege on a promise of such magnitude?"

Emma felt tears welling up; she beat them back. "Do you think I did it on a whim?" She tried to steady her voice.

"I cannot imagine why you did it," said her father. "But now that you've done it you must accept the consequences. You are a divorced woman. You are a single mother. You have broken your promise, destroyed your marriage and deprived your child of a father."

Furious, speechless, Emma struggled to compose herself. What her father had said was what she herself most feared to be true. Her father watched her, his eyes narrowed, triumphant.

Peter straightened in his chair, lifted his chin, cleared his throat. "Emma," he said formally.

Grateful, Emma turned. Her father frowned.

"Will you marry me?" Peter asked.

11

If there was one moment in which Emma fell in love with Peter it was then, the moment in which he dropped the jib on her father.

For a long, vivid pause there was silence at the table. No one moved. Mrs. Kirkland's fork had neared her mouth; it stopped, she set it down. She and her husband stared at Peter. Peter looked steadily at Emma. Emma looked back.

"Yes," she answered calmly. She straightened her spine.

Mr. Kirkland snorted, in an outraged way, and looked at his plate. His mouth went straight down at the corners. Emma's mother raised her water glass, with an awkward, spirited gesture.

"Bravo!" she said, her full cheeks faintly pink.

Then Mr. Kirkland, now outraged by his wife, raised his glass as well. He said stiffly to Peter, "Congratulations." He gave a formal nod.

Peter nodded back. "Thank you."

Then they all lifted water glasses to the moment. They looked at each other, smiling, surprised, even Mr. Kirkland.

It was done.

The next evening in the car, driving back to New York, Emma said to Peter, "You were very brave."

"Me! What about you?"

"You were brave. You took on my *father.*"

"He doesn't scare me. And I'm on your side," said Peter. "Remember that."

Emma looked at Peter for a moment, then away, out the car window.

They were driving through Connecticut somewhere, though it could have been anywhere. Outside was a strange landscape, springing alarmingly into sight within the strong beams of their headlights. Weeds, scrub trees, steep banks shone forth, radiant, then hurtled backward and were lost. At the tops of the banks were high blank noise barriers that concealed whole towns, concealed the passing geography. Cut off from the land it passed through, the road became a tunnel, featureless, infinite, lit only by the long swift glare of their passing selves.

Peter looked ahead, driving steadily, unmoved by the bleak passage, focused homeward. Emma thought of him walking back across the scrubby lawn with her father, carrying the grimy canvas bag of gear, the two of them windblown, ruddy, relaxed. She could see she had been wrong about the shouting: it *was* different for men. They didn't mind it. She wondered if all human activity were like this, everything, every gesture, every comment colored faintly by gender. Each side continually astonished, confused by the other's misperceptions.

Peter had told her that he had once come into his office to find his secretary crying at her desk.

"The poor thing," Emma said. "What did you do?"

"What do you think I did?" asked Peter, indignant. "I went into my office and shut the door."

"How could you? She needed sympathy."

"She needed time to pull herself together," said Peter firmly.

It was like hearing customs from an undiscovered race: what men thought was unimaginable. How could they not mind being shouted at? Wasn't that the point of shouting, intimidation? Why wouldn't they be affected? Why would they do it? And it started early, they were like this as children. Emma had seen them at Tess's playgroup, at two years old. The girls sat in a tidy row, their legs crossed at their plump ankles, helping each other as they played. The boys tried to kill each other. Wrestling, pounding: they thought this pleasant. The teacher presided calmly, intervened rarely. "No biting, Robert," she said. "Remember what I told you about biting." But why not biting? Why not machetes? It was what they wanted.

She wondered what Robert at work would say about her marrying Peter. It would be something unexpected. Robert was curious about other people, but not really interested in them. He had a rock-solid self-absorption that rendered him incapable of empathy, though he was good-hearted.

She wondered what the Chatfields would say. She had liked them at once. Mrs. Chatfield had been out in the garden, wearing a pair of huge droopy jeans which she called dungarees. Stepping forward, she had surprised Emma by putting both arms around her and hugging her, a real, warm hug. "I'm so glad to meet you," she said, then shaking her hand, and Emma had felt embraced. Peter's father, his eyebrows bristling kindly, had asked her if she would like to come birding with him in the marshes.

When she and Warren had gotten engaged he had told his parents alone. His father asked, "What clubs do her parents belong to?" Warren told her this in a tone of cheerful contempt: he knew his parents were outrageous snobs. Emma had never liked them, but she had thought Warren was different. She'd thought he saw them as arrogant, gossipy, mean-spirited. She'd thought he condemned that in them. How could she have been so naive? But she had been so young then, young enough to think that if you could see your parents' flaws you could avoid them. To think that you were different from your parents. Now she knew that, no matter how her parents exasperated her, she was cast in their image. She would duplicate, unwittingly, in a new manner, the ways she least admired.

The car surged steadily along the highway. Peaceful, Emma shut her eyes. She was surprised by her happiness. She hadn't realized how different it felt, this emotion, from what she had felt for Warren. This was without question; it came from everywhere, the air she breathed. It was what she wanted. She reached out and put her hand on Peter's knee. He covered it with his own and squeezed it.

"I'm right here," he said.

"I'm glad," said Emma.

When they reached the apartment Tess pushed through the front door and ran down the hall and into the kitchen. Emma followed more slowly. As Tess ran she called Rachel's name in a blissful shout. Rachel shouted back. When Emma came around the corner, Rachel was crouched on the floor, with Tess between her knees. They were staring deep into each other's eyes, their foreheads nearly touching.

"I missed you," Rachel was saying. "Did you have a good time with your grandparents?" Rachel's hands were clasped behind Tess's back, and she swayed the child back and forth as she talked.

Tess nodded. "And do you know what?"

Rachel shook her head. "Tell me."

"My mommy and Peter are getting married."

Rachel looked up at Emma. "Is that so?"

Emma nodded, smiling, and Rachel picked up Tess and stood. Holding Emma's child in her arms she leaned forward and kissed Emma's cheek, formally, hard.

"Congratulations," Rachel said.

"Thank you," said Emma.

"And I," began Tess, but stopped.

The two women were looking at each other and smiling.

Tess patted Rachel's shoulder insistently. "Rachel, you are not looking at me."

"What is it?" Rachel rocked her.

"And I," said Tess, "am going to be *in* the wedding."

"No!" said Rachel.

Tess nodded, proud.

"When will it be?" Rachel asked Emma.

"In September. We thought the eighteenth," said Emma. "We need some time to get organized."

"September eighteenth," Rachel said, and laughed. Her smile was suddenly huge, her old smile. "That's a good day. A *very* good day. That's my mama's birthday."

"Your mama?" Tess said, sidetracked.

"Would you like to go down to see her for her birthday?" asked Emma impulsively. "Shall we give you the trip as a wedding present?"

"Oh," said Rachel, smiling.

Emma would have offered Rachel anything, anything.

The next day, at her office, Emma called Francie to tell her. She waited until noon, to be sure Francie was up. Emma was by then on her second mug of coffee. She drank this with cream, from the carton she hoarded in the small office refrigerator. Two mugs was all she allowed herself; Emma would have liked to give up coffee altogether, and drink only herb tea. She would have liked to give up the chemical jitters for a more peaceful state of mind. She would have liked to eat only whole grains and organic vegetables; she would have liked to heal the whole polluted planet herself, but so far all she had been able to do was to cut down on her coffee to two mugfuls a day. Actually, she liked the chemical jitters.

While she was waiting for Francie to wake up, Emma had been trying to edit an article called "Connecting the Vertices: The Early Iconography of Jedson Cray." It was senseless. "These early pristine images—unintentionally self-conscious—exquisitely presage the abrupt and deliberately, almost fiercely conventional interiority of the later, more subtly convoluted work." Why couldn't art historians write a title without a colon? And what in the world were vertices? And why not write in English?

At twelve Emma took a chalky chemical sip and dialed. Francie answered.

"Hi," said Emma. "It's me. I wanted to tell you I'm getting married."

"Again?" said Francie.

Emma frowned. "For real."

"Who is it?"

"You know who it is. The man I've been seeing. Peter Chatfield."

"But what's he like? Another stockbroker?"

"Actually, Warren wasn't a stockbroker," Emma said coldly. "And Peter isn't either."

"You know what I mean," Francie said. "That *type*."

"What *type*?" Emma asked, nettled.

"Come on," said Francie. "Does he wear a gray suit and black wing tips to work?"

"No," said Emma. "He wears a bathrobe and a jockstrap. He's a sumo wrestler."

There was a pause.

Emma looked up to see Robert in the doorway. She waved, pointing at the phone. Robert raised his eyebrows. Emma shook her head and turned her back.

Francie finally laughed. "Good. We could use a little genetic diversity."

"So, will you come to the wedding?" Emma asked.

"When is it?"

"September. The eighteenth."

"Are Mother and Daddy coming?"

"Well, yes," said Emma.

"Then I'm not," Francie said firmly. "I'm not speaking to them at the moment. You can't believe how rude Daddy was to Rex."

"Oh, yes I can," said Emma. "He took a couple of swings at Tess, when we were there, and at Warren, and there was a moment when he sort of thought about going after Peter. He's a nightmare."

"Then why are you asking them?"

Emma closed her eyes. "Come on, Francie. They're our parents. We can't just cut ourselves off. Even if we never spoke to them again, they'd still be our parents."

"Thank you for reminding me. But we don't have to put up with them, and I, for one, am sick of it."

"Okay," said Emma. "Fine. But I still want you to come. You don't have to talk to them."

"I don't want to be in the same place with them." Francie sounded pleased.

There was a pause.

"So you won't come to my wedding," Emma said.

"I came to the last one," Francie offered. "I'll come to the next one. I'm only skipping this one."

"Very funny," said Emma. "This is the real one. This is the last time I'm getting married."

There was a silence. Emma took a sip of her coffee.

"I really wish you'd come," she said. "You're my only sister. You're my only anything."

"Emma, those people are harmful. They are out to do damage. I choose not to put myself in their way."

Emma rolled her eyes. Why did people start talking like that as soon as they crossed the California border? "You make them sound like the body snatchers," she said. "They're just our parents. And they have no control over you. You're a grown-up. Why do they upset you so much?"

"Don't be so smug," Francie said. "Don't pretend he doesn't make you mad."

"Okay, he does, I admit it," said Emma. "He makes me furious. But so what? He's still my father."

"You're afraid of him," said Francie. "You don't have the nerve to cut yourself loose."

Am I like Warren, Emma wondered suddenly, admiring something despicable? Should I be cutting myself off? But her parents were annoying, her father infuriating, still they were not bigots or snobs, they were normal infuriating people.

"I don't think cutting yourself off is the answer," Emma said. "I think you just put up with your family. Okay, they're flawed. So what? So are we."

There was another silence.

"Look, I came to your wedding," Emma offered. "I'll come to your next one if you have one."

"If?" Francie repeated coldly.

"When," said Emma. She would, too: nothing could be worse than Francie's first wedding. It had been in an orange grove, in the blazing sun. It was a hundred degrees. Everyone had been stoned, stumbling across the dusty furrows: the ground under the trees was plowed, not lawn. There was nowhere to sit down, and nothing to drink but bottled water, since at the time Francie had taken against alcohol and used only drugs.

"But how do I know Daddy isn't going to throw a scene?" demanded Francie. "How do I know he won't insult Rex again?"

"I'll talk to him," Emma promised. "Mother and I will talk to him. I really want you to come."

"Okay," Francie said, "but you're responsible. And you have to find us somewhere to stay."

"Fine," said Emma. "Fine."

Emma hung up, pleased. She was moving forward. She would start making lists, she would tick things off. She could now tick Francie off.

"Em?"

She turned. Robert was still there.

"Come in," she said, waving her mug. "Congratulate me. I'm getting married."

"Again?"

"That's what Francie said," said Emma. "I have to tell you it's not polite. You're supposed to say something nicer than that."

"Sorry," Robert said, interested. He came in and stood with his hands in his pockets. "Who is it?"

"His name is Peter Chatfield." She liked saying it.

"What's he like?"

"An angel in human form."

"Well, you *are* lucky," Robert said. "As well as realistic."

"I think you ought to think your spouse is perfect, at the start, don't you?"

"No," said Robert. "You should think your spouse is a nightmare. Then, if you want to marry them anyway, you have some chance of its working out."

"If I thought Peter were a nightmare I wouldn't consider marrying him," Emma said. "I did that once already."

"They say you repeat your mistakes. Is he different from the last one?"

Emma shook her head. "In every possible way. You cannot imagine. For starters, Warren was a child. Peter is a grown-up."

Robert shrugged. "Okay, then. But is he nice? Rich? Unmarried? Smart?"

"All those things."

"Good," Robert said, nodding. He tipped his chin up and looked at the ceiling. "I wonder how my wife described me, before we got married."

"Just like that," Emma said, "I'm sure."

Robert grinned at her. "Doubtful," he said. "Okay. Now. The article," he said, looking down at her desk. "What do you think?"

"Unreadable," said Emma. "Like his last one."

Robert frowned.

"Just a joke," she said. "It's fine." Stupid of her to make fun of something Robert took seriously. And if she thought this stuff was unreadable, why was she here?

"The David Salle show," Robert said. "We need someone to review it."

"Let's get a woman," said Emma.

Robert gave her an admonitory look. "I'm not running a bad review."

"I just think a woman might have interesting things to say about it," said Emma. She herself thought Salle's work was callow and sexist.

"Emma, I'm not going to run a review that makes a fuss over sexist issues. This is art, not sociology. Picasso was a shit to women, it's a fact. He's still a great painter."

"I'm not talking about Salle's private life," Emma said. "I don't know if he's a shit to women in private or not. It's his paintings I mind. I think they're prurient and humiliating to women."

"You're taking the images literally. There's more to them than that."

"But the literal images are *there.* You can't ignore them, just because there are metaphorical ones too. Deeper meanings don't contradict the literal one, they expand it. These paintings are about brutalization. They're big and voluptuous and they celebrate the brutalization of women. Everyone pretends they're ironic comments on it, but how do you tell the difference? Blacks wouldn't let a white artist paint big voluptuous images of blacks being trussed and lynched—there'd be a huge fuss." Emma's heart was pounding; she alarmed herself by disagreeing. "Women should complain about it, but they don't dare. Women in the art world are jeered at unless they sound like men. They've trained themselves to think like men."

Robert shook his head dismissively. "Salle does powerful stuff," he said loftily. "Maybe it's too much for you."

"I don't think it's powerful, I think it's just shocking in a superficial way."

But Robert only shook his head. "You see everything as moral issues, Emma. The world is full of ambiguity. Yours is not the only way to look at this. And I don't want a woman to review this. Women take everything personally."

"Women take personally things that are meant to demean them," Emma said. "Try substituting another minority group for women in these images, and see if anyone complains."

Robert shook his head again. "You're so intolerant," he said mildly, and left.

Alone, Emma waited for her alarm to subside. Her voice probably had been shrill. I probably am intolerant, she thought, disheartened. I suppose I do take things personally. But was she wrong about Salle? It was so unsettling for her to disagree with a man that she couldn't tell, afterward, if what she'd said had any merit, or if it were foolish. Pull yourself together, she told herself. You have an opinion, Robert has his. Why do you feel so threatened? But she did.

She thought again of Francie. She no longer felt pleased and effective about her conversation. Now she felt dismayed: why had she promised to restrain her father? She imagined his outrage at her broaching the subject. His mouth would draw down at the corners, his chin would lift. She could no more control her father than she could Rex, with his mangy ponytail, his unbuttoned mule driver's shirt, his crystals and his New Age certainties about channeling and other lives. She should have made Francie promise to make Rex wear normal clothes, and behave like a human being.

Her mother had told her that when Rex and Francie had been there, her father had innocently mentioned that his neck was stiff. Rex had sprung into action, given him a loony gaze and offered to lead a series of mind-body exercises that would allow him to "unclench" and rid himself of his poisons.

Emma could imagine her father's cold stare.

"My poisons? Would you mind explaining to me what you imagine my 'poisons' to be?"

The inconceivable suggestion: her father upstairs, stretched out on the bed—naked? would even the insane Rex go that far? Her father lying stiffly supine, holding his long bony feet together, tensely upright. Her father taking orders from an undertrained, overfamiliar pipsqueak who chanted tyrannically at him to let everything go. Emma saw her father pink with outrage at the idea of having poisons, or of giving them up on command. She saw his outrage at the idea of letting anything go, letting one single unimportant thing slip from his grasp.

Poor Rex, she thought, thrilled at last to think he could make a contribution, use his skills and powers. Emma sipped the last cold creamy dregs from her mug and decided not to call her parents right away.

Nor did she want to tell Warren. He had no secretary, and she wondered, in a cowardly way, if she could leave the news on his voice mail. Reluctantly she decided she could not, and instead left him a message asking him to call her. He didn't call back for several days. He never called back the same day she called him, he always made her wait.

When he did call, his voice was jovial and paternal. "Emma!"

"Hello, Warren," she answered, cool.

"You called me," he said.

She could see him, half-smiling into the air, his chin lifted. Warren often closed his eyes, in a supercilious way, when he talked on the phone. When he did this it wasn't so he could concentrate on the conversation, it was to demonstrate that he could do this with his eyes closed.

"Right," said Emma. "I just wanted to tell you some news. Peter and I are getting married. I wanted you to hear it from me."

"Ah-hah?" said Warren. She could almost hear him closing his eyes. "Well, congratulations. Or, no, you don't say that to women, do you. That would make it sound as if the blushing bride had achieved a strategic victory, instead of being the passive and innocent prize which a woman always is."

"Right," said Emma.

"It's the man you say congratulations to, on his great good fortune. On attaining his prize."

"Right," said Emma again, testy.

"And of course, I know what a prize you are," Warren said.

"I'm not going to fight with you, Warren," Emma said.

"I hope you're very happy," said Warren, his voice loud and artificial. "I really do. I mean that."

"Thank you," Emma said.

There was a pause.

She said gently, "I'm sorry it didn't work out for us, Warren. I still feel bad." She closed her eyes: she knew exactly how he looked. She knew what his gesture would be, brushing his hair off his face with his first two fingers, like a salute. She knew the smell of his skin, how it felt to hold him, where he was ticklish. It was inconceivable that she should be separate from him: she knew him.

"Why?" Warren asked, loudly. "Look, we've learned something, we're moving on. Much better this way. You've done us both a favor, that's how I see it."

"Don't be so pleased," Emma said. "You act as though it was wonderful that we got divorced."

"Emma, you left me. I think it was a mistake. I think you've never made a worse mistake. But I'm moving on. I'm moving on. I'm not going to weep every time you call me up, and I'm certainly not going to weep every time you ask me to. The time for you to expect me to tell you how I love you is past."

There was a silence.

"You're right," she said. "Okay. The wedding will be the eighteenth of September. So if you can mark that on your calendar, I'll want Tess that weekend."

"The eighteenth of September. Great," Warren repeated, slowly, as though he were writing it down. "Got it. Done. No problemo."

Emma did not believe he was writing it down. "Do you want me to send you a fax or something?" she asked, "so you have the date on your calendar?"

"No, I've got it," Warren said. "Great. Great. Look, I'm very happy for you but I've got to go. The senator will be here in two and a half minutes. I'll talk to you. Congratulations." He hung up.

It was different for Peter. He thought it would be unkind and cavalier to tell Caroline over the telephone, so he took her to dinner. They went to her favorite restaurant, Lutèce. It was dreadful.

Peter reserved a table in the garden room at the back, with the skylight, and the trellising on the walls. The French waiters bustled bossily about them. Surrounded by this—the soft light, the flowers, the heavy starched linen, the big transparent goblets—by the sense of great luxury, and the absolute conviction of its importance, Caroline glowed.

She wore a silk suit he had never seen, a deep black-green. Her skin was creamy, her hair immaculate. She wore her pearls, the necklace and earrings. She glittered with a sort of terrifying glamour. She held herself very straight, more formal than the waiters. She frowned at the menu, scanning it seriously, as though food were the important issue.

When their drinks came, Peter lifted his glass. "Cheers."

He meant the dinner to be friendly, understanding, a farewell to their marriage, after the rage had passed.

But Caroline raised her glass and answered, "Cheers!" in a very different tone warm, expectant.

They both drank, then set their glasses down. And Peter, who had been so certain of the need to do this, did not now know how to proceed.

"You look terrific," he said, as an opener.

"Thanks," Caroline said lightly, pleased. She took a long sip of her vermouth. She smiled at him. "You too. Maybe this was a good idea."

There was something complicitous about her tone; did she understand what was happening? Did she think he was considering something besides remarriage? And what was it she thought was a good idea—their splitting up, or having dinner together? But he didn't want to ask her, didn't want to engage her in this conversation, didn't want to make intimate forays into her mind. He wondered why he had been so determined to do this. The black-green suit, he realized, was new. She had gone to the hairdresser for this. His heart sank.

"How's Amanda?" he asked. Caroline's face changed at once. Reserved and cool, she shrugged her shoulders. She took a long sip.

"You know, this has been very hard on her," she answered. "She's having trouble at school."

Peter frowned at his drink. This was worse than the complicity. "Amanda has always had trouble at school."

"Not like this," Caroline said smoothly.

Peter sighed. "What's the problem?"

"She may be cheating on tests," Caroline said.

"Cheating?"

Caroline nodded. "It's not uncommon, apparently. During a divorce."

"Is that what the school said?" Peter asked.

She nodded.

"Who did you talk to?"

"The counselor. A psychologist."

Peter shook his head. "When I was at school there were no psychologists. There were no counselors. There were teachers, and there was us."

"And there was no divorce," said Caroline. She spread her hand onto the tablecloth. Her fingers were long and smooth, elegant. The nails glistened pinkly.

Peter looked down at his menu. "Are you ready to order?" Caroline nodded. "What would you like?" A waiter, arrogant, impeccable, paused beside them.

Unexpectedly, Caroline smiled at Peter, dimpling like a child. "You know what I like," she said. "I always have the same thing here." She waited for Peter to laugh. He did; he had forgotten.

The first time they had come here together, Caroline had been taking French lessons. Each week she spent an earnest hour at Berlitz. That evening, at Lutèce, she had tried out her new language on their waiter. She wanted chicken breasts, and asked carefully for them in French. She had looked it up in her dictionary before they went out. "*Je voudrais des seins de poulet, s'il vous plait,*" she said meticulously: chicken bosoms. The French waiter had been outraged, as they always were, by everything. Peter and Caroline were, he felt, barbarous, uncivilized. It crossed his mind, they could see, to call the maître d'hôtel and let him deal with this unpardonable behavior. Peter and Caroline, who hadn't then understood his outrage, had looked at each other and begun to laugh. There had been something exilharating about outfacing the waiter at Lutèce. Remembering, Peter felt a shadow of that triumphant alliance; it saddened him.

But now Caroline smiled broadly, and after they had ordered she leaned forward and took the heavy napkin from the table, spreading it on her silken lap. The suit was V-necked, and the dark green set off the milky skin of her throat. She moved her shoulders, and spread out her long fingers, so he would notice them.

"I had lunch with Marella Compton last week," she said, beginning a gossipy anecdote.

Peter listened, curious in spite of himself. Being with Caroline he was back again in the world he had lived in for the last decade, among the people he was used to seeing. Emma's friends were fewer, less close-knit, and he was only beginning to know them. Also Emma gossiped less. He admired this, but it made for less interesting dinners.

"Harrison wanted it both ways," said Caroline. "He wanted to stay friends with Frank Bailey *and* have an affair with his wife. So he asked Frank to lunch to talk it over."

"And what did Frank do?"

"He stood up in the middle of lunch at the Century and said 'Fuck you' to Harrison and walked out."

"Good for him," Peter said, laughing. Caroline smiled, and sipped complacently at her drink.

But this was wrong, Peter thought. He was trying to separate himself from her, not to fall into this camaraderie. And though Caroline's gossip had a ghastly attraction, he always felt grimy listening to it. One of his partners at work was like Caroline, always putting his head inside the door to tell Peter something he felt afterward he shouldn't really want to know. He talked about bad behavior, episodes that made you dislike everyone concerned. He delighted in them, and couldn't wait to spread them around. Peter felt it undignified to listen, low; but still, when he saw the man, a part of him quickened with interest.

Without gossip, though, it was hard to know where to direct the conversation: it was Caroline's main subject, her preoccupation. Peter wondered what Emma was doing now. He pictured her reading to Tess, sitting cross-legged in bed, a plate of inedible food in her lap. A heap of roast beef hash from a can, burned black on the bottom, a pool of rancid ketchup beside it on the plate. Emma had no sense of food. He wondered if this were hereditary, or whether she might have turned out normally if she had been brought up among people who took eating seriously. Perhaps it was genetic, perhaps there was a food gene missing from her double helix. He thought of her father, wolfing down sandwiches like a fierce old crow. He thought of her father, out sailing, Emma's worries about his shouting. He hadn't shouted that day, in fact he'd barely raised his voice. He'd been excessively polite with Peter.

When the food arrived, Caroline was talking about Amanda, a summer program she'd heard about: French and tennis lessons. Christ, Peter thought. Where was playing in the sand? What had happened to kites? Jump ropes?

"Betsy Edgerton told me about it," Caroline said with authority. "It's supposed to be *very* good." She sounded as though she and Peter were still a couple, still partners. As she talked she flashed her long pale fingers. She was vain about her hands; they were beautiful. She was still wearing her engagement ring, he saw: his grandmother's old-fashioned diamond. She saw him look at it, and held her hand up, displaying it elegantly. She batted her eyelashes at him, teasing, mock sultry.

"I'm not giving it up," she said.

Peter frowned. "What?"

"Don't worry," she said. "It's going to Amanda. It's hers."

Peter frowned again. "Amanda is seven."

"You don't need it," Caroline said. "Why would you want it? You're not going to give some other woman the ring you gave me. Another woman wouldn't wear it."

It was true; still, he wanted his grandmother's ring. When he had given it to Caroline it had seemed a gift. Now it seemed so obviously, unarguably a loan: his grandmother's ring! It belonged to his family, it was his heritage. There were two of them, actually: they had been made from a pair of diamond earrings. His father and his uncle had each inherited one: a faceted diamond set within a circling band of enamel. His ring had dark green enamel, his uncle's was dark blue. Caroline had been rather patronizing about the ring.

"You never even liked it," Peter said. "You didn't like the enamel."

"I think it's charming," Caroline answered. "What are you talking about? I've always loved it." She held her hand out again, admiring the ring, her slender fingers. She looked up at him again, smiling. She lowered her head in a charming, provocative way. "We haven't had so much fun in years," she said, arching her eyebrows.

This was going very badly. Peter wondered suddenly if anyone they knew was at the restaurant. Were they being seen together? Did it look as though he was flirting with his ex-wife? Caroline leaned back, using her shoulders, displaying her throat, arraying herself against the chair.

Peter put down his knife and fork. He set his elbows on the table and laced his fingers. "What I wanted to tell you," he said, "is that Emma and I are getting married."

Caroline said nothing. She looked at him.

"That's why I asked you to have dinner."

Caroline took a swallow from her wineglass.

"I wanted to tell you myself," Peter said, hoping for some credit. "I didn't want you to hear it from someone else."

Caroline still said nothing, and looked down at her plate. To his horror he saw tears in her eyes. She picked up her fork and began to pick dismally at her chicken. The tears began slowly to roll down the pale slopes of her cheeks.

"Caroline," Peter said anxiously, "Caroline."

Caroline put down her fork. She leaned back in her chair, careless now of her neck, her shoulders, her long white fingers. She leaned back haphazardly, like a monarch deposed, nothing left to lose. She stared directly out at him, her eyes level, tears brimming, rolling steadily down her cheeks. She did not bother to wipe them away. She folded her arms across her beautiful silk jacket and stared at him.

"You shit," she said levelly.

"Caroline," Peter said. He felt uncomfortably aware of the other people around them. Caroline was not behaving discreetly. Her chin was raised, her face was gleaming with tears. She stared steadily at him. The waiter came near, hovered disapprovingly, went on.

"Caroline," Peter said again.

Caroline said nothing more. She stared at him without answering or moving. Peter, receiving no response to any of his entreaties or questions, including those about dessert or coffee, finally called for the waiter and asked for the check. Caroline went on weeping as they stood up. Waves of tears followed each other down her face, without pause. She preceded him through the rooms of Lutèce, making her way among the linen-covered tables, the vases of flowers, the candles, weeping, her face raised like a glistening beacon. Around them people looked discreetly up at her, then looked away, then looked up again at him, wondering what sort of cruel husband this beautiful woman had, to have brought her to this state of misery.

Threading his way through the tables, Peter said nothing either. He felt ambushed: what he had meant was kindness. He had tried to be kind, but perhaps there were no kindnesses left to him. Perhaps the one great unkindness to Caroline made all his smaller gestures to her null, forever. He was a villain, she had declared it. He had ruined her life.

Peter said good night to the maître d'hôtel, who smiled formally. He bowed his head crisply. They both ignored the weeping woman.

Peter stood on the sidewalk with Caroline, watching for a taxi. She stood very straight, her head high. Her crying was now audible; she sniffed. She would not look at him. It was chilly. He felt the wind on his chest, through his shirt. He should have brought a coat. He stared out into the dark. It had not been Caroline's fault. It had been he who had changed. She was the person she'd always been. He had declared he wanted her, then changed his mind. How could he defend it?

A black woman, homeless, walked slowly toward them. She pushed a supermarket trolley, piled high with bulky mounds. From its handlebar swung plastic bags, stuffed full. What would you take with you, when you moved at last onto the street, he wondered. Only useful things, bedding, coats, if you had to push everything you owned, you abandoned sentiment. Not even a toilet kit: where would you use a toothbrush? The terrible meanness of such a life struck him, the humiliation of being always dirty, the fear of being always vulnerable. The woman wore a stained gray overcoat, long and filthy. It hung open down the front. She felt Peter's gaze on her, turned, muttering, and stared straight at him. Her face was round and lined, the forehead ridged, the eyeballs white and bulging. Her look was so direct, so full of dark and liquid hatred, that Peter turned away. Beside him on the sidewalk the woman he had married wept openly.

Should he relent, go back to Caroline? Would that stop her weeping? But at the thought, he saw his life spread out sickeningly before him, a gray misery. He would never go back to her.

He held the thought of Emma, waiting for him, her bright clear face. He hoped that this—she—was not a mistake. He hoped she was truly what he wanted, the person who would make him happy, the one he could make happy too. He knew Emma was stubborn, tense, censorious; she was also kind, scrupulous, thoughtful. How could you tell which things were important? He believed that he loved her. He thought of her vivid slanting eyes, her smooth body.

Beside him, Caroline shook with sobs. She became larger, more splendid, as she cried. Her body straightened regally, gave off heat. There was something sumptuous and magnificent about this, the plenitude of the tears, their infinite supply, their liquid, gleaming fullness. They would never stop, it seemed.

If this were a mistake, his marrying Emma, he was done for, Peter thought. He would never go through a divorce again.

12

On the day of the wedding Emma woke early. Peter had spent the night at the new apartment, at her superstitious request, and Emma was alone in her bedroom for the last time. The room was still dark when she opened her eyes. The small electronic clock by her bedside, mysteriously lit by a dim greenish glow, said 5:42. Nothing moved on the clock face, there was no narrow golden wand, sweeping grandly and endlessly toward the next moment. Instead, the cool neon number was fixed and immutable, as though this precise moment, 5:42, were the only minute this clock would ever acknowledge. Emma, lying alone in her bed in the dark morning, on the morning of her second marriage, felt she watched the only minute in all of time. The clock gave no reason to hope for 5:43, no reason to remember 5:41. This was all there was. As Emma watched, the neon lines suddenly shifted, the configuration changing too swiftly to follow. The moment was past.

The clock now declared silently and immutably that the time was 5:43. Emma was one minute closer to her wedding. She could feel it drawing nearer to her, she felt the tremors of a nearly audible rumble. The Wedding: it seemed large, ornate, shimmering white, unreliable, terrifying and unnatural, like a coach made from a pumpkin. It was coming toward her from the distance, growing larger as it approached. Slowly and inexorably it was blotting out the rest of the horizon, the landscape, the rest of Emma's life. It would roll right over her, she could see that; it would engulf her, subsume her. It was her doing, but it was now out of her control. It had grown larger than she, and unstoppable. By the end of that same day she would once again be coupled, paired, someone's wife. The Wedding, shuddering, creaking, shedding bits of finery and dropping flowers, would have overtaken her and then lumbered by. It would then be behind her, in the quiet past forever, and she would again be married.

It was still too early to get up. Emma tucked herself tightly into a muscular egg, drawing her legs close to her chest and lapping one bare foot over the other for warmth. Her stomach felt deeply anxious. It was normal to be nervous on your wedding day, she told herself. You couldn't help it. She wondered if it were normal to be twice as nervous about your second wedding day.

What it would be like, this life with Peter? How could you be sure you had made the right choice? What were the most important things? Peter had such energy, and he was bright and interesting and funny. He was generous. He loved her; he would be kind to Tess. She trusted him; he did not lie. And then he was wonderful in bed. Was that enough? Were those the important things? Because on the other hand he could be tense, fussy, demanding. He could turn pompous and judgmental. He frightened Emma when he was angry. He was touchy about his parents, and about money. And he played squash: would she have to spend her weekends in those cramped galleries, staring down at the tops of people's heads and a ball whizzing about like an insect?

There might be other things about Peter that should alarm her, things she didn't even know about, or things she knew about but which she didn't know now were important. Those things might turn out to be disastrous. How did you know?

She would never know what his life with Caroline had really been like. All she knew was the small raised spine of that continent, the narrow rocky range of unhappiness that Peter had exposed. The rest of it was vast, submerged, dark, and shared by Caroline. It was everything else: the decisions they had made about painting the hall, choosing a car. The quarrels they had had in airports, or at breakfast, or in other people's guest rooms, trying to keep their furious voices down. The unforgivable things they had said to each other, later forgiven. The times when they had laughed helplessly out loud in a public silence, or the times when they had both been angry at someone else, the man at the hotel who refused to acknowledge their reservation. The times they had been frightened, moments when they were suddenly afraid for their lives, or for Amanda's. All those things—sex, late at night, dry mouthed and desperate among the tangled sheets, missed planes, awful meals, wonderful ones—Emma would never know. She would never know these things even when she and Peter shared their own continent. The things from the first marriage would be concealed from her, first from loyalty, then from indifference and finally from forgetfulness. And no matter what Peter told her now, he had once loved Caroline. And that was good, she must remember that, no matter how painful it was, it was good that her husband was a loving man.

She hoped she was doing the right thing, she believed she was. You turn your choices into the right ones, you live them into being the right ones, by faith, by commitment. Looking back and agonizing was self-indulgence. You denied yourself that, it was useless and damaging. Conviction: she held to that thought. Emma closed her eyes and tucked her head down, under the covers, pressing her forehead against the domes of her warm hard knees. She was doing the right thing.

Certainly she no longer wanted to be divorced. Divorced was different from unmarried; unmarried could be voluntary, but divorce was failure. No matter who asked for the separation, it was your marriage that had failed. Divorce held a faint, indissoluble stigma, an ancient stain, like blood on a sheet. She hadn't realized how much she had wanted to be married. She wanted once again to feel that she was within society's fold. She wanted Tess to have two parents. She wanted to be part of a whole, something shapely and symmetrical. She didn't want this unnatural, lopsided, truncated form, the single-parent family. She felt its awkwardness constantly. She felt her own responses to Tess uncurbed, unconfirmed. There were times she lost her temper, when a husband would have calmed her and sheltered Tess. There were times she lost her nerve, when a father would have held firm against Tess's tyrannical demands. The task required two, for balance. She wanted to restore that for Tess. She hoped she could restore it for Amanda as well. Poor anguished Amanda: consoling her was Emma's task, her penance.

Emma lay rolled up tightly beneath her covers. The clock shifted again, without warning. Another minute, fallen away. Emma wondered if there were a chance of her getting back to sleep; she concentrated on breathing, tried to relax. She drew in a long breath, held it within her, and let it slowly out. She thought of the breath, of air flowing out of her lungs, all the small, soft, irregular, honeycombed hollows collapsing peacefully into themselves as the air left them, membrane meeting membrane, the deep red sea-creature cavities emptied. She felt the air from those moist caverns drawn into a warm stirring column, rising through her chest and up her throat, a current from the interior, passing, with a soft whisper, through her nostrils and at last dispersing outside her body, filling the close musky cave under the covers with her own vaporous essence. Emptied, Emma lay motionless, trying to coax herself to sleep.

The Wedding was lumbering toward her. Emma opened her eyes.

It was to be small and quiet, in a nearby church. The reception would be larger, at the Knickerbocker Club. Emma thought of Francie and Rex and her parents, and closed her eyes again.

She had finally gotten up her nerve to talk to her father, but when she called, it was her mother who answered the phone.

"Hi," said Emma cautiously.

"Oh, hello dear," said her mother.

"I'm calling about the wedding," said Emma.

"Oh, yes, good," said her mother. "In September."

"I know when it is," said Emma.

"I know you know. I'm just saying it to remind myself."

"Okay," said Emma. "Right. Well, I'm really calling about Daddy."

"Your father?" Her mother's voice changed slightly; tension entered it.

"Well, and Rex." Now Emma felt tense.

"Your father and Rex?" Her mother sounded baffled and alarmed.

"Francie's Rex," said Emma. She started talking faster, as though this would aid comprehension. "Francie asked me to call you, actually. She says that Daddy was not very polite to him."

"Not very polite to Rex?" Her mother's voice rose in denial, as though Emma were accusing her father of robbery.

"When he was staying with you. Last spring. Didn't he try to get Daddy to lie down upstairs?" Emma could not now exactly remember what she had heard. "With his clothes off?"

"Rex took off his *clothes*?" Now her mother sounded horrified.

"Not Rex's, Daddy's," said Emma, rattled.

"Rex took your father's clothes off? Is that what Francie told you?"

"No, Francie didn't tell me that," Emma began.

"Well, then who told you? I don't know what you're talking about. I don't remember anything like that."

"It didn't happen, Mother," Emma said, exasperated.

"Then why did you bring it up?" asked her mother crossly. "I thought you said someone's clothes were off."

"No one's clothes were off," Emma said loudly. "Daddy was rude to Rex."

There was a pause.

"Well, he might have been. But I don't remember it," said her mother. "I don't remember anything like that."

"You told me Rex tried to get Daddy to do some sort of New Age exercises to get rid of his stiff neck. Francie says Daddy was rude to Rex. She says she won't come to the wedding if he's going to be rude again."

"I don't think your father was rude to Rex. I don't think he'll be rude to anyone. And I don't think we're getting anywhere in this conversation," her mother said abruptly. "I'm going to hang up now."

"Wait, Mother. Would you talk to him? Would you ask him to be friendly to Rex?"

"Would *I* talk to him?"

"Mother, don't repeat everything I say. You make me feel as though I'm talking gibberish."

"I don't think that's how you should say it."

Emma closed her eyes. "I'm trying to say it the best I can."

"I mean *gibberish*," her mother said. "I believe it's a hard *g*. Not *jibberish*."

"Okay," Emma said. "You're probably right. But do you think you could talk to Daddy about Rex? Francie won't come unless you do."

"I don't think your father is rude to anyone," her mother said. "And Francie will have to make her own decisions. Now, I'm going to have to get off the phone, I have things to do. Good-bye, dear." She hung up.

Emma stared angrily at the phone and repeated, "Good-bye, dear." She squeezed her eyes shut, chagrined.

Now, lying in bed, Emma remembered the phone call, the infuriating blank wall that her mother presented. It had always been like that; her mother always took her father's side, always told her daughters they were mistaken. All complaints were redirected back at them. It had always made Emma wild with frustration, as though she were invisible, mute. What she saw and heard was denied, not allowed to be true.

But now, in her peaceful nest, it occurred to Emma that her mother might feel trapped between her husband and reality. Perhaps she could not help herself. Her silence and vagueness might be self-protection, she might not feel equal to the struggle between her husband and the world, her husband and her daughters.

Emma remembered once coming into the big kitchen of the house in Cambridge. She had been eleven or twelve. Her father was at the table by the window. He sat very straight, his lunch on a plate before him. He was looking directly forward, eating his sandwich. There was something bel-

ligerent and challenging about his posture, and he did not look at Emma,
or speak to her when she came in. Emma's mother was by the stove, her
back to them. Her movements were clumsy. She did not turn to greet
Emma either.

"All right then, Everett," she said without looking at him. "Fine.
Whatever you say. I'm wrong." Her voice was low and dead sounding,
and, horribly, it held tears. Emma had never seen her mother cry before.
The voice was terrifying; the air in the room splintered.

Mr. Kirkland did not move. "There's no point in getting upset about it,
Aline," he said. "Politics is just something you don't understand. There's
no point in *crying* about it." He took another bite of his sandwich, facing
straight ahead.

"I'm not crying," Emma's mother said, and she turned, still without
looking at her husband or at Emma, keeping her face away from them,
lowered. But as she said the words her voice broke frighteningly: she was,
she was crying. She put her hand to her face as she left the room, letting
the swinging door rush closed behind her. Emma stood frozen, feeling the
cold draft from her mother's departure. The kitchen felt empty. Her father
stayed at the table, unhurriedly finishing his sandwich. Emma watched
the angle of his jaw as he chewed. He did not look at her, or speak. Emma
could not move, it seemed: the air was filled with the glittering fragments
of catastrophe, it would be dangerous to move.

Now Emma thought again of that scene: her mother fleeing, her father picking up his sandwich. Her mother, with her vague gestures and
her anxious eyes, her faded sweaters, her torn turtlenecks, keeping quiet.
Her poor mother, Emma thought.

The clock was moving things along. It was now four minutes past
six. The Wedding was closer still, it was coming. At least the Chatfields
would be benevolent presences. She imagined Dr. Chatfield at the wedding in his threadbare linen suit and dark blue sneakers. She had never
seen him without the ragged leather strap of his binoculars around his
neck, and wondered if he would wear them to church, in case he caught
sight of a high shadowy flutter within the dim vault of the ceiling. She
saw him, straight backed in the pew, leaning discreetly sideways, his
head cocked for a better look. He whispered quietly but audibly to his
wife, "Cedar waxwing, winter plumage." At the reception Mrs. Chatfield
would kiss everyone comfortingly, her high cheeks rosy with pleasure.
She would wear a blue tweed suit and her pearls. And there would be

other people, aunts and uncles, cousins, friends of both Emma's and Peter's, people who had known them before, in their other marriages, but who had not taken sides, who were generously ready to wish them well again.

Rachel would be there, Rachel who had become Emma's friend again. They had found a new apartment, on Central Park West, and when Emma showed Rachel through it she had held her breath. The new place was bigger, the ceilings higher: there was more of it to clean. Emma hoped Rachel didn't feel like baggage, carried here and there, from marriage to marriage. But Rachel's change of attitude had been complete. She had walked calmly through the new apartment and exclaimed with pleasure. Rachel, tall and shining, would be a dark regal presence, reminding everyone of propriety. Or at least Emma hoped so. And Amanda? She thought of Amanda's small pale frozen face.

At seven o'clock, Emma gave up. She got out of bed and opened her closet to look at her dress. At her first wedding, to Warren, in the late seventies, she had worn a white pantsuit. Then she had wanted to look dashing and unconventional, but now she felt differently. For this, her real wedding, she had chosen a white silk suit with an ankle-length skirt. The jacket was close fitting and high necked, with long tight sleeves and tiny diamond buttons down the front. It looked, Emma thought, like an old-fashioned lady's riding jacket, like something her grandmother might have worn. Wearing it herself, she felt demure, and serious, as though she would be received again into the bosom of the world. At the sight of the long white shape, soft and lustrous, her heart lifted: it was all about to happen.

At noon, Emma went up to the Knick, where the reception was to be. She stood in the handsome high-ceilinged library, with its tall windows overlooking Fifth Avenue. Daylight filled the big rectangular room, muting the richness of the brown leather spines of the books that lined the walls, the Oriental carpet that covered the floor. On the mahogany table in the center of the room was a mass of flowers. The great risk of being married in September was chrysanthemums, with their fetid smell and rusty colors. Emma had ordered lilies and roses, white stock, fragile anemones. Now they stood in a lush mass, tendrils and vines curling through them, heavy green leaves petticoating the bottom. Everything was serene and orderly. Andre, the headwaiter, smiled and assured her that all was ready. There was nothing for her to do here.

But still she felt butterflyish: the Wedding was approaching.

They were to leave for the church from the apartment at three-thirty. At a little past two they all began the process of dressing, preparing themselves for the ritual.

Tess wore a pink Liberty cotton, patterned with fragile interlocking flowers. Her innocent chest was crossed by rows of smocking—even, intricate puckers—topped by the starched white collar. The long sash was tied in back by the patient Rachel. Tess twisted her head, struggling to make sure the stiff bow was made properly, the loops symmetrical, the hanging tails even. Dressed, the frail white socks folded neatly over themselves, the black ankle-strap party shoes creaking with newness, Tess walked slowly and solemnly after Rachel, subdued by her own splendor.

Rachel was dazzling in ankle-length orange silk, the color radiant against her deep chestnut skin. Her tiny braids were brought in a smooth swirl to the nape of her neck, and she looked powerful and serene.

Peter sat in the living room, reading. He looked clean and nervous. He was in a deep blue suit with tiny pinstripes, very dark and very dressy. He had just had a haircut, and it was too short. At the back of his head the twin cords that reached from neck to skull were exposed, and the shorn plush looked surprised and vulnerable. In his buttonhole was a gardenia, white, tender, its scent ravishing.

Rachel stepped out into the living room, holding Tess by the hand. Peter looked up at them.

"Don't you two look terrific," he said. "What pretty dresses."

"*And* party shoes," Tess said, pointing her toe.

"Thank you," Rachel said, giving him a wide white smile.

Emma, who had started first, took the longest. She never went to the hairdresser, and had been afraid to go to one for her wedding. What if they did something awful and you hated it? What if you hated the way you looked on your wedding day? She had washed her hair the night before, the way she normally did. Getting dressed, she looked at herself in the mirror. Maybe she should have gone to a hairdresser after all, she thought. But it was too late, and it would be all right. She pulled on the long slip, sliding it carefully up over her stockings. By three, Emma was finally dressed, moving her head carefully in the high tight silk, taking small steps in the long hobbling skirt. She loved the strange length and narrowness of the skirt, reminding her of this event, making it real, inevitable. The Wedding was approaching.

At quarter past three, Amanda had not arrived. She had been expected at three. Emma asked Peter, "Do you think you should call?"

"Already?" Peter asked.

"Well, when do you think?" said Emma gently. He must be nervous too.

"A few more minutes," he said. They were standing in the tiny dining room. They had nothing else to do. Tess stared up at them. In one hand she held the bouquet she was to carry. With the other she twirled a curl of hair. They waited. Emma walked with tiny steps the length of the room, then turned.

"What if she's not here by three-thirty?" she asked.

"Do you want me to call Caroline?" Peter's voice was tense.

"Don't you think?" asked Emma. "If we wait, and then you call, and Caroline says she thought we'd said three-thirty, then Amanda is so far uptown she'll miss the wedding."

"No, then she and the nanny can go straight to the church."

Emma said nothing, unhappy. She turned away and began to pace again. The house telephone rang, and Peter's face cleared. He left to answer it. He came back a moment later, tense again.

"The limousine is here," he said.

Emma looked at him and said nothing.

"Emma," he said, "just remember this is hard for Caroline. This is a difficult thing to do, to send Amanda off for my wedding."

"I know," said Emma. "I know it's hard for her. I'm sorry. But please find out."

"I'll call her," he said, and left the room.

Emma walked in a slow ellipse around the living room, her arms folded on her chest. She looked at her watch: three-thirteen. She thought of Caroline, dressing Amanda for Peter's second wedding. Poor Caroline. Perhaps they should have invited her, included her somehow.

Tess came into the room, holding her bouquet. "Mommy, I don't know if I can carry these flowers," she said. But Emma could hardly hear her.

"Of course you can," she said.

"I do not think I can, Mommy." She held the corsage away from her, a small knot of dark velvet violets set in heart-shaped green leaves. Narrow ribbons, pale blue, hung down from it.

"What do you mean, you can't?"

"I think I might drop them," Tess said solemnly.

Emma knelt down. "No, you won't," she said, trying to be calm. But her heart was pounding. It was like terror, she thought, though she did not think she was terrified of marriage. But her heart was pounding. She put her arm around Tess comfortingly. Peter came into the room. "Where is she?" Emma asked.

"She's on her way," Peter said, but his voice was odd.

"When did she leave?" Emma asked suspiciously.

"She's on her way," Peter repeated. "She'll be here in time."

"Peter—" Emma began. She felt helpless, breathless with anxiety. All the possible risks, the hovering, incipient calamities seemed now centered on this one thing: Caroline was going to keep Amanda from being on time. Caroline was going to interfere in Emma's wedding.

Peter took her in his arms. He held her close to him, patting her back. "It's all right, Emma," he said earnestly. "No matter what happens, it's all right." He held her tightly. "Shh, shh, shh," he whispered into her ear. "You and I will be married, no matter what." Emma closed her eyes, as though she were dancing, feeling him wrap himself around her.

Amanda and her nanny, Maeve, arrived, at three thirty-five. The others were standing in the hall downstairs with their coats on. Emma handed Amanda her bouquet, and they all bundled into the sleek black limousine at the curb. The door shut solidly. Rachel and Maeve sat, not looking at each other, on the jump seats. The two little girls sat in between Peter and Emma. The car was luxurious, with polished mahogany paneling, immaculate dove gray upholstery. Once inside they were quiet, subdued by the sudden silence and intimacy. Emma leaned back carefully against the seat. She took a long breath: there was nothing more to be done. Now things would progress regardless. She smiled at Peter. He smiled back and took her hand. It was almost here. The rumble was now deafening.

The car drew up at the Church of the Heavenly Rest. Peter got out first. He leaned back in and blew a kiss to Emma. "I love you," he said, and went off to find the minister. Emma waited in the car with the girls while people arrived and walked into the church. When the sidewalk was empty, they all got out of the car. Rachel and Maeve went inside to find seats, and Emma waited with the two girls in the damp stone hall. In the center stood a table, with a book for signatures on it, and a huge mass of flowers, the twin of the one at the Club. Her heart was pounding.

Inside the darkened church, the organist was doing quiet trills, and their friends and relatives were sitting silently in the pews. The moment was almost here. Emma felt quieter and quieter, weightless. She smiled at the two little girls. They wore identical dresses, their hair was brushed and shining. Amanda looked grim, and Emma wondered how it had been for her, getting ready. Had Caroline cried? Been angry? Emma knelt down next to the child. She wanted to start this off right, she was determined to draw Amanda toward her.

"You look beautiful," she said. "Your hair looks so shiny."

Tess pressed jealously close. Emma smoothed Amanda's hair; Amanda twisted slightly under her hand.

"Amanda, I'm so happy to be marrying your father," Emma said. "I know it's hard for you. I'm sorry for that. But we want to make you part of our family, with Tess and your father and I."

Amanda stared straight at her, unblinking. Emma stroked her head again; again Amanda recoiled.

"I love your father very much," Emma said. She wondered if she should tell Amanda she loved her very much too. She was afraid it would not sound genuine; she was afraid it was not yet quite true.

"And me," Tess said greedily, pressing her stomach toward her mother.

"And you," Emma agreed, absently. She was looking at Amanda again. The girl's hands hung down at her sides. "Where's your bouquet?" Amanda, not meeting her eyes, shrugged her shoulders. Tess stared at her sanctimoniously.

"Amanda, where is it?" Emma asked again.

Amanda met her eyes, but said nothing. Her hands were empty, they had left their coats in the car. She did not have it; the bouquet was gone.

"Is it in the car?" Emma asked. Amanda raised her eyebrows, slowly shrugged her shoulders. Emma marveled at her resolution. Emma looked outside, but the car had pulled smoothly off to wait on a side street. Amanda stood frowning into the distance.

"You'll have to walk without one," said Emma, looking around the stone hall. Inside the church the organist had begun a longer, more serious piece, preliminary to the Event.

"I know," Emma said. She held her skirt up off the damp flags and stepped over to the huge vase of flowers. Delicately she teased out a single white rose, extricating it from the hidden stems. The rose was small, perfect, blush white. She held it out to Amanda. "Here," she said, "carry this."

Now the Wedding was rattling forward, its rumble overwhelming, its bulk looming over her, vast, engulfing. Details no longer mattered, all was out of her hands.

The white rose held negligently in her hand, Amanda stood next to

Tess. Tess's bouquet was clutched conscientiously in both hands. Emma could see what she was thinking: she was not like Amanda. She was good.

Emma looked at small tense Amanda, defiantly holding her solitary flower. No matter what Emma hoped, Amanda could not be happy that her father was marrying Emma. Or that he was living with Tess. How could she feel happy about any of this? She was already, at seven, in mourning for her life, for her past and happy life, that other world. She was in mourning for the time before the fall, a blissful life in which order prevailed, things were in their rightful place, and her parents shone together in their proper settings, high in the firmament. Now this would be in the past, forever. But Emma was determined, too. She would rescue Amanda from her misery, draw her into something new.

The organ music grew bolder, forceful, demanding Emma's steps. The dark cool interior of the church waited for her, the deep powerful mystery of the ritual was almost upon her. Emma felt the frightening nearness of it, felt herself about to be engulfed. She turned to look outside, as if for the last time. The doorway was a bright rectangle onto the street. A woman, oddly hunched, wearing a tan raincoat, was standing at the edge of the sidewalk. She stood behind a parking meter, as though the narrow metal pole would conceal her. Emma's glance paused, her attention caught by the woman's tension, her frown, her anxiety. Her surreptitious air. It was Caroline.

The music now insisted, rising, gathering strength, and Emma turned back, facing the doorway into the dim vaulted space. She felt herself straighten. She looked down at the two little girls and smiled. She was prepared. At the end of the aisle stood the tall figure of the minister, exotic and powerful in robes, layers, brocade. Next to him she saw Peter's serious face as he stood, his hands joined formally in front of him. They were waiting for Emma. The Wedding was here.

PART TWO

13

Maeve Jones, Amanda's nanny, was from Wales. She had very white skin and very dark brown hair. Her hair was short and springy; a tracery of white laced through it. Maeve had a long nose and gray eyes, and she wore colorless glasses. Except on her day off, Maeve wore a brown-and-white-checked dress with a white collar and cuffs. In the summer the dress had short puffy sleeves, in the winter the sleeves were long, and Maeve wore a tan cardigan sweater with it. Cardigan was the real name for a button-up sweater, and it was a place in Wales. Maeve told Amanda that.

Maeve knew everything, and how to do everything. She was also very beautiful: she had beautiful lines in her face. There were two curves that cupped the corners of her mouth, even when she was not smiling. At the corners of her eyes there was a little nest of lines, light and airy, as though they had been drawn with feathers. Those grew deeper when she smiled. In between her eyebrows was a short perpendicular line, and on her forehead were wavy horizontal lines. Sometimes, when Maeve was sitting and sewing, Amanda climbed up on the arm of her chair and stroked the lines on her forehead, tracing them on Maeve's white skin. Maeve would duck her head, after a minute, or shake it, and ask Amanda what she was doing up there, if she was searching for gold, or what. But actually Maeve didn't mind, which Amanda could tell from her voice.

In those days, the days before everything changed, it was Maeve, already dressed, brushed, perfectly tidy in her uniform, who came briskly into Amanda's bedroom in the mornings, when Amanda was still asleep.

And that day, the day everything changed, began like all the others, with Maeve opening the door from the hall.

"Rise and shine," Maeve said when she came in. She always said that. Maeve spoke with a quick musical lilt: it was the way people spoke in Wales. As she crossed the room she tapped Amanda's foot, under the covers. At the window Maeve gave a quick authoritative tug to the shade and let it roll itself noisily up. She turned to Amanda, who lay in bed blinking at the light.

"Who's that still in bed?" Maeve asked. "Who's that Slugabed? Who's that Lazy Amanda?" Her voice was indignant, but there was a small smile at the edges of her mouth.

"Maeve, I'm not *lazy*," Amanda said. "I'm just *tired.*"

"Oh, just tired, I see." Now Maeve set her hands on her hips, her brown-and-white-checked arms making a pattern of exasperation in the air. Energy radiated from her, she nearly hummed. Maeve nodded. "Just tired," she repeated. She looked intently at Amanda. "That wouldn't have anything to do with staying up late last night, would it?"

Amanda remembered, and began to scramble herself out of bed.

"No, it doesn't," she said. She had promised, the night before, that if she stayed up past her bedtime she would not be tired in the morning.

In those days, Maeve always made Amanda's breakfast. She started the oatmeal before she came in to wake Amanda, and it would be ready by the time they arrived in the kitchen. While it was cooking Maeve helped Amanda get up and dressed. She had laid everything out in Amanda's room the night before: the white round-collared blouse, the plaid jumper, the navy kneesocks, the brown oxford shoes. Amanda's school clothes came in a box at the end of each summer: new dark blue socks, new blue plaid jumpers, new white blouses, each crisp and neat in its own plastic bag, pins holding it in its orderly folds. The new clothes were always too big, the jumpers drooping mournfully over Amanda's knees, the collars loose around her throat. That was so Amanda could grow into them, and, amazingly, without effort, she always did.

That morning Maeve knelt before her on the rug to help Amanda dress. Amanda set her hand on the knotty bone in Maeve's shoulder, to steady herself as she stepped into her bloomers, first one foot, then the other. Still kneeling, Maeve buttoned up Amanda's white school blouse. Amanda stood peacefully under Maeve's sure hands. Maeve tilted her head back as she worked, eyeing the buttons through the bottom of her glasses. With each button the small line between her eyebrows deepened, then relaxed.

"Maeve," Amanda said, watching her eyebrows, "when did I meet you?"

Maeve reached the top button, slid it through, and smoothed the collar down with a swift pat, finishing Amanda off. "You met me when you came home from the hospital," she said. "You were only a bundle."

"I wasn't a *bundle*," Amanda protested, pleased. "I was a *baby*."

"Not then you weren't," Maeve said. "Arms up, please."

Amanda raised her arms obediently and Maeve slid the jumper over her head.

"Then you were only a bundle." Maeve snugged the jumper into place, swiveled Amanda, raised the child's elbow, and pulled the side zipper down.

"What am I now, then?" Amanda asked. She was entranced by Maeve's authority, by her firm charge of Amanda's life.

"A scalawag," said Maeve. "Don't move." She went into the bathroom with the hairbrush, and Amanda heard a powerful blast from the faucet. Maeve came back, the brush dripping.

"Why do you put water on it?" asked Amanda, looking doubtfully at the sodden brush.

"So your hair won't fly away," Maeve said, raising it to Amanda's fine hair. Amanda thought of her hair lifting, strand by strand, up, off her scalp and lofting itself airily into space. She struggled to hold her head upright against the buffet of Maeve's quick determined strokes. The brush slid into a snarl.

"Ow," Amanda said, arching her body sideways.

"Sorry, Madam," Maeve said, not sounding it. She lowered the brush and picked delicately at the snarl with her fingers.

"Maeve," Amanda said.

"Madam."

"When you were little, did your mother call you a scalawag?"

"That's private information," Maeve said at once, curling her tongue around the *r*'s. She spoke with brisk precision, but Amanda knew from her voice she wasn't angry.

Amanda thought of the photograph of Maeve's parents which sat on her bureau. Amanda knew it, of course: she knew every object in Maeve's tiny room. The room was much smaller than Amanda's bedroom, and narrow. It held only Maeve's single bed, a bureau, a small bookcase, an armchair and a standing lamp. Maeve's bed was always made, the white coverlet always pulled smoothly up over the high rounded pillow. The room was always perfectly tidy, and it smelled of the bath salts Maeve used: Rose Geranium.

Amanda's room was large, with two beds in it, and two windows. She had once asked Maeve to sleep in the bed next to hers. "No one sleeps there," she had pointed out.

"I've got my own bed," Maeve said. "And you need your beauty sleep."

"But this could be your own bed," Amanda persisted. "And I would get lots of sleep."

"I stay up late with my reading, and writing letters. I'd keep you awake," Maeve said.

"I wouldn't mind," Amanda told her eagerly. "I'll just lie there with my eyes closed. I won't even hear you." Right then she had waited hopefully for Maeve's reply, believing there was a chance, thinking that only a slim layer of discussion lay between her and what she wanted. When she heard Maeve's voice answering she understood that this was not the case. She heard that no matter what she said, and no matter what Maeve said, there was no chance of this happening, and that Maeve would never tell her what the real reason was.

Still, she wished that Maeve's room were next to hers. She wished they slept side by side, even if they were separated by walls, so that if she had a bad dream she could slip next door, quickly, lightly, invisibly, without risking the long, heart-thudding, nighttime journey down black hallways. But Maeve's room was in a completely different part of the apartment, distant, remote: next to the laundry room, off the narrow back hall that led from the kitchen to the service elevator.

Amanda loved Maeve's room. It was like an enchanted country, and she roamed through it, when she was allowed, with rapt concentration, as though she were on a mission. Respectful, ravenous, she examined everything, scrutinizing, trying to memorize. She was trying to learn Maeve's life. She, Amanda, had only one life, and Maeve had been with her through the whole of it. But Maeve had another life, one that held her own family, her parents and her sister, Susan, and other places, even other little girls that Maeve had lived with. Amanda could not imagine Maeve living with other little girls, coming into their rooms in the morning, calling them Madam. It seemed impossible to her, but Maeve had told her it was true. Maeve had always been a part of Amanda's life, but Amanda had not always been a part of Maeve's life. The other parts of Maeve's life were amazing to her, fascinating.

Amanda knew the tortoiseshell brush and comb set that sat on the bureau. She knew the neat sewing case, with its woven handle and the small, gleaming, irresistible scissors. She knew the modest row of paper-back books, with beautiful women on their covers, with long hair and full sweeping skirts. She knew the copper luster pitcher that stood on the bed-side table, which was a present from Maeve's mother.

She knew especially well the photographs of Maeve's parents and of her sister. They stood blinking and smiling in an unknown Welsh yard, tall dense unknown bushes crowding behind them. Maeve's parents stood awkwardly side by side, their hands self-conscious, their faces smiling and anxious. Maeve's father, balding and thin lipped, was portly in a rumpled dark sweater that buttoned halfway up his front. Maeve's mother, small, wore a flowered full-skirted dress, tight across her bosom. Her smile was rigid, and her eyes were squeezed nearly shut, as though the camera's click, the shutter's fall, might hurt. Her eyebrows, though, were raised in a kind of private delight. Susan, standing alone in the same yard, was larger than her mother, more massive. She wore glasses, like Maeve, but her face was fuller, her nose smaller. Her hair was flat and smooth on top of her head, fluffy around her ears. The photographs were in a scuffed leather frame, navy blue, that folded like a book, and shut with a small metal snap. Amanda liked to snap it shut and then open it, but she was not allowed, because the click it made would drive Maeve loony.

"Maeve. When you write your mother, do you tell her about me?" Amanda's head jerked with the strokes of the brush. Maeve wrote her mother once a week. Her mother lived in Abergavenny, with Susan, who worked for the school board. Maeve's father was no longer on this earth.

"What would I tell my mother about you?" Maeve's voice was soft and fierce. "That you're a scalawag, mainly. A waste of paper, that." The brush snagged again on a tangle, and Maeve stopped brushing and began to work at the snarl with gentle fingers. Amanda said nothing. Her hands at her sides, she waited trustfully, suspended in the powerful current of Maeve.

Maeve disentangled the last confusion in Amanda's hair and gave her whole head a vigorous final round.

"There," she said, her voice full of satisfaction. She put her hands on Amanda's shoulders and walked her like a doll to the big mirror on the closet door.

Maeve's hands still on her shoulders, her guardian presence close above her, Amanda regarded her own image in the mirror. Her hands were flat against her skirt, her feet neatly side by side. Her hair hung stiff and straight, dark in streaks from the water. Her face was solemn; below it was her too-big white blouse with the rounded white collar, her dark too-long jumper hanging over the tops of her kneesocks.

"*Now* don't you look nice," Maeve said.

It was not a question but a declaration. Amanda could hear that whatever she looked like in the mirror—this face, these clothes, this flattened hair—was exactly the right way to look. It was the way Maeve wanted her to look. Each morning, when Amanda heard Maeve say that, with such certainty, such approval, Amanda understood that she did, truly, look nice. She knew that Maeve, through her competence, had turned Amanda into something that was in accordance with the world. It was a process over which Amanda had no control, like growing into her clothes. In Maeve's hands she became right. She felt as though she were in a great hammock in space, rocked, secure, sheltered, both swayed and anchored by powerful, benign forces.

In the afternoon of that day, the day everything changed, when school was over, it was raining. The mothers and nannies waited inside the big front hall instead of out on the sidewalk. When Amanda came down the wide staircase with her class, she saw Maeve near the front door. Maeve wore a tan raincoat and a see-through plastic rain hat, which fanned across her head in transparent pleats. Maeve was watching her, and when Amanda met her eyes Maeve lifted her eyebrows and raised her chin in greeting. When Amanda reached her Maeve leaned over.

"It's cats and dogs out there," she said. "You're to put these on." She held out Amanda's yellow slicker, stiff and clammy, and her red boots.

They walked home through the wet streets. Maeve carried the big umbrella, and it joggled with her steps, sometimes covering Amanda's head, sometimes allowing a sudden drop to fall on her hair, her neck. Around them the city whispered, its noises muted and hissing in the rain. Amanda watched her boots as she walked. She liked the sound they made, a hollow rubbery knock. She liked sloshing them in the water, and at the wide rivulet at the curb on Park Avenue she stepped rapidly twice, stamping, to make a splash.

"Amanda," Maeve said, giving her hand a tug. The stamping had delayed them. When they were only halfway across Park Avenue the light changed, and they were caught on the island. "You see," Maeve said. Cars sped heavily past them, hissing, spraying high glittering fans of water. Amanda stepped back, holding Maeve's hand. Maeve always made Amanda take her hand, crossing the street.

At home, Maeve set the dripping umbrella in the stand by the elevator. She unbuttoned her raincoat, then opened the front door. She moved inside slowly, and Amanda, impatient, jostled behind her. Pushing past, Amanda asked, "Can I come to your room?"

She was not usually allowed in Maeve's room, and never on Maeve's days off. Amanda's mother said, "Leave her alone. She's got you in her hair the rest of the week. Leave her alone on Sunday." Amanda was hurt by the way her mother said this, as though Maeve didn't like spending her days with Amanda, as though this were not what they both wanted. Amanda said nothing to her mother. She knew the rules. She was not allowed even to stand in the hall outside of Maeve's door, listening to see if she was there.

She did this anyway, slipping through the door from the kitchen and along Maeve's hallway. She tiptoed along the carpet, slower and slower as she approached Maeve's door. Outside it she stopped and stood still, her head bent, her eyes squinted, her breath held, listening. She heard little. Sometimes footsteps, a faint rustling. A mysterious silence. What did Maeve do when she was alone? Without Amanda? It was unimaginable.

But on rainy days Amanda was allowed in Maeve's room, as a treat. Maeve would make her cinnamon toast, and sweet tea with milk in it, which was called cambric tea. Amanda would bring in her Archie comics and lie on her stomach on Maeve's bed, reading and littering Maeve's bedspread with cinnamon crumbs. Maeve would sew on Amanda's buttons, or mend tears in her jumpers. Sometimes Maeve could be persuaded to play Go Fish.

That day the front hall was filled with suitcases, stacked and leaning against each other: Amanda's father, going on another business trip. Maeve knelt on the floor to help Amanda off with her boots.

"Can I?" Amanda asked again.

Maeve put one hand on Amanda's calf, the other on the heel of the boot. "Settle down, Miss Wiggly," Maeve said.

"But can I?" Amanda asked. She leaned against the suitcases and surrendered her foot to Maeve.

Maeve tugged. "We'll see," she said. "Hold still."

Amanda put her weight on her elbows, leaning back on her father's suitcases as if they were a throne. She pretended to be sad when her father went away, though actually she liked it. He called every night to talk to her, and when he was away she was allowed to sleep with her mother, or at least to start off in her mother's bed.

Her parents' bedroom was large, hushed. The thick carpet was gray, the ceiling distant and pearly. The wallpaper was covered with blue-gray shepherds and shepherdesses. At the high windows there were curtains with the same design, the blue-gray shepherdesses on them soft. Amanda was allowed to come in only if she was quiet. She was not allowed to bring anything to eat or drink, or anything that bounced. Sometimes her mother declared that Amanda herself was too bouncy, and then Caroline called Maeve to come and take Amanda away.

But if Amanda was quiet, she was allowed to bring her comics and lie on her mother's bed while her mother read her magazines, or talked to friends on the telephone, or watched TV. Amanda's mother was beautiful too, but in a different way from Maeve. She had thick bouncy hair, dark underneath but with pale blond streaks, that was held back from her forehead by two curved tortoiseshell combs. It swept almost to the tops of her shoulders, where it curved slightly. Caroline always looked just right. Her hair was always smooth and her fingernails polished. Her clothes always looked new, and she did not have to grow into them. When Caroline was at home in the apartment she wore black turtlenecks and black pants. She always looked planned, composed, complete. Amanda understood that this was exactly the right way for a mother to look.

When her father was away, often they both had supper in her parents' room on trays, and they watched TV together, laughing with the sound track. When Amanda's father was away, Caroline didn't cook. They ordered out, or had greasy grilled cheese sandwiches with American cheese. "Don't tell, Nanna," her mother would say, "junk food junkies." Sometimes, even when her father wasn't away, her parents had dinner on trays. Peter had his in the library, where he sat in his big armchair with a book, and read while he ate. Caroline had hers in the bedroom, where she lay on the bed and watched TV. Sometimes when Amanda was finished with her dinner she went and lay across the bed with her mother.

The bed was big, with a white bedspread and four long white pillows with lacy edges. The pillows were fat, and stacked two deep against the mahogany headboard. The bed was really two beds, pushed tightly together. The white coverlet was spread across them both, as though they were one wide bed, but underneath they were made up as two. The sheets and blankets were tucked in separately, under each mattress, down the middle. On the nights when Amanda fell asleep there, lying on her father's side of the bed, she could hear her mother's breathing, she could hear the rustle of her movements, but she could not, asleep or awake, feel the warmth from her mother's body, or the beating of her mother's heart.

In the evenings, while they were lying on the bed, her father would call home. Caroline picked up the volume control and turned down the TV. Amanda always talked first: she loved talking to her father when he was away. First she asked him where he was. It was always somewhere she had never been, and she asked what it was like.

"I'm in Los Angeles," Peter said. "It's full of cars and pink signs."

"Cars and pink signs?" Amanda imagined a huge parking lot, like the one at the airport, jammed with rows and rows of parked cars, each one fluttering with Easter-colored announcements.

"And what about you?" her asked. "What did you do today? What happened at school?"

Amanda would tease her father, making things up. He believed everything she said. Once she told him a friend had learned to fly, and once that a dinosaur had gotten into their classroom at school.

"A dinosaur!" her father said. "That's really dangerous, Amanda. I hope that didn't really happen."

"I'm sorry, Daddy," Amanda said happily, "but it did."

"Oh, no!" Peter said. "Was anyone hurt?"

"It ate Miss Bernstein," Amanda said, ruthless.

"Oh, no!" her father said, in despair. "Oh, no!"

At last Amanda relented, giggling.

When Amanda had finished talking, her mother took the telephone. While she talked to Peter, Caroline went on watching the TV screen. She never talked long. As she hung up she turned the volume back up again.

That day, standing by the suitcases, Amanda pulled her leg free from the second boot, Maeve holding it by the heel. Amanda kicked her foot in the air, ridding herself of the clammy boot chill.

"Don't jump around," Maeve said tartly, setting the two boots side by side. "We'll have the Great Lakes all over the floor. Hold still while I do your raincoat." Her voice was surprisingly cool; she sounded cross at something. Subdued, Amanda stood motionless while Maeve undid the metal latches of her slicker.

The voice behind her was completely unexpected. "Amanda." It was her father's voice, coming from the living room. Her father was never here when she came home from school, never. Amanda turned to look at him.

He stood in the doorway, not smiling. "When you've got your coat off, would you come in here a moment? Thank you, Maeve." His voice was somber.

Maeve's mouth, as she opened Amanda's raincoat, was tight and puckered. She looked at what she was doing, frowning, fierce, and said nothing.

Amanda, uneasy, nodded. Maeve finished with the raincoat and drew it off Amanda's shoulders, holding it, dripping, between her thumb and forefinger. The short vertical line between her eyebrows had deepened. "Off you go," she said to Amanda, nodding toward her father without looking at him. Then Maeve turned and left, carrying Amanda's boots and slicker, heading down the hall toward the kitchen. Amanda watched, but Maeve closed the door behind her without looking back.

Amanda was left alone with her father. She looked back at him: he stood tall and grave in the doorway. She was frightened.

"Come on," Peter said, holding out his hand to her. This was worse: why would he want to hold her hand to walk into the living room? Amanda took his hand and they went in.

The living room was huge, dim, alarming, filled with fragile objects Amanda was not allowed to touch. The walls were violent with leopard spots, the heavy gleaming curtains oppressive. Gold tassels hung down at their sides like sacred bell pulls. Amanda was not expressly forbidden to come here, but whenever she did, Maeve or her mother told her to come back out.

Now it was silent and shadowy. Peter, still holding her hand, walked with her to the big sofa, with its smooth rounded cushions. He sat down and patted the cushion next to him for Amanda. She sat carefully, feeling the soft down give way beneath her. She slid her hands underneath her thighs, for safety, and looked up at her father, waiting for him to begin this frightening thing.

Peter leaned forward and folded his hands. He looked down at his hands, and then at Amanda. "First of all, I want you to know I love you," he said, "and I'll always love you." Amanda felt a chill. "It's not your fault," her father said. Her heart began to pound.

"I'm going to move away," Peter told her. "It's not your fault, and it's not your mother's fault. It's no one's fault. Your mother and I don't make each other happy anymore."

Amanda stared at him. Behind him, across the room, in the background, was a huge swoop of green-gray curtain, hanging in smooth curved folds, fixed, immutable. After a long silence she heard herself ask, "Where will you live?"

"I have a new apartment," he said. "A small one," he added, and Amanda understood that he felt bad about this, guilty. "You'll come and see me there."

"But your things are here," Amanda pointed out. He lived here, with her and Maeve. All his things, his books in the library, his special lamp to read by, the painting of the lake where he had gone when he was little, his coats in the closet, his pictures: everything was here. His life was here.

"I'm taking some of them with me," he said. "They're in the suitcases in the hall. Some of them your mother will keep."

His coats? wondered Amanda. What?

"We'll still see each other a lot," Peter said. He put his hand on Amanda's wrist and stroked it, back and forth. His thumb felt rough on her skin. "I'll call you all the time. You'll come and see my new apartment. I'll come and take you out to dinner."

Amanda looked at him. She did not want to see his new small apartment, where he wanted to live without her, and she did not want to go out somewhere strange for dinner.

"Can I have sundaes?" she asked.

"Sundays?" her father repeated. "For visits?"

"For dessert," Amanda said. It was like talking to a stranger.

"Oh, for desserts," her father said. He nodded, unsmiling. "Anything you like," he said.

This too was frightening: Amanda was rarely allowed to have sundaes.

"But why are you leaving?" she asked.

"I've told you, because your mother and I don't make each other happy anymore."

She stared at him. On the mantel an ormolu clock ticked heavily in the silence. What her father said meant nothing. You didn't decide whether you were happy or not: you lived your life, that was how it worked. She and her father and mother and Maeve all lived together. They were happy because that was their life. You didn't *make* someone happy or not happy, you just lived your life. They were all happy, that was how it was. What could he mean? The people in your life were your people. You didn't decide about them, they were there.

Amanda looked down at her foot. She saw it was moving, a small urgent jiggle. She looked up again at her father. He was leaning forward, watching her. When he left for business trips he always hugged her, lifting her up and putting his arms around her so that she was close against his chest. She shut her eyes and hugged him back. She could smell him, warm and comforting, through his shirt.

Now he did not hold her, he only watched her, and rubbed his rough thumb along her wrist, over the bump of bone. Her father wanted to leave them. Thinking of this made Amanda feel very small, a tiny figure against a melting dim landscape with a distant horizon. Against that landscape she was barely visible, a speck. There was something dark all around her; there was something dark inside her. Things were vanishing all around her. No one, now, would point her toward the mirror and say that she looked nice. She was hardly visible now, she was hardly there at all.

Amanda stared at her father. She felt sick. She felt a swift lurch in her stomach, and was afraid she would throw up. She heard herself breathing, a strange sound; she wanted Maeve. She did not move. She had sunk so deeply into the cushion; she felt its softness had swelled up around her, puffed, yielding, dangerous, as though it were something from which she might never be able to rise.

Her father took her hand and gently pulled her up. Out in the hall he opened the closet door and took out his raincoat. She watched each thing he did. His face was fixed and terrible. Deliberately he put on his coat, settling the collar around his neck, without looking at her. Then he stooped down in front of her. He took her in his arms and pressed her against him. She felt something in his chest knock suddenly, like a sudden tight breath, then another. His arms were very close around her, he was so big, so close around her she couldn't move. She didn't hug him back: she was too small, enveloped by his embrace, to matter. Pressed against his chest she could smell him, but it no longer seemed the same. His smell no longer seemed hers.

"Good-bye, Nanna, I'll see you very soon. I love you," he said. She did not answer, her voice was too small.

In the foyer her father pushed the elevator button. All around him were his suitcases, loaded with his things that he was taking away. While he waited for the elevator he took the change from his pocket and played with it. He made a funnel with his fingers, and dropped each coin through it onto the next, making a chinking sound. Amanda watched him. She could still feel her heart beating, knocking around in her chest, hammering hard. She knew there was something she could say, some word, some sentence, that would stop him, make him take off his coat again. She could not think what it was.

The elevator door slid open, and Richie, the Irish elevator man, stood there, smiling. He was small and bald, with bold black eyes. "Hello, Mr. Chatfield, hello, Amanda."

"Hello, Richie," said Peter. "Could you help me with these?"

"Of course, Mr. Chatfield," Richie said, jumping forward. "Lot of bags," he said. "Long trip!" He winked at Amanda. She stared at him.

Together Richie and her father slid the heavy bags into the little room of the elevator. Amanda watched her father get in after them; he turned to face her. Richie stepped into his place at the controls. He smiled at Amanda.

"Bye now," Richie said unctuously. He winked at her again.

Behind him was her father, standing against the dark mahogany wall of the elevator. He was not smiling. "Bye, Nanna,"

Amanda said nothing. She could not think of the word, the sentence. The elevator door slid closed, slid over her father's dark unsmiling face, and then she heard its sudden smooth fall, the elevator's swift descent, down the shaft.

14

Amanda was seven when she and her mother moved. The new apartment was uptown, and it was not on Park Avenue, but on Eighty-seventh Street. The lobby was smaller in the new building, it was only a long narrow hallway. To reach the new apartment you walked past the first elevator and down to the end of the hallway, to the back, to the elevator there. When Amanda heard Caroline describing the apartment, she said that they were on the back elevator. Her voice sounded different when she said that, so Amanda asked her about it.

"Is it bad to be on the back elevator?"

"No, of course not," Caroline said right away, sharply, not looking at her. "It doesn't matter at all." So Amanda knew that it did matter, and that she and her mother were now in disgrace.

Amanda's new bedroom was smaller than her old one. There was still room for her twin beds, but there was really no room at the foot of them for her to play on the floor. Everything in the new bedroom was closer together, cramped. The checked curtains were too long for this window, and there was only one window here, not two. The curtains were hung anyway, drooping below the sill. "We'll have them taken up later," Caroline said, but in the meantime they drooped. Amanda's old rug was too big for this room, and she had the rug from Maeve's room. Amanda asked her mother where her own rug was. "In storage," Caroline said. "In a warehouse." Lots of things were in storage, it seemed, all the things they couldn't fit into the new apartment. The way Caroline said it, it seemed as though everything there had moved to a new life. Everything was safe, but they would never see it again.

Just before Caroline and Amanda moved to the new apartment, Maeve left them. When Maeve told Amanda she was leaving, Amanda did not ask her to stay. Amanda understood that if Maeve were leaving, like her father, it was because she wanted to leave, it was because she did not want to stay with Amanda and Caroline.

When Maeve said good-bye to her, Amanda saw small tears trickling around the lower rims of Maeve's glasses. Maeve took off her glasses and squeezed the bridge of her nose with her thumb and forefinger. She blinked her eyes quickly several times. Then she looked up again. She said she would come and see Amanda often: she would be living nearby. She was going to work for another family on Park Avenue, looking after another little girl. Amanda thought of Maeve in someone else's small bedroom, the folding leather picture frames spread out on another bureau. She imagined Maeve sitting in another armchair, the light falling on her hands as she sewed the buttons on someone else's cardigan sweater.

That night Amanda woke suddenly. Her room was dark. Urgently she climbed out of bed. She bolted for the bathroom. Barefoot, she stood on the cold tiles. Leaning over into the white porcelain bowl, Amanda retched over and over into the cold white basin. In between heaves she felt herself drooling slime, and her eyes teared. The smell was loathsome, and the retching was frightening. She could not stop. She felt as though she had been taken over by something. When she was finally through she was shaken and drained. She knelt in front of the toilet on the bath mat, shivering, one foot folded over the other for warmth, waiting for the shudders to pass. When it felt safe she wiped her dripping chin and slimy mouth on her towel. But still, when she went back to bed the smell hung sickeningly about her—it had somehow gotten into her hair—and she sank her nose in her pillow, trying to breathe through her mouth. Maeve was gone.

They moved on a Friday. On the first school morning in the new apartment, Caroline came into Amanda's room in the morning. She was not dressed yet; she was in her long quilted bathrobe with flowers on it. On her feet were blue fuzzy slippers, like pale blue lambs. "Amanda," she said briskly, "it's time to get up." Amanda opened her eyes but did not move. Everything was in the wrong place. Caroline stood on the rug, her hands in the deep pockets of her robe. She did not turn on the light, or move to raise the window shade.

"Nanna?" she said. "It's time to get up. Come on, let's go."

Amanda waited for her to open the shade, to come over to her bed, but her mother just stood with her hands in her pockets. Amanda looked over at the chair, but her school clothes were not there.

"Where are my clothes?" she asked.

Caroline looked blank. "What clothes?"

"My school clothes."

"Well—" Caroline looked at the closet. "I guess they're in your closet. Where did you put them when you took them off?"

Amanda had last worn her school clothes on Friday, when the movers had come. She had gone home that afternoon to the new apartment, where everything was in boxes. They had spent the weekend unpacking, but nothing was neat yet. She had no idea where her school clothes were. Before, Maeve had always taken them from her.

Caroline went over to the bureau, where there were two big square boxes, one on top of the other. "Well, let's see. What do you need?" she asked. "Your blouse, your kneesocks, let's see."

Amanda got out of bed, worried. "Where's my jumper?" she asked.

"Where does Maeve keep it?"

"In the closet," said Amanda anxiously. It didn't matter where Maeve had put it before; Maeve was not here now. There was no chance of the jumper, now, hanging neatly in the closet with her other dresses. Together they looked in the closet; a line of cotton summer dresses hung there limply. There were no plaid jumpers.

"It doesn't matter. We'll find another one in your boxes. These have all your things," Caroline said. She began to pry at the plastic tape sealing the box with her fingernails. Amanda watched. Caroline tore at it, frowning. She tugged at the reluctant tape, which was crisscrossed over itself, snarled and resistant. When she peeled the tape back from the top she lifted the two sides open and leaned in. Amanda was not tall enough to see inside; she watched her mother's face as she put her hands in, ruffled through the contents, still frowning.

"Shit," Caroline said, not looking at Amanda.

"What's in that?" Amanda asked.

"Towels," Caroline said. On the outside the box said, "Amanda" in Magic Marker. Caroline lifted it to the floor and bent over the second one. She began tugging on the plastic tape. That box held Amanda's sweaters. Caroline stood up.

"What will I wear?" Amanda asked anxiously. "It's a rule to wear the uniform."

"Well, you can skip one day," Caroline said. "I'll call them. I'll give you a note."

"No," Amanda said, alarmed. "I'm not skipping a day. No one goes to school without a uniform. It's a *rule.*"

Caroline looked again in the closet. "I know you have more than one," she said. "Maybe we should call Maeve."

"Maeve always puts it out the night before," Amanda said.

"I know that," Caroline said crossly, "but Maeve isn't here."

Amanda waited.

"Well, you go and brush your teeth while I look some more". Amanda did not move. "Go on, Amanda, go on in and brush your teeth."

Amanda went in alone to the bathroom. She didn't know exactly how to do this by herself. Maeve always put toothpaste on the toothbrush, and watched Amanda while she brushed. Then Maeve took a washcloth full of warm water, wrung it out, and put it over Amanda's whole face. The washcloth was hot and rough. Amanda closed her eyes and let her face be taken over, scrubbed, polished like a jewel, like crystal.

"Squeaky clean," Maeve said, and Amanda felt her face emerge, pure and pristine. It tingled airily, as though it were sparkling, as it dried.

But now, alone in her dark bathroom, Amanda did not want to brush her teeth or wash her face. She was worried about her uniform. She could feel the worry like a knot in her stomach. She wanted to move slowly, do as little as possible, do nothing to increase this. She turned the water on loudly, as thought she were brushing her teeth. She stood still, staring at herself in the mirror. She clenched her teeth and opened her lips. Her teeth looked white, no different from the way they would after brushing. She opened her mouth and stuck out her tongue, as far as she could. It looked mottled red, normal. She licked her lips and turned off the water. She came out of the bathroom again.

"Did you find it?" she asked Caroline.

"You can just wear a skirt," her mother said. "For one day it will be all right."

"I'm not wearing a skirt," Amanda said. "I'm not. Everyone else wears a uniform. It's a *rule.*" She saw herself in class, the white blouse rustling, her chest achingly bright, the agonizing center of the classroom. She saw herself enduring the bright white snowfield of her blouse through each class, everyone else's chest demurely covered by the plaid jumper. She thought of the wrongness of herself, the whole day. The questions she would receive from every teacher. The looks from the other girls.

"I'm not," Amanda repeated.

Her mother opened up a bureau drawer. "Here's your blouse," she said, pulling it out. "Here's a clean pair of socks."

"I'm not going to school in a skirt," Amanda said. She folded her arms. She felt sick to her stomach.

"Here, Amanda, put these on, anyway," her mother said. "I'll figure something out. What do you want for breakfast?"

Maeve had never asked what she wanted for breakfast.

"French toast," Amanda said, angry about the uniform.

"French toast?" her mother repeated. "That will take too long. We don't have time." She was in the closet again, going through Amanda's dresses, hanger by hanger. "Maybe it's underneath something else. I know you have more than one. It could be in any of the boxes." The hall outside was stacked high with cardboard boxes, still sealed.

"I'll see if it's in the laundry room, with the things that came back from the cleaners," said Caroline. "Come in when you're ready and I'll make you some toast." She left for the kitchen.

Amanda slowly put on her socks. She didn't know how she would decide she was ready, she could not be ready without her uniform. She pulled her socks tightly up to her knees, folding the tops over evenly. She put on her white blouse, starting at the bottom and buttoning it all the way up to the neck before she realized she had started wrong. She undid each button and started over. It seemed as though everything had changed. Now, simply putting on her clothes seemed fraught with peril. Every gesture seemed wrong, everything she did seemed a mistake.

Amanda looked at herself in the mirror. Her hair was not brushed. She never brushed her own hair: the handle of her hairbrush was too big for her hand, and the bristles hurt her scalp. Maeve knew how to brush without hurting. Now Amanda's hair was still in sleep-pressed mats, and it was dirty: no one had washed it on Sunday night. She was wearing navy blue bloomers and her voluminous white blouse, without an undershirt, which her mother had not noticed. Her socks came neatly up to her knees, and she set her feet carefully side by side. She pressed her hands against the sides of her legs and looked at herself in the mirror the way she always used to. She stood up straight, but the picture was not the same. It was wrong, the picture was wrong. No one would look at her and say now that she looked nice. She could see she did not.

After Maeve left, when Caroline went out at night she left Amanda with different baby-sitters. Maria still worked for them, coming twice a week to clean the new apartment, and sometimes she came back in the evenings to stay with Amanda. Maria was in her midtwenties. She was from El Salvador, and had narrow black eyes and thick inky hair. She had a broad, pale yellowish face, with wide smooth cheeks. She wore colored headbands and black tights, white blouses and cardigans—though she would not know what their proper name was, Amanda thought. Maria's English was minimal. She was fierce and strange; Amanda was afraid of her.

When Maria stayed, she spent her evenings on the telephone, speaking very fast in Spanish. For dinner she heated up a frozen pizza. There were no rules with Maria: Amanda took a bath alone if she felt like it, not if she didn't. At nine o'clock Maria appeared in Amanda's doorway and said, "Nine o'clock. Time for bed, okay?" Amanda would look up from her comic, or from the TV, and nod. Maria would come in a few minutes later to say good night. Amanda was by then under the covers. She needn't have changed into her pajamas, her teeth could be unbrushed.

"Okay, good night," Maria said, and turned out the light. Amanda waited until the footsteps faded and then turned her light back on, or the TV. Maria never came back. She went to the kitchen and picked up the telephone. She shut the kitchen door.

When Maeve put Amanda to bed she sat down with her for a moment, and smoothed the hair back from Amanda's forehead. Then Amanda closed her eyes and lay still, and Maeve traced a slow figure-eight pattern on Amanda's skin. Amanda could feel Maeve's calm fingertips move lightly, back and forth across her face. It felt like a kind of magic, as though she were perfectly connected to Maeve then, through that steady pressure against her forehead, as though Maeve's fingers were her connection to the rest of the world, the dark foreverness of space, and that Amanda was now a part of it, safe, whole, ready, because of her connection to Maeve.

Now, after Maria had said good night and gone back to the kitchen, sometimes Amanda lay with her eyes shut and pretended that Maeve's slow fingers were moving across her forehead. Sometimes she put her own hand up and traced the pattern on her face. It made her feel better, though it did not feel the same.

One night when Amanda could not sleep she came into the kitchen, blinking in the harsh light. Maria was sitting at the counter with a mug of coffee. She was on the phone. Amanda stood in the doorway and waited until Maria saw her. Maria jerked her chin up at once.

"What you want?" she asked, unsmiling. She still held the phone to her mouth.

"I'm thirsty," Amanda said finally.

Maria eyed her. Amanda did not move.

"*Espèrate,*" Maria rattled into the telephone. She turned again to Amanda. "What you want to drink? Want some water?"

Amanda shook her head.

"What you want?" Maria repeated.

"Coke," said Amanda, testing. Maeve would never have given her a Coke. Maeve would have scolded her back to bed at once. If Amanda were sick or upset, then Maeve would fix her a cup of warm milk, with a spoonful of honey dissolved in it. Then Maeve would come in and sit with her in the dark while Amanda drank it.

Now Maria set down the phone and went rapidly to the refrigerator. Everything she did she did very fast. She pulled out a can of Coke and handed it to Amanda.

"Okay?" she asked.

Amanda took the Coke and nodded. "Thank you."

Maria picked up the telephone again. She sat down on the stool and drew herself close to the kitchen counter. Her back was turned to Amanda. She put her elbows down on the counter and leaned into the phone.

"*Oyeme,*" Maria said, her voice low and urgent. She began again, rattling off a stream of unknown words, peppery and staccato, sending them out into an unknown world.

Amanda turned and left. The metal can of Coke was cold in her hand, its thin red sides springy and yielding. Drops of cold water formed on it and trickled uncomfortably over her fingers. Back in her room, Amanda shut the door and turned on her light. She snapped open the top of the Coke can: the dark liquid hissed, and dirty foam curled up out of the opening. She took a swallow, but the soda bubbled up too quickly in her mouth. It stung; it was too cold, too active in her throat. She felt it suddenly, alarmingly, in her nostrils.

Amanda set the can down on her bedside table and sat down on her bed. She was wearing pajama bottoms, a white cotton turtleneck, which was torn around the cuffs, and a sweater. She reached down and pulled a stack of old comics from underneath the dust ruffle. When Maeve was there, she had always looked under Amanda's bed. She hiked up the dust ruffle and dragged out whatever it was Amanda had stuffed there.

"Are you storing up treasure under here, or what?" Maeve demanded sternly. "There's a place for everything, and everything in its place," she said. She always said things like that, bossy little rules about everything in life. Amanda felt as though they held her in place, they held her world in place. There were those rules, always, forever, running along next to her, showing her the boundaries.

With Maria there were no rules. She never looked under the bed, and Amanda now kept all her comics there, in a bright slippery heap. Now, in bed, leaning on one elbow, Amanda flipped open a comic and began to read. Archies were her favorites. She loved reading about freckled, bright-eyed, ingenuous Archie himself, with his mysterious two-horned hairdo. And blond, ingenious Betty, just as pretty as dark-haired Veronica but inexplicably less successful. She liked hating the scheming and untrustworthy Reggie; she liked liking the eccentric Jughead with his duck-bill nose and hamburger habit. Amanda read all this soberly and with interest. She absorbed information about chocolate shops, senior proms, double dating, as though she was schooling herself for her own adolescence, though Riverdale—with its small, neat, separate houses; its quiet, unlittered streets; its public high school; its proms and football games—was utterly unlike the landscape Amanda knew. In Riverdale there were no strangers.

Immersed in Archie's life, Amanda forgot about the Coke. When she remembered it again the can was no longer cold, and the bubbles had vanished. She took a gulp but did not swallow. For a moment she held the sweet tepid liquid inside her mouth. The soda was inside her but it was not yet part of her, as it would be in the next moment. When she swallowed, it would become lost, part of her, indistinguishable from her stomach, her lungs, all the parts of her in her interior that she could not feel. The soda turned warm inside her mouth, the sweetness took on the taste of the insides of her cheeks. The light from the bedside lamp made a warm pool in the dark room. Swirling the Coke over and over in her mouth, Amanda turned a limp yellow page. As she did so she heard the front door slam softly.

Amanda swallowed the mouthful at once and put the can back on the table. Quickly she slid the comics under the bed and turned out her light. Her mother went into the back hall, toward the kitchen. Faintly Amanda heard her mother talking to Maria, then she heard her mother come back alone. Maria left by the service elevator.

Amanda lay in bed, her eyes tightly shut. She listened to her mother's footsteps, muffled by the hall carpet. The footsteps went past Amanda's door, and she heard her mother's bedroom door shut. Amanda opened her eyes, but she did not turn the light back on; her mother might come in to say good night when she herself was ready for bed.

Amanda lay still. Her new window did not look out on Park Avenue, so at night she no longer heard the smooth steady swoosh of cars when it rained. This room looked out on a side street, where the traffic was always stop and go. Instead of the quiet dreamlike sounds of solitary cars pausing for a light in the middle of the night, she heard the loud anguished strain of the garbage trucks, over and over.

Now it was quiet outside, and Amanda listened in the dark for sounds from her mother's bedroom. But both doors were shut, and she could hear nothing. She lay without moving, listening in the dark until she fell asleep.

One night, the winter Amanda was eight, she woke suddenly. A nightmare still had possession of her; threat and terror swirled inside her head, and her room was filled by something frightening. At first she lay in her bed listening to the sounds outside her window. A garbage truck was groaning down the block, and there was the faint cry of a distant siren, but neither sound was what had started her heart pounding. She watched the lights shift on her ceiling. Fear held her fixed in place, her arms and legs still. The shadows on the ceiling. And the shadows in her closet, behind the partly open door. The silence of the hall outside her bedroom.

When the fear of staying still outweighed the fear of moving, Amanda climbed quickly out of bed. Heart pounding, she ran to her door. Her mother's room was just down the hall. Amanda opened her door and, without looking into the darker reaches in either direction, bolted diagonally across the hall to her mother's door. She could feel terror racing through her. She opened the door, ready to sprint through the dark into her mother's bed. As she opened the door, she had already started, she had already taken the first step.

Her mother's room was lit. The small lamp on bedside table threw shadows from the bed hangings onto the ceiling. The rest of the room was dark and vague. The door was directly opposite the four-poster bed, with its heavy curtains. Amanda, standing in the doorway, was looking straight at the illuminated bed. It did not have her mother in it. There was instead a huge nightmare body under the sheets. Amanda stared straight at the rumpled excitement of this figure, at the confusion of heads on the pillow. Frozen with horror—it was like her dream—Amanda stood in the doorway, staring at the figure as it heaved and fought under the covers. Suddenly her mother's face appeared, detaching itself from the rest of the unruly bulk.

"Amanda?" she said. The figure was still at once. It had another head, but without a face. The other head was covered in dark hair.

"Amanda, go back to bed," her mother said. Her voice was furious; Amanda had never heard her mother sound like that before. "Go back to bed right now!" Amanda turned and left, shutting the door behind her.

Back in her own room, Amanda pulled the quilt off her bed and picked up a sheaf of comics. She took these into the closet, where she turned on the overhead light and closed the door behind her. Beneath the row of dresses, she pushed aside her shoes, making a clearing in the deepest recesses of the space. She put down her quilt and sat on it, pulling it up around her shoulders. The floor was cold, and Amanda was shivering, but inside the small closed closet it was quiet, and inside the cocoon of her quilt it slowly became warm. In the dim light from overhead she picked up the top comic on her pile, holding it on her knees. She began to reread the stories, already memorized, about Riverdale, about convertibles and cheerleaders.

The next morning, neither Caroline nor Amanda mentioned the night before. On her way to the kitchen for breakfast, Amanda looked through the open doorway into her mother's room. The bed was empty, the pillows punched and disorderly, the sheets rumpled and ghastly, one trailing on the floor. Amanda did not stop but kept on going to the kitchen. What her mother made for breakfast was cold cereal. Her mother bought whatever ones Amanda said she wanted.

15

On Friday they left New York late, after Tess and Amanda had had dinner. It was summer, the evening was long, and when they started out it was still light. Peter drove, with Emma beside him in the front. Amanda, who was eight, and Tess, four, knelt, facing each other, in back. The long slippery backseat was a separate country, wild, filled with adventure, inhabited only by them. They were playing Wonder Woman.

Amanda described the action as it occurred, in an urgent undertone. She clung precariously with one superstrong hand to the back of the seat, dangling in space from the side of a skyscraper. Tess watched, avid: she was Wonder Woman's helper.

"*Now the kidnappers are leaning out the window above me,*" Amanda whispered. "*They're trying to cut my magic lariat.*"

"They can't," Tess said, shaking her head firmly. "You can't cut it."

"*I let it out further,*" Amanda said, ignoring Tess. "*I slide down the skyscraper until I see an open window. I'm forty-seven stories above the street.*"

"And the wind comes up," Tess suggested.

"*They're banging at the rope from above, trying to wham me against the side of the building,*" Amanda said. She pushed herself back from the seat, her hands springing against the cushion.

Emma turned around to look at them. "How are you girls doing?"

"Fine," Amanda said.

"We're playing Wonder Woman," said Tess, bouncing once on the seat. "I'm the helper."

"Good," Emma said. "And what's happening?"

"We're winning," Tess said. "The kidnappers almost trapped us, but we're getting away."

"Good for you," Emma said, and turned again to the front.

"*Now he leans way out the window,*" Amanda whispered. "*He's trying to shoot me.*" Amanda flattened herself against the seat.

"Use your magic bracelets," Tess suggested.

"*Wonder Woman puts up her magic bracelet,*" Amanda said, not looking at her. She held her wrist up. "*Ping! Ping! The bullets bounce off it. Then I make the other end of my lariat into a noose, and throw it at Black Bart.*"

"It goes over his head!" Tess said triumphantly, clapping her hands.

Amanda looked at her. "Tess," she said, in a different voice, "I'm telling this."

"Okay, *okay,*" Tess said fiercely.

Amanda went on in the secret whisper. "*The magic lariat pulls him out of the window. Wonder Woman reaches out as he passes, and catches him with her superstrength!*"

"Why did you catch him?" Tess asked, in her normal voice.

"Because," Amanda said, in hers, "Wonder Woman is good. She never kills people. Anyway, it's too soon for it to be over."

Amanda stretched an arm out clinging with her other hand to the backseat. "*Wonder Woman holds on to him as she bangs against the building.*"

"When am I going to do something?" Tess asked.

"Soon," Amanda said, "as soon as Wonder Woman gets inside."

"You always say that," Tess said.

"*She's got hold of the windowsill,*" Amanda whispered, "*she's just about got it.*"

Tess sat up, pulling her knees up to her chin, her feet apart. She banged her knees together impatiently.

"*She gets inside!*" Amanda said triumphantly. "*She gets inside and sees her helper!*"

"What do I do?" Tess asked.

"*Wonder Woman gets Black Bart in through the window,*" Amanda said, struggling and pulling, "*and her helper is waiting with a big huge book. A dictionary. The helper hits him on the head with it as he comes inside. She knocks him out!*"

"*Amanda,*" said Tess, "I want to use the magic weapons. I don't want to use a dumb old *dictionary.* Why can't I ever use the magic things?"

"Because, Tess," Amanda said, her voice urgent. "They belong to Wonder Woman. They only work for her. Anybody knows that. No one can use them except Wonder Woman."

"Then I don't want to play anymore," Tess said. She turned away and stared straight ahead, her mouth set. "Or I want a game where I'm Wonder Woman," Tess said. "I want to be Wonder Woman."

"Tess, look," Amanda kept her voice down. She did not want Emma to hear this. "I'm bigger. Wonder Woman can't be smaller than her helper."

"Okay, fine, Amanda," Tess said. "You be Wonder Woman. I'm not playing anymore." She folded her arms, her face stony.

"Okay, fine, Tess," said Amanda. "But you're going to miss the big important thing that the helper does. She *saves* Wonder Woman."

"I don't care," said Tess angrily. She leaned into the front seat. "Mommy?"

Emma turned her head.

"Can I come in the front with you?"

Emma lifted her arms, and, traitorously, Tess clambered into the other world, with the grown-ups.

Amanda, alone, sat in the backseat. The world that had populated it—vivid, crowded, demanding—suddenly vanished. She was nowhere now. She was alone in the backseat. She looked out the window. Cars streamed past, in the relentless monotony of the highway. Amanda kicked her legs. She put her finger to her mouth and chewed on her nail. Boredom rose in her like a wave.

She leaned against the back of the front seat, behind her father. She looked at the back of his neck, the collar of his plaid shirt. The hair was cut short and plushy down at the base, and it grew longer and featherier as it went up on his head. Amanda brushed the back of his head with her hand.

"Dad?"

"Hi, Nanna," Peter said.

"When is it my turn to sit in the front seat?" she asked.

"You mean on Emma's lap?" Peter said. Tess, her thumb in her mouth, eyed Amanda suspiciously.

"Tess always gets to sit there," said Amanda. "I should have a turn in the front."

Tess pulled her glistening thumb from her mouth. "No!"

"It's not fair," Amanda said to Emma. "Why does Tess always get to sit in your lap and I don't?"

"Because she's so much smaller than you," Emma said, her voice light and brisk. "My lap isn't big enough for you, Amanda, you're such a big girl!" Emma smiled at her brightly.

There was silence for a moment.

"Amanda is too big to sit in your lap?" Peter said to Emma.

"Amanda is actually quite big," Emma said. Her voice was still brisk, and she didn't turn to look at Peter. "Amanda is growing up. Her arms and legs are longer than you think."

Amanda waited, her head pressed against the seat behind her father, but her father said nothing more. Tess lay against Emma's chest, her thumb back in her mouth. Amanda looked at her, and Tess pulled her thumb out and stuck out her tongue at Amanda. Amanda made a mean face, squinting her eyes. Then she sank away into the backseat. She threw herself down on the seat, flattened by boredom and resentment. She hated Tess. She hated both Tess and Emma. Emma always did that. One time when her father was away and Amanda had been staying with them, Emma had let Tess sleep with her. Amanda had asked if she could sleep there too, and Emma had said there wasn't room.

Amanda lay in resentful silence, watching the wild headlights slip past. She hated her father for saying nothing. The car slid from lane to lane, from one stream of headlights to another. Cars rushed past in the other direction, endlessly, slipping past forever. The car beneath Amanda surged along through the night. Alone in the backseat, in the roaring darkness, she slept.

She awoke at the silence, when the car stopped.

"We're here," Peter said, and opened his door. Outside it was dark and quiet. There was only a quiet rushing sound from the wind. Amanda could smell the sea. Tess had been asleep too. Her eyes were bleary.

"Everyone take something," Emma said, but she really meant Amanda. She and Peter were carrying things anyway, and Tess was too small. Amanda carried her own suitcase, and they set off on the little path toward the house.

The Kirklands were waiting for them at the front door. Mr. Kirkland, who was tall and frightening, kissed Emma and Tess. He shook hands with Peter and Amanda.

"Hello, Kirk," Peter said to him, setting down a suitcase. "You remember Amanda, my daughter."

"Hello, young lady," Mr. Kirkland said, looking down at her from underneath his eyebrows. He was very tall.

"Hello, Amanda," Mrs. Kirkland said. "I'm glad to have you here." She leaned over and put her arms around Amanda. Her arms felt strange and uncertain. She kissed Amanda's cheek. Amanda waited without moving for her to stop.

"Gonny!" Tess shouted loudly, showing off. She threw herself against her grandmother, closing her eyes to show rapture.

"Well, I don't know what you'll find to do here," Mr. Kirkland said loudly to Amanda.

Emma stopped and turned to her father.

"She'll find lots to do here, Daddy," she said. "She and Tess will do things together."

"Good, good," Mr. Kirkland said. He frowned all the time.

Upstairs, they crowded along the hallway. Tess, holding on to her grandmother's hand, led the way, bossily. "This is my room, Amanda," she said, looking back at Amanda. They were to share it. There were two beds and a faded rag rug. Between the beds, in a battered gold frame, was a picture of a girl in old-fashioned clothes: a black cloak and hat, with a fur muff. Shelves, built into the walls, held china mugs, a pincushion, a collection of shells. All the furniture was painted white. Nothing looked new.

Tess sat on the bed closest to the door. She bounced on it and declared, "This is mine. I get this bed."

"Now, Tess," Mrs. Kirkland said, "remember that you're the hostess. You ask your guest what she would like."

Tess looked at Amanda. "Amanda, would you like that bed?" She pointed to the bed near the window.

Amanda shrugged her shoulders. "I don't care," she said.

The next morning, Amanda woke first. Resisting, her eyelids shuttering against the light, she finally opened her eyes. It was the light that had wakened her; the room was awash, aglare, with brightness. There was nothing to keep it out: at the windows were only thin white curtains, not drawn. Flimsy white shades kept out only the sight of the ragged pines and sandy flat lawn outside. Nothing at all kept out the sun, which had entirely invaded the small room with brilliance.

At home, Amanda was never awakened by light. In her bedroom, the blue-and-white-checked curtains were always drawn at night, and the heavy white shade was pulled securely down to the windowsill. The window itself was tightly shut against the night. The enclosed air moved peacefully through her lungs again and again through the night. She was surrounded by a breathing, murmuring web she wove herself, warm, familiar, close.

The nights were different when Amanda was with Emma and her father. Nights with them were not safe. Emma always made Amanda sleep with the window dangerously open: anything could get in from outside. The dark wind came into her room at will. And last night Amanda had heard strange noises. There were rushing noises outside, and inside there were creaks and incomprehensible patterings. At home in New York there were no sounds like that. There was only the sound of traffic, or the rising song of a distant siren, or normal noises like that. In the mornings there was the strident familiar racket of heat rising powerfully through the pipes. All of these sounds were known and comforting.

Amanda slid further up on her pillow and looked around. Tess, of course, was asleep. Tess slept all the time, she took naps, she went to bed early, she woke up late. Her head was pressed deep into the pillow, her eyes tightly closed, her mouth slightly open.

Amanda looked around the room. It was shaped wrong: the ceiling, instead of being flat, slanted down on either side of the window, cutting the space into strange uneven shapes. But everything here was strange.

The house made Amanda uncomfortable. It was old and the furniture was rickety, the rugs were frayed and there were holes on the chair arms. Amanda's mother would never have lived in a place like this. Amanda had been to her real grandparents' house, Caroline's parents', to their whitewashed brick house. There, the floors were smooth and polished, and the walls had no cracks in them. The furniture was not faded, and there were no holes in the chair arms.

This house, Emma's parents', was poor. Emma seemed unembarrassed by it, but to Amanda its poverty was shaming. She held herself aloof from it: the faded slipcovers, the shabby floors, the dusty corners. None of it had anything to do with her. She was only marking time here, waiting to leave. She had to be here. Her father made her come. The games with Tess were the only times she was not waiting to leave.

Amanda looked around the room: there was nothing for her to do here. There was nothing in the room but books. Books made her restless. Emma made Amanda listen while she read to Tess when she put them both to bed, too early. Emma made Amanda go to bed at the same time Tess did, even though Tess was four years younger. When Amanda told Emma that at home she went to bed at nine, Emma said, "Your mother lets you stay up until *nine?*" Her voice rose as she asked this. She looked concerned, as though Amanda had said her mother let her play with guns.

Emma acted as though the bedtime reading was a treat. Tess lay under the covers, and Emma sat by her pillow. Tess listened breathlessly, her eyes fixed on her mother, her face intent, as though she were picturing every word Emma spoke. Amanda lay on her back, her hands clasped under her head, and stared up at the ceiling. As Emma read, Amanda's foot jiggled, a steady restless beat. Emma read slowly, as if it were exciting, changing her voice affectedly for the different characters.

Emma looked up often at Tess; she turned often to smile at Amanda, too, but Amanda never looked back at her. Emma read about the unpleasant girl in the horrible dark house in England, the stupid robin and the so-what garden. The long incomprehensible words, and nothing to watch but the ceiling. Amanda tried to block it all out, to concentrate on something else, a TV movie she liked, instead.

At home Amanda never had to read or to listen to reading. Her own mother never read books to Amanda, and seldom to herself. When her mother did read, it was a new book, something with a bright cover, usually with a beautiful woman on it. Those were what Amanda felt were the right kinds of books to read. But mostly Caroline read magazines. She liked to watch television with Amanda. Sometimes she made a bowl of popcorn, and she and Amanda lay together on Caroline's bed, making a nest out of the down quilt.

Emma never watched television, and neither did Tess. They never knew what Amanda was talking about if she said something about one of her favorite shows, something that everyone else knew. Emma just shook her head and smiled, as though it were normal to be so stupid. But Tess eyed Amanda, envious. She was not allowed to watch television, and Amanda would have even felt sorry for her if she had permitted herself.

Amanda got out of bed. She was wearing pajama bottoms and the short-sleeved striped jersey she had worn the day before. Amanda liked sleeping in the clothes she had spent the day in. Emma disapproved, and told her not to. When Amanda did anyway Emma got cross. Her mouth turned angry and she said, "I told you not to do that, Amanda!" Maeve would never have let her wear day clothes to bed either, but she wouldn't have gotten angry. Maeve would have called her a monkey and told her to get right out of bed and into her pajamas, but she wouldn't have been angry. Maeve never got angry at her, never. Emma got angry at everything.

The Kirklands' house was quiet, and it felt early. Amanda was too awake to stay in bed. She would go and find the television. She would watch cartoons, keeping the sound down low. Even though Emma's parents were poor, they would have a television set, even very poor people had television sets. Maria had a television set.

If Amanda were at home now, she would put on her red plaid dressing gown that her mother gave her for Christmas. She would go into the library and watch cartoons. Amanda had always watched cartoons on Saturday mornings. When she was little she had carried around with her a yellow blanket with a smooth satin binding. She would lie on the library rug with pillows from the sofa, wrapped in her yellow blanket and watching the Road Runner. She held her blanket up to her face, folding the satin edge of it around her nose and mouth, and breathing in its familiar smell. She lay like that, squinting at the TV, sometimes watching it and sometimes closing her eyes, letting the chatter of the Road Runner and the Coyote wash over her, all of it blending into a comforting hammock of sound. And sometimes, while she was lying there, her eyes half shut, wrapped in her blanket, breathing through its tattered satin edge, Amanda would feel the sole of her foot slowly invaded, a delicate trail of sensation, a diabolical feathering across her skin, warning of delight and hysteria: the unbearable bliss of tickling. Her mother had found her. Then her mother would sit down next to her, wrapping the two of them in the blanket. Her mother had watched cartoons when she was little, the Road Runner, and Tom and Jerry, rampaging across the screen, and that made Amanda feel safe, comforted to know that she was growing up in the same world as her mother.

Amanda stood watching Tess, but Tess did not stir. She went to the bedroom door and looked out into the hall. She considered going back into her room and sitting on Tess's bed, staring at her until she woke up. Tess was company, even if she was only four. She was also protection from Emma. Amanda would be blamed for anything that happened if she were alone, but if there were two of them, Emma would relent. Still, waking Tess was totally forbidden. Even if Tess said she wouldn't tell, Emma would be suspicious if Tess got up early. And if Tess and Amanda had a fight later, Tess would threaten to tell, and if she did tell Amanda would get in trouble.

When Amanda got in trouble Emma would say, "Amanda, would you come in here for a second? I'd like to speak to you." Emma's voice would be light and brittle. Amanda would go into the room with her, and Emma would close the door. Then Emma would sit down, slowly and carefully, to make sure Amanda understood how serious all this was. Then she would fold her arms across her chest and look at Amanda, her face hard and dark.

"Now, Amanda," Emma would say. "I want to talk to you about waking Tess up in the morning." She would pause, looking straight at Amanda. "Tess is younger than you. She needs more sleep than you do. She is a little girl." She would pause again.

Amanda, standing up, would shift her weight from one leg to the other. One knee would jiggle, waiting.

"But I've told you this before. How many times, do you think, have I told you that you are not to wake Tess up?"

Amanda knew that she didn't have to answer this question. She would sigh, as loud as she dared. She would be waiting for this to be over.

Emma would sit still, staring at her. "It's not just waking Tess up," she would go on. "It's the fact that you do it over and over, even though I've told you not to."

Of course Amanda did it over and over: Tess was always asleep when Amanda woke up. Amanda would look sideways, then back at Emma. She would be waiting for Emma to finish. Emma acted as though Tess were the most important person in the world, and as though waking her meant the end of the universe, as though Tess were some wonderful princess who could not be touched, who would shatter into pieces if Amanda woke her up half an hour early. It was safer to leave Tess asleep.

Amanda tiptoed down the hall and down the front stairs. The TV would probably be in the living room, she thought, though she hadn't noticed it there last night. She looked around now in the daylight: there were more bookcases, but no TV in sight. Turning back into the hall, Amanda quietly explored the rest of the downstairs. She prowled through a small room by the front door, with one armchair in it and an oak desk. She opened a door onto a huge closet, jammed with stuff: sailing gear, slickers, tennis racquets, jackets and rubber boots. Another back room had a big white metal rack with plants on it, and an old striped sofa, but no TV. Amanda wondered where they kept it.

She went back through the living room and dining room, then through the swinging door into the kitchen. Mrs. Kirkland, in a faded cotton dressing gown, was sitting at the table. An open book was propped up in front of her, against a jar of marmalade. She was wearing glasses that came only halfway up, and she was reading as she ate. On a plate sat an egg in a cup, and she was scooping its insides out with a spoon. She looked up, over her glasses, as Amanda appeared in the doorway.

"Well, good morning, Amanda," she said. "You're up early."

Amanda came all the way into the room, and Mrs. Kirkland smiled at her.

"Would you like some breakfast?"

Sidetracked, Amanda nodded, and slid into a chair across from Mrs. Kirkland.

"What would you like?" On Mrs. Kirkland's plate was a blackened piece of toast, with a cold slab of butter partly smeared across its surface.

"French toast," answered Amanda.

"Oh," said Mrs. Kirkland doubtfully. She looked up at Amanda. "French toast."

Amanda said nothing, kicking her heels against the chair.

"I guess you'll have to wait until Emma comes down for that," Mrs. Kirkland decided. She smiled again at Amanda and returned to her book. Amanda watched in silence.

"Where's the television set?" asked Amanda finally.

"What television set?" asked Mrs. Kirkland, looking up.

"The one here. I couldn't find it."

"Oh." Mrs. Kirkland smiled deprecatingly and shook her head. "I'm afraid we don't have one. You'll think we're very old fashioned, I guess. We've never wanted one here. It changes the evenings. It's good for some things, I know. We have one at home, in Cambridge. We watch the news on it, but we don't really want it here." She smiled again at Amanda. She seemed pleased.

"You don't have one?" asked Amanda, still confused.

"Not here."

Amanda turned and looked out the window. Even Emma had one, in her apartment. It could be turned on for special things. The thought of a whole house without a television set discouraged Amanda. She had not really paid attention to what Mrs. Kirkland had said, but to choose not to have a TV, and to smile proudly about it, was mystifying to her. It was like cutting off your foot and boasting about it: two feet were all right for some things, but they made it too easy to get around. What was wrong with spending the evening watching TV, wondered Amanda.

It was warm already, later it would be hot. Amanda stared out at the summer-dead lawn. Beyond the lawn were the wooden railings going down to the dock, and a flagpole. The flag was moving gently, dreamily, in the early breeze.

"Is the flag yours?" Amanda asked.

Mrs. Kirkland nodded.

"Why do you have it?"

Mrs. Kirkland looked outside. "Oh, just, you know, out here along the water. Lots of people have them, for some reason."

Amanda stared at her. "Does it stay up all the time?"

"It stays up all summer. We take it in for the winter. Would you like some regular toasted toast?" She held up the flattened, blackened rectangle. "We have some honey," she offered, as a special treat.

Amanda shook her head, but she now felt hungry. "Is there cereal?"

"Oh, I think so," said Mrs. Kirkland. "Look in the larder. Right back there, that door, no, that one."

Amanda found the door.

"On the second shelf. Do you see some?"

"Yes," said Amanda, but did not reach for it. It was a tasteless kind, sugarless, without interest. The kind you had to chew all morning. Emma had tried to give her some once. The cover of the box had only writing on it, no cartoon creatures, no colors, no excitement. At home there was a whole shelf of different cereals, with interesting names, Honey this, Captain that. They were all sweet, bright, colorful, launching themselves into her day. Now Amanda shut the cupboard door and came back, dispirited, to the table.

"Didn't you find it?" Mrs. Kirkland pushed back her chair and stood up to help.

"I don't like that kind," said Amanda.

"Oh dear," Mrs. Kirkland said. "I'm sorry there's nothing you like here." She sat down again.

Amanda went over to the refrigerator and opened it.

"Don't stand with the door open too long, Amanda, you're letting out the cold air, you know." Mrs. Kirkland sounded anxious. Amanda, staring at the chill contents of the shelves, did not answer.

At home, the refrigerator was full of things Amanda might want. Her mother kept treats for her in the kitchen: Oreos, and sodas, and ice cream bars in the freezer. Amanda was allowed to have one ice cream bar in the morning before her mother got up. Often she cheated and had two, hiding the stick and the wrapper of the first under the bedskirt. At Emma's, in spite of the fuss Emma made about good food, there was nothing good to eat in the refrigerator. There were no cookies, no sodas, no ice cream. There was nothing sweet. And if Amanda asked why she didn't buy snacks, Emma's face would get that I'm-better-than-you look. Her voice would get light and hard, and she would say that sweets weren't good for you, and that's why she didn't buy them. Then she would offer Amanda a cold green apple, which Amanda hated.

Amanda shut the refrigerator door. There was nothing there for her either—nothing delicious, nothing comforting.

The swinging door opened and Emma appeared.

"Hello, Mum," she said cheerfully. Then her voice changed, just slightly, into a harder, higher tone. "Good morning, Amanda! I didn't know you were up."

Emma smiled, first at her mother, then at Amanda. Amanda watched her warily. Emma came over to her by the refrigerator.

"Where's Tess?" she asked.

Amanda shrugged her shoulders.

"Still asleep?" Emma asked, and when Amanda nodded she said, "Good." Emma leaned over and lowered her voice. "Now, Amanda, what about that jersey you're wearing? Didn't you bring your pajama top? I thought we'd talked about that already, not wearing clothes to bed." Smiling, she looked at Amanda, who did not answer. Peter came into the kitchen behind her. He was dressed for the day in jeans and a polo shirt.

"Well, hello, lovey," he said to Amanda. "You're up early." He smiled at her. He looked at Mrs. Kirkland. "Good morning, Aline."

"Oh, good morning, Peter," said Mrs. Kirkland. "Isn't this awful, here I am in my bathrobe. I get so used to being alone, you know, I'm just not used to visitors." She smiled at him shyly, lifting her shoulders.

"Why don't you run up and get dressed, too, Amanda?" Emma said. "Remember to brush your teeth. And make your bed if Tess is awake." She stood up and patted Amanda on the head as though she were a show animal.

At home Amanda never had to make her bed. When Maeve had been there, she had made it. Now, during the week, Maria did. On weekends it stayed unmade all day. If her mother saw it unmade, she would frown and say, "Your room looks like the glacier stopped here," but then she would forget about it. The bed didn't really matter.

With Emma things were different. Emma smiled at Amanda all the time, but not the way Maeve had smiled at her, and not the way Emma smiled at Tess. Emma smiled at Amanda as though they were in a play, and the smile was for the audience.

Amanda always forgot about making her bed when she was at Emma's. She didn't care about remembering, it was stupid. She stood leaning against the counter, sliding one finger back and forth along the chrome edge. She watched Emma and did not answer.

"Oh, dear," said Mrs. Kirkland brightly. She looked around, smiling, at them all.

"Amanda?" said Emma. Her voice was a little louder, now. She was inviting Peter to listen.

"Amanda," said Peter, meaningfully. Amanda said nothing. She looked down at her hand, then looked up at her father. He and Emma were both staring at her, their faces were turning hard.

"Amanda?" her father said again. His voice was now angry.

"What?" Amanda said. She raised her eyebrows, aloof, indifferent.

"Did you hear what I said?" he asked. "Did you hear what I said?"

Amanda ducked her head and did not answer.

"Now, wait," said Emma, in a calming voice. Amanda could hear that she was now trying to undo what she had started. "Amanda, let's not make this into a big deal. Just run upstairs, get dressed and make your bed." There was a pause. Amanda did not look up or speak, but Emma, instead of noticing, deliberately turned her back on Amanda. She began pulling pots out of the cupboard. "Off you go," she said, her back still turned. Mrs. Kirkland smiled at Amanda, raising her eyebrows and blinking.

Amanda drew herself slowly upright. Her father was still standing angrily in front of her. Ignoring him, Amanda turned.

"Let's go up together, Amanda," said Mrs. Kirkland, standing up. Amanda didn't answer, and Mrs. Kirkland raised her eyebrows kindly and said, "Anyway, I'm going up. Why don't you come with me?" She left the room.

Amanda walked behind her, sauntering. As Mrs. Kirkland climbed the stairs. Amanda hung back. From out in the hall, she heard her father in the kitchen. His voice was low and tense, and Amanda stopped, listening.

"Don't give me that look," Peter said. "She drives me crazy too."

"She doesn't want to be here," Emma said. "Why do you make her come to you every weekend?"

"I want her," Peter said stubbornly. "She's my daughter."

When Amanda heard her father say that, "I want her," she felt a strange painful jump in her chest.

"You're making her miserable," Emma said.

"Thank you," Peter said. He gave a short horrible laugh.

There was a silence, and then Peter asked, "Do you think *you're* making her happy?"

Right away, as though she'd been waiting for this, Emma said, "Do you think she's making me happy?"

"She's a child, Emma," Peter answered, his voice angry and loud. "You are a grown-up."

"And you are a bully," Emma said. "You shouldn't do this to her."

"I'll decide what I should do," Peter said. There was a pause, and then he said, "I wish you loved her."

Amanda waited, holding her breath, but Emma did not answer. There was no more talking. Amanda heard more pots banging, she heard the cupboard door slammed, and then she heard water running at the sink. No one spoke, and finally Amanda turned and went on, very quietly.

She climbed the stairs and opened the door to her room. Tess was still asleep. Amanda walked in and sat down, harder than necessary, on Tess's bed. Tess lay on her side without moving, her head tucked into her pillow, her hands spread open, one palm up, one down. She breathed without making any sound at all.

Experimentally, Amanda rose slightly and sat down again, slightly harder than before, rocking the mattress. Tess frowned. Her fingers clenched, then spread. She relaxed into sleep once more. Amanda drew closer. She put her hands on either side of Tess's face and leaned over it. She stared down at Tess's soft open mouth, her closed eyes, the bluish veins beneath the skin. Tess was a baby, really, thought Amanda. She put her hand out; it hovered over Tess's face. It descended, directly over the nose; delicately she pinched shut Tess's nostrils.

Tess frowned and shook her head. She opened her mouth to breathe, then opened her eyes. She saw Amanda and frowned more, her mouth tightening angrily.

"Amanda, you're not supposed to wake me up," she said, peremptory.

"I didn't," said Amanda, cool and scornful. Her hand was back at her side. "I was just sitting here and you woke up. I was just waiting to see if you would. Your mom is downstairs already."

Tess sat up quickly, blinking, trying to catch up with the day. Amanda stood and drifted toward the door.

"Where are you going?" asked Tess, anxious.

"To the bathroom," said Amanda, indifferent. She turned away.

"Wait," said Tess, scrambling herself out of bed. "Can I come with you?"

"You can't. You have to make your bed first," said Amanda, without looking back.

"No, I don't," Tess answered. "I'm not going to." She pattered barefoot out into the hall after Amanda. Amanda, moving swiftly, went into the bathroom and shut the door just as Tess arrived. Tess knocked. Inside was silence, irresistible.

"Amanda!" said Tess.

Silence. Tess knocked again, urgently.

"Amanda!" she said, her voice rising.

Amanda heard the rising voice. Emma would hear it if she weren't careful. She stepped closer to the door.

"What?" she asked, her voice low.

"Can I come in?" Tess asked, her own voice lowered in response.

"What's the password?" asked Amanda.

There was silence.

"You can't come in without the password." Amanda moved audibly away from the door.

"Amanda!" Tess said loudly, frustration in her voice. "I don't know the password. Let me in!"

Amanda moved quickly back to the door. "Okay," she said. "Listen, Tess. Put your head down next to the door." She put her own next to the other side. "Can you hear me?" Amanda was whispering.

"Yes," Tess whispered back.

"Okay. Now, listen," Amanda said. "The password is"—she paused—"*caramba.*" She said the word with a rolled *r,* making it foreign and exotic.

"Caramba," said Tess obediently, her *r* hard.

There was no response.

Tess, anxious, repeated the word, louder. "Caramba!"

There was still no sign from inside the door, where Amanda stood listening.

"*Caramba,*" screamed Tess, the word filling her throat. She was desperate.

Without a word Amanda opened the door, and Tess stepped quickly inside. Amanda closed the door behind her. Tess stood waiting, her hands docilely behind her back. She watched Amanda, eager, worshipful.

"Okay. Now," said Amanda slowly, sternly, "this is the game."

16

Amanda pushed opened the door to her mother's bedroom and stepped inside. She wore her school uniform: the green plaid jumper with dropped waist and box pleats; the long-sleeved, round-collared white blouse, the green kneesocks. Everything but shoes was regulation. Amanda, who was thirteen, and all her friends wore a certain kind of brown lace-ups, with a dull matte finish that was unpolishable. The shoes were made of thick leather, with heavy metal eyelets. They were meant to support growing arches—that was what the box said—but this intention was entirely subverted by the way Amanda and her friends wore them, with the shoelaces untied, carefully loosened into a series of useless loops. The shoes slapped noisily against the floor at every step.

Caroline's room was dim and quiet; the morning light was sifting in around the shades. Caroline was always in bed when Amanda left for school.

Amanda spoke from the doorway. "Bye, Mom, I'm leaving." Her voice was loud, an announcement, not the beginning of a conversation.

Across the room, Caroline's head rose from the pillows.

"Oh," she said fuzzily. "You are?"

"Yeah," said Amanda, still loud. She came closer, dragging her untied shoes on the rug.

"Oh," Caroline said again. "What time is it?" She squinted at her bedside clock. "Oh, of course you are." Her voice turned brisker. "Come give me a kiss."

Amanda bent over quickly to kiss her mother. She was careful about this: sometimes Caroline sniffed her breath, and asked if Amanda had brushed her teeth. Today Caroline only said, "Did you have something for breakfast?"

"Yes," said Amanda, who had not.

"I'll see you this afternoon," Caroline said, then remembered. "Or no I won't. I'll see you later. Bye-bye, sweetie." Her mother said *sweetie* to all her friends, even people she hardly knew, and in just the same tone that she used to Amanda.

"Okay," Amanda said. "Can I have some money?"

"Didn't I just give you some?" Caroline said.

"No. That was last week."

"What do you need it for?"

"We want to go to the movies."

There was a pause, and then Caroline said, "In my purse." She lifted her head up from the pillow and pointed. Her purse was on the desk chair.

"Thanks," Amanda said. She crossed the room to the purse and opened Caroline's smooth black leather wallet. It was bulging, and she took out a twenty, folding it quickly into her hand. "Okay, bye. Thanks," she said again, and waved.

"You're welcome," Caroline said, sounding irritated. She dropped her head back onto the pillow.

Amanda slid out of the room, closing the door. She went rapidly down the hall, grabbed her jacket and book bag from the chair in the front hall and left the apartment at once, so that her mother would not think of something and call her back.

Out in the hall she put on her blue-jean jacket and slung her heavy canvas book bag over her shoulder, hoisting it up so that its weight hit her in the right spot. She pushed the elevator button. Now she was free, the rest of the day belonged to her.

When Amanda came home in the afternoon, the apartment would be empty. Caroline got up late and spent the morning at home, most of it on the telephone. She went out to lunch with friends. Four afternoons a week, she worked at Sotheby's, the auction house, where she arranged their flowers. It was a big job. She did all the arrangements in the exhibition galleries, the auction rooms, the boardrooms and the executive offices. When Caroline had first started doing this, when Amanda was little, Amanda would tell people that her mother worked at Sotheby's. Their faces always brightened at the name. "Sotheby's, how interesting," people said. "Your mother must be very smart. What does she do there?" When Amanda told them that her mother arranged flowers, the faces changed. People nodded, and what they said next was about something else. Now Amanda didn't say where her mother worked unless she had to.

Downstairs in the lobby, Amanda said good morning to the new doorman. The old doorman, Tommy, had retired. Tommy had a narrow rocky face and an Irish accent. He had told her rhymes, taking her up and down in the elevator. *Did you hear about the old woman,* he would ask her. *Oh, there was an old woman who lived in a shoe,* he would say as the elevator rose. Tommy's accent reminded her of Maeve's, though it was not the same. But now he was gone, and the new doorman barely spoke. He was named Alberto, but he wanted to be called Albert. He had black hair, black eyes and a Spanish accent.

"Good morneen," Alberto said. He was caramel colored, small and brisk, very formal. He pushed the door open for Amanda, looking past her.

"Thanks, Albert," Amanda said, and stepped out onto the sidewalk.

Outside, the early light slanted along the street, and the air was chill and fresh. It was the first week of December, and the sun was pale and colorless. Amanda walked over to Madison and then north toward school. She walked quickly, the air cold against her bare thighs. Her unlined denim jacket was little help: the cold air funneled down her chest and sifted chillingly up her arms from her loose cuffs. She went into the coffee shop on the corner, grateful for the warmth. The shop was full of people, of the sharp smell of coffee and the sizzle of frying breakfasts. The tall silvery coffee machines glowed, steaming. People sat on stools, leaning elbows on the counter; the thin, dark-skinned waiter listened to the orders and said nothing. He wore a white uniform and moved fast.

Amanda ordered coffee to go. Back out on the sidewalk, she held the cup, in its small brown bag, in both hands. She could feel the warmth spreading into her palms, her cold fingers. She walked slowly, to keep from spilling. At the corner of Ninetieth she turned toward Fifth. Set grandly back from the street was the big Carnegie mansion that was now the Cooper-Hewitt Museum. Amanda sat down on the low stone wall that surrounded it, leaning against the iron railing. She took out the cup and lifted its plastic lid. She bent her head to the cup's warmth, its smell. A tiny cloud of steam rose from the coffee, and Amanda squinted against it as she took her first sip. The stone wall was warm, and the pale winter sun fell across her face.

Down the street Courtney Miller appeared, walking fast. Courtney was Amanda's best friend. She had long limp blond hair, blue eyes and colorless eyelashes. She was often in trouble, and Caroline did not like her. She wished Amanda would find a more suitable friend.

Courtney's book bag hung heavily from one elbow, banging against her leg with each step. In her other hand she held a take-out bag. She stopped in front of Amanda.

"Hey," she said.

"Hey," said Amanda, moving over. Courtney sat down beside her. Concrete pillars rose at intervals from the stone walls, and the girls each leaned into a corner made from the railings and the pillars, as into the corner of a sofa. Courtney took the plastic lid from her coffee.

"What's up?" said Amanda.

"Not much," said Courtney. They sat in silence, taking noisy sips of the hot coffee. "I had another fight with my mom last night," Courtney said. She leaned down and pulled at her sock.

"What happened?" Amanda asked.

"Same as always. She pisses me off," Courtney said. She leaned back, facing Amanda, and set one foot up on the stone wall.

"Now, now," said Amanda in a teachery voice, and they both laughed. "But she's still going to let you go to the dance," Amanda added, to make sure.

"Oh, yeah," said Courtney. "*Ob*viously. No, this was my mouth. And she uses worse language than I do, which she knows perfectly well." Courtney shook her head. "Last time they had a fight I heard her yelling at my dad in the middle of the night. *You asshole, you asshole!* And now, to me, she goes"—Courtney dropped her voice to imitate her mother— " 'Courtney, I really do not want to hear you using that language,' because she heard me say *shit* on the phone. I just can't believe her."

"Just don't get grounded," Amanda said. "If you're not going I'm not."

The Cosmopolitan Ball was held at the Palm Club, in late December. Invitations were sent to girls at the age of fourteen, and to boys at fifteen. Courtney had a late birthday, and was nearly a year older than her classmates. She was fourteen, and had received her invitation as a matter of course. Amanda was still thirteen, but she had talked Caroline into getting her on the list. Caroline had called a friend who was on the committee, and Amanda had already received the thick white envelope, the heavy engraved invitation.

"I'm going," said Courtney. "Don't *you* fight with your mom."

"I never have fights with my mom," Amanda said.

"You're lucky," said Courtney.

"Only with my dad," Amanda said.

"And your stepmother," Courtney added.

Amanda made a face and did not answer. They drank in silence.

"Emma says drinking coffee will stunt your growth," she said, her voice rich with scorn. She looked at Courtney and shook her head. Both girls began to laugh.

Courtney looked at her watch. "Come on," she said. Amanda drank the last of her coffee, noisily, tilting the paper cup high. She drained it and stood up, sticking the empty cup between the iron railings.

"You still coming after school?" Amanda asked as they set off again.

"Yeah. Are we going to do it?"

Amanda raised her eyebrows. "Unless you're going to chicken out."

"Right," Courtney said scornfully, and butted her shoulder against Amanda's.

Inside the school building, the girls clattered down the big front stairs to the upper-school cloakroom. This was in the basement, a low-ceilinged room with a checkerboard linoleum floor. Tall metal lockers lined the walls. Now it was quiet; in the mornings the girls were still muted from sleep, still subdued by the recent weighty presence of their parents. They were still tidy. Glossy hair was drawn sleekly back. Kneesocks were still high, blouses still unwrinkled, personalities still docile.

In the afternoon, when Amanda and Courtney met there after classes, the atmosphere had changed. The girls were now messy, unraveled by the challenges of the day. Hair hung in loose filmy strands, escaped from the tortoiseshell barrettes, the bright elastics of ponytails. Kneesocks had slid down into comfortable piles around ankles. Personalities had emerged. Girls leaned on locker doors, pushed at each other, used their bodies in expansive ways. Voices were raucous, the noise in the low room deafening.

Amanda opened her locker and put on her blue-jean jacket. She jammed her books brutally into her bag. Courtney, her jacket on, her book bag already full, leaned against the next locker. She stared closely at Amanda.

"You nervous?" she asked finally in an undertone. She brushed one hand beneath her hair, resettling it on her back.

Amanda paused, not looking at Courtney. She pretended to shake. She said slowly, "Nervous?"

Both girls laughed. Both girls were nervous. Amanda turned brisk. "Okay," she said, resolute.

She slammed her locker shut with a metal clang, and hiked her book bag up onto her shoulder. "Come on."

They walked down Fifth to Seventy-second Street. On the east side of the avenue, buildings towered toward the sky, orderly and majestic. The grand apartments rose rank upon rank, commanding the great New York views: the pastoral splendor of Central Park. The doormen stood under the crisp awnings, erect, immaculate, militant.

"There's Tina's building," Courtney said, pointing.

"Whoo-pee," Amanda said scathingly. Then, in a high silly voice, she said, "Oh, girls, I'm *so* rich. Aren't you impressed?"

Courtney stared up at the building, squinting. "I went there once. In fifth grade, to her birthday party. She's on the sixteenth floor. There's her window."

"Juuump, Tina, juump!" Amanda called.

They walked, long strided, on the park side of the avenue. Trees leaned over the stone wall, invading the city street, dropping leaves, twigs, seed-pods, onto the stone-paved sidewalk. In the summer the leafy branches formed a cool, damp canopy over the sidewalk. Now bare, the branches made a woody network, a shield from the stinking blasts of cars, and the Fifth Avenue buses. These steamed periodically away from the curb, to lumber southward, ponderous and self-important.

As they neared the park entrance at Seventy-second Street, Amanda slowed.

"Wait," she said, "let's go over it again, what your brother said."

"Okay," said Courtney. "Dirty blue coat. Sneakers. Goatee. Always grinning. His name is Harold."

Amanda nodded, uncertain. This had seemed entirely straightfor-ward when David had told them about it. Then, in the privacy of Court-ney's bedroom, the three of them sitting on the rug, leaning against Courtney's bed, watching MTV, it had seemed exquisitely simple, a world they knew, could handle. Now things were different: now there were only the two of them, standing on the cold sidewalk, surrounded by noise and strangers. Now it seemed perilous, full of variables and risk. Amanda found the plan hard to hold in her head.

"Okay," she said bravely. They walked on. "But what if the blue coat's at the cleaners?"

"What if he's shaved his goatee?"

"What if he's changed his name? What if we go, 'Harold?' and he goes, 'Not anymore'?"

At Seventy-second Street they slowed more, and turned indecisively into the park. Just inside the entrance was a broad curving sidewalk that descended into the park's interior. The walk was lined with benches, and the girls looked covertly at the few people sitting on them.

"What if he's not here today?" Courtney whispered.

"It's his *job*," said Amanda firmly. "He has to be here." She hoped this were true.

They walked, slowly, along the sidewalk. They both saw him at the same time. He was sitting on a bench, leaning back, his legs stretched out in front of him and crossed casually at the ankles. His arms were spread out along the top of the bench. He was grimy, with a small horrible goatee. He wore a gray sweater and jeans. His coat was unbuttoned and flung open. It was dark blue.

"There he is," Courtney said.

"Shhh," Amanda said, urgently.

"We can still *talk*," Courtney whispered. "Just because we've seen him, there isn't an order of *silence* for half a mile."

Amanda didn't answer. They were getting closer, and he had noticed them. He took his arms off the back of the bench, folding them over his chest. He looked straight at the girls.

"Is that a signal?" Courtney whispered.

Amanda didn't answer.

"Are you going to talk to him?" Courtney asked.

"I have the money," Amanda whispered back.

"Are you going to *talk*?" Courtney repeated.

"*Yes*," Amanda whispered angrily. They had almost reached him. The man sat up straighter, watching them boldly. The girls walked up to him, wavered, stopped, and stumbled on past, not looking at each other. Courtney jostled Amanda's shoulder with hers. Then, two strides past him, Amanda swiveled abruptly, as though she had forgotten something. The man was staring at them.

"Harold?" Amanda said.

He nodded. His dark eyes were very bright, his mouth small and thin. There was a pause.

"My brother told me about you," said Amanda. Her voice sounded

strange, as though she were out of breath. "Or, her brother, actually."
There was another pause. Harold stared. "We'd, uh, like to buy some stuff
from you." She swallowed.

Harold smiled at her, his small mouth red and moist above the dust-
colored fur of his goatee.

"Great, great," he said fast, nodding. "Let's just step into my office."
He led the way out onto the grass, into some trees.

Amanda kept her eyes on the ground. Her heart was pounding, she
felt the danger of the open space. She felt suddenly, overwhelmingly, the
presence of the city police force all around her. She was filled with dread,
with certainty. Over and over she heard the approaching buzz of the little
scooter, saw the plastic windshield, the helmet, the implacable black and
white sign: POLICE. She saw the neat black boots of the policeman appearing next to her. She did not look up.

When they reached the trees Harold stopped.

"Okay," he said, "great." He watched the girls too closely. He shook his
head interrogatively, baring his teeth in a tight-edged smile. "What are
you, prep-school girls?" His overcoat was long and dirty, with military
stripes.

Courtney nodded. Amanda, hating him, said nothing.

"Great, great," Harold said, talking fast. "Now, look, this is really great
shit I've got here. I want you to know that Harold always has good stuff.
The best. Tell all your little friends." He turned severely from girl to girl, serious. "Got that? The best."

The girls said nothing. Courtney nodded again, squinting.

"Great," Harold said. "You got the money?" The smile had gone.

In her pocket Amanda's fingers were already curled around the
twenty-dollar bill. Her heart was pounding. David had told them how to
do it, but suddenly it seemed impossible, a roaring chasm lay between her
and the act itself. The tiny folded bill in her hand now was something she
could not lift, in fact she could not move it at all. If she pulled it out it would
fall to the grass, would suddenly be carried off by the wind, the policeman
would appear, the shining blackness of his sunglasses concealing his eyes.
Taking the plastic bag she would fumble, it would open, everything would
spill out, the policeman would arrive as her fingers tightened around it.
This was excruciating, she thought, she would never do this again. Her
chest felt tight, cramped. She looked into Harold's eyes. He was watching
her closely.

Amanda nodded stiffly, and Harold's mouth slid into a smile, a real smile this time. "Great," he said softly.

The apartment was dark and silent. Amanda called out, "Mom?" when they arrived and went down the hall and looked in her mother's bedroom, to be sure. It was empty, the bed unmade.

"It's okay. She'll be gone until six," Amanda reported. "We have almost two hours."

In the kitchen they turned on the lights and dropped their jackets and book bags on the floor. They turned on the small TV on the counter and tuned it to a soap for company. Courtney found a bag of Fritos. Amanda found matches and brought the china ashtray from her mother's room. Her mother was always planning to stop smoking but so far had not. The girls sat down on either side of the small kitchen table.

"Okay," Amanda said, ceremonial.

Apprehensive, Courtney lifted her hair from her shoulders with both hands, shook her head and resettled her hair. Amanda put the plastic bag between them: it was half full of dried weedy-looking bits. Brown seeds drifted through the mass. Courtney put the book of papers on the table, and the two girls began awkwardly to roll cigarettes. The marijuana formed awkward heaps, the seeds stuck to the girls' tongues when they tried to lick the paper's edge, the paper did not meet properly.

"How do you do this? It looked so easy when David did it," said Amanda.

"Shit," said Courtney, starting over.

Finally Amanda made a cigarette, bunched and bulging, that stayed rolled.

"There," she said. She set it down. The girls stared at it.

"I can't believe we really did it," Courtney said.

"I can't either," said Amanda.

They looked at each other. Amanda shook her head.

"I kept hearing policemen," she said.

"I kept thinking *he* was a policeman," said Courtney.

"Don't tell anyone," Amanda said.

"Oh, I'm really going to," Courtney said, rolling her eyes.

"Just don't," said Amanda. "Don't tell your brother." She picked up the lumpy cigarette and put the end gingerly in her mouth. She took it out again and looked at it. "Does it matter which end you put in?" she asked. They both stared at the joint.

"No," Courtney said, uncertain. "I don't think so."

Amanda put it back in her mouth and lit it. She drew in a long hot breath, held it, and handed the joint to Courtney. Courtney drew a deep breath of her own. The two girls stared solemnly at each other, the blue smoke expanding inside their chests.

"I meant to tell you," Amanda whispered, trying to hold on to her breath. "Emma's asked me to go Christmas shopping with her on Friday."

"*Emma?*" Courtney frowned. "Why?"

"I don't know," Amanda said. "Will you come with me?"

"But you hate her."

"I have to go."

Courtney frowned. "But she's awful."

"I know," said Amanda, "but she won't be to you. Please, Courtney," she said, and closed her eyes. "If I have to go alone I'll commit suicide." She opened her eyes again. "If you come it will be fine. She'll be really nice to you. It will be fine, I promise." She put her head down on the table again. "I can't go alone."

Courtney frowned. "I don't know," she said. "What will you do for me?"

"Anything. There is no favor large enough," Amanda said, her head still down on the table. "Plee-ease, Courtney," she said again. "I'll commit suicide, and then you'll have to be friends with Tina."

Courtney shuddered. "Okay," she said. "When do we do it?"

Amanda raised her head from the counter and took a Frito. "Friday," she said again. "She's coming here at five. Mom won't let her up in the elevator, so we'll have to wait in the lobby."

"Why can't she just call upstairs?"

"Mom won't speak to her on the phone. We have to be in the lobby. Tell your mom you're coming."

"She'll be delighted," Courtney said. She frowned earnestly, imitating her mother. " 'I just wish, I just wish you had *more* friends. It's not that I have anything against Amanda. I just wish you had *lots* of friends. Don't you have anyone else to do things with? Not that I have anything against Amanda.' " They both laughed.

" 'I just wish you were more *suitable*,' " Amanda said. " 'As a friend.' " Imitating her mother, she said, " 'I think it's a good idea to have a *circle* of friends. It's more broadening.' " She picked up the joint and drew in another hopeful breath. She handed it to Courtney, who sucked on it hard. They stared at each other.

"Do you feel anything?" Amanda asked.

"I don't think so," said Courtney.

"He's such a nerd," Amanda said suddenly.

"Who?" Courtney said. They spoke in high little gasps, trying to talk without letting the smoke escape.

"Harold," gasped Amanda. They both began to laugh.

"This is really great shit, Amanda," said Courtney, nodding like a marionette. She waved the joint grandly in the air. "Really."

"Great, great," Amanda said, nodding back, frowning. She pressed her lips together tightly. She took another breath, sucking in the hot smoke, holding it inside the hollow of her chest, holding and holding it. Inside, she could feel it expanding, burning mysteriously, enlarging and darkening. At last she coughed, letting a gout escape.

"What are you, prep-school girls? You know, you girls are *so great,*" Courtney said. She had stopped nodding and was now shaking her head goofily from side to side. She closed her eyes and leaned her head back against her chair. She began to laugh, her eyes still shut. "You girls are really something," she said. "What are you, *prep-school* girls?"

They both laughed helplessly.

"What are you, slime?" Amanda said, and they laughed more. "*So* great."

They each took another long gasping breath on the cigarette. Amanda's vision seemed strange, her eyes were beginning to lose focus. She took another belt of smoke and looked around the kitchen. She was surprised to realize that things were changing, in fact they were completely different, all around her. She felt an overwhelming need, both to let everyone know about this—about the hilarious absurdity of the great white refrigerator, humming by itself in the corner, for example—and at the same time to keep all this to herself, to hoard and savor it, as she— alone, she saw now—could do.

But if she tried to tell all this Courtney would not hear her. Courtney was leaning back against the kitchen chair, her eyes closed, nodding to a rhythm only she could hear.

They finished the Fritos, got out the sodas. They gorged. David had told them about the munchies. They sat chewing solemnly, staring straight into each other's strange powerful eyes. They watched a soap, laughing uncontrollably. They had never understood the soaps before, never realized how breathtakingly funny they were. The things they all said to each other were uproariously funny, or amazingly profound, sometimes both at once. They talked and laughed and closed their eyes. Amanda went to sleep in little intermittent dips.

Later, it slowed and stopped. The room returned to its normal proportions. Everything was once again ordinary: the kitchen furniture, the soaps. Their eyes were now well known, familiar, no longer magical. Amanda stood up and slid open the kitchen windows, wide. The cold evening air swept through the room. She stood in the open window, waiting, shivering. Outside it was dark, and the kitchen was full of shadows. The room seemed altered, contaminated by their afternoon there.

"You think we should spray with air freshener?" asked Amanda, uneasy.

"Won't your mom smell it and wonder?" Courtney asked.

"Won't she smell the grass and wonder?"

"Tell her it's room freshener? A new flavor? David says that at boarding school they hold the joint out the window. They pull it inside to take a puff, and then they exhale into socks, so all the smell goes into the socks. Then they put the socks in the wash."

"Yuck," said Amanda.

"I *knew* David's socks always smelled bad," Courtney said.

"They're high," Amanda said, but nothing seemed funny now.

The kitchen had turned bleak and desolate. It was past six, and the afternoon was over. Amanda carried the ashtray to the garbage can and threw in the crumbly ashes, rustling the papers around so the ashes would sift invisibly into the trash.

At the sink, she held the empty ashtray under a heavy stream of hot water. It was her mother's favorite, a white porcelain saucer. In the center was a bouquet of dark pink roses. From this fluttered a few petals, a leaf or two; ribbons trailed from the stems. Amanda hated it, and she hated hearing her mother say it was sweet. Amanda hated hearing her mother say things like that. It made her feel pulled back, against her will, into the time when she, Amanda, would have looked up at her mother's face and agreed with anything her mother said. She would have said that she loved the roses too. She hated that, she could not even bear the thought of it anymore.

A dark smudge of greasy ash stubbornly spread across the center of the ashtray, resisting the hot water. Amanda, one corner of her lip curled up in concentration, scrubbed hard at the stain with the sponge. She felt the ashtray slip in her fingers. She felt it slide from her grasp; grabbed at it, found it, clutched it, and felt it—smooth and slippery—slide again from her fingers. Amanda's fingers closed desperately on themselves and she saw the ashtray hit the white porcelain sink, saw it split, beautifully, into clean narrow shards, as simply and quickly as though it were meant to.

Amanda stood in front of the sink, the cold kitchen behind her. The ashtray lay in pieces, the bouquet with fluttering leaves and streaming ribbons now shattered, indecipherable. The water ran over the jittering shards, steadily, as though all of this were all right, this sudden terrible sense of aftermath and letdown. As though Amanda were meant to stand here like this, the kitchen bleak, and flooded with the evening chill, she herself flooded with failure, with this black black grief suddenly crowding around her, enveloping, everywhere.

17

On Friday, at five o'clock, the girls were not waiting for Emma down in the lobby. They were upstairs in Amanda's room. This still had the blue-and-white-checked curtains and bedskirts that Amanda had had as a child, in the old apartment, when Maeve and her father still lived with them. They had been in the new apartment for five years, but the curtains still drooped below the windowsills. Caroline had stopped saying she was going to have them taken up.

It seemed that there was plenty of money for some things and none at all for others. In the summer, Caroline and Amanda flew to Louisville to visit her parents, and sometimes to a ranch in Wyoming with Caroline's brother and his family. At Christmas they flew down to Barbados, where Caroline's parents rented a house every year. There was money for these trips, which were expensive, and there was money for expensive clothes. But it seemed that there was no money for things like Amanda's curtains. Amanda would not bring it up, because asking for anything that cost money made trouble. Caroline gave Amanda pocket money whenever she asked, but if Amanda asked for an allowance, or for money to be spent on something larger, then Caroline's mouth grew tight.

"Your father should really be paying for this," she would say, and the way she said the words made them sound poisonous. Amanda hated hearing her saying those words in that way. She didn't want to hear Caroline talk about her father at all, she didn't want to think about her father. Hearing Caroline refer to him in that voice made Amanda feel as though she were being whipped. She didn't want to think about her father, or hear his name spoken, or see him, if she could help it.

Amanda didn't care about her curtains being too long. She didn't care what her room looked like. It was always messy. Three days a week Maria made Amanda's bed and picked up her clothes. The other days the room stayed untouched. Amanda liked having the bed made for her, but she wanted the clothes left where they were. She liked knowing where everything was, finding her clothes just as she had left them. She hated order, disorder seemed safer. Caroline rarely said anything about Amanda's untidiness—she seldom made her own bed. But sometimes, for no reason, Caroline came into Amanda's room and flew into a rage. She stood with her hands on her hips and shouted at Amanda, and then Amanda had to pick up everything, every single thing that was visible. What Amanda did was throw all her shoes into the closet, and then stuff everything else into the laundry hamper, everything: clothes, belts, comic books, tapes, magazines.

At five o'clock, when Emma arrived, Amanda and Courtney were sitting on Amanda's bed. They were wearing their school uniforms. Their book bags and jackets lay on the floor, and their shoes were scattered on the needlepoint rug. They each had a can of Coke, and a box of Oreos stood on the bedside table. They were arguing over a model in a magazine. "It is *clearly* Cindy Crawford," Amanda said, leaning forward to look. She knew her models.

Courtney was sitting cross-legged at the end of the bed. She was unconvinced. "I don't think so," she said. "Look at the nose. That's not how Cindy Crawford's nose goes. It goes like this." Courtney drew a line in the air.

"You know nothing at all about it," said Amanda loftily. "Her nose goes like this." She drew a different line in the air.

"No, it's like this," said Courtney, redrawing her own line.

"Like this," Amanda said, pushing at Courtney's hand in midair. Courtney pushed her hand, and they began to laugh. Down the hall the buzzer sounded.

"Oh, my God," Amanda said, sitting up. "It's Emma. We're supposed to be downstairs." She jumped up. The magazine slid to the floor, and she scrabbled wildly for her shoes with her stockinged feet.

"So what?" Courtney said, watching her. "We'll just go downstairs."

But Amanda had already left, her feet stuffed halfway into her shoes, running on tiptoe down the hall to the kitchen. She pushed open the swinging door and saw Caroline already standing there, by the wall telephone that went to the lobby. Caroline had just come in from somewhere, and she was in a dark suit with gold earrings. She stood very straight, holding the phone to her ear. As Amanda pushed into the room Caroline looked at her and opened her fingers. The telephone receiver fell with a hard clatter from the height of her head onto the counter. Caroline walked past her daughter without looking at her.

"It's for you," she said, pushing through the door and walking out.

Amanda picked up the battered phone. She heard a tiny voice repeating, "Hello? Hello?"

Amanda said nothing until Caroline had left the room and the door had swung shut. Then she put the phone to her ear.

"Hello?" she said. She was listening for her mother. She heard no footsteps retreating down the hall; Caroline was standing outside the kitchen door.

"Amanda?" Emma said.

"Yes," said Amanda.

"*What* is going on?" Emma asked her, cross. "Didn't you say you'd be down here at five? The doorman called upstairs and then he handed me the phone, and when I said hello someone dropped it. My eardrum is practically shattered. What's going on?"

"Sorry," said Amanda, watching the swinging door. "I dropped the phone. I'll be right down." She hung up.

Courtney, looking scared, appeared in the doorway, pulling on her jacket.

"Does she know I'm coming?" Courtney asked.

"It'll be okay," Amanda said. She rammed her heel into her shoe. "Come on. She'll love you." She headed back down the hall. "Wait a sec, I'll be right back, I'm getting my jacket," she called back to Courtney. Her mother's bedroom door was closed, and on her way back from her room, holding her jacket, Amanda stopped outside it, listening.

The door was paneled and solid. The white surface was smooth and gleaming. Amanda put her cheek next to the wood. She held her breath. There was no sound at all from inside. After a moment Amanda straightened up and stepped back from the door.

"Mom?" she called, as if from a distance, her voice hurried. "We're leaving now. I'll be back in an hour or so. See you later."

Amanda stood, her head down, frowning, waiting for an answer. She put two fingers into her mouth. Her tongue sought bare exposed nail. She found a tiny half-moon strip and closed on it with her teeth. She tore it off, feeling the soft peel of it curling away. She waited, blinking, wincing, for a moment, longing to leave, hoping to hear nothing. She never said the name Emma to her mother. She had never heard her mother say it.

"Okay, bye," she said loudly. She turned and went noisily on down the hall, her footsteps heavy. Courtney was waiting by the front door, her face subdued.

"Is it okay?" she asked.

Amanda nodded, then shrugged her shoulders: as if she knew.

In the lobby, Emma was standing by the door. Her dark hair was short this year. She wore black pants and a quilted jacket. She had gold hoop earrings in her ears, and she looked irritated.

"Hi, Amanda," Emma said, and kissed her quickly, hard, on the cheek. Amanda did not kiss her back.

"Hi," Amanda said, moving away from her. She nodded at Courtney. "This is my friend Courtney Miller. This is my stepmother," she added.

"Hello, Courtney," Emma said, wheeling to face Courtney at once and smiling. "I'm Emma Chatfield." She shook hands with Courtney. "Nice to see you. Are you at school with Amanda?"

"Yes," Courtney said.

"That's nice," Emma said.

"It's nice to meet you," Courtney said, shy.

Amanda stood without speaking, waiting. Her shoulders were slumped, her face passive and blank.

"So, Amanda," Emma said briskly, "where shall we go first? Who do you need to get presents for, and where would you like to go?"

Amanda gazed at the front door of the lobby. "Well," she said, frowning slightly, "I don't really care where we go." She paused. Finally, when Emma seemed about to speak, Amanda shrugged her shoulders. "Wherever you want."

Emma waited for a moment. "Well," she said, "this trip is for you. I thought we'd go wherever you need to go. Who do you need to buy presents for? Who's still left on your list?"

Amanda stared out the lobby doors as though she were hypnotized by the evening traffic outside. She shook her head slowly. "No one really," she said. "I have something for everyone."

Emma paused for a moment, then said, "Well, okay. You're very organized." She smiled at Courtney. "She's much more organized than I am."

Amanda, still looking out the doorway, said, "Courtney still has shopping to do, though."

Courtney looked stricken; Emma did as well.

Emma looked first at Courtney, then at Amanda.

"Did you invite Courtney to come with us, Amanda?" she asked.

Without speaking, Amanda nodded slowly. Then she said, "Courtney has a lot of shopping to do."

There was a pause.

"Not really," Courtney said anxiously. She shifted her weight from one leg to the other. She slid her hand behind her neck, under her hair and shook it free, down her back.

Emma looked at her and smiled. "Well, how nice," she said. "We'd be glad to have you. Where would you like to go, Courtney?"

Amanda's gaze unlocked from the door and slid to Courtney's face. Courtney stared at Emma like a deer trapped in headlights.

"Who's still on your list to buy presents for?" Emma asked.

"My mom," Courtney offered desperately.

Emma turned to Amanda. "And what about your mom?"

"I already have something."

"Good for you," said Emma, pleasantly. "What did you get her?"

Amanda frowned. "A silk blouse."

"Oh, nice," said Emma. "What color?"

"White," said Amanda.

"That sounds very pretty," Emma said. "Well, what do you think? Shall we just start meandering and stop when we see someplace that looks interesting?"

Courtney looked anxiously at Amanda. Amanda nodded blankly, and they pushed out through the door.

They set off into the darkening evening. It was turning cold; Emma hunched her shoulders. They walked to Lexington and walked south, against a steady tide of people. Men were coming home from work, carrying briefcases, their overcoats buttoned, the collars turned up. Women passed, wearing bright wool coats, scarves at their necks. A cluster of girls approached, Amanda's age, in uniforms and jackets, walking fast and talking loudly; behind them was a cluster of boys, parkas over their blue blazers, talking more loudly, and roughhousing.

Emma and the two girls walked abreast until they passed another group of girls, who walked in a ragged line across the sidewalk. Emma stepped back to let them past, and at that moment Amanda nodded coolly to one of them. The other girl nodded just as coolly back. Amanda pulled Courtney to her side and whispered in her ear. Courtney giggled loudly and said something Emma did not hear. The two girls kept their heads together, walking closely, shoulder to shoulder, just in front of Emma. Emma tried once to catch up and walk abreast again, but the oncoming stream was too strong.

They crossed the next street, with Emma an awkward step behind the girls. Waiting at the red light was a high-wheeled Jeep wagon, shiny black, with dark tinted windows. The windows were closed, but pounding music pulsed through them. The giant wagon throbbed with malevolent energy. Drug dealers, thought Emma, sweeping through the city streets, chemically crazed, impervious to humans. She felt the chill of their nearness. The light changed, and the wagon surged forward, blasting across the avenue. Emma looked at the girls ahead of her: did they see the wagon as part of their world, their ally? When she, Emma, had been a teenager, the dealers were casual—usually friends—and the drugs were benign— grass, a little hash. Now it all seemed terrifying. The drugs themselves were so dangerous, and the dealers were killers. But perhaps Amanda saw it all as simply exciting, her generation's escape, their secret bliss.

Passing a tall black woman in a dark coat, Emma was reminded of Rachel: she missed her. Rachel was now living in Brooklyn, where she worked as a word processor. Emma didn't know exactly what that meant but assumed it was sort of like a secretary. Rachel seemed happy, when she called. They exchanged Christmas cards and occasional telephone calls, but Rachel almost never came into Manhattan anymore. Their friendship, their time of closeness was over. When Rachel did come into New York, it was clear that everything had changed. The person she had come to see, the person she had loved, was gone. Tess was different. She was now shy in front of this tall black woman who smiled at her with such affection.

But right now Emma missed her: Rachel had been the only person who knew what it was like with Amanda, how bad. Loyalty to Peter kept Emma from telling her friends, and she could not tell him. She could not tell her parents, who still disapproved of her divorce, to say nothing of her remarriage and her stepdaughter. She could not tell Francie, who had herself suddenly remarried at City Hall and moved to Minneapolis so both she and her new husband, Carlos, could go into rehab. Now she was a model mother, spending all her evenings at either AA or PTA meetings. She was full of advice on parenting, talky and smug.

But Rachel: Emma hadn't had to tell Rachel about Amanda. Rachel had seen everything. Rachel had heard Amanda's sullen answers, she had whisked the plate away when Amanda refused Emma's food. She had looked at Emma over Amanda's head and slowly shaken her head at Amanda's behavior. Emma had not had to speak a disloyal word, she was wholly understood. Right now, walking down this crowded sidewalk, she wished Rachel were striding purposefully along beside her.

The wind was chill against her face, the night was deepening around her. Emma pulled her scarf closer around her throat. How had things gotten so bad, that she was here, walking along this cold street, struggling against the passersby to keep up with this hostile child who was no kin to her?

If she had known how bad it was going to be, would she have gone through with the second marriage? But she would never have believed how bad it would be. She couldn't have believed it, because she had faith in herself. She'd believed she was a good person, kind and warm. She'd felt sympathy for the child, and she'd believed that she could heal the wound. Love, understanding, sympathy: these were all that was needed, and she could supply them. She had been confident in herself. And she'd been wrong.

After a few blocks she called to Amanda. "Amanda, where shall we start? Do you want to try Chez Vous, at Seventy-sixth? They have some funny things."

Amanda looked back at her. "Funny?"

"Well, you know. Amusing." Emma waited. "If you want. It's right near here. Or would you rather go somewhere else?"

Amanda turned away. "No, that's fine," she called over her shoulder.

Amanda wanted the whole ghastly afternoon, the sham treat, to be over. She wanted to be back at home, lying on her own bed, reading an old comic, alone. She closed her eyes, willing the trip to be over, as though by blotting out the long dark sloping avenue before her, the steady rush of car lights moving south, the grid of traffic lights extending downtown, the pedestrians pushing past them, the chill creeping inside her open jacket, Amanda could blot out her own life, the things that made up her own landscape, endless and excruciating.

Chez Vous was small but brilliant. Its window was filled with light, and piled with luscious, whimsical objects: flowered porcelain, lace-edged pillows, beribboned bath salts, tortoiseshell picture frames. The two girls went inside, Emma behind them. The shop owner stood behind a counter.

"Hello, good evening," she said, smiling at them. The woman was in her fifties, not tall, with dark brown, henna-tinged hair, piled up loosely in a knot. She wore dangling earrings and glasses with big square red frames. She was plump, and her clothes were loose and woven, dull colors. Her smile was professional. "How may I help you?" she asked.

The girls did not answer, turning away at once.

"We're just looking, thank you," said Emma, smiling back at the shop-keeper. She looked down at a little table covered with a starched linen cloth. On it was an old-fashioned bureau set made from fake ivory: a round hand mirror, a soft-bristled hairbrush, a shoehorn. Emma picked up the shoehorn. Hard to imagine, now, a shoe so rigorous in its fit, that you needed this curve to gain access. Hard to imagine hair so smooth, so fine, that these yielding bristles, caramel colored, weak, would take it in charge, would have any effect at all on tangles. Nowadays people were kinder to their feet and crueler to their hair: they wore big soft-soled sneakers, and combed their hair with vicious-looking metal-toothed dog brushes. She set down the shoehorn.

The shop owner moved in on her. "Lovely, isn't it," she said. "And perfect condition."

"Very nice," Emma said, not meeting the woman's eye. She drifted sideways, away. The woman smiled into space.

Across the room Amanda and Courtney stood before a table. Amanda picked up an object and showed it to Courtney, saying something Emma could not hear. Courtney snorted with laughter and the two of them leaned against each other, giggling. The shopkeeper turned to glance at them.

Emma moved away from the bureau set. The shop owner looked back at her, hovering. Emma gave her an oblique undirected smile, and picked up a pottery teapot in the shape of a pumpkin.

"What about this, Amanda?" she said, holding it up.

Amanda and Courtney turned around to look. They stared at it and said nothing.

"Don't you think it's funny? And kind of sweet, I think."

The girls did not answer, and Emma held the teapot up in silence, twisting it in her hand as though she needed to examine every inch. "What about this for your mother, Courtney?" she said finally, brightly, looking at Courtney, smiling.

Courtney nodded politely. "It's nice," she said. Amanda stared at the teapot, her face blank. There was a silence and Courtney added, "I think she has one, though." The girls did not look at each other.

Emma put the teapot down and turned away.

They're teenagers, Emma told herself. It's no fun to shop with grown-ups. It's no fun to be with grown-ups at all. This behavior isn't aimed at me. They just don't want to be with grown-ups. It's their age. She looked at the flowered pot holders, the old-fashioned lace pillows mounded into a luxurious mountain, the fringed hand-woven angora wool throws in jeweled colors.

It was a failure, of course.

Lying awake at two o'clock in the morning, Emma had imagined it differently. She had imagined that, alone, without Peter or Tess, she and Amanda would be able to lay down their weapons, approach each other. Lying in the dark, Emma had pictured the two of them doing what Amanda and Courtney were doing: walking shoulder to shoulder, looking at things and laughing. She had imagined taking Amanda afterward for hot chocolate, the two of them sitting knee to knee in a small steamy coffee shop. She had imagined them, alone, talking, making each other laugh.

"That's a lovely one," said the shop owner loudly, nodding and smiling at what Emma was holding.

Emma looked down. She was standing over a wicker basket full of lacy white pillows, each with a cross-stitched motto. She had been picking absently through the pile. The pillow she held said, in valentine-red letters, I LOVE MY MOM.

18

Their car, a white Volvo station wagon, was one of the last to drive onto the ferry. There were already twenty or thirty other cars on the deck, gleaming in the late afternoon sun, set out in a tight grid like a game of metallic solitaire.

On board, Peter turned the car around and waited. At once a grizzled ferryman advanced on them, his face red-baked from the sun, sea-grimy jeans hanging below a pendulous belly. Standing before the Volvo he raised his hands and began to direct it, like a conductor with a familiar score. His gestures were rapid, practiced: finger twirls, brisk two-handed shunts, the beckoning flap, the palm-upright halt. Peter focused only on the gesturing hands, ignoring the perilous closeness of the gleaming cars on either side. He cut, straightened, rolled forward, back, without once looking around. It was an act of faith. The Volvo, flawlessly conducted, slid neatly backward into its own slot, a perfect ten inches from its neighbors on all sides.

Peter turned off the ignition, yanked on the hand brake and said with finality, "Okay. We're here." He was still in his gray business suit, wrinkled and sweaty from the trip up, but he had unbuttoned the collar of his crumpled shirt, taken off his striped silk tie and folded it into his breast pocket.

His voice was filled with relief, and he raised his arms and stretched, as far as he could in the cramped space, though they were not really any-where yet. They were only parked on the deck of the ferry, a forty-minute passage across the sound still ahead of them. But for Peter the real trip was over. The deadening high-speed drone of the highway was behind him. Now, as the little ferry begin to move beneath him, he felt a loosening, a lifting of his heart. The things that furnished his mind—that consumed it—at work, during the week, were gone. He was here, the damp breeze against his skin, heading out to sea.

Peter and Emma had first come to Marten's Island five years earlier. It was a small place, quiet, peaceful, full of families. There were two shops and a post office. Most of the summer people were from New York, and Peter and Emma had first visited friends there, then rented their own house. Two years ago, they had bought a small piece of rising ground, inland but looking out on the ocean. Last winter they had built a modest shingled house. They had come up several times, during the winter and spring, while it was being built, but Amanda had been away at boarding school. She had never seen the house, and she had never spent a whole month with them on the island, in one of their rentals. The year before this she had gone to tennis camp, the year before that they had gone down the Snake River together, and come to Marten's only for a week.

For this first summer, they had rented the new house out during July, to defray the building costs. August was their first whole month in it, and Amanda would be there with them. Emma had left the magazine and was in graduate school. She would be there all the time. Peter would come up on weekends, and stay for the last two weeks, through Labor Day.

Thinking about the new house pleased Peter. He loved so much about it, its simple lines, the bright shingles that would turn soft and various grays. He loved the interior spaces, the tall handsome windows looking out toward the water, the big stone fireplace. He felt exultant, that he was responsible for these spaces, that he had contributed this to the sum of the earth's shelter.

He felt buoyant and hopeful about this month with Amanda. It was true that she had been sulky for several years, but she was an adolescent. They all were like that. The dyed hair, the little row of miniature gold rings in the ear, the unsmiling face, the baggy pants that dragged on the sidewalk, those frightening black boots: they were all fads. They were required to look like this.

He remembered the girls of his adolescence: then the look was ethereal, great spills of shining hair, hanging down bare backs, that English model with those huge wistful eyes, endless legs. Elvira Madigan: virginal and flowerlike, that was what they had been like, or trying to be. Tender glistening mouths, dewy yearning eyes, His girlfriend, Annette Stevenson, had ironed her hair to make it flat and lustrous. He'd seen her do it, in her family's laundry room, kneeling on the linoleum, her ear pressed against the edge of the ironing board, her eyes screwed anxiously shut as she pressed the iron dangerously close to her skull. She brushed her hair out then, and it was straight. But afterward, at Singing Beach, where they sat around a fire and smoked dope, her long brown hair did just what it always did: turned soft and fuzzy in the damp air, growing a fine misty halo around her thin face.

Amanda right now was not thin, she had put on weight at boarding school. She wasn't fat, but she moved heavily, sluggish and reluctant. Peter hoped that this month would be a release for her, a chance to get away from whatever kept her so unhappy, so unwilling to move. The year at boarding school might have begun that process, he thought, made her not quite so solipsistic, opened her eyes a bit to the world. He wanted for her to unclench herself, release her good mind, to give up being so angry, so withdrawn, so stuck in that closed hostile room. He thought that this summer could be the beginning of that, he felt sure of it.

There had been some cautiously optimistic comments from her teachers. It was too bad that she had dropped field hockey, as she had dropped so many things, but field hockey itself was not so important. And her art teacher said she had made some very provocative comments. He was sure that this was the beginning, that Amanda was starting to blossom. He wanted her to unfurl her fragile petals, to turn toward the light, to turn toward him. He longed for her to turn to him.

The house would make a difference to her. He had told her all about it, he had showed her the plans, he had sent her photographs of it during the building. He had explained her room to her. In New York, when Amanda spent the night with them, which was seldom, she shared Tess's room. Here she would have her own pretty room, which Emma had done up for her carefully. The house would be a place that they all shared. There were other kids her age; she would make friends, have her own world here. He saw her riding her bike around the island with the others, part of a big swooping crowd, wheeling along the narrow roads in the sun.

He and Emma had tried to think of everything to make it happy for her. The main thing was a teenage tennis clinic at the club, three mornings a week. "All the kids her age will be in that," Emma said. "Once she's in that she'll meet everyone. And from then on it will be easy, she'll be part of everything. And I'm going to go on excursions with the girls. I'm going to take them on separate outings, alone, on different days. We'll find things to do." She smiled. Emma seemed so eager about this, so certain, so full of anticipation. And she had showed him with such pride the room she had prepared for Amanda—the flowered bedspreads, the white curtains, the bright rugs.

"It's pretty, don't you think?" she said shyly, standing in the doorway. "I hope she'll like it. I tried to make it more grown-up than Tess's."

Emma had cut her hair differently that summer, with heavy bangs. In back it was very short, like a boy's. She looked like a teenager, with her cropped hair, and wearing clogs, khaki shorts and a T-shirt. Her tanned legs were slightly bowed, and she stood with her hands in her pockets, her feet set neatly together like a good child's. Peter had been touched by her shyness, her eagerness. He hoped Amanda realized how much Emma was doing for her. He put his arm around Emma, fervently. Please, he thought, please.

"Ow," Emma said.

"Sorry," he said. "I'm thinking how much she'll love it." Amanda would love it, he thought, he would make her love it.

Now Peter and Emma began to shift in the front seat, unbuckling, collecting themselves for the passage. Amanda, behind them, was already collected. As Peter turned off the engine she was sliding across the backseat, and as he set the brake she was opening the door as far as it would go, nudging against the glossy curve of the gray Mercedes next to them. She slid through the narrow opening, not looking back, and pushed the door shut behind her, or at least tried to. A strong uneven resistance made her turn: Tess's face was poised in the doorway, tense, pleading.

The two girls had barely seen each other that year. Tess was still living at home in New York, but Amanda had moved on to a new world. On the drive up that afternoon they had sat in the backseat together, as they had always done, but had barely spoken. As soon as they were under way Amanda opened her knapsack and took out her new Walkman. She untangled the cords and put the metal arc over the top of her head. Leaning back against the seat, she settled the speaker pads over her ears with relief: she could hardly wait for the sound to seal her off from the world. Tess watched respectfully.

Emma turned around, leaning over the back of the seat with a book in her hand. She spoke, smiling; Amanda could not hear the words but knew she was offering to read aloud. Emma always did this in the car; they had gone through all of the Madeleine L'Engle trilogy on long trips, with Peter listening too, at the wheel. Amanda wondered what book Emma was now holding—what book she thought was appropriate for a fifteen-year-old, an adult. It didn't matter. Amanda leaned back, the music sealing her off against the world. She was safe.

Emma waited, smiling, for an answer. Amanda stared at her, frowning slightly, as though Emma were speaking gibberish. Tess, her face unhappy, answered. Amanda didn't hear what Tess said, but Emma's face changed. She turned around and closed the book.

Amanda leaned further back and turned the sound up. She closed her eyes: the music rose, bold and intimate, inside her head. She felt as though the music itself were a room she had entered, full of dark pounding motion, dangerous and metallic, a demonic machine shop in full swing. She imagined herself standing inside this wild dark room, standing right in front of Sting, watching him as he sang, his wild hair, his urgent eyes, his electrifying movements.

During the whole trip Amanda sat still, remote and absorbed, the vibrant music deep in her head. Tess sat silent beside her, staring at the roadside rushing past. Amanda said nothing to Tess, she no longer had anything to say to her. She felt changed, adult.

Now, her hand still on the car door, Amanda looked briefly at Tess's face, poised urgently in the opening. She could see what Tess wanted—to be partners again—but the gap between fifteen and eleven was too great. Amanda turned away, not bothering to speak. Tess, uninvited but not prohibited, scrambled after her. Behind them Emma called, "See you upstairs!"

Neither girl answered. Amanda pretended that Emma was calling Tess. Tess pretended she hadn't heard.

The girls threaded their way across the deck, through the maze of tightly packed cars, clambering awkwardly over the nearly touching bumpers. By the time they reached the stern rail, the ferry was under way. In the time it had taken them to park, to climb out of their car and make their way to the rail, everything in the world had changed.

When they had driven onto the ferry, the deck had seemed only an extension of the dusty landing. Not even a mild defining bump had marked the frontier between land and sea. But now the ferry was revealing its true nature. Without even a preliminary lurch it had begun, disconcertingly, to move. Slow, calm, the ferry's motion was so majestic that it seemed at first as though the dock itself might have quietly disengaged and begun a retreat from the stationary boat. But now it was clear: the ferry was under way, setting out for Marten's Island, eight miles offshore.

Already a widening stretch of gray-green water lay between the ferry's broad stern and the dock. On land, figures, so recently large and important—the ferryman among them—were becoming miniature and insignificant. Already, the whole center of things, the vivid, immediate stage of the world had shifted to here—seagoing, transient, unstable—instead of there, where it had just been—landbound, fixed, known.

The girls leaned in silence against the rail as the ferry passed the shabby factories, the low rooflines of abandoned warehouses. At the river's mouth the ferry skirted the government submarine works, its nuclear secrets submerged in the cold shifting waters, between huge metal stanchions. Then the land gave way altogether, and the ferry headed out into the open sky and expansive reach of Long Island Sound. To the west, the sun was lowering behind a dark mass of clouds, their steamy centers truculent, muscular, their scalloped edges light-shot.

Amanda rested her forearms along the metal rail, her weight on one hip, the opposing knee cocked. Beside her, Tess, inches shorter, strained upward to strike the same casual pose, glancing sideways at Amanda for comparison, carefully setting her arms along the rail like Amanda's, cocking the same knee. Noticing, Amanda irritably shifted to the other knee. Silently, frowning steadily out to sea, Tess did the same.

Amanda turned to her. "Tess," she said, in reproof.

"*What?*" Tess widened her eyes, disclaiming, disingenuous.

But Amanda only shook her head, scornful. It didn't matter what Tess did, or how she stood: Tess was eleven years old. She looked it. She still wore the clothes Emma chose for her—bright-colored jerseys, well-washed jeans, clean sneakers. She had Emma's mournful slanted eyes, her pointed chin. Her glossy honey-colored child's hair was in two neat ponytails. Tess looked tended, glowing, like someone's beloved child.

Amanda did not. She wore blue jeans, faded and baggy, a wide fraying hole across each knee. Her black T-shirt was worn to a grayish sheen, partly covered by a thin black sweater, buttoned halfway down. Her black shoes were thick soled and clumsy. Even her hair was now dyed black, glintless matte, with a pale green streak along one temple. She wore it short and messy, tucked behind her ears.

Standing next to Tess, Amanda could feel the pull from her, her mute request, a plea for Amanda to return to the life they had shared. It was not possible. For Amanda, all that was now blurred and unimportant, like someone else's dream. She could hardly believe her memories of the things they had done with such intensity, the complicated games they had created. Remembering them now made Amanda cringe. It was hardly credible, and she rejected it. All that was like the time before she was born.

Amanda stared out at the retreating shoreline and the darkening afternoon. The shore was now no longer a real place but an abstraction, a somber band on the horizon. She felt hope ebb, her heart slowly sinking, her spirits darkening with the afternoon. Amanda had not wanted to leave the mainland. It would be a long month before she was permitted to make this trip back across the water, to return to her own real life. She was a captive here, on this boat, on her way to an unknown place. At school she had been wholly in charge of herself, and in the city, with her mother, she was independent. Caroline seldom asked where she was going, or gave her a curfew. She was on her own now, but no one had asked her about this month with her father, no one had asked if she wanted to go to his new house on Marten's Island. She resented being told by her parents she was going, she resented this involuntary visit, this exile. She was being treated like a child, forced back into an earlier part of her life. She felt now infinitely remote from that life, from her father and from Emma. She felt light-years away from Tess. She resented the idea that she and Tess were peers, playmates, She turned on Tess.

"So," Amanda said, her voice languid, unkind. "What's it like, at Marten's? Do you like it there?"

Wary, Tess nodded, shrugging her shoulders. She was used to coming here. Marten's was where she was. It had not occurred to her to wonder if she liked it.

"What do you *do* all day?" Amanda sounded challenging, derisive.

Tess shrugged again. "I don't know," she said, guarded. "Bike. Go to the beach."

The beach: under no circumstances would Amanda go to the beach. It meant revealing her body, and she would not do that. Amanda hated her body. She never undressed near a mirror. Glimpsing herself naked was excruciating, she hated every angle of herself. She felt as though she were under a terrible curse, trapped in an alien form.

"What else?" asked Amanda.

"Well, tennis," said Tess, casting about.

"Tennis," said Amanda. "Clinic?"

Tess nodded.

Amanda squinted out at the Sound. "Clinics," she said. She closed her eyes. Clinics were almost worse than the beach. The jaunty little pleated white skirt that showed off your white thighs, and the heavy boatlike tennis shoes, and the little white socklets. Worse than the clothes was being there, in the clinic itself. Standing in the full blast of the midday sun, the heat all around you, bearing down on your head, radiating up from the gritty gray-green court. You stood at the back of the court, waiting in line for your turn, staring at the pro but bored and stunned by the sun, so that when your turn finally came you didn't notice. "*Next! Let's go!* Amanda, that's you! Let's go, now!" The pro bawled out your name, and you made a clumsy scramble across the court, up to the net as the yellow ball floated toward you in a low, insulting curve. You rushed at it, your racquet stretched out as you tried to swing, though you were too late for that, you simply lunged and you heard, as you struggled to swing anyway, the pro's voice, "*Punch*, don't swing, Amanda! Remember what I've been telling you. Don't swing, *punch.*" But it was too late, you had already swung, and you were off balance, so you hit the ball on the rim of your racquet, and it bounced into the net and then rolled into the court so that you nearly tripped on it as you moved off.

"Better," called the pro shamelessly, "much better, Amanda." You turned and jogged off; once out of the alley you slowed, carrying your racquet head-down and tapping it with your foot, kicking it, actually, with every step you took. You returned to the back of the court, where you waited, sweating, enervated, for your next turn.

Tess watched Amanda's face intently. "I *hate* clinics," she offered.

"You do not," Amanda said, scornful.

Tess nodded energetically, but Amanda shook her head. Tess was lying. Tess was a goody-goody, who liked everything her mother told her to. Amanda changed the subject.

"How often do you see your dad?" she asked, unfriendly.

Tess's face altered. Wary again, she shrugged her shoulders.

"How often?" repeated Amanda, bullying. "Every weekend? Every month?"

"I don't know," said Tess, twisting her head to one side. "Not every weekend. Sometimes they take me on vacations with them."

"Is it fun?" asked Amanda, curious, not kind.

Tess looked at her and did not answer.

"Is it?" Amanda persisted.

Tess turned her head and looked out at the Sound. "Yes," she said, not turning.

"What's your stepmother like?" Amanda asked.

"Mimi," Tess corrected.

"Mimi," said Amanda. She waited.

Tess shrugged again, not looking at Amanda. "She's pretty."

"Does she like you?" asked Amanda, relentless.

Tess glanced at her but did not answer. She looked out at the water, intent, her eyes narrowed, her mouth set. She now seemed deeply preoccupied, her gaze shutting Amanda out. Amanda could see that the question was one Tess had never considered. She could see that Tess still believed the world was safe for her, everyone in it kind.

"Does she?" Amanda said, pursuing. "Does she like you?"

Frowning, not looking at Amanda, Tess nodded.

Amanda stared at her boldly, but Tess would not look back.

The ferry churned steadily seaward, leaving a broad flattened path of subdued water behind it. Seagulls had gathered in a ragged band as the boat moved out into the sound, and they now made irregular circles over the wake, screaming, accusatory. They drifted slowly over the boat, past the rail, their wings motionless. The girls could see, close up, their polished black heads, the hard curved beaks with their hooked tips, the merciless yellow eyes.

The new house stood on a wooded rise. The driveway made a circle before it, and wooden steps led up to a long deck. The shingles were still golden, the trim bright white.

Peter and Amanda, carrying bags, were the first to climb the back steps. Peter set down his things and put his arm around Amanda.

"So what do you think?" he asked. "Pretty neat, don't you think?"

He was excited: in spite of herself, Amanda smiled.

"Come out with me and see the view." They walked along the side porch to the back. Below, a golf course spread smoothly down a gradual slope, disappearing and reappearing as it made its way to a distant beach, beyond that blue water, now barely visible in the gathering darkness.

"That's the Atlantic down there, not the Sound," he said, proud. Amanda wondered why this made a difference. She could feel her father's pride in everything here: the ocean view, the house he had built, even the ferry ride pleased him. She felt his pride in the whole island. But Amanda felt a stranger here; she would not share in any of this. It all excluded her, she was not part of this life. Peter stood next to her, his hands in his pockets. Smiling, he turned to her.

"I'm so glad you're finally *here*, Nanna," he said, putting his arm around her. Amanda felt suffocated.

"Ow," she said, pulling away.

"Ow," Peter mocked, good-naturedly, "ow, ow, ow." He released her. "Sorry, Nanna. Didn't mean to torture you. It was meant to be a hug." He kissed her on the top of her head.

Amanda didn't move. She hated this, the spotlit glare of his attention, the demand for response. She raised her shoulders slightly and craned her neck, freeing herself from his presence.

"Peter!" called Emma. "Do you have the key?"

She stood by the back door, holding two big white canvas bags. "The key!" she repeated.

"Hold on," said Peter at once, feeling in his pocket.

He hurried off, leaving Amanda alone on the porch. She could see indistinctly the white wicker chairs, pots of white geraniums at the bottom of the broad railing. In the near-dark, Amanda could feel the ocean in the distance, beyond the sloping green mat of the golf course. The air, rising from it, was chill and damp against her face.

Suddenly the house was radiant. Amanda found herself in the dark, invisible. The porch window gave into the living room, clean and new looking. It glowed with bright colors, flowered furniture, framed posters on the wall. On every table were photographs: Amanda wondered who the people in them were. All this was new to her.

Inside she heard the heavy shuffle of her father's feet on the stairs, carrying the biggest suitcases. Outside she heard Tess, slowly mounting the back steps. Amanda walked toward her, along the side porch, and saw her appear in the shaft of light from the screen door. Tess took each step carefully, as though she were on a tightrope. She couldn't see in front of her. Her arms clasped the deep belly of a clay pot; against her face was the palmy foliage of a fern. As she mounted the steps and approached the door her steps quickened, desperate.

"Mum!" she called. "Come get the door!"

"Coming," called Emma from the interior. She sounded rooms away.

"Quick!" shouted Tess, "I can't hold it!"

Struggling for balance, she raised one knee, to support the pot's dead weight, and took one hand away to open the door. With all her weight on one foot, her ankle wavered. Her bare foot swiveled desperately back and forth, reaching for equilibrium. She grabbed for the screen door.

Amanda, coming from the dark behind her, caught at the screen door just as Tess did, pulling it open for her. Tess was leaning forward, bracing herself to pull against the sucking resistance of the door closer. At Amanda's unseen tug from behind, Tess rocked heavily forward. She tried to catch herself and went down hard, saying in a high voice as she fell, "*Amanda!*"

The pot hit the sill squarely, shattering. Big terra-cotta shards scattered across the white tiles. The fern lay among them, its webbing of frail roots exposed, its arched fronds now broken into stiff angles. Mealy clumps of black potting soil clotted on the floor.

As Tess raised her head Emma appeared in the doorway. Tess climbed slowly to her feet, raising her hand to her face. Amanda, still holding the door, could see Tess's face, lit brightly from above. The light bleached all color from her; Tess's skin glowed, white. In that light the sudden scarlet rush looked dark, near-black: down from her nose, down in a wild swift stain over her mouth, down her throat. It was shocking: the fluid brilliance, the unstoppable rush of it.

Tess stepped, wobbling, over the mess of the shattered fern. "Mum," she said, her voice quavering. She began to cry. Her hands were covered. It flowed like liquid shadow, glittering, down her throat. Her wrists were coated by it.

"Tessie," said Emma. She knelt down, "Come and let me clean you off." Her voice was frightened.

Emma leaned over, hugging Tess as she led her back toward the kitchen. Fat red splotches dropped hotly onto the white tiles, marking their passage. Emma did not once look at Amanda, who stood on the porch, still holding the screen door open.

Amanda heard Peter's footsteps as he jogged easily down the stairs. He stopped at the fern.

"What happened?" he asked.

Amanda picked up her suitcase and began to lug it over the whole mess, the pot, the broken fern. "Tess fell," she said.

Peter said nothing, and when she looked up Amanda found his eyes on her.

"How did she fall?" he asked.

"I was behind her. I pulled the door open and she didn't know I was there," said Amanda.

Peter waited, but she said nothing more. "Is she all right?" he asked. His face was closed, his voice not friendly.

"She has a nosebleed," Amanda said. "Emma took her into the kitchen." She began to climb the stairs, dragging her suitcase.

Behind her she felt her father standing. She felt his anger rising toward her, his will pushing at her. He took Tess's side, and Emma's. He blamed everything on Amanda. But she would not yield, she would not apologize. She would not be soft, as he wanted her to. She hated him. Everything that was wrong in her life was his fault. The things he did, the things he said were the things that had ruined her life. Everything was his fault: the school she went to, which she hated, her bad grades, the way her face looked, the small dark apartment where she and her mother now lived, the small dark life she and her mother now had, everything was his fault. Everything, all the dark unhappiness that filled the air around her like mist. It was her father's fault. He was the source of everything. He could never make up for what he had done.

Looking at her father from the top of the stairs, she felt herself close down, seal herself off from him. Peter stood silently at the foot of the stairs, his hands on his hips, his face threatening. Amanda said nothing, and at last he turned and followed Emma and Tess. Amanda waited. She did not know which room was hers, and besides, she wanted to hear what they said. She could hear low voices, but no words. She would be blamed for this. She didn't care.

She set down her suitcase and made her way back down the stairs, and down the short white hallway lined with storage shelves, to the kitchen.

"How did she fall?" Peter asked.

Emma's voice was muted, noncommittal. "I wasn't there."

"What happened, Tess?" Peter asked.

Tess sounded scared, sorry for herself. "I was starting to fall, because of the pot. My arms couldn't carry it anymore. I called for you, and you were too far away. I pulled the door open, and Amanda grabbed the door behind me and I lost my balance."

There was a silence. Amanda stood in the hall, the shelves beside her stacked with lunch hampers, thermoses, paper plates. She could feel Peter and Emma in the next room, consulting each other wordlessly, confirming something, agreeing.

"It wasn't Amanda's fault," she heard Tess say.

No one answered her.

"Mum?" Tess said. "It wasn't Amanda's fault."

But still no one answered.

Tess would be looking up at them intently, her eyes moving from face to face, watching for clues. She would be trying to learn how to read the world. The three of them would be sitting and looking at each other in silence, like a family portrait.

19

Amanda lay on her bed, reading. It was after dinner, a Thursday night, two weeks after their arrival. Peter was in New York. Emma, Amanda and Tess were alone in the house. Amanda was stretched out on the white bedspread with all her clothes on, including her sneakers, which was against the rules.

Amanda did not look up at the knock on the door. "Who is it?"

"Me." Tess peered in. "Can I come in?"

"Okay," Amanda said, "but I'm reading. You can come in but don't go banging around."

"I'm not going to go *banging around*," Tess said, and slipped inside. She closed the door behind her, eyes roving around the room. Amanda ignored her. Tess stepped away from the door, rocking, heel and toe, her feet stiff. She stood in front of Amanda's bureau, staring greedily.

The two girls shared a bathroom, but Amanda kept everything interesting, all her private things—bottles, tubes, jars—in here, on her bureau. Tess glanced at her in the mirror, but Amanda did not look up. Tess began to browse among the cosmetics, delicately picking up each jar. Frowning, she read each label, unscrewed each top and carefully sniffed the contents. She squeezed a tube, receiving a pink viscous curl on her fingertip. Glancing again at Amanda, who was still reading, Tess transferred the curl to the tip of her nose. She regarded herself in the mirror, turning her head from side to side. Her face was smooth, slightly tanned, with pallid freckles along her cheekbones. Her upper lip rose into two small peaks. Her green eyes, like her mother's, slanted down. Tess puckered her mouth self-consciously. Amanda, in the background, looked up. Tess waved ingratiatingly at her.

"Hi," she said.

"Don't," said Amanda.

"What?"

"Don't go through my stuff."

"I'm just *looking* at it," said Tess.

"You're using it."

"Just this. What is it?" She held up the tube.

"It's for my zits," said Amanda.

"Oh," said Tess, respectful. She looked again at her decorated nose in the mirror. "What are zits?"

"Pimples," said Amanda. "You don't have any."

"Oh," said Tess, gratified. She looked at herself again, then back at Amanda. "You don't either."

"I do sometimes," said Amanda. In a falsetto voice she added, "I'm a teenager!"

Tess held up a bottle of pale blue lotion. "What's this?" she asked.

"A kind of mousse," said Amanda. "Don't put it on your nose. It's for after you've washed your hair."

"Just a little," said Tess, dabbing an oozy dot on her nose. "I'm starting a collection here."

Amanda shook her head and went back to her book.

Tess held up a black plastic cylinder. "What's this?"

"Mascara," said Amanda. "It goes on your nose."

When she had finished sampling the cosmetics, Tess wandered over to the bed. She sat down quietly next to Amanda's feet. Amanda did not look up. Tess put her hand out, palm flat, over Amanda's bare calf, not quite touching the skin. She held it there in an experimental way, as though she were testing for warmth. She looked frequently at Amanda, who ignored her. Tess ran her hand, like a small pinkish hovercraft, slowly up and down Amanda's leg. Amanda did not shave her legs, and Tess's palm grazed the furry hair.

"Quit it," said Amanda, without looking up.

"What?" Tess said, innocent.

"Quit what you're doing."

"I'm not doing anything."

"You're touching my leg," Amanda said, looking up.

"I'm not," said Tess. "You can't feel it. I'm only touching the hair, not your leg."

"Don't tell me I can't feel it, I can feel it. Now cut it out." Her voice was fierce.

Tess removed her hand and made a face that Amanda could not see. She sat on her hands and bounced twice on the bed, hard, in protest.

"Quit," said Amanda, not looking up.

Tess stopped. She sat for a moment, restless. She twisted her shoulders violently, then peered at Amanda's magazine.

"What are you reading?"

Amanda held it up: *People.*

"Yuck," Tess said.

"You don't have to read it," said Amanda.

Tess bounced again. She saw the paperback on the bedside table.

"What's that?" she asked.

"Look at it," said Amanda, without raising her head. Tess picked it up.

"What's it about?"

"A murderer."

There was a pause. "Is it good?"

"*Really* good."

Tess examined the cover. "Can I read it?"

Amanda looked up. "You wouldn't like it."

"How do you know?" Tess said.

"You'll get scared."

"No, I won't."

"Yes, you will. You'll get scared and go running into your mom's room in the middle of the night, and I'll get in trouble."

Tess put her hands in her lap and shook her head.

"Yes," said Amanda, reading.

"No," Tess said. "I won't, Amanda. Don't tell me what I'll do."

There was a silence. Amanda turned the page.

"*Amanda!*"

"What?"

"*Don't tell me* I'll get scared."

"Okay, fine, you won't get scared," said Amanda.

There was another pause.

"So," Tess said cautiously, "can I read it?"

Amanda looked up. "Are you going to go running into your mom's room in the middle of the night and get me in trouble?"

Tess shook her head slowly, frowning.

"Okay," said Amanda, looking back at her magazine. "Take it. There's a whole bunch of them on the shelf. They're all scary."

But Tess was suddenly distracted. She leaned toward Amanda.

"Amanda," she said, "are you chewing gum?"

Amanda glanced up, indifferent. "Want some?"

"We're not allowed," said Tess.

"Do you *want* some?" Amanda repeated.

There was a pause. Slowly Tess nodded.

Amanda stood up at once. The gum was in the bureau. She held it out, offering Tess an open pack.

They heard Emma's footsteps coming up the stairs.

"Tess!" Emma called. "Are you ready for bed? I'll come in and read to you, if you're ready."

"I am," said Tess loudly. This was not true; she was still completely dressed. "I'm in Amanda's room. I just have to brush my teeth."

She took a stick of gum from the pack and vanished into the shared bathroom.

When Amanda finished her magazine, she tossed it onto the floor. She lay still for a moment. Tess finished brushing her teeth, and through the wall Amanda heard Emma begin to read. The drone of her voice rose and fell. Tess was too old for this but neither she nor Emma seemed to know it. They would go on interminably; Amanda picked up a paperback and began reading again.

Finally the reading voice stopped, and Emma and Tess began to talk. Their voices were quick and uneven, interrupted often by laughter. Apart from Tess and Emma talking, the house was silent. Amanda could hear their voices, but she could not make out the words through the wall. The voices went on and on, intimate and mysterious. It was as though Amanda were listening to a foreign language, as though Tess and Emma spoke their own private tongue.

Amanda lay on her side, one hand propping up her head. She was reading a Stephen King novel. It was one she had read before; she had read all his books. She would rather read one Stephen King over and over and over, forever, than read, even once, one of the books Emma had left for her. These stood, a bright gaily colored row of hints, in the bookcase near Amanda's bed.

When Amanda had first arrived at the house, Emma, helping her settle in, had made a fuss over these books. "I've chosen these for you, I hope you like them," she'd said. "I know you'll like this one, it's really wonderful. I envy you for not having read it." Emma gave the book a twinkly look, as though she and the books belonged to a wonderful little club, where they all wore pink and hugged each other. Amanda did not want to join Emma's club. Emma gave Amanda books year after year, for Christmas and birthdays. Amanda never read them, she never opened them, she never even read the titles.

Now, through the wall, Amanda could hear a different note in Emma's voice, premonitory. This signaled Emma's departure, the closure of Tess's evening. Emma's voice began to rise slightly. As soon as this happened, Tess's voice became wheedling, and she pleaded for Emma to stay longer.

Amanda heard the final words clearly. "Okay, good night, now, Tessie." It was repeated several times. The voice was louder; Emma was leaving, and was near Tess's door. When Tess's last-minute pleadings were exhausted the door was shut, though not completely. Tess was afraid of the dark, and her room had a crack of light all night. Even so, she had nightmares, and when she was small, used to appear, terrified, in Emma's bed.

Emma's footsteps now sounded briefly in the hall. Amanda tucked one sneakered foot more safely under her ankle and settled herself more deeply into the mattress, as though preparing for a high wind. She heard Emma in her doorway, but did not look up until Emma spoke.

"Amanda? May I come in?"

Emma's voice had changed again. When she talked to Amanda, there was something hard in it. It was like a bird's, shrill, unanswerable. Her face looked different, too: guarded and wary, her queer slanted eyes watchful.

Amanda looked up as though she hadn't noticed Emma's arrival. At Emma's question she raised her eyebrows, as though she could not imagine a reason for Emma to come in her room.

"Sure," Amanda said, her voice indifferent. Amanda had no choice about Emma's coming into her room, night after night, about Emma pretending they were friends.

Emma advanced, smiling stiffly. "So, how are you?" she asked. She was barefoot, in jeans and a dark red turtleneck. The turtleneck hung loose, just grazing the top of her jeans. She wore no belt. Her new haircut showed her ears. She stood in the middle of the room, her bare feet together, her arms folded, her shoulders hunched.

"Fine," said Amanda. She saw Emma's gaze rest briefly on her sneakers, nestled dirtily against the white bedspread. Every night Emma reminded Amanda of the no-shoes-on-beds rule. Every night Amanda ignored it. Tonight she waited, her own gaze locked on Emma's face. She saw Emma's gaze pause, move on. Amanda did not move her feet. Emma smiled at her brightly.

"What are you reading?" Emma asked.

Without speaking, Amanda held up her book for Emma's inspection.

"Stephen King," said Emma.

Amanda did not respond.

"Do you like him?"

"He's my favorite author," said Amanda.

Emma nodded slowly. "What is it you like about him?"

"The violence," said Amanda. "I love violence. And being frightened."

There was a long pause.

"Oh," said Emma. She glanced at the books she had put on Amanda's shelf. "Well."

Amanda waited for her to leave.

"Well," said Emma again, "I just came in to say good night."

"Good night," said Amanda. She smiled for Emma.

Emma did not move. It seemed as though she wanted something else to happen. Amanda stared steadily at her.

"Well," said Emma, and stopped again. She took a breath. "You know, Amanda, if you'd like to have a party or something, have some friends over for dinner—a cookout, or something like that—I'd be glad to do it with you. We could rent a movie, or something." She drifted into silence.

"A party," Amanda repeated. She would never invite anyone here, to her stepmother's house. Finally Amanda made herself smile. "Thanks," she said.

There was a pause. Emma seemed to be waiting for more, but Amanda was finished. At last Emma took a breath.

"Well, I just wanted to let you think about it. Or if you have another idea, we could do that. Something on the beach. Or have a bunch of girls here for the night."

"Thanks," Amanda said.

"I hope you're having a good time here," Emma said. "I hope you like the other kids. I know it's hard to move into a new place at your age."

"It's fine," Amanda said, and waited.

The girls here were blond, lithe, cheerful, with thin thighs. When they smiled, their braces glittered, their smooth straight hair sliding off their shoulders. They had invited Amanda to the beach club for sandwiches. Amanda had refused. She had nothing to say to them, girls in neat bright clothes, girls who still believed that rules were there to protect their world. And the boys were jerks, horsing around goofily on their bikes, yelling. They did not talk to Amanda, none of them had even looked at her. She despised them. The kids here made Amanda feel somber, urban, heavy. They were from a different tribe, one without doubts. They were fools.

She said nothing to Emma.

Emma waited, her arms folded across her chest.

Go, Amanda told her stepmother silently.

"Well," Emma said finally, "you can think about it."

"Okay," said Amanda, forcing another smile.

"Good night, Nanna," Emma said.

Nanna was the nickname her father used. Only he was to use it, and her mother.

Emma bent down to kiss her, putting her hand on Amanda's shoulder. Her touch was light and jittery. Amanda heard the sound of a kiss, in the air by her ear. Emma straightened, her hand still on Amanda's shoulder. She gave Amanda two little pats.

"Sleep tight," Emma said, smiling.

"I will," said Amanda, smiling back. "Good night." Go, she thought, go.

Emma turned to leave, but at the door she stopped. "Shall I open the window for you?" She asked this each night.

Amanda shook her head.

"Do you want the door shut?" Emma now asked.

"I don't care," Amanda said. Go.

Emma smiled at her. "Am I driving you crazy?" she asked.

"No," Amanda said, giving her a vague smile. Yes.

"Okay, well, good night," said Emma. "I'm finally going to go." She was still smiling, as though she and Amanda were having fun together.

"Good night," said Amanda. Two more weeks. Emma turned away, and Amanda raised her eyes. She heard her stepmother go down the hall, into her own room. She heard Emma's door shut.

The house finally silent around her, Amanda took a long breath. She settled herself comfortably against the bed. She still had to wait until

Emma had finished reading and turned out her light, but she would wait in peace. No one would come into her room again. She read on in her novel, absorbed: the terrified woman, the chilling signs of pursuit, the growing horror.

Toward eleven, Amanda heard Emma's footsteps, then the rush of the plumbing. Amanda waited for a moment, then got up quietly. Standing in her doorway, looking down the hall, she watched the strip of light under Emma's door. When it went dark, Amanda turned silently back into her room and closed her door. Her own night had finally begun.

She knelt on the rug beside her bed and slid her arm deep between the box spring and the mattress, between the flowered blanket cover and the white dust ruffle. From this secret interior Amanda withdrew a plastic bag containing a flattened box of Marlboro Lights, a cheap yellow cigarette lighter, a metallic pink ashtray, and another, smaller plastic bag. This was folded over and over on itself, and held her stash, about a dozen limp hand-rolled joints. She smoked these sparingly; they had to last the month.

Amanda now opened her window, though she hated the damp cellary air that crept in from the ocean, and the banging of the dry furry moths against the screen. She had to open it, because of the smoke. She sat on her bed and put on her Walkman, setting the charmed arch of metal over her head as though its deep sound would insulate her from the whole rest of the world. At least she wouldn't hear the moths.

Amanda kicked off her sneakers, set the ashtray down on the bedside table and lit a flattened Marlboro Light. She drew in a long breath of hot smoke and closed her eyes. She felt the burn, rough and delicious against her throat.

Now, alone, Amanda was herself. Around her was silence. Safe in her own room, surrounded by her own music, her own smoke, her own breath, Amanda was living her own life. She leaned against the flowered headboard and blew out the first soothing bloom of smoke, a warm hazy current that drifted intricately, in silence, into the air of her room, like the slow fluid movements at the bottom of the ocean.

Some nights, after the Marlboro, she smoked a joint, or part of one. Some nights she wanted that hot stoked feeling, of being secretly in charge of everything, or at least knowing secretly how funny everything was. Some nights she smoked only the Marlboros, sometimes putting the cigarette to her mouth and pulling that deep invasion inside her, sometimes just sitting with the cigarette burning between her fingers, letting it grow shorter and shorter as she turned the pages of her book. She liked letting the cigarette burn, letting the luxuriant smoke from it move softly through space.

The nights were long, in her father's house. Amanda could not sleep in this house; she did not try. She lay on her bed, smoking and reading, sometimes all night, until the outside light took over from the inside. Sometimes she finished a whole book in one night, the black hours passing unnoticed. Sometimes she listened to tape after tape, the plastic cases littering her bedspread as she moved from one musical world to another. Some nights she only wanted one tape, and played the same music over and over. The music and the night surrounded and sheltered her. She could feel the house silent. She could feel the whole island silent. She could feel the Atlantic Ocean, lapping along its shores, silent. It was four o'clock in the morning, and Amanda was the only person awake, real. She drew her own private smoke into her lungs, deep, and slowly blew it out, a peace.

What she felt was sadness, and she let herself at last sink slowly into it. It was a relief. All during the bright excruciating day, with its jittering talk, its interference, she waited for this moment, at night, when she was alone, surrounded by darkness. Now she could let go, and descend into this deep space she yearned for, this place where she knew she belonged, silent, vast; this deep lake of sadness.

In the morning Emma knocked on her door.

"Eight o'clock."

Amanda did not answer. Her head was still dark and full of smoke, and her brain would not move.

"Amanda?" Emma said. "Time to get up. It's eight o'clock."

Amanda cleared her throat. She had to say something or Emma would come into the room.

"Okay," she said. Her voice was strange in her ears, low, and somehow split.

"Amanda?" Emma said again.

"*Okay*," Amanda called, summoning all her energy.

"See you downstairs," Emma said.

Amanda lay without moving. She had not yet opened her eyes. Her face was plowed deep into the core of her pillow. She had to get up. Her clinic was at nine, and she would have to leave at ten of, on her bike. If she was late Emma would drive her, which she could not risk.

Amanda pulled herself up, her eyes still shut. Her limbs were dead. She still felt stoned, her mind sequestered in another place. She stood unsteadily, keeping her eyes shut against the room, which would now be garishly bright and full of salt air. She took a step, staggering slightly, and cracked her eyes open onto the unkind blare of yellow flower-sprigged wallpaper. She closed them again and groped her way to her bureau. She felt in the top drawer for socks, the heavy tennis underpants. She had no clean socks. She could not remember where anything was: her tennis shoes, her racquet, her skirt. She moved slowly, concentrating. She found things one by one: the skirt on the floor in the closet, under a T-shirt, a pair of dirty socks at the bottom of the wicker laundry hamper. Dressed, Amanda stared at herself in the mirror. There were dark half-moons under her eyes. She brushed her matte black hair briefly and shoved it behind her ears. The idea of water on her face seemed too challenging, and she decided against washing her face or brushing her teeth.

Emma was down in the kitchen, dressed and cheerful. She was on the phone, leaning against the white counter. When she saw Amanda she smiled and blinked at her, then held up one finger to show how much longer she'd be. Amanda stood, waiting.

"Now I have to go," Emma said loudly, her voice warm. "Amanda has just come in and I have to get breakfast into her before she goes to tennis." There was a pause and she smiled again at Amanda, nodding. "Okay," she said. "I'll tell her. Okay, bye."

Emma hung up and turned to Amanda. "Mrs. Cartwright says hi."

Amanda said nothing. Mrs. Cartwright was an old friend of her mother's and father's, who had now become a friend of Emma's. Amanda didn't like hearing her mother's friend talking to Emma. It seemed to her as though Emma were greedily trying to take over everything, not just Amanda's father but as much of his life as she could, including things that were really Caroline's.

"Now, you sit down and I'll bring you what you want," Emma said, and Amanda sat down at the scrubbed pine table. There were three places set, with oval straw mats, folded white napkins and deep blue glasses. The silverware had bamboo-shaped handles. Amanda knew the straw mats: they were from before. Maeve used to use them for Amanda's breakfast. The mats were not Emma's, she had no right to them, thought Amanda. There were other things here, too, that she remembered from before. These things belonged not to Emma but to Amanda's mother. Even the new things, the things that had been bought just for this house, like the bamboo-handled silverware, all these things should really have been Caroline's. Everything in the house should have been Caroline's: everything in this life Peter was leading should have been Caroline's, and Amanda's. It should have been their life. Nothing at all should have been in this house, it should not exist.

"Talley Cartwright is in the clinic with you, isn't she?" Emma asked. She was at the sink, filling the kettle.

"I don't know," Amanda said.

Emma turned to look at her. "You don't know?" She frowned, but Amanda shook her head indifferently. "Well, maybe Talley's a bit younger. But I thought you were the same age. How do they divide you at the clinic, by age or by ability?"

"Age," said Amanda, guessing.

"Well, then," said Emma, "that's why." She began opening cupboards. "What would you like? Toast? Cereal? Grapefruit? I've just got some pink grapefruit for your father. Would you like one of those?"

"I don't like grapefruit," Amanda said. She hated grapefruit. Her mother knew this. Maeve had known it. Peter knew it, and so did Tess.

"Oh, you don't?" Emma's back was turned, she was peering into the refrigerator. "I thought you did."

"I hate it. I've always hated it," said Amanda. The sour smell, the biting taste, the treacherous spurts from the little glistening wedges.

At Amanda's tone, Emma turned to look at her.

"Have you?" Emma said. She closed the refrigerator. Now she talked fast. "I can't keep everyone straight. Peter loves grapefruit, Tess hates strawberries, you hate grapefruit—I can't keep it all in my head."

Amanda said nothing. Emma had no trouble keeping Tess's tastes in her head, or Peter's.

"So, what would you like?" Emma asked. "Toast? Cereal? Yogurt?"

At home, Amanda had whatever she felt like for breakfast. Often she had nothing. Here, Emma made her eat something, and it could never be anything sweet, like doughnuts or cinnamon rolls, which Amanda loved. Also Emma wouldn't let her drink coffee. This was all supposedly for Amanda's good, but if Emma was so concerned about Amanda and her good, why didn't she remember what Amanda liked? Amanda had spent weekends with Emma since she was seven. Emma pretended to be such a great mother, but why did she remember everyone's likes and dislikes except hers? Emma's lapse, her nervous response to it, seemed revealing to Amanda, important. Amanda felt suddenly powerful.

"Amanda? It's twenty of nine. Tell me what you'd like."

"I don't really want anything to eat," said Amanda. "I think I'll just have coffee."

Emma frowned. "Coffee! Don't have coffee, Amanda."

Amanda shrugged and stood up. "Okay, then," she said. "I won't have anything. I'm not hungry. I'll see you later."

"No, wait," Emma said. "You should eat something, especially if you're going to play tennis."

"All I want is coffee," said Amanda.

There was a silence.

"Does your mother let you drink it?" asked Emma.

"I drink it at school," Amanda said, impassive.

"Well," Emma said, "you're awfully young to get in the habit. It's really not good for you."

"Whatever," Amanda said. "I'm not hungry."

She turned to go before Emma could answer. Amanda wanted to be gone from here, really gone, elsewhere. She would have liked to twist a glowing dial and find herself three weeks from now.

"I've got to go or I'll be late. Bye," Amanda said, her voice loud. She picked up her sweatshirt and left the kitchen. She went through the back way, the laundry and the mudroom. Speed was crucial, or Emma would say something, try to stop her.

Amanda got out onto the back deck without stopping, the screen door slammed lightly behind her. She picked up her bike from where it lay on the driveway and swung her leg over the saddle, standing up on the pedals and pushing off hard. She bumped heavily along the driveway, the wheels grinding through the gravel, to the edge of the road. Still no voice from the house. One more push on the pedals and she had left the gravel. Now she was out of the shrubbery, onto the dark smooth paved road. She had made it.

At first the road rose slowly in front of her, and Amanda stood up on the pedals with each push, feeling the bike sway lightly back and forth between her legs. At the top of the little rise the road curved to the right, and Amanda sat down on the saddle. She coasted silently through the long green tunnel: high privet on either side, summer-thick maples overhead. The landscape was summer lush; the fields were full of tall grass, and the trees shimmering with green. The lanes were overgrown, and the houses hidden from the road by trees and hedges. The island was full of small hills, and the roads twisted mildly up and down, revealing brief verdant views at each turn.

Past the little store and the cluster of buildings around it, a few slow cars, past the small open green, and the road became emptier again. Amanda turned onto a smaller lane, then coasted down a brief wooded slope, pedaled fast through an S-turn. She turned off the road into a sandy farm track that led to an open field. There the bike slowed, and Amanda stood again with each push, the sand dragging at her tires. The field itself was long sweet grass, now in high feathery plumes. Around its circumference was a rose hedge, huge, impenetrable. Amanda had never found anyone else here. She rode bumpily along the edge of the field to the far corner, where she laid her bicycle on its side. As she set it down, she realized she had forgotten her tennis racquet. She wondered where it was, if Emma would notice. It was too late to go back; she would tell Emma she had borrowed someone else's.

Amanda had laid her bike down by a rough circle of flattened grass. Taking her sweatshirt from her basket, she folded it into a bundle. She lay down on the flattened grass, setting the sweatshirt under her head like a pillow. She pulled one sleeve loose and laid it over her eyes. It was still early, the sun was not yet hot. She would be able to sleep here for two hours, until the sun was overhead and blazing. She pulled her knees up close to her chest. Around her were the dim rustlings of the long grass in the wind, insects. The sunlight was blotted out, and a dark peace came over her. She was alone; she had vanished. No one in the world knew where she was at that moment. She was free.

Amanda felt herself expand into the air, as though she had blissfully dissolved, like the curling gray smoke vanishing into the air of her room, only she was expanding into the warm summer sky. She slept.

20

As Amanda slammed out of the kitchen, Emma found herself leaning forward, her body tense and urgent, as though she were about to do something: to reach out and catch Amanda. Draw her back into the warmth of Emma's arms. Hit her.

But Emma did nothing, did not move or speak. She stood motionless, tilted forward in that odd way. She heard the quick hiss of the screen door opening, heard the tense light slam as it shut. The rapid footsteps down the wooden stairs. The kitchen now was silent, though not calm: it felt roughly abandoned. The violent departure left the air turbulent, as though a motorboat had just churned through it. Emma, caught in the wake of the girl's flight, folded her arms and drew a breath. The breath caught, scalded, in her chest. Rage and shame: she closed her eyes and leaned her head against the refrigerator door. She pressed the tips of her fingers against the hard sockets of her eyes. She wept.

I am your father's wife, she thought.

"'A party?'" she thought. "'A party?'"

Light sloped through the window to lie in long brilliant rectangles on the white counter. A row of green glass canisters stood against the windowsill, their tops molten and fiery in the shaft of sunlight. A patch of light fell against Emma's back, hot and insistent.

Emma picked up a napkin from the counter and put it up to her eyes. She held it there for a moment, covering her eyes with both hands, her mouth open in a silent cry. She crumpled the napkin. It will never end, she thought. She drew a long breath.

She pulled a tall canister out of the row, sliding it without sound across the counter. She poured granola into her bowl, and filled its dusty hollows with milk. She left the hot shaft of sun and sat down at the table, in cool blue shadow. She began to eat, looking out the window.

Outside, along the house, were the lilacs Emma had planted. She had brought up the shrubs herself from a nursery in Connecticut. Wrapped in burlap, laid carefully on their sides, the rough scratchy gang of them had ridden in the back of the Volvo. It had been early spring then, mud season, cold and raw. The whole landscape had been dead, the wind unkind. Emma, in rubber boots and parka, had carried the heavy bundles to their places and pushed her spade into the chilled and gritty soil. She had set them along the side of the house. Now their heart-shaped leaves, matte green, brushed against the window.

Emma ate her cereal in silence, hearing again the screen door's little slam, the clumsy thudding footsteps on the deck. Next to her was Amanda's place setting. It was pristine: the clean circle of the blue-rimmed plate. The smooth white napkin, folded, corner matching corner. The dark lustrous glass, empty.

She should have remembered that Amanda hated grapefruit. Now, of course, she did: she could see vividly Amanda's familiar grimace at the very word. She should have remembered. And even if she hadn't remembered, she should have been nicer about it. She had been unkind, her voice rough. Now, in the silent kitchen, Emma whispered, I'm sorry, Amanda, I'd forgotten you don't like grapefruit. That was what she should have said, but she had not. She had been defensive, peremptory. She had been hateful. She had answered scornfully, as though she, Emma, could not be expected to remember what Amanda liked. As though the likes and dislikes of this child were insignificant. As though the life of this child, her whole being, the complex map of herself, made up of all her thoughts and interests and ideas, all was irrelevant to Emma, unwanted. She had treated Amanda like an outsider. Sitting at the table, out of the sun, Emma now felt chilled. Cold blue shame filled her. Desperate to get away, she thought, sickened. She had driven her husband's child from his house. Her husband, who had trusted her with his only and beloved daughter.

The kitchen reproached her: the row of handsome glowing canisters, the bright tiles above the sink, all the smooth surfaces, the points of color. The flowered pottery jugs, the checked pot holders, the striped dish towels. What was the point of this charm? She had driven her husband's child from his house. That was the sort of mother she was, just this warm, this maternal, this kind. I will do better, she promised.

Carrying her dishes to the sink, she heard a sound behind her and turned. Tess stood in the doorway, in her nightgown; her face was still sleep crumpled.

"Hi, Tessie," she said. Emma heard her own real voice. This was the person she really was. "Come have something to eat."

Tess rubbed her eyes and sat down without speaking. Emma fixed her cereal. Tess sat slumping, gazing out the window. Her fine honey-colored hair, unbrushed, hung in messy hanks. She was not fully awake, still dazed by dreams.

"Mom," she asked, "are there dogs around here that have rabies?"

"No," said Emma. "Dogs around here all have shots." She poured milk into Tess's cereal.

"If they didn't have shots would they get rabies?"

"Probably not," Emma said. "There isn't much rabies around anymore to catch." She paused. "Actually, that's not true. There is some rabies around now, it's killing the poor raccoons. But most dogs are inoculated, so even if a dog were bitten by a rabid wild animal he wouldn't get it." Emma carried the bowl to the table.

"But if he hadn't had a shot, and he was bitten by a raccoon, he would get it?"

"If the raccoon had it."

Tess looked at her cereal. "I don't like it when you put the milk in for me," she said, squeezing her eyes shut, puckering her mouth. She was still too close to sleep to be rational, part of the real world.

"I forgot, sorry," said Emma.

"I *hate* when you do that," said Tess crossly.

"I'm sorry," Emma said again. "I forgot. Did I put too much?" She waited, watching Tess's darkening face. She was ready to cry.

There was a pause. "I don't like it," Tess said. She made a whimpering sound.

"Tess," Emma said. She threw her hands in the air. "Shall I throw the whole thing out?"

Tess sat without moving, her head stubbornly bent.

Two fights in one morning, Emma thought. What am I doing wrong? How does this happen so easily? Why do we find ourselves pitted against the wills of our children?

Should I give way, throw the cereal out and start over? Would that be flexible and understanding? Or lax and indulgent? What signals do we send our children?

They waited. Each felt the other's will—powerful, stubborn, braced. The silence lengthened. Not looking at her mother, Tess picked up her spoon, her face stormy.

"Okay, *fine*," she said bitterly. "Fine." Tess began to eat, sloppily, her mouth resentfully open. Under the table she kicked her feet against the chair leg.

"Thanks, Tessie, for being a grown-up," Emma said.

Tess didn't answer. She went on eating but closed her mouth. She stopped kicking her feet.

Tess's clinic started an hour later than Amanda's, but by the time Tess had finished breakfast, gone back upstairs, washed her face, brushed her teeth and hair, and dressed in her tennis whites, it was too late for her to ride her bike. When she came down the second time, Emma was standing at the bottom of the stairs. She watched Tess descending toward her, her trim little-girl body barreling down, her neat tan limbs flying. Tess jumped down the last two steps holding out to her mother elastic bands and a hairbrush. Emma began to brush Tess's hair into two ponytails.

"It's too late for you to ride," she said. "I'll drive you over."

"And my bike too," Tess said.

"And your bike too. And I love you," Emma added.

"I love you," Tess said. The quarrel was over.

She stood perfectly still before her mother, offering herself up trustfully. Emma stood over her, brushing her hair. This age was still perfect, the culmination of childhood, she thought. At ten there was a flowering, before the awkwardness of adolescence: Tess was still there. The limbs were long and smooth, the skin flawless. The hands and feet were still neat, diminutive. And the lovely candid gaze, the ingenuous sweetness: these children still love you without shame. The thought burned into Emma, and she closed her eyes for a moment, in gratitude, seized by love.

"Mum," Tess said impatiently.

"Okay," Emma said. She drew Tess's hair into a smooth brown waterfall over her face, then made a neat line down the middle. The pale skin of Tess's skull shone meekly through her hair. Emma pulled first one half of the hair into a ponytail, drawing it into a silky fountain behind Tess's ear.

"Mum," Tess said, tilting her head up. "Why do you always get so mad at Amanda?"

Emma said nothing, pulling Tess's hair into the second ponytail. She slid the elastic off her wrist and over the slippery hair, and pulled the tail down behind Tess's pink, whorled ear. She wondered if Tess had been awake that morning, if she had heard their raised voices. Had they raised their voices? She remembered rage, but not shouts.

"I don't always get so mad at Amanda," Emma said.

There was a pause.

"You do a lot," Tess said, diffident.

"A party?" Emma thought, "A party?"

"You're all set," she said, patting Tess's collar. "Maybe I do," she said. "Amanda has a hard time with the rules in this household. She's not used to them."

Tess lifted her head and looked up. She looked now like a person, not a child: her features were small but finished. Her brow was clear, her gaze direct and candid. She was not yet self-conscious. She looked straight into her mother's eyes. She waited.

"I can't explain everything to you," Emma said. She turned away. "Get your racquet. Let's go."

Outside, the morning was clear and fresh. The leaves were still dewy, and the air in the shaded driveway felt cool and mysterious. Emma breathed deeply, drawing the sweet calm air into her lungs. The wooden steps rang under her heels. She picked up Tess's bicycle and wheeled it across the resistant gravel to the Volvo. The rear door rose with a brisk pneumatic *whoosh*, and she heaved the bicycle onto the carpeted plateau. As she slid it in, the front wheel doubled back on itself; the bike lay twisted, a jumble of metal parts. Emma's push set the rear wheel unexpectedly spinning, and the spokes suddenly glittered, crisscrossing dizzyingly in the dark interior. The narrow angles met, meshed, dissolved, too fast to follow. The wheel's swift motion, silent, hypnotic, was a small gift, lovely, a vision. Tess appeared at her side, and Emma turned to her.

"Look," she said, making a peace offering of the silver shimmer.

Now Tess, looking past Emma into the dark car, saw the silver spinning glitter, and slowly smiled.

There were two clubs on Marten's Island, the Big and the Little. At the western, ferry-dock end of the island was the Little Club. This was for tennis and children. It had ten red clay courts, a sheltered beach and an old rambling clubhouse. The Little Club was informal. Lunch there was a picnic down by the water, or a sandwich, ordered at the modest snack bar, and eaten standing on the porch among teenage boys in sweaty tennis clothes, lounging against the railing, wolfing down food and laughing raucously.

At the other end of the island was the Big Club, for golf and grown-ups. It had an eighteen-hole course, a long ocean beach and a proper restaurant. Lunch at the Big Club was sit-down, with umbrella-shaded tables and flowered tablecloths. The men wore golf shoes and pink pants, the women sunglasses and expensive straw hats.

The Little Club driveway led straight in at right angles from the road, past tennis courts on both sides. The clubhouse was to the left of the driveway, long, low and white shingled, with deep porches along two sides. Before it was a flagpole and a dusty circle. The driveway passed the circle and then continued down toward the water, and a long quiet beach on a sheltered cove.

It was now midmorning, and the air was turning warm and light. A breeze drifted easily in off the water. The flag by the clubhouse lifted and rippled, dropped again. Tess's clinic was at the upper courts, where a stand of honey locusts laid filigreed shade onto the scrubby lawn. Under the trees was a scattering of young girls, all in clean whites and sneakers, all holding racquets, all aimless, waiting for the clinic to start.

Emma parked the car and turned off the engine. She put her hand on the door handle, and Tess spoke.

"Mum," she said.

"What?"

"When I go to Daddy's can I take my bike?"

Emma looked at Tess. Her face was troubled, the fragile eyebrows drawn together. It would be a nuisance, getting the bike off the island, sending it with Tess, but the more serious question was Warren. Would he be offended if Tess brought her own bicycle? Everything offended Warren now, since he had married the difficult Mimi. Mimi was from Greenwich, and was right about everything. She would not talk to Emma, but she talked to Warren about her. It turned out that Emma was wrong about everything.

Emma stroked Tess's face, smoothing her golden eyebrows.

"Why do you want to take this one? Don't you have one there?"

"I do, but it's a baby's bike. It's too small." Tess made a face, delicately hideous. "It has pink plastic streamers on the handles."

Warren would definitely be offended. He would see this as a criticism, and he would accuse Emma of making trouble. He would light into Emma on the phone and then hang up on her. Then he would be too busy to take her calls. But why should Tess be the one to suffer?

It would inevitably cause a fight. If Emma insisted on sending the bike, Warren might take it out on Tess. Which was worse, making Tess ride on the babyish bike, or making her bear the brunt of Warren's anger? Why was Warren always, always angry at Emma? Why wouldn't he simply, at last, subside, let go?

"I'll talk to your father about it," Emma said. Tess looked worried, and Emma patted her knee. "We'll work it out," she said.

Tess smiled and slid out the door, her attention gone. Her best friend, Sarah Rogers, was approaching. Sarah had a solemn oval face, with heavy eyelids and a high freckled forehead. Her hair was in tidy, red-blond pigtails, and her white shorts were pulled up high, above her waist.

"Hi, Sarah," Emma said.

"Hi," Sarah said, polite, preoccupied. She walked slowly and woodenly, her tennis racquet held in front of her at an angle, face-down. With each step, she gently kicked the taut strings. "Bonk," she said, in an undertone, as her toe hit the strings, "bonk. Bonk."

Tess sped past Sarah, grabbing her friend by the arm, spinning her around and hustling her. Sarah swiveled unprotestingly, allowing herself to be carried off. Emma dragged Tess's bicycle out of the back of the Volvo and laid it on the lawn.

"I'm leaving your bike here," she called. "Come home for lunch or call. Bring Sarah if you like."

Tess did not look back but called, "Okay," as she and Sarah made their way across the lawn, into their own world.

Emma walked back to the car. Beyond the low hill, stretching gradually down to the beach, the cove was spread out, green and glittering, in the morning light. The flag in front of the clubhouse snapped, dropped and rose slowly in a restless billow. Emma was liberated, the morning was hers. For the next several hours the girls were safe, industrious and someone else's responsibility. Stretching out before Emma, luxuriously, was silence.

Driving back out, now feeling calmer and kinder—guilty, actually—Emma slowed the car to wave at Amanda. She looked for her among the clusters of players, but the courts were at some distance, and each had its own shifting groups, teams playing out a doubles point, or a line of figures dashing singly up to the net. Emma, looking several times as she drove slowly past, had not found Amanda among the others by the time she reached the end of the driveway. She went on, turning out onto the road. She would say something conciliatory to Amanda later.

At home, Emma stood again in the silent kitchen. The house no longer felt abandoned, it felt hers. The silence was now peaceful. She put on the kettle. She stood dreamily near the stove, waiting for the water to boil. Now the vicissitudes of the morning began to slide away. She began to forget the room, the girls, herself. Her mind, released, moved like a smooth wave unrolling across white sand, to her work.

When Emma had decided to leave the magazine Robert had offered her a promotion.

"I need a woman in a senior position," he told her earnestly.

"But you want a woman who will write like a man," Emma answered. "You don't want me to write anything nasty about the boys."

"Now, Emma," Robert said, grinning, holding his bare elbows.

Emma grinned too, but she meant it. Most of the successful women in the art world—painters and dealers and critics—acted like men. Particularly the artists: God forbid that a woman artist should paint like a woman, that she should paint tenderness, rapture, bliss, or babies, intimacy, family. All that was viewed as minor, secondary, while the subjects of men's art—rage, war, politics—was seen as crucial and central.

Emma was working now on her master's degree. Her field was twentieth-century American art, and her thesis was on women painters of the nineteen thirties. There were a lot of them, but most were obscure, and part of her task was simply discovering them and their work.

Emma loved this. She loved the research, sitting in the subaqueous gloom of a microfilm room, in the spinning silence of the machines, watching images and text slide past, each frame radiant as she focused her gaze on it. She loved the New York Public Library, with its vast, handsome rooms, the spaces dignifying their inhabitants by their beauty and symmetry. Here everyone spoke quietly, out of respect for scholarship. The hushed words seemed to rise up to the high ceilings and dissolve there into a dim comforting protective murmur. Emma loved the huge Public Reading Room, with its long oak tables, the heavy brass reading lamps. She loved the unknown colleagues, all silent, absorbed by their texts, each drawing private sustenance from words. She loved handing in her requests for books, the excitement of seeing her number appear in glowing numerals on the electronic board over the desk, announcing the arrival of her books from the stacks. She loved receiving them, the worn and tattered catalogs, the old dog-eared books, the bound magazines: they were treasures.

For a year Emma had browsed, reading dealers' records, exhibition catalogs, auction catalogs, newspaper reviews and correspondence. She had examined paintings; tracking down grimy canvases in the basements of museums, in the attics of descendants, in the warehouses of dealers. She loved the moment of discovery, as someone, an indifferent museum employee, an excited relative, held up to her eyes a picture ignored for decades. Here was the tangible reality of its dry scumbled surface, its dust-dulled colors. Here the artist was revealed at this particular moment, with all her strengths and shortcomings, struggling with her task. Emma loved this: the decoding of the efforts, the explication of the images. She loved bearing witness to the struggle itself.

Emma particularly liked the extra layer of questions that came with women artists. There was always the issue of whether or not women's art was intrinsically different from men's. If you believed, as Emma did, that women's sensibility was different and that therefore their work should be different from men's, then their historical mediocrity made sense. For it was true that there were shamingly few great women artists. But if they had always labored under the handicap of trying to paint like someone else, this seemed inevitable. They had been instructed to assume an alien consciousness: they had tried to paint like men. The good ones, like Morisot and Cassatt, had painted very well indeed, and very much like the men of their circles, though they hadn't offered much that was new. But a great one, like O'Keeffe, painted like no one else, no men of her time and no women before her. She was attacked for that, for not painting like the men of her era. She was accused of being obscure, arcane. But to Emma she was simply being female, painting from a different kind of sensibility. O'Keeffe was painting how it felt to be a woman. Emma thought that women were still trying to paint like men, just as big and bold and power-ful, as political, as insulting and angry as men. As though that were all there was, as though there were nothing else worthwhile. Certainly those were the women who were encouraged by the art world, and not those who "painted like women," no one who painted intimacy, or rapture, or babies. But why weren't images of babies as important as those of guns?

There weren't other painters like O'Keeffe, but Emma hoped to find some who came close. She was looking for someone who drew on her own sensibility, who produced images that magnified her own feelings, some-one who was not ashamed to paint joy as well as rage. Emma loved thinking about these issues. She wanted to take on each of these philosophical problems, work on it over and over until she had solved it like a geometry theorem. She wanted to leave it behind her, perfectly clarified.

Standing by the stove, waiting for the kettle to reach its harsh fluttering note, Emma could feel all this lying before her, a feast. When the water boiled, she carried her mug upstairs to the tiny study. She closed the door behind her; the room was filled with quiet expectation. The desk was a rich stew of papers, photographs and art books, with the blank computer screen hovering over it all. It looked wonderful.

Emma took the first long swallow of coffee. She let the mouthful slide smoothly down. She felt the caffeine begin its work, warming her gullet, loosening her brain. She picked up the first photograph.

It was a black-and-white interior of a post office. On the long wall, high over the windows, was a semiabstract mural: farmers and construction workers, on a heroic scale. The noble laborers, toiling away at agriculture and technology, the twin supports of the economy. It looked like Communist art of the same period, Emma thought. The same iconography, the same idealized view of labor.

She held the photograph close to her face, examining the pattern of forms, the interconnected figures, the imagery. Her first draft was always longhand; the computer, with its disorienting scroll of text, came later, after the ideas were fixed in an orderly progression. She pulled a yellow pad over, and on the smooth, empty surface she began to write.

21

The ferry landing at Marten's Island was in a small sheltered cove. On one side of it was the dock, and a sandy parking lot. On the far side of the cove rose a small steep bluff, covered in a dense tangle of long grass. At the top, the ground flattened abruptly, and the grass there was cut decorously short and became a back lawn, shared by three brick bungalows. The brick houses had been built by the Army, during World War II, when Marten's Island had been used as a surveillance post. Day and night, from concrete bunkers that still huddled against the dunes, American eyes had scanned the shifting gray ocean waters for the shafts of German submarines. The brick military houses, small and utilitarian, were in marked contrast to the rest of the local houses. The island had become a summer colony around the turn of the century, and the old houses were shingle style, with turrets and gables and wide wraparound porches.

On Friday evening, when Emma arrived at the ferry landing, cars were already lined up along the dock. The parking lot was nearly full. Women stood together in chatting groups, and streams of children galloped among the parked cars.

Waiting for the ferry, the women looked different: tonight they were dressy, tended, glowing. Clothes were crisper, more colorful. Hair shone silkily, freshly washed. Legs were immaculately smooth, just shaved. The mood was festive and anticipatory: on Friday night the husbands arrived, and when the husbands arrived, the season changed. The evenings lengthened, the island clocks changed to Adult Time: it was the start of the Weekend.

The weeks on Marten's were quiet and domestic. Daily, the mothers wound the giant ticking clock of the house. The children were like small suns, at the center of everything. The deep and steady gaze of the mothers was focused on them. During the week, the mothers were only mothers. Elsewhere, the rest of the year, most of the mothers worked, full-time or part-time, paid or volunteer. But here on the island, during the week, they were only mothers.

On Friday nights, the mothers became wives. Their steady gazes shifted: now they focused on larger, more demanding stars. In the weekend sky, the fathers eclipsed their children effortlessly. Excited by their fathers' presence, resentful at the shift, the children turned rowdy and demanding. The mothers turned annoyed, the fathers admonitory. The fathers turned their own gaze on the children, but it was not the deep and steady one of the mothers. The fathers' gaze was loving but lordly: they demanded precedence by right. They had spent the week in the hot asphalt city. During the fathers' time, the activities were adult: Golf. Cocktail parties. Sex.

But the season of the husbands was brief. By Monday morning the heavens had shifted again, and the galaxy of husbands was gone. The children ruled the firmament once more.

It was after seven when Emma made her way across the lot, smiling and calling out greetings. She knew everyone she saw. Marten's was large enough to have different circles, but small enough so that everyone knew everyone. When Emma had first come here, she had worried that it might be claustrophobic, but now she saw it differently. The population was larger than it seemed. Each house was used by not just a family but an extended family—grandparents, siblings, in-laws and cousins. The summer population was fluid, people came and went all season—relatives and houseguests and tenants. Now Emma liked the sense of community; she had made real friends here.

Tonight she felt cool and crisp. In honor of the ferry she wore a fancy ironed long-sleeved jersey, deep purple, and clean white ironed jeans. She had put on dangly silver earrings: one of the benefits of very short hair was earrings. Getting out of her car, she joined Susan Cartwright in a cluster of women. Susan taught Spanish at a girls' school in New York. She was big-boned and generous looking, with a wide freckled face and long friendly eyes. She wore a white linen shirt and raspberry-colored shorts. Her sunglasses, set on top of her head, held her dark straight hair in place.

"We're complaining about our children," Susan told Emma.

"I can*not* get Sarah to do her summer reading," Alison Rogers said. She had her daughter Sarah's earnest hazel eyes, the high smooth forehead. She was wearing red heart-shaped earrings. "I don't know what I'm going to do. She has two whole books left, and it's almost the end of August. I'm going to have to lock her in her room for the rest of the vacation. It's like this every year. It drives me crazy. We fight every day."

"You're lucky Sarah's read *one*," Carol Morris said. Carol was short and stocky, with a wide mouth and heavy eyelids. "Nick won't read anything at all." She sounded triumphant. "Not one single word. I mean it. But I think the schools expect too much. This is supposed to be *vacation.* The books they give them are too long. *I* wouldn't want to read them, myself."

"All mine will do is watch TV," said Ricky Thompson, who was fair, nearly albino, with pale thick skin and strawy eyelashes. "I wish the schools would test them on old *Star Trek* episodes."

"I've given up. I'm not going to fight with Jamie anymore. I'm going to cheat," announced Nancy Williamson. "I'm going to read all the books and tell him what they're about. Then I'll take his SATs and apply to college for him. Probably won't get in."

Alison turned to Emma. "Has Tess done her reading?" she asked accusingly. "I bet she has."

"Oh, she's doing all right," said Emma, noncommittal. Tess had finished her reading, but Emma would never have said that. You never boasted about your child, any more than you boasted about yourself. You sidestepped praise, you offered flaws. You praised others, and let them sidestep praise.

"Oh, of *course* Tess has finished her reading," Susan said cheerfully. "Tess is a genius, we all know that."

"It's true," said Alison, scolding. "She probably read the books on her own. It's really revolting, Emma."

"Oh, come on," said Emma, proud. "She's hardly a *genius.* She just likes to read."

"What about Amanda?" Alison asked, her eyes narrowing. "I suppose she 'just likes to read,' too."

"Not so much," Emma said.

About stepchildren the rules were not so clear. Criticizing your stepchild was not the same as criticizing your own child. Everyone knew the place your own child held in your heart, but no one knew what place your stepchild held, or if that child had any place in your heart at all. Complaints about your own child showed modesty, but about your husband's, malice.

"I don't really know how Amanda is doing on her reading," Emma said, untruthfully. "Peter's in charge of that."

"Smart," said Carol Morris, emphatically. "It's his responsibility. Why ruin your summer? I have to say, Emma, you're brave to have her here, for the whole month. Brave or crazy."

"Oh, I don't mind," Emma said. "It's fun."

Carol shook her head. "I put my foot down about Ted's daughter. I won't have her here on Marten's," she went on. "I told Ted, 'Look, this is where I came when I was little. It's my family's place, and our family's place. I want someplace where she doesn't intrude. You can see Cynthia in New York.' "

"And what did Ted say?" asked Emma.

"He didn't *like* it," Carol said vengefully, "but he got *used* to it. It was a *nightmare,* having Cynthia here. She'd fawn all over Ted. 'Daddy, what was it like at your wedding to Mommy?' " Carol's voice rose to falsetto. " 'Was Mommy really pretty when you married her?' One time she brought their wedding photographs out here! That's when I said, 'Okay, that's it. Out.' " Her voice rose again in imitation: " 'Wasn't Mommy beautiful when you married her? Weren't you happy then?' " Carol went on, in her own voice, "I said, 'See her all you want in New York.' " She shook her head. "Not here. I'd had it."

"Well," said Emma. "It sounds difficult."

"That child was a horror. I don't know about Amanda." Carol looked at Emma expectantly.

But Emma would not offer her the horrors of Amanda. "Oh, Amanda is fine," she said vaguely, and turned away, looking out to the water.

It was so baffling, being a stepmother, so difficult to figure out. Who are our role models? Emma wondered. There are no nice stepmothers, they're all cruel. We have to make it up as we go along. We make up motherhood too, but we have great examples of that, all over the place. And as mothers we have maternal instinct on our side, urging us to cherish our children. But as stepmothers, we find that maternal instinct is busy telling us to turn the kids loose in the forest, and keep the bread crumbs for our own children. Besides, the premise is different. We choose motherhood, for itself, but not stepmotherhood. We may welcome stepchildren, we may learn to love them, but what we chose was their father. No one agreed to marry the father because she fell in love with his children.

Emma gazed into the glinting evening sea, out to where the ferry would appear. "Is it going to be late, do you think?"

"Oh, God, I hope not," said Carol. "I have people coming for dinner."

There would be dinner parties all over the island tonight, the tables set with jeweled colors. There would be candles, tall columns of white set at measured intervals; there would be little flickering votive pots scattered among the dishes. There would be flowers: masses of stiff hothouse blossoms, in formal constructions. There would be fragile messy wildflowers, dripping petals on the cloth. There would be clusters of glasses and goblets, crowded around the tip of each knife. There would be serious food.

"Are you cooking?" Emma asked.

Carol made a face. "I've already cooked," she said plaintively. "I cooked all during my twenties and thirties. Isn't that enough?"

Emma laughed. The others were still talking about the summer reading.

"I said to Talley, 'Fine, don't do it,' " said Susan. " 'Don't read at all. Ever. What does it matter if you get into college? Waitressing is good, steady work.' " Susan shook her head, gritting her teeth. "She drives me *crazy*."

The other women laughed companionably. Their children were, all of them, infuriating, intractable, all determined to live their own incomprehensible lives. The mothers were thwarted, helpless against their children's worst instincts. Comforting, comforted, resigned, the mothers turned toward the water, waiting for their husbands. Emma waited with them, silent.

The evening was not quite calm. An offshore breeze flipped up the waves into a mild chop. Low in the sky hung a long rumpled bank of herringbone clouds. Emma realized suddenly that she could hear the ferry, that it was approaching, unseen, and she had been listening to it, unaware. There was a steady, distant thrumming. The sound slowly increased.

The women stopped talking. The engine noise grew louder, thunderous. The ferry hove into view, rounding the point, filling the small entrance of the cove, ponderous, commanding, like a potentate arriving in the throne room. In the mouth of the cove the ferry paused, and the engine pitch changed to a high roar. The boat pivoted with a majestic swirl.

It churned powerfully backward and then, with another change in tone, lunged neatly sideways. It surged to a halt, precisely at the dock's edge. The water in the tiny cove foamed. Ropes were thrown over pilings, snugged tight. The movement of the boat ceased, and the ferry stopped, caught and quieted. On deck, behind the ropes, was the herd of husbands. Rumpled, tired, they stood massed and motionless, like immigrants, arriving on this island of wives and children. Emma looked along the line of faces: at this distance, they all looked like strangers. But as the boat drew closer, the faces grew clearer, familiar. There was Susan's husband, Jackson, with his intent, myopic stare, his odd rectangular glasses. There was Ted Morris, with his soft, unformed features, as though he hadn't quite finished being baked.

There were not only husbands onboard; there were now lots of working women. There was Julia, the eldest Sykes girl, a lawyer, in crumpled red linen, her blond hair wild from the crossing. Beside her, the same height, was her husband, upright, square faced, Soo-Yung Kim, who worked in the same Wall Street firm. The Sykeses loved Soo-Yung, regardless of his foreignness. And how could they not? He had gone to Harvard and Harvard Law. The Sykeses' only son, Charlie, had dropped out of three colleges, none of them Harvard, before he'd been sent off to rehab in Minnesota, and he'd been in and out of that at least twice. This summer Charlie was drifting goofily around Marten's. Emma had run into him at lunch at the Big Club one day. Smiling and empty eyed, he had told her in a hippie drawl that he was "working on a screenplay." How could the Sykeses not love the steady, brilliant, focused Soo-Yung?

The Anglo-Saxon homogeneity of Marten's was disappearing. It wasn't only Julia Sykes who had gone splashing boldly into foreign gene pools: Angus Witherspoon had married a black classmate from Yale Law, and the Wilsons' son had married a pretty Mexican girl. Blue-eyed blond babies with paper-white skin were sharing the sand with sloe-eyed, black-haired, caramel-skinned babies at the Little Club beach. A generation earlier this would have been unthinkable, but now no one complained. These were not interlopers who had somehow snuck into the club, these were third-generation members, born into it. No matter how tightly closed your mind was, how could you close your heart to your own liquid-eyed, soft-skinned, beloved grandchild, gazing peacefully up at you from the circle of your own arms?

Emma searched through the crowd of tired faces for Peter's. She found him, and felt a tiny shock of pleasure. He saw her; they smiled. She watched him, with a surge of anticipation. He stood taller than the other men but looked just as rumpled. His shirt collar was open, his tie off. So slatternly, Emma thought happily, a business suit and no tie. He was usually so neat, so formal, it tickled her to see him so charmingly rumpled. She waved at him. He was so handsome, it still surprised her. His hair was summer-blond, and a big lock of it was loose, flopping rakishly on his forehead. His wide white smile came straight at her. The crowd of passengers began to move, surging forward onto the dock.

Back in the car, Emma said, "Hold still for a moment," and put her arms around him. Peter hugged her hard, squeezing her ribs. He smelled wonderful, tired and sweaty, a faintly bronze whiff. Emma breathed him in, reminding herself.

"Let's just stay here in the car," she suggested, her eyes closed. "Everyone'll be gone in a few minutes. We can spend the evening here." No dinner, she thought, no girls, no tension.

Peter tightened his hold. "Let's."

But they separated, smiled. Emma started the car.

"I can't tell you how glad I am to be here," Peter said. "The guy next to me on the train hadn't brought anything to read. I thought I'd go mad. He kept peeking at my *Times*, over my shoulder."

"What did you do?"

"I asked him if he'd like to look at it, to shame him into stopping. He said no, and then went right on doing it. I asked him again, and he acted as though he didn't know what I was talking about. So I moved into the other corner of the seat, and folded the paper up into quarters, so he really couldn't read it. He kept peeking around under his eyebrows, to see what I was doing. I think he was hoping I'd give it to him when I finished it."

"And did you?"

"Of course not. I folded it up and put it in my briefcase."

Emma laughed. "The poor beast," she said. "He must have been salivating. Why were you so mean?"

"Why was he so stupid? I offered it to him twice, the silly bugger."

"Men are so strange," Emma said.

"What would women have done?"

"Oh, you know. It would just be different. They'd be trying to empathize with each other. Evan Bradbury was complaining that now that women are at the editorial meetings, at his paper, everything has changed. Apparently we've ruined everything."

"How have you done that?"

"Everyone used to shout. That was how they resolved things, by shouting at each other. But now, he says, if you shout at the women editors they start to cry. It's ruined everything," she repeated.

"Quite right," Peter said. "What do you want us to do, be polite?" He was beginning to relax. "God, that ride is long."

"It's the last one for the summer," Emma said. He was here now until Labor Day. She patted his leg. She felt happy: maybe everything would be all right, now Peter was back. "I'm glad you're staying." She did not add, "to take charge of Amanda."

But Peter heard it. "You've had everything on your shoulders," he said at once. He patted her leg. "You've been great."

"Oh, I don't know," Emma said uncomfortably, knowing she had not. "I'm glad you're here now."

Their car was part of a slow vehicular mass, all converging on the exit at the far end of the parking lot.

"Tell me what's been going on," Peter said.

"Not much," said Emma. "Carol Morris told me she supports Bush."

"Does that surprise you?"

"I guess I just assume that women will be Democrats," Emma said.

"Even I couldn't vote for Bush," he said. "The convention was sickening. Not that I think Clinton is a whole lot better."

"I know," Emma said. "He's so obviously unprincipled." Those bad-boy blue eyes, that self-consciously charming smile. The awful blow-dried hair, like a dentist. "He has that 'come on, honey,' look. But he's still better than Bush. He's pro-choice, and he's better for poor people and the environment."

"Did you tell Carol that?"

"She says he's going to ruin the economy. She says it like that, 'Oh, Clinton's going to ruin the economy.' I don't think Carol knows anything about the economy. I think that's what she hears Ted say."

Emma looked at Peter, waiting for him to laugh with her, but he looked out the window.

"Just because the people here are Republicans," he said, "it doesn't mean it's a terrible place. You're so intolerant, Emma."

"I am not," Emma said. "I don't think all Republicans are terrible. I like you, for example."

"Thank you," said Peter. His mouth was still tight.

"Peter, that was just an idle comment," Emma said. "I like it here. I like my friends here. You don't have to defend Marten's to me, you know."

"It was my idea to come here," Peter said. "If you make fun of it, I'm unhappy."

"I agreed to come. And now I like it. We're here together."

He looked at her. "I hope so," he said.

"Everything is not on your shoulders," she said. "You feel responsible for everything. You take on too much." She stroked the back of his head, and after a moment he yielded, leaning his head toward her palm.

"On the train I was planning things we could do together, these two weeks," Peter said. "I thought we could play family tennis, doubles. What do you think?" He looked at her hopefully.

"Fine," Emma said. "Let's." She wondered what Amanda would say.

"Will Tess be up for it, do you think?"

"Tess will be fine about it. She's not a star, but she's a trouper. She'll do it."

"Good," said Peter, encouraged. "Amanda ought to be pretty good by now, after all these clinics. Actually, she was always pretty good. She always walloped the ball."

Emma glanced at him: this happened every Friday. In New York all week, away from Amanda, Peter created in his mind another daughter. He was thinking now of that longed-for child: how good she was at tennis, how much fun it was to be with her, how sweet she was at being a daughter, how loving she was.

A car slid up next to them: the Morrises. Ted was in the passenger seat, and Emma smiled, lifting her hand. Ted waved back energetically. His tortoiseshell glasses slid down his nose as he smiled, and he pushed them up sloppily with his middle finger, the other fingers splayed across his face.

"There's Ted Morris," Emma said.

"I saw him on the train," Peter said, not turning. "He's got some terrible deal he wants me to look at." Peter thought Ted was a fool.

To make up for Peter, Emma smiled again at Ted. Past him was Carol's profile, her chin high and firm.

"Carol won't let Ted's daughter come to Marten's. She's too difficult." Emma spoke without turning. "She says Ted can see her in New York."

"Nice of her," Peter said.

"She says Ted didn't like it, but he'd learned to live with it."

"Aren't I lucky," Peter said, looking at Emma. "Is that what you want me to say?"

Emma said nothing.

"Well, it's true, I am," Peter said. "I know you wouldn't ever do that."

He leaned back, stretching his neck. "Ahh. I'm looking forward to these two weeks. It's the first time we'll all have spent any time together in the new house." Emma heard in his voice his anticipation. He saw them all happy there.

They had reached the mouth of the parking lot and passed through it. Now they were in a line of cars, winding slowly in single file along the narrow road, under a canopy of trees.

"One other thing that happened," Emma said carefully. "Amanda and I had a discussion at breakfast." She paused. "It got rather heated, I'm afraid." As soon as she had spoken she regretted it. It was a poor moment to tell Peter this. But she was driven by guilt: not telling at once made her feel as though she were concealing what had happened, lying by omission.

Peter did not answer.

"She got upset," said Emma.

Peter waited. The line of cars moved ceremonially along the road.

"It was about coffee," Emma said. "Whether she should be allowed to drink it when she's here. I think she's too young for it. Apparently she's allowed to have it at home."

Peter looked out the car window.

"At fifteen," Emma said.

Peter turned to her. "I know how old Amanda is," he said.

Emma looked straight ahead.

They did not speak again until they were home. Emma jogged up the steps without looking back, and held the screen door for Peter without turning.

"Thank you," he said.

"You're welcome," said Emma, still not looking at him. The girls were upstairs. She went straight to the kitchen and listened to Peter slowly mounting the stairs. She had gotten everything ready before she left, and now she took from the refrigerator the covered bowl of sliced vegetables, the bag of washed feathery greens, the pale blubbery slabs of swordfish.

When Peter came down, he was showered and changed, still angry.

"How do you think it makes me feel when you say things like that?" he asked. He opened the refrigerator and stood before the cold glowing interior, staring into it. "Do you think I want to hear about how badly Caroline has brought Amanda up?"

"Is that what you think?" asked Emma. "That Caroline has brought Amanda up badly?" It gave her a thrill to say this.

"Don't ask me," Peter said, "to criticize the mother of my daughter." He took out a bottle of white wine and set it loudly on the counter. "But if Caroline is doing a bad job, I can do nothing about it. Do you understand that? Caroline makes the decisions. She has custody. She pays no attention to what I say."

Emma said nothing. She was standing in front of the stove. In one pot was rice, in another a summer stew: glistening strips of peppers—gray-green, yellow, deep red—and slivers of translucent onion. Below the pots trembled low blue circles of flame. The rice simmered beneath its lid, the vegetables were slowly approaching a hiccupping boil.

"But even if Caroline did listen to me, that's not what you want," Peter went on. He set the corkscrew onto the neck of the bottle. "You want Caroline to listen to you. You want her to take *your* advice about coffee, not mine."

"But *you* don't think Amanda should drink coffee?" Emma asked. "At fifteen?"

"How should I know when Amanda should drink coffee? I don't give a damn when she drinks it," Peter said angrily. He screwed the cork violently out of the bottle. "I think there are more important things to argue about."

The rice, suddenly, boiled over. Water foamed furiously under the lid, hissing and steaming. As Emma slid the pot off the burner the broth slopped down the side, sizzling against the stainless steel.

"Of course there are more important things than coffee," said Emma, angry now herself, and flustered by the rice. "It's just an example: Amanda has no rules. She's allowed anything she wants."

"Maybe that's true," Peter said. His voice was loud and angry. "Or maybe Caroline has her own rules, ones you don't know about. But in any case, please stop complaining to me about it. I can do nothing. Just as Warren can do nothing about how you bring up Tess."

"I listen to Warren about Tess," said Emma.

Peter made a skeptical sound in his nose. He banged open a cupboard door and took out two wineglasses.

Emma put down her spoon and turned to face him.

"Peter, who am I supposed to be, with Amanda? Am I meant to be the mother? Am I meant to be in charge, here in my house?" Emma paused.

Her own voice rose. "I'm not in charge. I have no authority over Amanda, she won't permit it. If I say, 'Don't put your shoes on the bedspread,' she puts her shoes on the bedspread. If I say 'You shouldn't have coffee,' she says, 'Then I won't have breakfast,' and she walks out the door. Everything here is temporary for her: she doesn't care. She's just killing time, she's waiting to go home. I've never had much control over her, and now I have none. Now I feel how precarious everything is. At any moment she may blow everything up."

"You're just feeling sorry for yourself," Peter said.

"Maybe I am," Emma said. "But I've tried feeling sorry for her for years, and it doesn't help. The only way I can think to help her is to be a mother to her, and neither you nor she will let me do that."

There was silence. They stood looking at each other.

When they had arrived from the ferry, there was still light in the fading evening. The windows had revealed shadowy trees, the darkening lawn, the mysterious descending undulations of the distant golf course. Now the evening was over, and the summer dark was settling heavily around the house. Through the broad kitchen archway, the big dining room windows were gray and opaque. They had become ghostly mirrors, reflecting the bright colors of the interior in pallid grisaille. Outside, the damp night air pressed against the panes.

"What do you want me to say?" Peter asked, his voice quieter, but not friendly. "I can't control any of you. Do you want me to say I wish Caroline were more strict? I do. And I wish you were less strict. I wish Amanda were less resentful. I wish she were happy here with you. I wish you were happy here with her. I wish you loved her." He laughed suddenly, unhappily. "Christ, I wish you *liked* her."

"*Don't* try to blackmail me," Emma said, in a fury. "Don't you try to bully me into feeling the way you want me to feel. I can't control how I feel. I can control what I do, but not what I feel. Don't do this to me. I never did it to you."

"Don't *you* tell *me* that my daughter feels being here with me is temporary, and that she hates it," Peter answered.

"When have you ever given her a choice?" Emma asked. "You've never given either one of us a choice, a chance to decide for ourselves what we'd like. You've forced us on each other from the beginning. You've forced us to do what you wanted us to do, and now you're trying to force us to feel how you want us to feel."

"Don't hide your behavior behind mine. Don't pretend that I'm to blame for what you've done," Peter said. He had picked up the wine bottle to pour it, but now stood holding it in the air, gripping the neck of it, as though he could strangle it. "*And don't try to tell me that you've tried to be a mother to Amanda.*"

Emma did not answer.

"This is the worst thing in my life," Peter said. His voice was terrible, now, filled with grief. "You and Amanda."

The stew had just begun sloppily to boil, and Emma turned back to it. She stood over it, thrusting the spoon against the dead weight of the vegetables, their slithery mass. The heat now rose from the big iron stove in dense, suffocating waves. It was hard for her to breathe.

22

The four big windows were wide open, and the sweet night air moved freely through the bedroom, filling the space of it. Earlier the room had been shelter, enclosed and private, filled with lamplight and conversation. It had been transformed. Now, in the silent dark, the windows wide, it was as though the walls had dissolved, and the room was opened up to the night. Now it seemed a part of something larger. Now the room was an open space in the midst of the grand passage of the cool nocturnal wind, sweeping across the body of the small island before it moved beyond the land and, out over the water, rising, into the slow movement of the upper airs, lifting across the spaces of the night sky, shifting and tingling above the silent ocean.

Emma became aware that she was awake. The room was dark. There was no sound. Peter lay next to her, asleep. She heard his slow quiet breaths. Her eyes, she found, were open, and she lay still. She was waiting for something. She could see the muted glow from her tiny clock on the bedside table, its private illumination: the radiant numbers announced three-fourteen. Beyond the bedside table, the curtains shifted faintly.

Emma listened; she felt the cool drift against her face. Outside, the trees moved slightly in the night air. There was another sound, something else. Someone was in the room with them. Emma raised her head, trying to see. A darkened patch hovered next to the bed.

"Tess?" Emma whispered.

The patch nodded. Emma pulled back the covers and slid over toward Peter. Her gesture drew a swirl of cold air into the cave of warmth beneath the covers. Tess climbed in, and Emma pulled the covers down again, close. Tess curled tightly inside the curve of her mother, drawing up her cold feet, huddling hard against Emma. Emma felt the bony ripple of Tess's spine against her own front. Tess no longer fit neatly against Emma as she had as a child; her torso was beginning to lengthen toward adulthood.

Emma whispered into Tess's ear. "Did you have a bad dream?" She mouthed the words, her voice a faint thread of sound. She was afraid of waking Peter.

Against her face Emma felt Tess's nod. Emma said nothing, but folded herself more tightly around the child. She heard the faint words.

"*Rabbit dog,*" Tess whispered. She shivered.

Emma hugged her again. What was a rabbit dog? she wondered. A mix, half dog, half rabbit? Or a dog bred for killing rabbits? Was there such a thing? Some kind of terrier? A rabbit dog. She rubbed Tess's forearm, slowly, soothingly. But Tess stayed tense, her limbs taut. From time to time she shivered, and then Emma kissed the back of her head, and hugged her more closely. The top of Tess's hard head was her chin, strands of Tess's fine dry hair lifting against her face. Finally Tess's trembling ceased, and Emma began herself to tilt slowly toward sleep. *Rabbit dog?* It was not until sleep was partly upon her, not until she found herself, confusingly, in two places at once—a chaotic picnic on a hillside somewhere, under dark skies, and also here, in bed, against her pillows—that the word drifted into her mind, suddenly clear: *rabid.* Rabid dog.

In the morning, Emma woke to daylight. Tess, beside her, was stretched out, her limbs now loose and sprawling. Behind her Emma could feel Peter, awake and disapproving. His body touched hers nowhere. Emma lay still. Peter sat up, then went into the bathroom.

Emma picked up Tess, still sleeping, and carried her back to her own bed. Tess's room was no longer frightening. It was day-safe; the sun glowed boldly around the edges of the window shades. When Tess woke again, alone, she would not be afraid.

In her room, Emma shut the door quietly behind her and sat down on the bed to wait for Peter. He emerged, shaved and clean. His face shone with dampness. His hair lay in cold wet furrows. He was naked, his pale pelt glistened across his chest, down his flat belly, down to the fat slack curl, dangling over the jostling pink pouch. Emma averted her eyes. Ordinarily it seemed unkind, unfair, to look when everything was so limp.

Now, when Peter was angry, it seemed dangerous to look, bad luck some-how. Peter strode to his bureau, his heels thudding on the wooden floor. Loudly he opened and shut the drawers, his movements brusque.

He spoke with his back to her. "She's too old for that, you know," he said.

"I know you think so," said Emma.

"I do think so," Peter said forcefully. He shut a drawer hard.

"I know," Emma repeated.

"I see," said Peter, turning around. "You know how I feel, but you ig-nore it."

"I know how you feel," Emma said, "but I disagree with you."

"I see. And when we disagree, we do what you want. Is that it?"

"No," said Emma. "Not always."

"She only does it because she's allowed to," Peter said.

"She hasn't done it in a long time," said Emma.

"She'll go on doing it as long as you let her. You have to draw the line somewhere."

"I don't think you draw the line across fear," Emma said. "I think that if a child is frightened you comfort her."

Peter rolled up his sleeves fastidiously. "It's a question of discipline," he said. He left the room.

Emma went into the bathroom, closing the door behind her, closing herself off from Peter's disapproval. She felt the burden of his dislike, the familiar fear that it would turn against her daughter. She stood before the mirror in her crumpled lavender cotton nightgown. She stared at her thin neck. Her hair was wild from sleep. There were bluish shadows beneath her eyes, and a frown line between her eyebrows.

She turned on the water and took her toothbrush from the glass. A line of anxiety ran down inside her, like a ribbon unrolling, glittering, rapid.

At breakfast Peter did not speak to her. He was sitting at the table when Emma came down, eating his grapefruit. Without comment he fin-ished it and carried his plate to the sink, stepping carefully past her, draw-ing politely back so she could move by. He made himself real coffee, and sat down with the paper. He did not look at her. Emma made herself toast and instant coffee and carried it into the living room to eat. When the girls came downstairs, Peter and Emma looked up and smiled. They became animated, each talking cheerfully to the girls, though not to each other.

This was the day Peter had planned the family doubles. After lunch he and Amanda took on Tess and Emma. Peter and Amanda won the toss.

"You start, Nanna," Peter said, and tossed her a ball. "I just got the bill for the second half of your clinic. I want to see what I'm getting for my money." He moved up to the net and leaned forward, waiting for Amanda to serve behind him. He grinned at Tess across the net. "I'm going to poach," he warned her.

"Don't," ordered Tess. She shook her head at him.

Amanda stood, frowning and slouching, at the service line. She was wearing a dirty tennis skirt, though her T-shirt was clean. When she had come downstairs in the dirty skirt, Emma asked if she didn't have a clean one, but Amanda said this was the only one she could find.

"I'm sure there's a clean skirt for you to wear," Emma said, touchy. Was Amanda implying that the laundry didn't get done here? She felt silent reproach from Peter, for sending his daughter off in dirty clothes.

But Peter stepped forward and put his arm around Amanda's shoulders. "She looks fine," he said, not looking at Emma. Now Emma felt reproached for being too fussy. "Let's go."

Amanda's shoulders drooped, her matte black hair seemed greasy. She looked so forlorn, thought Emma, so unhappy. Right now her heart went out to Amanda. I'll do better, Emma promised. I'll change things.

Amanda threw the ball up too high, and off center. She drove it into the net.

"Fault!" Peter called, short and high, like a referee.

Amanda threw up the second ball and walloped it into the net.

"Fault!" barked Peter again. He walked jauntily across the court. He looked back at Tess. "I'm still going to poach."

"Don't," said Tess happily.

Amanda double-faulted again, then managed to get a weak second serve to Tess, high and deep and slow. Tess backed up wildly, swung off balance, and sent the ball straight up into the air.

"Where will it land, where will it land?" sang out Peter. "World's Smallest Grown-up Sends Ball into Orbit." They all watched it hurtle upward, finally pause, and drop down, outside the court.

"Good try, Tessie," Emma said.

"We got a point, Nanna!" Peter shouted. He threw up his arms triumphantly as though they had won the U.S. Open. Emma and Tess laughed. Amanda said nothing. She walked back to the service line. Peter turned around to watch her.

"Okay, another patented Amanda Chatfield serve! Can they handle it! Nothing else like this in all tennis, folks, it's never been returned yet! She learned it that summer she took a tennis clinic on Marten's Island, it all started there, folks, the career of"—Amanda threw the ball up— "Amanda 'Tiger' Chatfield." Amanda slammed the ball into the net.

"Fault," Peter said.

Amanda threw the ball up again. It went into the net.

"Fault," Peter said, more quietly.

"*Dad*," Amanda said.

"Sorry, Nanna, I'm distracting you," Peter said. "I won't say anything more."

Amanda lost the game with another double fault, and Peter called to her.

"Good try, Nanna," he said. "You've got a great swing."

Amanda said nothing. She took up her position to receive, feet apart, knees bent, eyes on the ball, frowning.

It was Tess's serve. She stood still for a moment at the service line, collecting herself. She threw the ball up high and straight, arching her back supplely, bending gracefully as she'd been taught. But she mishit, slamming the ball hard onto the court, on her side of the net.

"Oops," she said cheerfully.

"Good try," said Emma.

Tess's shirt had pulled out from her shorts, and her ponytails loosened. She danced and jiggled at the service line. The racquet looked too big for her, and her shots were wildly erratic. Tess grinned when she hit the ball in, grinned when she hit it out. Emma saw her connect solidly with a powerful two-handed backhand, her weight on the right foot, her arm in the right position. They all watched as the ball sailed out into the sky, toward the clubhouse roof.

Tess hunched her shoulders. "Oops."

Peter kept up a running commentary. "There she is, ladies and gentlemen, the world's smallest grown-up, serving one of the great games in tennis. First she's going to hit the ball with the racquet, then the racquet is going to hit the ball with her."

"*Peter*," Tess said. "I can't do this if you keep talking."

"Sorry, madam," Peter said cheerily. "I won't say a word." He made a face at her.

"Peter!" Tess scolded. "I'm going to start over."

Amanda said nothing. She moved reluctantly across the court, her face sullen. She looked constantly over her shoulder, as though she was expecting the arrival of someone more interesting. When Peter served she stood at net, yawning uncontrollably. Every time she hit the ball Peter said, "Good try! Great swing, Nanna!" Amanda never answered.

Afterward, Peter walked back to the car with his arm around her.

"You have gotten really good, Nanna," he said. "I think this pro has really helped you. Your swing is really fantastic, and when it starts going in, no one will be able to touch that serve, or that forehand."

Amanda frowned.

"Do you like the pro?" Peter asked.

"*I* like him," Tess offered.

But Peter wanted to hear from Amanda. "What do you think, Nanna?"

"Yeah," Amanda said, shrugging her shoulders. "He's okay."

"Only okay?" asked Peter. "I have to pay the second half of your clinic. If you don't like him, maybe we should move you to private lessons. Do you think this is worthwhile or not?"

"It's *fine*, Dad," Amanda said, and behind her, Emma heard desperation in her voice.

Poor Amanda, she thought again.

Peter, rebuffed, took his arm away from Amanda's shoulders.

Poor all of us.

At home, Emma followed Tess into her room and sat down on her bed.

"Tessie, what happened last night?"

"When?" asked Tess.

"The nightmare," said Emma.

"Oh, yeah," Tess said, looking troubled. "I had a nightmare."

"About what?"

"A rabid dog," Tess said. She began twisting her torso, swinging her arms against the pull, not looking at her mother.

"But why were you thinking about a rabid dog, Tessie?" Emma asked. "Is it something that bothers you?"

Tess shrugged her shoulders and raised her eyebrows. "I guess," she said.

"What frightens you?"

"Well, if a rabid dog came after you," Tess said, swinging hard, "it could kill you."

"But there aren't any around here," Emma said.

Tess looked at her sideways. "You said there might be."

"It's within the realm of possibility," Emma said, "but it isn't something to worry about. There are no rabid dogs around here. None."

Tess eyed her and did not answer. She swung her arms back and forth. "But why are you thinking about them?"

Tess shrugged her shoulders.

Emma stood up. "Well, don't, okay?"

She left, worried. If Tess came in again that night, Peter would be furious. It was strange, Tess being so frightened.

Peter and Emma had barely spoken all day. They were invited to a cocktail party that night, and they dressed to go out in cold silence. Emma stood in front of her mirror, in silky white pants, a deep turquoise top. She pressed the tip of her forefinger against the round open lip of the perfume bottle and tipped it up. She touched her neck, behind the point of her jaw, at the base of her throat. The rush of scent made her feel pretty, wanted, and she looked at Peter in the mirror, hoping he would look back at her and smile. She hoped that Peter would say she looked nice, that he would forgive her, but instead he stood by the door and asked distantly, "Ready?" Still in disgrace. Her heart hardened and she nodded. She pulled a shawl around her shoulders and followed him without speaking. Peter went ahead to say good-bye to the girls.

They were in Amanda's room. They were sprawled raggedly on the beds, still in tennis clothes, happily reading comics.

"Okay, guys," said Emma. "We're going to Mr. Taylor's, for drinks."

"We know," said Tess, not looking up. "You already told us."

"Well, blink if you understand," said Peter, nudging Amanda's foot with his knee.

Amanda looked up and smiled at them, peacefully, at that moment as though she were another child altogether, someone who loved them. Her short hair was slicked back, showing the shape of her head. Her blue eyes glowed. She's pretty, Emma thought, surprised. She'd be beautiful if she were happy.

"Have a good time," Amanda said, as though she were the grown-up, sending them off for the evening. "You look nice," she added generously to Emma.

"Thanks," said Emma, touched. "We'll be back around eight, eight-thirty, and then we'll have dinner with you." She smiled at Amanda.

Peter smiled, too, at Amanda. He did not look at Emma.

"Okay, we're off," he said to Amanda. "See you later, Nanna. Be good, Grown-up."

"Bye," said Tess peacefully.

"Bye," said Amanda.

Going down the stairs behind Peter, Emma was furious at him, for being so friendly to them, so cold to her. How dare he stay angry at me all day because I comforted my daughter? She hated the back of his head, hated his wide shoulders, hated the way he went downstairs with his hands in his jacket pockets.

Outside, the evening was still light, the sky high and luminous. The trees were silent, and as they walked across the gravel their footsteps sounded loud. They got into the car without speaking.

The road curved down the hill into the village, then out through a little wood. Beyond that, the landscape opened up onto the Point, which projected into the Sound. The road ran along the water's edge. Beyond a narrow rocky shingle was a broad sweep of quiet water washed by the settling sun. It was calm. Far out in the transparent evening air were gulls, gliding, silent. When they rose, out of the shadow, their dusky forms turned brilliant as they were struck by the rays of the dying sun, their shapes suddenly gleaming in the high light-filled sky. They seemed autumnal; Emma thought that the summer was nearly over. She wondered suddenly if she would see them next year, if she would be at Marten's next summer.

They turned the last corner, and the Taylor house came into view on the spine of the low ridge. The house was big and white shingled, with a deep wooden porch running all the way around. Lawns sloped away from it on all sides. There was a line of cars along the road. Peter pulled in behind the last one. They walked up the broad rising lawn, Emma on tiptoe, so her heels would not sink into the soft earth. Approaching the house they could hear the sound of the party: affable voices, laughter. On the porch was a crowd of people.

Old Mrs. Taylor had left the house to her two children, Christian and Edwina. Edwina used the house in July, and Christian in August. They each gave a big cocktail party during their respective months. They were highly competitive.

Edwina was married to a partner at Lehman Brothers and had more money than Christian. Her party was fancier, but she pretended that money had nothing to do with it. If you complimented her on the caviar, she said, "Oh, well, anything's better than what Christian gives you. You're lucky if you get salted peanuts, straight from the can, from Christian." She shook her head. "Christy was *always* like that. *Always*. He doesn't care what he eats. When he was little he ate kibble out of the dogs' bowls. He loved it. They nearly starved. Really. We had to start feeding them out in the kennel, instead of in the house, because of Christy."

But Christian's cocktail party was very good. He did not, of course, serve dog kibble, or peanuts from a can. His hors d'oeuvres were wonderful, and if you complimented him on them, he smiled and said, in his nasal drawl, "Well, I know it's not like *Edwina's* party, but we do our best. And, frankly, I've never thought liveried servants was in very good taste, in the summer, you know, at the beach. A touch pre*tentious*, don't you think? But Edwina was *always* like that, even when she was a child. That was always her little way." Edwina did not, of course, have servants in livery. Edwina hired the same four waiters that everyone else on Marten's used for cocktail parties.

Emma and Peter had gone to Edwina's party, in the beginning of July, and they were going, of course, to Christian's. Everyone went to both. Edwina's party marked the height of the season, and Christian's marked its close. And they were elegant parties: it was a great pleasure, exalting, to stand on the broad shining porch, the evening sun lowering, in the big handsome house overlooking the water.

Christy Taylor stood at the top of the steps. He was portly, broad-faced and dark-haired, with horn-rimmed glasses. His skin was deeply sunburnt, with white crinkles around his eyes. He wore a blue blazer, a striped shirt and bright green pants. He was a dandy, all his creases sharp, his colors bright, his edges crisp.

"Hello, Chatfields," he said genially. He held up a frosted glass. "Welcome." He took Emma's hand and kissed her theatrically on each cheek.

"Christian," Emma said, smiling.

Christian drew back, still holding her hand, and looked her up and down. "You're a lucky man, Chatfield," he said soberly, shaking his head. Christian loved women, though he had never married, and never appeared with a companion of either sex.

"I know that," said Peter. He smiled, but the smile was for Christian, not Emma. She looked at Peter appraisingly, as though he were someone she had just met.

Up on the ridge, they were again in the full glow of the dying sun. Peter was lit by its radiance, his damp hair shining, his blue eyes brilliant against his summer-darkened skin. He looked golden and triumphant, as he had when Emma had first seen him, at his own cocktail party. Then he had moved so confidently among his friends, warm, expansive, in his own beautiful rooms. He had seemed then shining, potent.

Peter was older now: creases deepened his cheeks, and his eyes looked weathered, with strong lines around them. Still he seemed to gleam. Now that Emma knew him, she still loved his looks, his wide-set eyes, the slightly crooked mouth, the upper lip's slant to the left. But Emma now knew his center, sullen valleys as well as sunny peaks. She hardly cared what he looked like: he was who he was, he was part of her. They had been married now eight years. She hardly cared that she was angry at him, or he at her, she felt so locked to him now, so joined, angry or not, handsome or not, it was his core that was joined to hers. Even their estrangement connected them. She longed now for his anger to subside.

"So, Taylor," Peter said, "what are the chances of getting a drink around here?"

"Damned sight better than at Edwina's shindig," said Christian at once. "The bar's inside, but someone'll be around in a minute." He held up his glass again. It was rimmed with pale glitter. "House specialty: margaritas."

"Yum," said Emma.

"You bet," said Christian, but his attention was going. Behind them someone else was climbing the stairs, and Christian looked past them to greet the next arrivals.

Under the wide porch roof, on the freshly painted green floor, was the party. Everyone was in summer clothes: fresh linens, bright flower-garden colors. There was glossy slithering hair, tanned skin. White smiles. The voices were eager. The guests stood in knots and clumps, while among them threaded waiters with silver trays. The waiters, in white shirts and black jackets, carried long-stemmed glasses of white wine, salt-rimmed glasses of margaritas. The waitresses, in black dresses with white aprons, passed food: neat rows of toasts, glistening savories, fresh crudités. Everything was small, gleaming, tempting. Mounds of vivid green parsley declared everything fresh.

A waiter came up for their drinks order. Peter and Emma moved toward the animated crowd. They were side by side, but they still did not speak to each other. Emma wished he would relent. She looked at him out of the corner of her eye. She'd have spoken if he did.

"I hear the blues were biting yesterday," someone said, "in the race."

"Emma! Will you be here next weekend?" a woman asked. "My sister is coming. She remembers you from last year."

The voices swirled around them.

"He's been posted, you know," a man said confidentially, "at the Racquet *and* the River Club. And they can't pay the maintenance on their apartment, so every morning he has to carry his trash down on the service elevator. In his business suit."

"He'd never even seen her before April," said a woman's gleeful voice, "and by July she had him moved out of his house and into divorce court. He never knew what hit him."

"No, he's back at First Boston again. Somehow. I don't know what kind of a deal he made. Nobody knows."

Peter and Emma drifted apart. They knew everyone there; moving among them was like rocking in a warm bay, washed by friendly waters. Some people they made their way carefully over to, some people they only waved to; some people they had seen too recently to have anything new to say to now, some people they never had anything to say to, and merely smiled at.

Emma was talking to Susan Cartwright when Peter came up. Big Susan looked like a goddess, in billowing green silk, a tunic and loose pants, and long green earrings that fluttered gently when she moved her head. Peter appeared next to Emma. He touched her elbow, not warmly.

"Let's go," he said. He did not look at her.

Irritated at his abruptness, Emma did not answer, and moved her arm away from his hand. She looked steadily at Susan, who greeted Peter happily.

"Peter! How are you! I haven't seen you all summer, it seems," she said, and kissed him on both cheeks. The margaritas had expanded her personality; she was now brimming with warmth. "How is your beautiful new house?"

Peter smiled at her. "We love it," he said, charmed.

"I *hope* so," said Susan. "I love it. I love those pillars on the porch, and the archways. I love the whole thing. And tell me about Amanda. How is she liking Marten's? Is it a success?"

Peter nodded. "I think she likes it," he said. "I think she does. She doesn't thank us every morning for being here—but you know what teenagers are like."

"And what is she doing every day?" Susan asked. "It's hard when they don't have a gang to go around with."

"Well, the clinic is the main thing," Emma said.

"Clinic?" Susan said. She reached out to a passing tray and took a water chestnut wrapped in bacon. "Aren't these great?" She looked around conspiratorially. "Last week I told Christian that the food at Edwina's had been really sensational this year. I think it worked. Anyway, I'm taking credit for it. Wait, wait," she called to the waitress, who was turning away. "One more." Susan smiled at her and reached.

"The tennis clinic," Peter said. "She has that three days a week. I don't know what she's been doing the other days."

Susan squinted her long narrow eyes and cocked her head. In one hand she held her margarita glass, in the other she had three toothpicks. "Hold on," she said. "I have to get rid of the evidence." She looked around and set the toothpicks on a passing tray. She turn back to them. "What tennis clinic?"

Emma and Peter stared at her. "The one at the Little Club," Emma said. "The one Talley's in."

Susan shook her head. "Amanda isn't in the clinic at the Little Club."

There was a pause.

"Amanda isn't in the clinic?" Peter said. "Yes, she is."

"No," Susan said. "I know she's not. I take Talley over every morning. Amanda came a few times in the beginning, but after that she stopped. I asked Talley. Then I asked the pro. The pro said the same thing. She came a few times and then stopped. I thought she didn't like it and you'd found something else for her to do."

The waitress swam into view nearby. Susan craned over a navy-blazered shoulder to see the tray.

"Phooey," she said, "it's that dry cheese on toasts. I should have told Christy that Edwina only has caviar." She looked more closely at Peter and Emma. "Is this a surprise? Did you not know this? I'm sorry if I've been indiscreet."

Peter shook his head. "It's all right," he said. "Don't worry about it. We're glad to know." He turned to Emma and said briskly, "Now, we have to go."

Emma nodded. They moved through the crowd together, smiling and saying good-bye. Taking her to the clinic, Emma was thinking as she smiled. Introducing her to everyone. Asking her every day how it went. Getting her up in the morning. Making her breakfast.

Smiling, they thanked Christian, saying extravagant things. Out on the lawn they stopped smiling. They did not speak until they were in the car.

"Damn her," Peter said, his voice devout. He closed his eyes. "Damn her." He sounded close to tears.

Emma said nothing.

Peter opened his eyes and started the car. "What do you suppose she's been doing?"

Emma shook her head.

"Does she have any friends here? Does she go off with someone?"

"No one I know of," said Emma. She remembered Amanda's response: "A party?"

They rounded a curve, passing another car with friends in it, on their way to Christian's. Everyone waved, smiling. When the other car had passed, Emma's and Peter's smiles faded.

"Do you suppose it's drugs?" Peter asked.

"How do you mean?" asked Emma.

"I don't know what I mean," said Peter. He drove on in silence. "I could strangle her," he said. His tone was deadly.

"Peter, wait," said Emma. "This isn't the worst thing. How bad is this? It's not really that bad. It's just skipping some tennis lessons."

"It's everything!" Peter said furiously. "It's lying to us, it's the attitude. It's this *on top of everything else!*" He pounded the steering wheel.

Emma thought of Amanda's contemptuous stares, her eight-year silence, her sullen face. She didn't answer.

He pulled into the driveway and got out of the car, slamming the door. He went first up the steps.

They could hear the girls in the kitchen, chasing each other, rough-housing. Furniture moving, a small shriek. Peter walked rapidly down the hall, Emma hurrying behind him, their footsteps ominous, like policemen. The girls were dodging around the table, throwing something back and forth, their voices high, full of laughter.

As Peter and Emma came into the room, Amanda, her back to them, shouted, "No! No!" She grabbed one of the chairs and ducked down, behind it.

"Yes!" Tess shouted. From across the table she threw something—a thick paperback book—at Amanda, just as her head went down. The book went over Amanda and straight at Peter, who grabbed at it in midair, missed it, grabbed again, and dropped it. The book hit the floot and skidded in front of Emma. Tess shouted, inarticulate.

Emma picked up the book. It was one of Amanda's. On the cover was a savage St. Bernard, his mouth open and snarling, saliva dripping from his jaws. Rabid dog, she thought.

At the sight of Peter's face, Tess froze. She saw Emma behind him and stood up straight. Amanda turned around. Bare legged, barefoot, in their rumpled tennis clothes, the girls drew themselves into positions of decorum. Their faces became cautious and solemn.

"*Amanda,*" Peter said, in a tone of awful commencement.

"What?" she said. Amanda stood next to the table. She leaned one elbow on it.

"Why did you tell me you'd been going to the tennis clinic?"

Amanda looked sullenly at the floor.

"Why did you lie to me?" he asked.

"I didn't lie to you—" Amanda began.

"Yes you did too lie to me," Peter shouted.

"I didn't lie," Amanda repeated.

"What do you mean you didn't lie?"

"I just said the pro was okay. I didn't say I was going," Amanda said angrily.

"How dare you pretend you weren't lying!" shouted Peter. "You were *living* a lie. Every day you lied to us. Every day Emma sent you off to the tennis clinic. Do you think you were behaving truthfully?"

Amanda rubbed one finger back and forth on the top of the table. She did not look up.

"Answer me, Amanda," Peter said.

Amanda said nothing, her head bent stubbornly.

"How dare you do this?" Peter said. He was leaning toward Amanda from the waist. His face was red, furious. "How dare you act like this?"

Amanda had frozen. Her hand stopped moving, her shoulders hunched. She was gone, she was nowhere. Peter took a step closer.

"Answer me!" he shouted. "Answer me! How dare you do this to me! You do this all the time! This is all you do! You reject everything we do for you, everything! You make my life a misery!" Peter's hair was in his eyes. His throat was corded, crimson with rage. He leaned closer to her. He waited.

She said nothing.

"All you do to me is this! How dare you! How can you do this, Amanda! Answer me!" His voice was wild with distress. Amanda looked stonily at the floor, and did not answer.

"Answer me, answer me, Amanda," Peter repeated. His hands were clenched, close to his body. Amanda stared at the table. She said nothing.

"Damn you, Amanda," he said, and turned from her, weeping.

23

Amanda sat alone on the back deck. It was more peaceful on the deck than in her room: it was four o'clock in the morning, and around her the night was very quiet. She felt safe in the silence. Below her floated the pale glimmer of the driveway, and the vague gleam of the car. Beyond that was the deep black of the trees, high and dense and murmuring. Beyond the black trees was the road, though she couldn't see it. She imagined it, hard and shining in the moonlight.

In the dark, Amanda held up her last joint, its jeweled tip glowing secretly. It was the only one her father had not found; Amanda herself had forgotten she'd had it. It had been in a plastic bag, rolled small and stuffed in an empty tape case. On the label Amanda had written DREAMS. She had hidden the joint there months ago, at school, and had only found it that afternoon, when she was going through her tapes. She had spread them all out on her bed. She'd picked each one up and looked at it, remembering the music. She couldn't play any of them, because her father had taken away her Walkman.

Peter had taken away her Walkman, her cigarettes and, of course, her dope. It had been a real scene, her father looming over her, his fists clenched, shouting. His knotted red face, his body sending out waves of fury. He was huge and hot: Amanda had felt as though she stood before an open furnace, the heat blasting against her own face, as though at any moment she might be devoured by that ravenous flame.

She tried not to think of it, but flickers of it kept recurring, playing in her mind like scenes from a horrible movie. Her father had been all dressed up for his cocktail party, in his striped tie and beautiful shirt, he'd looked so handsome, it made it worse, somehow. He had shouted at her, and his voice had been terrible, loud and flat and terrible.

Amanda had stood still, her jaw clenched, all her muscles locked, as though she had braced herself before a big wind. He had gone on and on, once he found her things. Dishonesty and betrayal and shame: he had shouted those at her. Amanda had said nothing. It was something she had learned. You just stood and waited, and let them yell at you. There was nothing they could do to you in the end. She did it with her mother, she did it at school. You said as little as you could get away with, and let them talk as long as they wanted. You waited for them to finish, and then it was over.

When he had said that since he could no longer trust her he was going to search her room, Amanda had wanted to scream at him. Her skin had burned at the thought of him pawing through her things, his big clumsy hands touching her private things—her cosmetics, her jewelry, her underwear, her things that were hers, set out in her own private order. She had wanted to run upstairs before him, stand in front of her door and stop him, her arms stretched out across it. But he would only have pushed her aside. There was nothing she could have done but wait. She'd stood with her arms crossed, watching him walk out of the kitchen. He had turned and looked back at her.

"You come too, Amanda," he said, and so she had to.

When he found the plastic bag under the mattress, she thought he would hit her. "Damn you," he said, for the second time, his voice thick as leather. It was a terrible thing to say, and Amanda felt her throat tighten, and tears start behind her eyelids, though she kept them back. She blinked. She was ready for him to hit her, in a weird way she *wanted* him to. It would be almost a relief, an end to this farce. She had always known how he really felt about her, and this would be proof. It would show that everything else was false, as she had always known. This pretense of affection. This insistence on her coming here, this pretending that they were, the four of them, a family, that he loved her. A farce, Amanda would whisper to herself. A total farce.

Her father did not hit her, in fact he stopped yelling. He had come to the end of his anger. He had gone as far as he could. He held the dope in his hand and said, "What have you done, what have you ever done in your whole life, Amanda, to make me proud of you? What have you ever done but disappoint me?"

The silence in the room was crystalline, revelatory. Tess, in the doorway, was frozen. Emma stood mute and still behind her, her eyes fixed on Amanda.

Then Amanda drew her breath and answered him. She wanted to rise proudly to her father's level. She meant to use his weapons—power and accusation. She wanted to speak as his equal, to challenge him and reveal his hypocrisy. She wanted to point out that the word *betrayal* was not one he could use any longer, that a man who had abandoned his wife could not talk about betrayal and shame and disappointing others. She meant to accuse him now, out loud, of all that he had done. She meant to list his un-forgivable acts, so that no one here would forget, so that here in his own little circle he would stand condemned, forever.

But when Amanda opened her mouth, none of that was possible. As she tried to speak, her throat closed, and panic rose inside it. Her eyes stung. All she could do was cry out, in a strangled voice, "Fuck you, Dad." Her throat closed up entirely after that, and of course she began to cry. He was too much for her.

But Amanda had since closed this off from her mind. She did not want to think about her father. It was so clear to both of them that she was not the daughter he wanted. He wanted someone else, someone like Tess—someone with perfect grades, who was so cute and charming, someone who was not Amanda. All Amanda could do was wait until she was old enough never to see her father again. That was what she longed for.

She had been sitting on the porch for some time. She had read up in her room until quite late, when she was sure everyone else was asleep. It was hot, and Peter had turned on the big attic fan. The cool steady hum drowned out the noise of Amanda's footsteps, but it also meant that the bedroom doors were wide open. She had to tiptoe past the dark unreadable space of her father's bedroom, the open doorway full of threat, his and Emma's invisible, imminent presence. She had done it, walked past, her gaze fixed ahead of her, holding her breath. Her pulse surged and she imagined her father's stern voice, coming suddenly through the sound of the fan.

But once she was down the stairs she was out of danger, and out here it was calm. Amanda listened to the small wind shifting the leaves and thought of the night air, rising into the brilliant spaciousness of the sky. She felt peaceful now. After smoking half a joint she was beginning to see a deep comforting connection between herself and everything around her: the murmuring trees, the grainy texture of the wooden steps, even the empty road beyond the trees, shining silently in her mind.

She looked up at the darkness, as it rose and expanded. She liked the way the sky at night came right down to the ground, right down to where she sat. In the daytime, the sky and the air were different: the sky was blue and the air transparent. But at night they were the same. The same luminous darkness was the sky and also the air you walked through. Right now Amanda was sitting in the night sky. All around her might be stars, drifting airily nearby, just out of sight. This made her smile. Alone in the dark, Amanda felt peaceful and free, as though she had no body at all, as though she had dissolved into the breathing darkness.

A car went slowly past, down the hill. She wondered who it was, so late. There was no restaurant on the island, no nightclub, nowhere to go but someone else's house. It must be kids, she thought, and wondered who. She wondered if she were to meet them now, out on the road, at this secret time of night, the car door opening and the interior light creating a private world just for themselves and her, if they would now recognize each other as kin, creatures of the night.

The other kids here were alien creatures. There was no one here whose eyes Amanda would meet. She lifted the joint and set her mouth to it. It was funny how you held joints differently from cigarettes. Cigarettes you held carelessly, dangling between two knuckles; joints you held tightly, pinched between your thumb and forefinger. There was something mean-spirited about that tight pinch; Amanda preferred the negligent knuckle clasp. She tried it; the joint felt lumpy and unbalanced between her knuckles, and she took it again in her thumb and forefinger. She took in a long slow breath, hot, harsh, exalting. She squinted against the smoke, holding it deep inside her chest, feeling it rise mysteriously into her head. She closed her eyes.

An image came slowly into her mind. She saw the dark road up the spine of the island, as though she were driving it. The long flat stretch, the pavement shining in the moonlight. On the ocean side, long grass bending in the sea wind. Silence. The image was stationary, like a photograph. In the headlights everything was bold and sudden in black and white.

Amanda opened her eyes and thought of driving. She could, actually, drive a car. She knew how. Earlier that summer she had stayed with a friend in Stonington, Alison Ferguson. Alison's father had taken them both out and taught them to drive. He had them start and stop, start and stop, all over an empty parking lot.

When it was Amanda's turn, she gripped the steering wheel tightly, as though she could control the car through the strength of her fingers. She put her foot down carefully on the gas, further, then further, then further still. Nothing happened. She turned and looked anxiously at Alison's father, and the car jerked and shot forward.

"Lift your foot up, lift it up," Mr. Ferguson said.

It seemed for a moment that Amanda had done something wrong, as she always did, something terrible, and that the car was rushing forward, roaring, unstoppable, carrying the three of them toward extinction.

But Mr. Ferguson's voice was calm. "Lift your foot," he said again, patient.

Amanda lifted her foot, and magically the car slowed to a purposeless roll. Amanda put her foot on the brake, and stopped the car completely. Her heart was pounding, and she looked at Mr. Ferguson, expecting him to frown.

But he said mildly, "Amanda wants to be a race car driver." He looked into the backseat at Alison, who was giggling, and said, "Your friend is a wild woman."

Then he taught her to press the pedal and move the car forward docilely. She had learned to start, to stop; she had even learned, unevenly, to back up, the car yawing artlessly across the parking lot.

Now Amanda lifted her head and squinted across the pale gravel at the Volvo. It glinted in the dark.

Inside Amanda's head was a song, and she laid her head down on her folded arms. With her eyes shut she sang quietly. "You, only see what-you-want-to-see," she sang. She heard the words, not in her voice, but in the voice she heard singing the words on the radio. The grass was now doing calm fogging things inside her head, and she felt peaceful. "You, only see, what-you-want-to-see," she sang to herself again. Her voice was high and gentle, a narrow ribbon of sound.

Amanda raised her head and stared out into the black trees. Again she thought of the long straight road up the island. The unswerving line unrolling rapidly, like in a movie. At high speed the peripheral landscape jumped, but the road itself kept hypnotically steady, centered, focused, rushing away before her eyes. She thought of it, surrounded by darkness, its mysterious path lit up by the headlights. Everything around it would be silent.

It was what she wanted to do: rush away, rush away from here. She wanted to rush ahead with her life, rush on until she was a grown-up and this was years in her past—these horrible times, her father's disappointment, the look in his eyes of blame, endless, endless, there forever.

A magical thought came to her: she could walk across the driveway and get into the car. The keys were always in it. She could drive it. She could feel herself walking across the driveway, the gravel cold and sharp beneath her bare feet.

She opened her eyes: she had not moved. She was sitting on the steps. She smiled to herself and put her head down again on her crossed arms. She imagined, again, walking across the gravel, feeling the stones against her bare feet. The driveway went in a curve; there were two entrances, and the car faced one of them. She wouldn't have to back it up. The sound of the fan in the house would, she hoped, drown out the sound of the engine starting. She would be on the road in a moment. She saw again that empty black road. Things were taking on a slow inevitability.

It was getting chilly, and Amanda wrapped her arms around her legs, hugging them. Now she felt affectionate toward her body. She liked her legs, even. She forgave them. She breathed in the comforting smell of her body. She felt the sudden roughness of her skin, rising into tiny humps of chilliness. *Goose bumps,* she thought. She rubbed her arms, but she wasn't cold enough to go inside. At least there were no bugs.

At Alison's house they had climbed out on the roof one night to smoke. They'd had a candle with them, and moths had flown into it. Excited, insane, they had tried clumsily to get at the flame. They had singed and blackened their wings, then staggered off, flying in horrible crippled patterns.

"What are they *doing?*" Amanda asked, trying to brush one away from immolation. She hated the feel of it, the buzzing vibration of its dry wing.

"Trying to kill themselves," said Alison. "Yuck." She swatted at one.

"They're not," said Amanda, making a face. "They're trying to *maim* themselves. It doesn't make any sense."

"And suicide does?"

"I mean, nerdhead," said Amanda, "if you wanted to get out of here, then you'd kill yourself. But why make things worse than they already are and then go on living?"

There was a pause.

"Have you thought of it?" Alison asked.

Amanda nodded. Of course she had, they all had. A girl in their class had run away from school. She'd been found a week later, at home. She had hanged herself in the barn. Amanda had thought of it over and over: the dim stillness of the barn, that dark silhouette.

She wouldn't do that. She wouldn't hang herself, turning suddenly heavy and terrified. You'd change your mind, and it would be too late. Your face would turn black, and you'd shit. No, she'd use pills. Her mother had sleeping pills, and Amanda had gone into her bathroom cabinet and poured them out of the bottle and into her own hand. They were shiny capsules; she'd listened to the dry weightless slithering sound as they piled into her cupped hand. They were yellow, blue, the colors intense, clinical. In her hand they had felt light but serious. She'd held one in her fingers and squeezed. It had yielded; it would give up its contents. What was inside could kill her. Amanda held her own death in her fingers. It beckoned. She was very close to it. It was in her fingers.

She had put all the pills back in the bottle and screwed on the childproof cap. She'd put the bottle back where she had found it, between a jar of Nighttime Rejuvenation and a lipstick called Mellow Mallow, which she sampled, rolling it smoothly along her lips and then smacking them precisely together. She knew where the bottle was. Sometimes she checked on it, to make sure; it was always there.

Amanda looked up now at the Volvo. It was still there, and she was still here. She still hadn't walked across to it. She put her head down on her knees and closed her eyes. The road. Halfway up the island, the road was flanked on one side by a meadow that stretched out to a little cove. There were oyster beds there, wooden trays of young oysters set in the shallows. She tried to imagine them. Were they in stacks, or spread out in rows like cookies on a sheet? Could they move? Did they mind being stacked up? How could you tell if they minded? She felt tender toward the young and helpless oysters, massed unprotestingly in the wooden trays. She hoped they were well treated; she feared they were not.

She had heard what was done to chickens, to veal calves. She had stopped eating veal. Not that she ever ate it anyway, but on principle. Lab animals. At school they had seen a movie showing what the cosmetics companies did to lab animals. First they took out the vocal cords, so the lab workers wouldn't be bothered by the sounds of their screams. After the movie the teacher talked to them about what they could do about this. Some of the girls wrote angry letters to the cosmetics companies, but it made Amanda feel helpless and sad. It seemed that the world was like this, that everywhere there were small creatures that were tortured. It seemed that there was too much of it for her to do anything about it. It was the way things were. She tried not to think about it.

Amanda wondered if the oysters could tell when it was night. Did they have eyes? She tried to remember how an oyster looked. She couldn't remember an eye anywhere. Was there an obvious one somewhere that she had missed? Maybe there were eyes inside the shell, maybe the oyster could only see when it was open. That made sense. It wouldn't need to see when it was shut. Or maybe that was exactly when it needed most to see. It was hard to tell, hard to imagine how oysters felt.

Behind her Amanda heard the back door click open. At once she cupped her fingers protectively over the joint and lowered her hand.

"Amanda?" It was Tess.

"What?" Amanda did not turn around.

"What are you doing?"

Amanda did not answer. Tess let the door sigh closed and came out on the deck. Her bare feet made a soft padding sound. She sat down next to Amanda. She was in her nightgown. In Amanda's hand the tip of the joint glowed.

"What is that?" Tess asked.

"Guess," said Amanda. She spoke slowly. The grass had slowed her tongue down, made spoken syllables roll off it delectably.

"Oh," said Tess, her voice changed. "Can I try it?"

"No," said Amanda. "You're too young."

"Come on," said Tess. "I am not."

"No," said Amanda. "Look at the trouble you got me into over that stupid dog book. Why are you up, anyway? Are you scared again?"

"I just woke up. I wasn't scared. Anyway, I'm sorry about the dog book. I didn't tell." She paused and sniffed. "I can smell it," she said, impressed at the rank strangeness of it.

"Really," Amanda said.

"Let me try it," Tess said. "Just a puff."

"All I really need," Amanda said, "is for them to find out I'd given you dope. That is really all I need. Dad would have me executed."

Tess frowned.

"Anyway," Amanda went on, "this is my only one, and I'm putting it out now. I want to save it." She stubbed the ember out carefully. She waved it in the air to cool it off and then put it back in the plastic bag.

"That's all you have left?"

Amanda nodded. "Dad took everything I own. This was hidden somewhere else. I'd forgotten I had it."

Tess sighed. She banged her knees together. The dark air around them was cool. She stared out into the darkness.

"No fireflies," Tess observed.

"They're all up there," Amanda said, pointing upward. Tess looked up.

"Those are stars," she said.

Amanda did not answer. There was no point in trying to explain things when you were stoned. She understood a lot of things right now, but she could not explain most of them. Tess banged her knees together again.

"Let's go for a drive," Amanda said.

"In the car?" Tess asked.

Amanda laughed.

"You can't drive," Tess said.

"Of course I can *drive*," Amanda said. "I just don't have a *license.* I can *drive.*"

Tess looked at her. Amanda looked out into the darkness. It came to her suddenly how easy, easy, it had been to drive. She could feel the steering wheel in her hands, that perfect circle of power, going around and around, held between her two hands. Moths would fly toward the windshield, and the airstream would swoosh them right past, they would turn into stars, effortlessly, beautifully, without pain.

She stood up. Tess watched her but did not move. Amanda started down the steps. It was so easy. She felt as though she were riding a secret invisible wave. She walked down the steps without feeling them. She forgot about Tess. She walked across the gravel, marveling at the feel of it, so sharp. Sharp beneath her bare hard soles, her toes. Sharp but it didn't hurt. This was her secret.

"Wait for me," Tess said. Amanda heard the rapid descending thumps of Tess's feet on the steps. "Yikes." Tess slowed to a hobble on the gravel. "Ouch."

Amanda opened the car door and got in.

"Cool," she said, settling herself. It felt great in the driver's seat. It was entirely different on this side of the car. The steering wheel was here. The road was in front of you. She thought of the black road, the soft grass beside it, bending in the sea wind. She closed her door as Tess slid in beside her. The girls looked at each other and laughed.

The keys were up on the visor, they fell into her hand as though they were her property—heavy, intricate, magic. She had no trouble with the ignition, the engine flared at once into obedient sound. She looked out into the blackness. Lights, she thought, charmed. She felt among the instruments along the dashboard. She nudged a stalk coming out of the steering wheel. The windshield wipers sprang eagerly to life, dashing back and forth across the glass.

"Amanda," Tess said, worried.

"Hold on," Amanda said. She turned off the windshield wipers. She turned on the turn signal. It blinked greenly to the left. "Hmm," she said. "Wait a minute." She found the knob. Ahead of them the row of spindly lilacs suddenly awoke, and in the corner by the road, the trunk of the big maple. "There," Amanda said, but she was not quite certain. There was something limited and restrained about the patch of light.

"It's supposed to be brighter," Tess said doubtfully. "Those aren't the real lights."

"Yes, they are," Amanda said. "These are what you use when you're not on the highway. I know how to drive, Tess." She could see well enough.

She put both hands on the wheel and set her foot carefully on the gas pedal. The car moved, obedient to her wishes. Amanda felt sublime. She had never felt so powerful, so easy in her strength.

Now everything began to gather around her, the smooth dreamlike parts of what was happening. There was the deep night, there was the perfect circle held in her hands. The lights revealed a magic path. The engine hummed its orderly incantation. It came to Amanda, her foot poised, that now everything would happen exactly as it was meant—perfectly, without error.

She felt something rising slowly inside, she felt brimming, exultant. Things were changing, right now. Things were now going right. The part of her life, the bad part, when everything she did was wrong, was over. Now things were altered, and she was in the part of her life when everything was right. Now everything was possible to her. She eased her foot down, and the car's energy rose obediently. She was part of something large and marvelous. The car rolled smoothly forward on the gravel. Amanda took her foot off the pedal; the car stopped.

"You see?" she said. "I told you I could drive."

"Cool," Tess said. She patted her thighs through her cotton nightgown.

Amanda put her foot down again, and the car nosed forward. She was exquisitely aware of everything around her, could hear the grating shift of each piece of gravel as the car's weight rolled forward. She heard the engine singing inside its heated cave. In her mind she saw the road shining under the high moon, reaching straight up the center of the island. She could see everything.

She eased the car out of the driveway and turned carefully up the hill. The road here was a dark tunnel, overhung with trees. The leaves were lush and dense, strange and sinister, lit up but colorless. They hung overhead in jagged intricate patterns, like stitchwork.

Nearing the turn at the top of the hill, Amanda slowed the car to a crawl. The curve here was sharp, nearly right-angled. A high privet hedge rose blackly along one side. She brought the car close to the hedge at a stately crawl and turned the wheel. She moved it too quickly and too far, and the car twisted unnervingly. But she was moving slowly, and she took her foot off the gas and corrected, turning the wheel back. The car steadied, responding. Amanda felt triumphant. Everything she did was right. The car settled into the journey. The white church shimmered past on the left, a pale angular apparition in the dark. The road curved again, less sharply here. Amanda was more confident now, and turned the wheel slower, more gently. The car turned perfectly smoothly. It was easier now, now she could feel how it was meant to be.

"You see?" she said to Tess. She felt as though she were inhabiting two states of consciousness. One was sharp and focused, like when she steadied the car, and from there she could deal with the hardness and urgency of the rest of the world. The other state was soft, vulnerable, sleepy, and from there she could not explain things to anyone, she could not even talk.

"Cool," Tess said again, but she seemed muted. She was craning forward, peering ahead into the darkness.

The car carried radiant space before it, like a lantern in a cave. The long straight road was empty, just as Amanda had imagined it. They reached the flat strip, and on the right were the wide meadows. The grass was feathery, and bright white as they passed. Insects, fiery in the lights—moths, creatures with heavy bodies—blazed suddenly, close, and then were gone, thudding into the windshield, or simply vanishing, yanked into invisibility by speed. Along the side of the road, telephone poles appeared rhythmically, upright, solid, too close to them.

Amanda was intent on the car. It grew larger and larger in her consciousness, it grew magically in her brain. The strange feel of it in her hands, the mysterious translation of her thoughts into its movement, transfixed her. A spell glowed invisibly around her. Ahead, the dark road gleamed under their rushing lights. Beside her Tess leaned forward, staring, rapt, as though they were crossing the untraveled surface of the moon.

They passed the high telephone pole where the ospreys had a nest. Amanda had seen it, an enormous, disorderly raft of twigs overhead. The ospreys were fierce looking, with their curved beaks and muddy feathers, black frowning brows, it was hard to think of them as domestic, as good parents. They seemed to her demons, ruthless, a family from hell, shrieking and tearing things out of each other's mouths.

The slow snakelike curves of the Big Club driveway appeared in their lights. Amanda slowed the car and turned sedately into the parking lot.

"Now what?" Tess asked. She was subdued, anxious.

Amanda shook her head. Speech no longer interested her. She could not explain to Tess that there was nothing to fear, that everything now would go right. It was something she just knew. The car in her hands was supple and obedient. The gravel lot sloped down before her into the darkness, mysterious, without color or context. The landscape was limitless, shrouded in night. In the parking lot she would be able to turn in a circle, she would not have to back up to turn around. It all worked perfectly. As they turned, suddenly the sound of the car on gravel stopped, they were making no sound, as in a dream. Amanda stared, puzzled: they were on the lawn. The car was driving on the grass.

"The car's on grass," Amanda said. "Like me." She looked over at Tess to see if she got it, but Tess said nothing.

Tess was too young to understand the things Amanda did. And the vast amusement Amanda felt, the benevolent complicity she felt from the world, was private. She shut her eyes for a second and discovered the rich deliciousness of the dark behind her eyelids, textured, layered, soft.

"Amanda," Tess said, scared.

Amanda opened her eyes. Tess was looking at her. Her hand was clenched around the door handle.

"What?"

"Open your eyes."

"I am," Amanda said, and laughed. She shook her head. She could not explain this. She was back on the gravel, back on the driveway, facing the right direction. They were going home. She congratulated herself.

They eased smoothly out to the road, and started back. On the right now was the mass of dense brushy woods that had taken over the interior of Marten's Island. Wild grape, wild rose, wild blackberry: it was a thicket of bristling growth. Amanda loved it. She loved the thought of the dense green tangle. She loved chaos, she felt like cheering it on. Go, she thought giddily. On the other side of the road was soft bending grass, and far out beyond the grass were the silent oysters.

"There are the oyster beds," Amanda said. "The oysters are asleep in their beds." She began to laugh.

Tess looked at her soberly. Tess was just a child, Amanda thought. She had left Tess far behind. She shook her head to herself and pressed her foot down smoothly. The car surged on. "Asleep in their beds," she repeated. It had a dreamy ring to it. Insects hit the windshield, faster than before. The thicket raced alongside. The black sky was high above them, rising and embracing everything. Everything was going right. The marijuana was singing in her head now, warm and luminous. She was singing, herself. The long black night was just outside her, and she could feel it inside her too, flowing through her in a dark fluid stream, the way the air was streaming past the windows.

The car was hers, humble, restrained, powerful in her hands. She had the perfect circle held in her hands. The perfect circle to hold forever. She thought of saying that out loud to Tess, but Tess was too young to understand it. She smiled to herself. Everything would turn out right. She was somehow protected, magically. She laughed out loud to think of this, laughed with happiness. She thought of her father, he would be pleased by this. He would be pleased by her.

The road kept coming up to them, fast, the line down the middle moving slightly from side to side, the way it did in a movie. Amanda tried to keep precisely in the center of the line. It seemed the right thing to do, it seemed symmetrical, fair. The line down the middle leapt up at her, shifting, thrilling.

"You're going too fast," Tess said. Her hand was on the door handle and she looked straight ahead, as if by watching the road she could control it.

"No I'm not," Amanda said, and to prove it she put her foot down further on the gas pedal. There was lots more speed that she wasn't using. The meadows flashed along beside her, the long dense grass, white in the headlights. Now it did feel fast, to Amanda. She could not remember what to do: what had Alison's father said? But she felt in a stasis now, flying along in the car, along the straight road, the meadow grass standing soft and fluid beside them. It seemed right, it seemed exactly right, but it was not exactly right; at the same time there was something else she was thinking of.

"Amanda," Tess said, her voice more urgent.

"What," Amanda said. She knew there was something else, but could not remember. What had Alison's father said? What had he said? She was a wild woman, but it was not that. They were coming past the church now, the white building, the sides sprang up suddenly into the black windshield.

"Amanda!" Tess said, now loud. She was frightened.

"It's okay," Amanda said. She heard her own voice now, high, mystical. She could hear all that she knew, it was all in her voice. "It's okay," she said again, to Tess.

The curve was coming up, after the church. There was the curve. She saw it in her mind's eye, saw it coming smoothly, the car sliding decorously around it the way it did when her father was driving, or Emma. She knew how the car would go around it, without slowing, like those tiny metal cars on metal game tracks, slipping around it hypnotically. She could not tell which she was watching, which was real and which was an image in her mind. She watched the road leap along in the light. She watched the road swing around, on the curve. But everything was going faster than she meant it, the curve was jerky, things swiveled, jerking, the hedge was not where it was meant to be and then everything changed, the tempo of everything changed, and the white line moved beneath the car, it went suddenly all the way around, spinning and pivoting, and then there was the hedge, springing powerfully toward the windshield, and the tree.

PART THREE

24

The room is semiprivate, which means that a pale green curtain could be pulled out between the two high metal beds, separating them for privacy. But the other bed is empty, and the curtain is pulled back against the wall. The room is a narrow rectangle, not large, and it is nearly filled by the two beds. A straight-backed chair faces the bed where Tess lies. Emma has been sitting in that chair since eight o'clock in the morning. It is now the afternoon of Tess's third day in the hospital.

For the first two days she was in the Intensive Care Unit. In the ICU there were no curtains to pull, no privacy. The beds stood exposed, away from the walls, so they were accessible on all sides to doctors, nurses, machines, the equipment of saving lives. The head of the bed did not stand against a wall, anchored there against the pull of the night. There was no bedside table, no lamp. No lamps were necessary: the overhead lights there were always on. There was no need for darkness, there, the patients had created their own night, their own darkness and silence. They slept on, in spite of everything, the noise, the activity, the unremitting light.

In the ICU, underlying all the other sounds, was the steady wheezing gasp of the respirator, forcing air relentlessly in, lengthily out, of the lungs of those patients whose bodies no longer breathed for themselves. Tess did bravely breathe for herself, but still she was put for a time on a respirator. This was to hyperventilate the brain, in case of swelling. Tess lay with her mouth stretched horribly open around a flexible ribbed hose. The hose was too big for her mouth, Emma thought, it was made for a grown-up's gape, not for Tess's soft lips. But there was no child's size, Emma was told.

The machine breathed loudly, and too hard, Emma felt, into Tess's narrow chest. It rose and fell mechanically under the hospital gown.

There were other machines. Tess was also connected to a black screen that tracked each quick living beat of her heart, recording it as a small meteor, bright and silent. While Emma stood by Tess in the ICU she was nearly afraid to touch her, afraid to do much more than stroke her arm. She was afraid that she would disturb the bandages on Tess's head, or the black cuff of the heart monitor that clasped her upper arm, or the small IV needle that pierced the delicate skin on the back of Tess's soft hand, or the clamp on her finger that measured, in some mysterious way, the oxygen in her blood. Tess was given CAT scans, and her blood, her urine, her reflexes, all were tested, to see what sorts of injuries there might be besides the hemorrhage. The tests showed nothing but bruising and the hemorrhage.

These things, the hospital, had taken over Tess's body. They fed Tess, tended her, kept Emma from her. This felt like punishment to Emma, for negligence, perhaps. For where had she been when Tess's body had so terribly collided with hard unyielding things? Where had her mother, her protector, been? Emma stood timidly by Tess in the ICU. She has always felt that she owned Tess's body; it has been hers since its birth. She feels that it is a part of her, an extension. She has touched it almost as often and as familiarly as her own, stroked it, washed it, tended it. She has known it with such deep and steady attention that it seemed indisputably to be hers. Now she has been shown to be wrong. Now she can barely stroke Tess's arm. She does that very carefully, afraid of disturbing the equipment. Emma is desperately afraid of disturbing anything. She holds the machinery, the doctors, the nurses, all of it, in superstitious esteem: these are the forces that are trying to save her child.

Now, Emma is alone with Tess in this small narrow room. Periodically Emma rises and goes to stand by the bed. She leans over her and strokes Tess's motionless arm.

Tess lies still, her eyes closed. Her face is swollen and battered. The blood has raged angrily everywhere, under the tender skin. There are darkened patches, welts, raised islands of bruise, small continents of deep discoloration—purple, a dreadful greenish brown. On the left side of her forehead is a wide lump, a line of dried brown blood along its crest. The shape of her mouth is distorted by swelling, the sweet line of her lips is changed. On one side of the upper lip there is a vertical line, where the skin has split.

Still, beneath the bruising and alterations Emma can find her daughter. Along the hairline are Tess's tiny blond hairs, fragile, shining. The eyebrows are smooth and unchanged: long pale arcs, soft and gleaming, like rabbit fur. Tess's freckles are still visible, pale apparitions among the deep reds. Her sweet light hair is glossy, her face clean. Someone else has washed Tess: not Emma. Someone else took a cloth and gently washed the blood from her face, cleaned her fragile translucent eyelids, the soft skin around the swollen nostrils. The thought that someone else did this is painful to Emma, she has been denied something.

Emma stands next to Tess and watches her closed eyes, resting deep in the sheltering sockets. Behind the swollen lids, the eyes are not always still. Sometimes Emma sees them move, a swift underwater flutter, staccato blinks. Sometimes the eyes open, and then Emma leans forward, her heart pounding. But the eyes are unfocused, the pupils sluggish, the stare vague. Even when the eyes move they do not see. Then they close, and then there is stillness, nothing.

Emma looks down at Tess's face. Tess's mouth is slightly open, relaxed, the beautiful cushiony lips just parted. She breathes without sound, but Emma can see the long slight rise of the chest as Tess inhales, the faint shift in the hollows of her throat, then the fall of her chest as she exhales.

Watching her daughter breathe is what Emma does when she stands by her bed. It is soothing. This is completely normal, this breathing. Emma leans over, watching intently, as though she must memorize this rhythmic motion. It is what Emma used to do at night when Tess was a baby in her crib. Emma remembers this, waking in sudden alarm, slipping out of bed, moving through the dark apartment, stepping softly into her daughter's room. Standing by the crib, leaning over the bars, listening, watching, until she was assured that Tess was breathing, her small body alive, secure.

It is this feeling that Emma tries to recapture as she leans over Tess now. She strives for that feeling of reassurance and relief, as she sees her daughter breathe.

A smooth clean bandage made of thin layers of white gauze has been wrapped over and over across the top of Tess's head. Except for this, Emma tells herself, and except for the bruising, which will fade, Tess looks asleep. She is just asleep, Emma tells herself. This is how she is determined to view it. Sleep is what Tess needs. It's the truest, most deeply benign restorative. Tess is deeply, powerfully, usefully asleep. Her brain is healing itself.

Emma tries to imagine Tess's brain. She pictures it: intricate and convoluted, the mysterious whorls fitting themselves precisely into the smooth perfect concavity of the skull. She sees it as beautiful and flawless. She cannot picture it as damaged, she will not.

Tess has had a hemorrhage of the dura, the layer of cells that line the skull. That layer, which should be clean and pale, like the translucent creatures in a drop of pond water beneath a microscope, has been suffused with dark violent blood. The blood, rushing into this landscape, has stopped now, and stilled, but it has not retreated. Those clear pure cells have been invaded, violated. But Emma sees them as only changed in color, as though a different filter has been set across the microscope, the cells still in perfect working order. She cannot hold in her head the images of these darkened cells and that of Tess's beautiful whorled brain and that of her swollen motionless face. The three together are too terrible.

Emma wavers between wanting to know all she can and being faint with fear at learning too much, learning something she cannot bear to know. She does not want to know certain things; if they are true she does not want to hear them. There are certain words she never wants to hear. She has, in a split second—the second in which Tess's warm skull met the dashboard of the car—become deeply, irremediably superstitious. She now believes fearfully and wholly in the power of thoughts, coincidences, bad luck. She believes in an ambient and potent malevolence which she does not want to arouse or attract. On some unexamined level she believes that if she allows certain thoughts into her mind she will be giving them permission to be true. She doesn't want these thoughts to have any existence at all, not even a silent, fleeting moment of consideration. Resolutely, she does not let herself think of certain possibilities. She does not permit it. She feels that this, at least, is something she can do. This is a willed act that she can perform. It's the only one. She cannot help Tess in any other way.

Emma knows that if she has to hear any mention of the worst, or even of the very bad, she will not be able to bear it. There is a kind of panic, tumultuous and overwhelming, that she can feel starting to rise in her as her mind moves toward certain thoughts. To avoid this panic, she asks only certain questions. She asks what the screens are for, what the electronic signals on them mean. She listens carefully to the answers; they are her lifelines. They are all she has. Those answers, and the manner, the looks given her by the doctors and the nurses. Emma watches the doctors and nurses, studies them like a lover. She has memorized and examined every gesture, every word, every subtle alteration of expression. She scans everything for meaning, for the meaning she wants.

This morning, when she arrived, the morning nurse looked at Emma before she looked at Tess. Jackie, a short broad white woman in her fifties, has a pleasant doughy face. There are deep lines from her nose to the corners of her mouth. Her short graying hair is cut in brief weightless layers, feathered like a bird. She is big hipped and big rumped. Emma loves her, as she loves everyone who has taken care of Tess, she loves them as a prisoner loves the wardens, cravenly, desperately.

"Good morning," Jackie said. Usually Jackie looked at Tess when she said this, but today she looked at Emma, and smiled.

"Good morning," Emma answered. She hoped her voice didn't sound too eager.

Jackie walked to the bed with her clipboard. She began writing down numbers, recording the information from the machines. There was nothing else that was unusual, just her look. Did it mean that Jackie knew something new, something that she did not want to tell Emma, something Emma could not bear to hear? Did it mean that Jackie pitied Emma, pitied her innocence in the face of this new, dreadful knowledge? Or did it mean that Jackie could now look first at Emma because Tess was slowly moving out of danger, and she no longer required such concern, such concentration, such urgency? Maybe the look meant that Jackie was allowing Emma more intimacy with her, because of this undisclosed good news. That Jackie no longer needed to keep Emma at a distance. Or maybe it meant that the door, this morning, had not been pushed all the way shut, and when Jackie came in Emma was in her line of sight. But Emma could not afford to think that. She needed signs to follow, meaningful symbols to interpret that would give her hope. The numbers on the monitors, the steadily rising and falling electronic lines, the brilliant, limpid impulses, like bright stars flowing across the black screen, are too frightening. She can hardly bear to look at them, for fear they will show her something that she cannot deny, cannot bear to learn.

Jackie lifts Tess's limp arm. She drives the glinting shaft of a needle into it and draws a syringe of bright blood. The color is healthy, Emma thinks, vivid and clear. They have taken so much blood from this small body. Jackie checks the IV bag. The soft transparent sac hangs high over Tess's motionless form, its fine plastic line carrying a narrow but infinite supply of fluid—medication, nutriments. How can this tiny line sustain

Tess? Three meals a day? But Emma has been told that it does. She must trust these people, the answers they give.

Jackie leans over Tess. She picks up Tess's hand.

"Good morning, Tess," she says. "If you can hear me, squeeze my hand." There is a long moment, during which Emma does not breathe. Jackie does not move, bent over Tess's poor bruised face. Emma watches, her whole body listening. Then Jackie sets Tess's hand down again, gently, next to her side. Without looking at Emma she pushes a button to raise the head of the bed. There is a hum, and slowly it rises. Jackie sets her strong arms underneath Tess and shifts her unresisting form, turning her carefully onto her side. Emma hates watching this, she hates seeing Tess's limbs fall about lifelessly. She cannot look away.

This happens every two hours. A nurse comes and turns Tess, moves her arms and legs. And periodically a nurse will ask Emma to leave the room. She is polite and friendly, but she makes Emma leave while she does something to Tess. Emma asked once what it was she did, but the nurse shook her head. "There are certain procedures that we only do without any visitors, even the parents," she says. "It's a hospital rule."

From her reading, Emma believes that this is testing for reflexes— pain. And they suction out the throat, to clear it. At some point, too, there is the risk of bedsores, and the nurses would cut those out. This is called decubiti, and Emma cannot imagine it. She cannot imagine Tess's beautiful lithe body breeding sores, or having those sores cut out, raw and oozing. She cannot imagine it.

She has asked the nurse if she can turn Tess herself: she, Emma, is there all day long, with nothing to do. She can turn Tess every hour, she can turn her every fifteen minutes, if that will help. She knows that circulation is important to a comatose patient. She has learned this through reading what Peter has brought her. She has not dared ask these questions directly of the doctor; she does not want these words spoken out loud.

At the foot of Emma's chair is a canvas book bag. She has two books for herself—a Trollope novel and some essays by Lewis Thomas—and three glossy magazines. She has, so far, not opened either book. She has read one of the magazines, but she cannot remember which. She has brought some of Tess's favorite books: *The Lion, the Witch and the Wardrobe*, and two Tintins. During the day, Emma periodically picks up one of the books and reads out loud to Tess, who lies without moving, her eyes shut. Emma reads for hours at a time, giving dramatic inflection to the story, giving each character a different voice. When she reads from Tintin, she barks for Snowy the Airedale in the loony words of the French editions: "Ouah! Ouah!"

Tess and Amanda used to laugh at Snowy's French bark. Emma remembered a car trip in which the girls both knelt in the backseat, pretending to be Snowy, and barking with French accents at everything they saw. "Ouah! Ouah! A McDon-ahld's! Ouah! Ouah! A breedge!" They barked in queer growly voices, and talked with ridiculous accents, and this made them laugh so helplessly and loudly that Peter, who was driving, told them irritably to quiet down, as though they had been fighting, not laughing. But they were laughing too hard to pay any attention, their laughter had taken over their world just then, it was all they could do, and they rolled backwards on the seat, their knees in the air, their eyes watering, shaking with laughter, helpless. And then Peter, because they were on a highway and he felt harassed and pressured by the speed and traffic, and resentful of the fact that he was bearing all of the family burden, and they were bearing none of it, shouted at them. Even then the girls did not stop, what had taken them over was more powerful than Peter's anger, and they crouched down behind the seat, whispering gutturally to each other and laughing, trying to muffle it, but unsuccessfully, snorting and choking, their hands held over their mouths, writhing with hilarity.

Emma, remembering this, finds herself smiling, thinking of that irrepressible laughter. But at once this becomes painful: as soon as she realizes she is smiling she remembers. This memory is so different from the way things are now that it is excruciating, and the idea of Peter shouting at Tess for laughter is intolerable, like sacrilege. And that car trip was so utterly different from what she knows now of the last car trip the two girls took together that Emma cannot allow herself to compare them without that feeling of rising panic.

She shakes her head to clear that memory from it—it burns—and she reads on steadily, at length. She concentrates on the story, which is about the Abominable Snowman, in Tibet, and a gang of international criminals, and kindly people of great virtue and courage, and of course the indefatigable, stouthearted, high-minded Tintin. When Emma lets herself think about the characters in the book—the nice ones—tears gather in her eyes. She weeps furtively for the lonely misunderstood Abominable Snowman, and for the kind Tibetan who risks his life for Tintin. Emma will now weep at anything.

Her reading voice, she believes, is soothing Tess. Emma believes that, on some level, Tess knows that Emma is there in the room with her. She believes that somewhere in Tess's hidden, quiet, resting mind she can hear her mother's voice. Emma believes that this steady sound will maintain the connection between herself in this world and Tess, wherever she is. Emma hopes that her voice will draw Tess back into this world, where her mother is waiting.

Just before three-thirty Doctor Baxter arrives. It is in the afternoon that he always comes, but usually earlier than this. Does his lateness mean anything?

Emma sits up straighter when he comes in. She leans forward in her chair, setting her feet neatly side by side. She feels that if she is very good, very polite to the doctor, perfectly courteous, if she can achieve a kind of perfection through her behavior, Doctor Baxter will tell her the things she wants to hear. This is another of her superstitions.

"Good afternoon," Doctor Baxter says, his eyes sliding over Emma at once and moving to Tess. He is polite but impersonal, it is clear that he is not here for conversation. He is here on his own business, and Emma's presence is incidental. He will tolerate it, he will be courteous, but that is all. Emma sits up very straight in her chair. She would stand eagerly, and come over next to him at Tess's bedside, but she has done this, and he has not seemed pleased. He seems to want to be the only person leaning over Tess. He seems to think that his right to Tess's body is now greater than Emma's. She cannot deny this. She cannot deny him anything. She must trust him.

Doctor Baxter is not very tall, only just taller than Emma. He is mostly bald, with deep horizontal lines in his forehead. His eyes are small, blue and very intent. He wears pale reddish tortoiseshell glasses. Now he moves past Emma and stands before Tess, his eyes on the heart monitor. He watches the screen as it flickers with that brilliant white tadpole, jittering endlessly along the black stream.

Emma, watching, tries to make her own face bright and interested, in case he turns to her. She tries to look alert and responsive, someone he can tell things to. Doctor Baxter does not look at her. He picks up Tess's hand and says, "Tess, if you can hear me, squeeze my hand."

Waiting, Emma feels her mouth suddenly go dry. She feels tears threatening, a lump in her throat. Panic hovers around her: she must not cry in front of the doctor, she must not. She presses down the lump in her throat, swallows, blinks. Then Doctor Baxter sets Tess's hand back down on the covers, and he straightens up. He makes a notation on the chart, Tess's chart, which he has on his clipboard.

"Well?" Emma manages. She can no longer endure the silence. "How does it all look?"

Doctor Baxter turns to her. "About the same," he says. He stoops slightly, bending over Tess's face. He pulls down her eyelids, separately, and flashes a tiny bright light into each one. He picks up Tess's hand again and presses his thumb deep into the pale flesh of her wrist. Emma watches him without breathing. She watches him as though he had water, and she were dying of thirst. She knows that he is listening, through his hand, to the deep murmurs of Tess's poor damaged body, that Tess's blood is speaking to him. Mute, Emma waits. She cannot bear to ask again.

None of Emma's thoughts has words. What she wants is what she is, it's all she is. She never forms to herself the sentence she's thinking; she's living it. That's all there is to her, that one sentence.

Doctor Baxter pulls down the sheet. Tess's small body, in its hospital gown, lies trustingly before him. Her feet turn slightly out, relaxed. He picks one up and runs his thumbnail up its outer edge. The foot twitches slightly.

Emma takes her courage in both hands. "What does that do?"

Without looking at her Doctor Baxter answers. "This is called Babinski's sign. It concerns the amount of blood in the brain."

Emma feels her heart pounding. "And?" she presses. "What does it show with Tess?"

"When I run my finger along her foot," says Doctor Baxter, "the toes normally respond by turning down, reflexively. If the toes turn up, there may be a dangerous amount of blood in the brain."

"Oh," says Emma. She is having trouble breathing, the information is so powerful, so momentous. She has no idea why the test works, why this response is so. She would not dream of asking him: she feels she is only allowed a certain number of questions. "And?" she finally says, fearful, desperate. "What do her toes do?"

Without speaking Doctor Baxter does the test again. His nail slides smoothly along the outside of Tess's foot. Emma stares at Tess's toes. Magically, as the doctor's nail reaches the upper half of the foot, Tess's toes suddenly curl downward.

"Oh," says Emma again. Gratitude floods through her. "It's good." She looks at Doctor Baxter. He doesn't look at her, but he nods.

"Isn't it?" she asks, insisting.

But he will not give in. He will not allow her to flood with hope. Ignoring her question he turns to her, his face neutral. An absolute barrier surrounds him. His mouth is set with his own thoughts.

"It's a satisfactory response," he says. "But there is no change," he finishes, reminding Emma that despite the beautiful rippling of the toes, that breathtaking signal from the interior, brilliant, commanding, like the sudden gleam from a lighthouse, Tess's mind is still shrouded, fogbound, silent.

Doctor Baxter waits politely. He does not want Emma to entertain unreasonable hope, she can see that, and he also does not want her to break down and weep. These are things he resolutely wants nothing to do with. He does not want her to ask him for anything more than information.

Emma blinks, and her mind turns panicky. All day long she has waited for this moment, her one moment with the doctor, who is her only hope. She depends upon him in order to be able to continue with her life. When the moment of her audience arrives, she is confused and overwhelmed. She is struck dumb with terror. She is afraid to ask technical questions, even when she has rehearsed them. In his presence, under his neutral, impassive gaze, her mind locks. She knows she will stutter, pronounce things wrong, sound moronic. She knows the words, the names. She knows about the dural hemorrhage. She knows that Tess tested at seven on the Glasgow scale of obtundation; she knows that ten is the worst, deep coma. She knows that obtundation means unconsciousness. She knows all these things; she cannot risk saying them, talking about them. Fear makes her stupid. She reverts to clumsy, childlike questions that suggest a deep and abiding ignorance.

"But what do you think?" she asks desperately. She now stands up, regardless of the risk of offending Doctor Baxter.

"There hasn't been much change," he says. His voice is not unkind. He slides his pen into the metal clasp at the top of the clipboard, but doesn't move. He waits. He's giving her this long moment of attention. Does this mean that he's sorry for her? Does this mean he's letting her know that she should not be too hopeful?

"But it doesn't mean anything bad, does it?" Emma says. "I mean, the brain may just be recuperating on its own, mending, but she'll still, she'll still . . ." she stops. Terror has seized her speech, and her voice breaks. ". . . come out all right?"

Doctor Baxter looks at her for a moment. She can't read his expression. Then he nods.

"It's possible," he says.

Emma can think of nothing more to say. After a moment Doctor Baxter steps politely toward her, making her retreat from him, since there is not room enough for him to get by unless she moves. She steps backwards, toward the hard-backed metal chair, and he passes her without looking, on his way to the door.

"Excuse me," he says, as he passes.

That's all. Her moment with the doctor is over.

At just past six, the hall door opens. Emma looks up: it is Warren. This is the first time he and Emma have been alone together since the accident. Warren's face is tense, his mouth tight.

"Hello," he says stiffly, and steps inside. He is beautifully dressed, dark pinstripe suit, broad lustrous tie. He looks polished, gleaming. How can he look, at six o'clock in the evening, so unrumpled, wonders Emma. Did he go home and change, after work? Emma resents his nattiness, deeply and instantly. She resents his dressing up, showing himself off, here, visiting his daughter, who is unable to see him. Emma feels vivid with hatred for him.

"Hello, Warren," she says.

Then, as she says his name, she begins suddenly and unexpectedly to cry. Cramping, powerful sobs take over her body, and she bends forward in her chair, her face covered by her hands. She cannot stop. Over and over she is shaken by long hideous sobs. Warren draws near, uncomfortable. She feels him standing next to her, and out of embarrassment, or out of consideration for him, she tries to stop crying. She cannot. The sobs hurl through her like blasts of wind. Warren leans past her, to the windowsill, where there is a box of Kleenex. He hands it to her and pats her awkwardly on the back. His touch is uneasy, as though he has never touched her body before in his life, as though he's never patted another human being before.

"Shh-hhh," he says, sounding insincere. "It's okay."

Emma doesn't answer. She is furious. *What is okay?* It's intolerable, absurd, for Warren to say that anything is okay. Her anger makes her cry harder. The crying has now taken her over completely, and she makes terrible sounds, great racking moans, loud and awful, as though she were near death—long shuddering gasps that shake her whole body. At the bottom of each sob her body is empty, airless. She sobs again, draws gustily in and the breath floods back into her, opening her lungs for the next cry. Her cheeks are flooding with tears, her chin is wet, her throat, her neck, her wrists.

When she manages at last to stop crying, when the heaving sobs slow and lessen, Emma stands up. She lifts her face to look at Warren. She takes a Kleenex, blots her eyes, blows her nose, sighs. She knows she is now red eyed, swollen nosed, which pleases her. She wants Warren to see how bad things really are, that everything is bad. That he can't simply put on beautiful clothes and make things all right. Warren's face is now close to hers, it is right in front of her. She is closer to him, physically, than she has been in years. She sees that, though his mouth is tight and pinched, unfriendly, his eyes, like hers, are sad.

He is Tess's father.

Emma puts her arms around him and lays her head on his shoulder. Warren doesn't move at all, he stands stiff and resistant within the circle of her arms. But she holds him close against her, she holds his grief to hers, and after a moment he puts his arms around her and holds her. Then he begins very gently to sway, holding her close and swaying very slightly, almost as if they were about to dance, holding her, rocking her back and forth.

Emma holds Warren tightly, in a way she has not been able to hold Peter since it happened. Warren's body now seems unfamiliar to her: the shape, the height, the heft of it are wrong. She has forgotten his smell. But still she feels right, holding him tightly in her arms, and she closes her eyes, swaying with him, letting him rock her, rocking him. She feels him begin to cry, too, his chest suddenly heaving against hers, a breath taken, then let out slowly, in miserable graduated gusts. When she hears this she begins to pat his back, slowly, gently, sliding her hand on his back in small soothing circles, as though he were a child, as though she loved him.

Emma stands facing the door to the hall, which is still open. Over Warren's shoulder she sees Peter appear in the doorway. Seeing her, he stops. She watches him, saying nothing. Her arms stay around Warren, and she goes on patting his back, gently. Peter stands with his briefcase in one hand. His clothes are wrinkled; he looks rumpled and undistinguished. Emma despises him for this: how can he come to see Tess in such a state of disarray, looking as if he cared so little?

Peter waits, but Emma does not change her position or speak. The two watch each other. Finally, Peter, his face dark, moves into the room. He sets his briefcase, with some emphasis, down on the empty bed. Warren hears him and pulls himself away from Emma, his head bent. Emma hands him the box of Kleenex, still looking at Peter. Warren blows his nose, wipes his eyes, tries to compose himself.

"Hello," Peter says, coolly, to Emma.

"Hello," says Emma. She does not move.

"Hello, Peter," Warren says awkwardly. He gives a sideways wave. His head is still down, he is trying to recover.

"Hello, Warren," Peter says courteously. He turns from them both and stands over Tess's bed. He leans over her silent form.

"Hello, little chickadee," he says quietly. He puts his hand down to stroke her hair.

"Don't," Emma says suddenly.

Peter looks at her.

"Don't touch her," Emma says.

Peter's mouth tightens. He withdraws his hand and straightens. "How is she?" he asks Emma. He speaks gently and matter-of-factly, as though Emma were a panicky animal.

Emma shakes her head, looking at the floor.

"What did the doctor say?" Peter perseveres.

"Nothing new," Emma says. She folds her arms.

There is a silence. Warren sniffs, wipes his face. He tries to blow his nose discreetly.

"How long do we go on waiting like this?" Peter asks.

Emma shakes her head.

"Is there anyone else we could talk to? Should we think about getting a second opinion?" Peter asks.

Emma stares at him. She can hardly answer. She feels deeply bound, immobilized, by inertia and fear. It is hard enough to get through each day. The idea of changing everything, doing something else, something different, seems terrifying to her. She does not dare disturb things here, she cannot imagine destroying the delicate equilibrium of this silent room, of the hope that clings lightly in the corners, like cobwebs. She does not dare risk angering Doctor Baxter. She cannot imagine telling him that she is challenging his authority with a second opinion. She cannot risk his anger.

"Maybe we should," Warren says. He looks at Emma.

"Who should we ask?" Emma says, helpless.

"I could ask my doctor to suggest someone," says Peter. "We could get a referral to the head of Neurology at Columbia-Presbyterian, maybe."

"At another hospital?" says Emma. "We don't want to move her, do we? And suppose he says we should do something different? Then what? Which doctor do we trust? *How do you know what to do?*"

There is a silence. Warren and Emma look at each other, then away. Peter looks at Emma. She does not look at him, she will not meet his eyes. Beside the bed, the heart monitor silently records the steady courses of white stars across its deep black screen.

Emma knows that Peter is looking at her. She does not want to look at him, or talk to him. It is too hard. She is concentrating on something. She is concentrating on how to get through the next moment. And then the moment after that. Peter is in the way of this. Everything is in the way of this, but especially Peter.

"Do you want me to talk to Doctor Hendricks about it?" Peter asks Emma.

Emma says nothing.

"Emma?" Peter says. Now his voice contains a trace, a very faint trace, of impatience.

Emma lowers her eyes, not looking at him. She shakes her head.

There is a silence in the room. Peter looks down again at Tess. He watches her face, steadily, intently, as though he were reading her. He draws nearer, leaning down slightly, though he doesn't stretch his hand out again. He gazes down at her. His eyes are tender. Emma looks up. She sees him watching Tess.

"Don't," Emma says without inflection.

Peter looks up. "What?"

"Don't look at her like that," Emma says.

There is a silence.

"Emma," Peter says, "don't go too far."

Emma does not answer. There is nowhere that is too far for her to go. She would do anything. She is trying to get through the next moment.

Warren straightens his shoulders finally, returning himself to the public person. His voice is now courteous, impersonal. He says to Peter, "How was the traffic coming uptown?"

Peter stares at him, then answers. "Not too bad, actually," he says coolly. "I'm not late because of the traffic. I'm late because I stopped at the apartment."

There is a silence. Both men have, at different times in their lives, said "the apartment" and meant the place they lived with Emma.

Emma says nothing. She does not ask Peter why he stopped off there, what he has brought. She cannot remember what the apartment is like, why he might want to go there. She cannot focus on it. She is trying to get through the next moment. It is exhausting.

She wishes both of them would go. She wants to get out one of Tess's books and read to her. She has a feeling that this, right now, might be a crucial moment. It might be. Right now, Tess's consciousness might be beginning to rise, light might be beginning to break across it. Right now might be the moment when Tess should hear her mother's voice, reading aloud words that Tess knows.

Emma thinks of brave little Tintin: maybe his image is the one that could reach Tess, break through to her. In his tidy V-necked sweater and droopy knickerbocker trousers, his argyle socks, his neat little quiff of hair: maybe Tintin will scale the distant peaks of Tess's sleeping mind, as he did the icy ridges of the Himalayas. He might, Tintin might do that.

Emma does not want Peter to look at her or speak to her. She does not want him to come near her. She does not want to hear his ideas. She is trying to get through the next moment.

25

On the fourth day, Tess is moved into a fully private room. It is on the same floor, seven, which is Pediatrics. The new room is square, and seems large, compared to the last one, since there is only one bed. The window faces west, and overlooks Central Park. The wide blank shimmer of the Reservoir is slightly to the south. The window is just above the trees. Whenever Peter looks outside, at any time of day, he sees small figures pounding doggedly around the perimeter of the water. The runners' bright shorts and T-shirts are vivid among the greens and browns of the path, against the surrounding shrubbery. It seems strange to him that they continue their daily runs, that they carry on just the same, as though the world has not stopped, as though Tess were not lying here, motionless.

The bed commands the room. It is imposing, high and squared off, with polished metal rails. Facing it are two chairs, with a low Formica table between them. In the window corner of the room, facing the bed and suspended high in the air, is the glazed blank gray screen of a television set. Emma has not turned it on.

It is Tess's fourth day in the hospital. Each of these days seems vast, enormous, apart from all other days. This evening when Peter came in, the first thing he saw was Emma, sitting in one of the chairs. She was leaning forward, toward the bed. Her chin was thrust out, her arms were folded on her chest, and her legs were crossed and wrapped around each other.

For a moment, seeing the intensity of her posture, the urgency of the angle, Peter thought Emma was listening. She looked still and focused, as though she was listening with great concentration. He thought she must be listening to Tess, who had not, so far, made a sound since the accident. As he realized this his heart lifted, for just a split second, before he saw from her expression that Emma was not listening to anything. She was leaning forward and simply waiting, waiting, waiting, in this silent room, for Tess to return.

"Hello, Em," said Peter gently. He was always the first to speak now.

"Hello," Emma said. Without moving she watched him come in and set down his things. He put down his briefcase, and the big shopping bag that held their dinner. He came over to Emma and leaned down to her. She lifted her face for his kiss without warmth.

"This is a much nicer room," Peter said, looking around.

Emma said nothing.

Peter moved to the bed. "How is she?" he asked, leaning over the bruised face.

"The same," Emma said.

The fourth day. Tess lay still, her breath slipping invisibly through her swollen lips. It was painful to look at her.

"Hello, chickadee," Peter said gently. He stood watching her. "She looks better to me." He turned to Emma. "Don't you think her color's better?"

Emma said nothing. He looked at her, waiting for a reply, and finally she shrugged her shoulders.

"The swelling's going down," he said. "Her eyes are less hidden. You probably don't see it, because you're with her all the time, but they look much better today, to me." Peter leaned over Tess again. He spoke to her very quietly. "Wake up, little chickadee," he said coaxingly. He was almost whispering. "Come on, Tessie, wake up. We're here waiting for you. We love you. We want you back." As he said the words, Peter imagined how it would be if, right then, hearing him, her lips parted slightly. He imagined how it would be if she opened her eyes, slowly blinked, saw his face. How it would be when she returned. His whole body focused on that moment, wanting it. He felt his chest seized with that feeling, with his wanting her back.

There was no sound in the room. Tess lay still.

Peter's eyes filled with tears, and he turned away from her, toward the wall, his back to Emma.

"I think she's better," he said, when his voice was firm. He turned to Emma. "What did the doctor say?"

"Nothing," said Emma. "The same."

Peter sighed. He came and stood next to Emma. He imagined Tess's small bright spirit, floating somewhere, waiting. He imagined it a sort of transparent image of her, perfect, intact. Unhurt, but out of reach.

"The waiting is the worst," he said. He patted Emma's head gently. Her head, beneath the springy hair, felt immediately warm: the brain, he thought, the blood. In this new world everything, everything around him spoke to him of Tess. He sighed and sat down beside Emma.

Grief was an actual weight, he thought. It felt like a physical burden. You carried it with you all day, unsheddable. Your shoulders, by nightfall, felt dragged down. Then he corrected himself. This that he felt now was not grief, not true grief. This was fear and sadness. True grief would be something that allowed no hope. He did have hope. He was waiting for Tess to get well. He waited for her improvement every day. The fourth day.

Every day, when he realized that there was no news, no good news, no change, he felt an ominous settling, a lowering feeling, the orchestra sliding down into deeper and deeper bass chords. Things somehow were descending, moving toward a dark, frightening, nether region that he did not want to explore. There was nothing you could do. You had to carry on, ignoring these terrible doom-filled chords, keep on with the business of living.

He leaned into the shopping bag.

"Dinner?" he asked.

Emma said nothing.

"We're Italian tonight," Peter said. He lifted out a stack of shallow aluminum pans with white cardboard lids. "I got one ravioli and one linguine with scampi."

"I can't remember what linguine is," said Emma. "Are."

"Have a look," said Peter. "Take whichever you want. I'll take the other."

He set the pans out on the table between them. The pans were still warm, in a vague, unfocused way. He folded back their flexible edges and pried off the cardboard lids. The dishes were revealed, the pallid chalky forms awash in gelid red sauce. He opened a plastic container of salad, which held pale shredded lettuce with drops of water clinging to it. There was half a loaf of Italian bread, sliced most of the way through.

Emma looked without interest at the two pans. She chose ravioli, the little pillows, half-submerged in red murk. Peter took the linguine, a snarled skein of narrow snaky cords. From the bag he produced two plastic glasses and a big bottle of mineral water. He twisted the top off with a tiny pneumatic hiss.

"I think you'll like this vintage, madam, it's the same one that you had last night," he said.

Emma, bent over her tray, turned to look at him. Her eyes were unblinking. It was a stare you might receive on a subway, from a stranger. Peter looked down at his food.

"Actually, I meant to bring some wine," he said. "Tomorrow I will."

"Don't," said Emma.

"Why not?"

"Not here," Emma said.

"There's no rule here against drinking. For visitors," Peter said reasonably.

Emma shook her head, not looking at him. "I don't want it in this room."

Peter, his heels braced awkwardly against the metal legs of the chair, his lap full of the messy pan, said nothing. He took another forkful of the linguine. The fourth day. There was no logic that you could use, he thought. Anything could happen, for any reason, and no one knew what it would be. The doctor said there was nothing to do now but wait. The longer Tess was unconscious, the graver it was. The less chance of recovery.

Peter tried to imagine the site of the hemorrhage: the tissues clogged with blood. Tess's brave cells struggling to rid themselves of this intrusive fluid, to cleanse themselves. In his mind Peter urged them on. Imaging: wasn't that what they called it? You imagined the body healing itself. But did it have to be the patient herself who imagined it, or could it be someone very close to the patient, someone sitting right next to the patient's bed?

The CAT scan, done on the first day, had shown hemorrhaging. The clearing of the blood would take time. That was all anyone would say. The neurologist said his tests showed some disturbance; he wouldn't say more. No one would say more than that. No one knew, he supposed, or perhaps they all knew and wouldn't say. Perhaps that was the way it worked: he and Emma were not ready to hear it, if it were something they could not bear. Maybe you were meant to live with this until it was borne in on you, slowly, that this was the way things were. That this was the natural order of things, this was the way nature made it possible to bear things.

No one knew what would happen now, that was what the doctors said. There was no more reason to think one thing than another, Peter believed. Who knew what delicate shift, what unknown factor, would bring Tess's soul back to them, unharmed? Who knew what might keep it away? Maybe Emma was right. Maybe alcohol would, in some mysterious way, be obstructive. They would never know, and how could they risk it? In any case, there was no point in upsetting Emma. Peter thought again of Tess, fleetingly, a sort of radiant ghost, drifting somewhere clear and blue, the soul fine, healthy, perfect. Waiting for something.

The linguine was tepid, and the sauce glutinous. The plastic spoon scraped unpleasantly against the aluminum. Peter sucked in his cheeks at the sound. He tried to eat slowly, drawing out the process, pleasureless though it was: nothing to look forward to, afterward. Dinner was the only event of the evening.

"Was Warren here?" he asked. Emma said nothing and he looked up. She nodded.

"He came this afternoon," she said. She lifted her glass and drank from it, still looking at him steadily. Her gaze was open and empty.

Hurt, Peter looked down again at his food. Before all this, before the accident, the mere speaking of the name Warren had drawn Emma and him together, in complicity. They were allies, and Warren was their mutual antagonist, the outsider. Peter did not voice his criticisms of Warren, but he felt them very strongly: Warren was a fool. Emma complained to him about Warren, and Peter sympathized.

Now all that had changed. The complicity was gone, Peter and Emma were no longer allies. Now Warren was the father of Emma's child. It was Warren whom the doctors consulted. It was Warren who helped Emma make the decisions. Now Peter was the outsider. He was the father of the person who had nearly killed Tess.

So Warren had come in the afternoon, when Peter was not there. Peter gave him credit for tact, at least. He felt another leap of rage, remembering how he had come in to find his wife in the arms of another man, *that* other man. At least that had not been repeated.

Peer took a long drink of the mineral water; it bubbled fiercely in his throat. He set down the plastic glass. In front of him was the hospital bed. Everything fell away before the silence in this room. This was Warren's child.

And really, Peter thought, he had no idea, now, what Warren was like. He had always thought of him as immature and selfish. Years ago, during the divorce, he had been those things, but they had all behaved badly, all three of them. What was more selfish than leaving your spouse? You were at your worst during a divorce. Not only did you behave at your worst, you were also at your most suspicious, judgmental, intolerant. You gave people no latitude. Each small thing your antagonist did was deemed intolerable, it seemed like final, crucial, irrefutable proof of something. Over and over this was proved, and amidst mounting animosity, you cried excitably to yourself, You see? More! More! Worse, and still worse. You forgave the other person nothing. There were no mitigating factors, there were no excuses. You were merciless.

Well, you had to be. If you were wrong about this, about your own guilt, then what you had done was intolerable. You would not be able to live with yourself. You were struggling for your moral life. The other person must be sacrificed, if you are to survive. Outrage is useful. During a divorce it runs at flood level, high and foamy. It is aroused by the smallest gesture: any lateness. The least request. Any change in plans. All financial transactions. Everything is final, irrefutable proof. Your own side, your own argument, seems so transparently reasonable and benign; the other's so patently absurd and malevolent.

Peter looked over at Emma. Her head was bowed. The line of her bare neck rose to meet the cropped hair, the map of dark plush, at the base of her skull. She ate slowly. Her knees were pressed tightly together, under the aluminum tray. Her feet were set pigeon-toed, toes just touching, heels apart. Her shoulders were hunched, drawn together as though she had been wounded, as though she were protecting herself from another blow.

He remembered Emma weeping with rage over Warren's behavior. He had taken her side, always. After she stopped crying she was bitter, vindictive. There are no margins for forgiveness during a divorce. You make no allowances for this person as you would for a friend. This person is not a friend but an enemy, an enemy with whom you must make the most intimate and revealing arrangements. There is no forgiveness on either side, and you operate in a continual state of astonished rage. Underlying it all, of course, is the true, great and unspeakable outrage of abandonment, betrayal—the withdrawal of love. There is the intolerable answer to the intolerable question: Do you love me? This is a question you cannot bear to hear, cannot bring yourself to answer. You cannot allow yourself to confront that. You choose to focus instead on immediate issues, the fact that the child is brought back late once again, the fact that the weekend plans have been changed without notice, things that are final, irrefutable proof of intolerable behavior.

Looking back at it all, Peter saw with lucid amazement his own self-ishness, his deliberate blindness, lack of compassion. Determinedly self-serving behavior. He could hardly blame Warren for acting the same way. If childishness would save a marriage, would prevent one's heart from being shattered, who would not stoop to it?

But he had never looked back, Peter thought now. He had never looked at his own behavior or at Warren's, really. He had seen Warren through Emma's eyes, and only Emma's eyes when she was angry, and never questioned that view. We see people in one set of circumstances, he thought, and we decide—we can see!—that this moment reveals their true characters. Though we know this is not true of ourselves: our unkind acts are aberrations, moments of duress, mistakes, much regretted. Moments in which we are not ourselves. There must be ways Warren revealed his generosity and kindness, his responsibility and humor. There must be people who know him like that. Peter wondered what Warren was like with the people who loved him: his second wife, Mimi, their adopted son. He wondered how Warren was when he was at ease, when he was at his best. And he, Peter, would never see it. It was like the uncertainty principle: Peter's presence would change the nature of the event.

But what was Warren's appeal? What had it ever been, for Emma? She had told Peter he was funny, charming, warm. Peter saw none of that. He saw Warren's silk ties, his lustrous shirts, his self-indulgent collapse on Emma's shoulder. He felt again the surge of anger at that image. The way Warren ran his hand through his hair, lifting his chin as he did so, arrogant, self-conscious. Peter disliked him again, detested him.

He took the last bite of the dull linguine, scraping at the corners of the pan with his spoon. Picking up the container of salad, he scrabbled half of the iceberg lettuce into his red-smeared pan. There was no dressing, and it tasted like nothing. Each bite was a brief succulent crunch that dissolved at once, into water, in his mouth.

He looked over at Emma. She had ignored the salad.

"Remember your greens," he said, pushing the container toward her. She did not look at it. She had eaten only half the ravioli. Earlier she had eaten a candy bar; on the table was a crumpled red wrapper. Usually she was strict about sugar, and he wondered if this were a part of an unspoken bargain, if she were abandoning her standards, offering her own health in exchange for Tess's. Trying to change the balance.

And who knew? Who knew what would work? Who could say for sure, after a recovery, that it had not been prayer, the kind hands of the nurses, the absence of alcohol? Who could say what subtle shift would alter this terrible suspended moment and bring things back to normal, would bring Tess's spirit back to them? He was not superstitious, but there was nothing now to be certain of, nothing to rule out.

After the sad meal was over, Peter put the aluminum pans back in the bag. He set his briefcase on his knees and unsnapped the brass locks. He took out *The Magic Mountain.* He had begun reading it before the accident, and now found it unhappily eerie to be reading about sickness, about the impassive responses of doctors, the medical environment, the dangerous seduction of illness. But everything now was like that, he thought, everything now seemed related to the accident, in some sort of ominous and horrifying ironic web. Now, headlines about car crashes, marijuana, teenage criminal behavior sprang piercingly into his awareness. He was surrounded by it. Everything seemed to refer to the accident, although he told himself determinedly that it did not. That was superstition, hysteria, the mad attempt to force coincidence and pattern onto something random and undecipherable. He refused to stop reading the book. He felt as though that would be giving in to something, something that it might be dangerous to give in to, something he could not allow himself to yield to.

He leaned back in the narrow, uncomfortable chair, trying to settle his shoulders between the cramped arms. He opened the heavy book, glancing first, again, at the silent figure in the bed. From where he sat, he could see only the silhouettes of Tess's feet, shrouded by the blanket. They did not move.

He looked down at his book and began to read, sinking slowly into the distant world of prewar Europe. The solemn mountains, the clear salubrious air, the innocent assumptions of order and continuity. He spent the evening with Hans Castorp and Clavdia Chauchat, against the background of the implacable Emma, the distant, sleeping Tess. Peter moved from one world to the other, drifting silently between the two, entering the chilly bright sanatorium, encountering the self-indulgent Castorp reclining in his deck chair, pulling his blanket over his legs. The delicious Clavdia appeared, with her strange name, the unexpected drawl of the *v*, the sensual dangerous Clavdia; then Peter emerged unhappily into this real hospital room, with this real child, who had no choice in her illness. The deep steady note of sadness reverberated through both worlds, through the majestic German mountainscape and the doomed love story, so that everything in the book, Hans Castorp's moments of greatest joy and ecstasy, was suffused with Peter's unbearable melancholy, and somehow deepened it.

Often, as he read, Peter raised his head and looked up at Tess's bed, listening. There was no sound from her; still, he found himself suddenly drawn to attention. Each time, Emma raised her head too, hopefully, as though he might have heard something she had missed. Each time, after a moment, without looking at him, Emma lowered her head again to her book. Sometimes she read silently to herself, sometimes she read aloud, to Tess. Sometimes she moved her chair over next to the bed and sat there, reading. Sometimes she stood by the bed, looking down at Tess's battered face.

When Emma read aloud, Peter listened to her steady voice. At times she seemed so calmly interested, so engaged by her text, that he wondered if she had forgotten who her audience was. He hoped she had. He hoped she had moments of relief. He hoped she had become caught up in the story, intent on the perfidious Edmund, the brave Lucy, the noble Aslan. He hoped she had forgotten, for a moment, the terrible space and time she actually inhabited.

Peter went to his office every day, and there were many times, for him, when he was talking to colleagues, drafting a document, having lunch with friends, when he forgot. He never truly forgot, this knowledge was always in his mind, but there were many times when it was not in the forefront of his mind, moments when he laughed. He didn't want to talk about it at the office, hated having people mention it. That drew it again, painfully, to the forefront. Hearing the accident spoken of out loud, by other people, pulled it closer to something he could not deny, something that might be permanent. As long as it was dark, unspoken, it might be temporary, nothing that need be addressed, a nightmare he did not have to discuss. He never brought it up, and there were times during the day when it was silent, quiescent, mostly absent from his mind. The times when he laughed were a relief.

At ten o'clock Peter closed *The Magic Mountain*.

"Well," he said, "I think I'll pack it in. Want to come home with me?"

Emma looked at him. The first two nights she had spent in the hospital. While Tess was in the ICU, she had stayed in the waiting room, dozing on the uncomfortable plastic-covered couches. In the semiprivate room, Emma had stayed on a mat on the floor. She was not allowed to use the other bed, even though it was empty. One night she had gone back to the apartment in the middle of the night, and slept a few hours.

Now she shook her head at Peter. "I'll stay here for a while."

"Are you going to spend the night here?"

"I don't know."

"Okay," Peter said. He leaned down and kissed Emma's raised and unresponsive mouth. He moved to the bed and leaned over Tess. He whispered good night to her, his words barely audible, as though now, at night, her sleep were normal, and he was trying not to wake her. As he left, he turned at the door to blow Emma a kiss.

"Good night," he said.

Emma looked at him. Her thick bangs covered her forehead; her long eyes, below them, were pink rimmed. Finally she said, "Good night."

Back at home, the darkened apartment seemed strange to him, brooding, unfriendly. Without turning on lights he walked through the square hall, past the darkened living room, with its small polished tables, its glowing rugs, everything poised for the brilliance of lamplight, conversation, laughter. Entertainment: he couldn't now imagine it. Another life, another world, not his. The rooms were now silent and gloomy, full of blame. Blame was everywhere.

In their room, in the big four-poster bed, he slept at once. He woke later, and in the dark he felt groggy and confused. He reached for Emma, to find her side of the bed empty, a wasteland of cold sheets. For a moment he groped, bewildered, unable to remember why his wife was gone; sickeningly, with wakefulness, it came to him. Tess's terrible wounded face, the bloom of bruise beneath her skin. Her silence. He closed his eyes at the memory.

He was asleep again, later, when Emma opened the door. He woke, hearing her undressing in the dark. She moved carelessly, not trying to be quiet.

"Em?" he asked, whispering.

"What," she said, out loud.

"You're back," he said. She did not answer.

Lying there, watching her in the gloom, Peter wondered how she saw her return here. Was it a defeat? A failure of the flesh? Or a practical decision, morally neutral? He wondered if it signaled despair or expediency.

"Come to bed," he said, but Emma did not answer. She went into the bathroom, and he heard the water running.

Peter lay waiting for her in the dark, listening to her shower in the next room. He felt deeply solitary, more so than he had felt before she returned. He was alone. His solitude seemed vast, endless, hurtful. He mourned Emma's absence in bed at night. He mourned her absence in his days, and in his life. Emma hardly spoke to him now at all. When she did, it was with barely veiled hostility, a crushing weight of blame.

Peter was waiting for this to end. He didn't want to know how much longer it might continue. He didn't allow himself to consider that things might be changed for them forever. He held that thought away from himself, but it lay darkly along the horizon. He was treating all this as temporary: how could he not? He wanted his wife back, he loved her. And he wanted Tess to get well. He loved Tess.

Peter remembered the exact moment when he discovered that he loved Tess. It had been years before, when Tess was still a small child, four or five. It was in the summer, at the first cottage they had rented at Marten's Island. They had all been outside, on a hot peaceful afternoon. The girls were playing in their hideout, beneath the low curved branches of the forsythia bushes. Emma had been doing something—what had it been? Not reading. She had had something, spread out in colorful pieces, all over a round metal table in the garden. Her short legs were stretched out beneath the table. It had been Peter who was reading, sitting in a chaise lounge, his feet up. Suddenly the air was split by a high piercing wail from Tess. She burst out of the sheltering mass of forsythia.

"I was *stung*," Tess said shrilly, agonized. She held her elbow in one hand. "There was a *bee*." She wore only shorts, and her soft little-girl torso was pink and vulnerable. Amanda came crouching out of the bushes behind her, looking anxious.

"*Ow, ow, ow, ow*," wailed Tess, running toward them, throwing her head up and down as she ran.

"Come here, Tessie," Emma said, opening her arms.

But Tess, for some reason, did not even look at her mother. Clutching her plump arm against her bare chest she ran across the lawn, crying in a high unbearable voice. Dodging around Emma's arms she sped past her to Peter's chair.

Surprised, he put his book down, and just in time. Tess threw herself onto his chest, burrowing against him like a small animal.

"Peter," she said sorrowfully, "I was stung."

Peter put his arms around her. "Ow," he said consolingly.

"It *hurts*," Tess said, speaking into his shirt. "Make it stop." Her whole body, warm, damp, solid, was collapsed trustingly onto his. The suddenness, the choice, and the trust undid him. Peter felt his chest fill unexpectedly with emotion, and for a moment there was no room in it for speech.

Swallowing, he looked over at Emma, who raised her eyebrows and smiled. Peter hugged Tess's small heated body. She made settling movements, fitting herself urgently against him, then lay still, sniffing.

"*Ow, ow, ow,*" she whispered.

"We'll put mud on it," Peter said. "That will make it stop hurting."

"Mud?" Tess raised her head.

Peter leaned over and carefully spat into the damp earth beside his chair. He stirred it with the tips of his fingers, and plastered a small clump of brown sod onto Tess's elbow. She watched, absorbed, still troubled. Then Peter rocked her again, holding her against him, and patting her silky bare skin. Her back was so short that he spanned it with his spread palm. He felt her heart beating quickly against his chest. She lay limp and confiding in his arms, snuffling. He tucked his chin over the top of her head and kissed the fine blond hair.

He felt strange, astonished by this unexpected spreading glow. He had never named, to himself, what it was he felt for Tess. Something large and vague: affection, responsibility—a sense of dutiful connection. But this, whatever it was, was different. He was in a wide new range of feeling. Something within him had let go, and he was flooded, engulfed by an emotion he hadn't known he owned.

It was her trust that had brought it on, her innocent certainty that he loved her. Her belief that it was true made it so. She had claimed him for her own.

Since that moment of choosing, Peter had loved Tess, though not in the same way that he loved Amanda. It wasn't more or less, but different. He felt pride and affection for Tess, seldom anything else. Vexation, but never anger. It was Emma who became angry at Tess, Emma who disciplined her. Peter always took Tess's side; his only task was to love her. For Amanda he felt different things, more complicated, all of them closer, more desperate. For her he felt anger, she trapped him in a kind of wild resentful love. He was knitted into Amanda, they shared the same root system. They could not be separated, no matter how much rage lay between them. It was a great deal. He could not now think of Amanda—walking around, talking to her friends, watching videos—without rage spreading across his mind.

Peter thought again of Tess, lying in the hospital.

Sometimes he imagined how things would be if she did not get well. Unlike Emma, he let this thought into his mind, he let it take up space. He imagined a room—would it be in their apartment?—with a wheelchair, heavy, with shining spokes on the wheels, and a special high metal bed. He imagined a woman with a white uniform seated near the bed. The woman looked up brightly whenever someone came in. But Peter could go no further than that. He could not bear to imagine Tess herself, changed.

While he waited for Emma to come out of the bathroom, Peter closed his eyes. He thought, God, let her get well. Please let her get well. Please. His body tensed in concentration, fervent. Please, he thought, please. He was praying.

He had never prayed before all this. It seemed hardly fair, having been so indifferent to God all this time, to ask his help now. But there was no one else to ask. Peter prayed all the time now, in between other thoughts, if that was what this was, this urgent surge of feeling, wanting. What else was there to do? Who knew what would make the difference? This might. Please, he thought again, let her get well. He was supplicant, humble, fervent.

Emma came back into the room. She was in her nightgown, a calf-length cotton T-shirt. The V neck showed the two bones at the base of her throat. Through the thin cotton he could see the two points of her nipples, the diagonal slants of her ribs, as she walked. Her ribs were surprisingly close to the surface, like a starvation victim's.

Emma's face, in the light from the bathroom door, was closed. Peter held up the sheet for her to climb in next to him, but without meeting his eyes Emma walked around the bed and climbed in on the other side, nowhere near him. She turned her back and lay tightly coiled on her side, close to the edge of the bed. She said nothing.

Peter rolled over and slid closer to her. He had not remembered the bed being so large, the other side being so distant. He put his arms around her and felt her go rigid.

"Emma," he said, whispering. He slid his chin along the curve of her shoulder. It was unyielding. She said nothing.

"Emma," he whispered, again.

"What?" Emma answered, not whispering. Her voice was loud in the dark.

"Let me in," Peter said.

Emma did not answer.

"I love you," Peter said. He slid his hand along the ridge of her shoulder, slowly, tenderly, back and forth. Not to arouse but gently, to comfort. He remembered this body when it was his, when he was allowed to arouse it. He remembered a time, in the house at Marten's, waking up in the middle of the night, and Emma turning silken and silver beneath his hands. He could hardly imagine this now. Sex, that expanse of generous delight, was something from another world, lost to him.

Emma said nothing. Her body, under his hand, was rigid.

"Emma," Peter said, "I'm part of this. I want her to get well too. We're in this together. I love Tess too."

In his arms, Emma stiffened more.

"Don't say her name," she said.

Peter took his arm from around her. He rolled over, turning his back.

Later Peter woke again. Emma was gone.

The room was now completely dark, the door to the bathroom was shut. He heard something, and raised his head to listen. Emma was in the bathroom. He could hear her weeping. The sobs were long and drawn out, the voice was low and exhausted. The sound of it frightened him, it was raucous and uncontained.

Peter listened, then climbed out of bed and padded over to the bathroom door. He opened it and, in the sudden dazzling light, he blinked.

Inside, the bathroom was radiant: the white tiles around the tub, the peach-colored walls. On the walls were delicate prints of ferns. The room looked like a bower, except for the woman. Emma was kneeling on the floor in front of the tub. Her arms were folded on its rim. Her head was laid down on top of her arms. The sounds she made were terrible and loud.

Peter knelt beside her. He put his arms around her.

"Emma," he said.

At once she stopped. Her body went limp. The sudden silence was alarming. She did not answer. She waited for him to leave. Peter held her. He tried to rock her with his body. She was rigid. She would not look at him. She waited for him to leave. He felt her willing him to leave.

In the office, during the day, Peter waited for Emma to call. Each time the phone rang he picked it up quickly, at once, on the first ring, no matter who sat across the desk from him.

"Chatfield," he said, hoping to hear Emma's voice telling him what he wanted to hear. In the brief moment before he heard the caller's voice answer, it might be true. During that moment it might be Emma, telling him that Tess had begun to waken, that his life had begun to heal.

26

They had both wakened at the sound of the crash, though they hadn't known what it was. They found themselves lying in a listening silence, hearkening to an unremembered sound.

"What was it?" Emma asked, sitting up.

"Some kind of . . . ," Peter said. Her sitting up made him get out of bed. He didn't know what it was. They both put on bathrobes and slippers, moving quietly. They went downstairs. The moon was full, and each room they passed was filled with its cold light. The nighttime silence was oddly alarming. They went out the back door, onto the deck. In the road, up the hill on the other side of the hedge, was a big vague light. They moved toward it.

"Where's the car?" Emma asked, as they crossed the driveway. Peter didn't bother to answer: the car's absence seemed minor then, something that could be set aside, explained later.

But it was not minor, and each discovery after that was worse. Out in the road, in the terrible gray moonlight, Peter saw something motionless at the curve. At first he couldn't understand it, couldn't read the dark shape. The strange light flooded the hedge, the tree. Everything was still and silent, but even so there was a sense of recent violence. They began to hurry: now he could see that the shape was a car, lying on its side. Its dark metallic underside was facing them, its nose was buried deep in the trunk of the maple.

The poor people, he thought. He felt compassion for them, these strangers, whoever they were.

Ah, but each thing he saw was worse, sickeningly worse. The car, as he approached it, as they came around its back end, became a Volvo, familiar, theirs. Incomprehensibly theirs. On its side, its headlights—oddly subdued—blared into the hedge. No sound came from it, no sound. A figure knelt at the side of the road, its back to them. The figure's arms hung down at its sides: this shape too was familiar.

"Amanda?" Peter said. She turned. In the bloody glare from the taillights he saw a long red abrasion on her cheek. Her face was bruised and muddy. She looked at him, dazed and silent, her eyes dull. He had never seen such a look. His heart tightened with fear.

"Are you all right?" he asked, touching her shoulder.

Amanda made a strange sound and flinched violently, pulling away from him. "Don't."

"What happened?" Peter asked, frightened.

"We crashed," Amanda said.

"Is it your shoulder?" Peter asked, touching her more gently. She nodded, squeezing her eyes shut. We, thought Peter.

"Who was with you?"

Amanda nodded at the car. Peter turned to look. Emma was at the car. The headlights lit up the trunk of the tree, and the dense mosaic of the privet hedge beyond. The dashboard lights were on. Peter heard her voice. It did not sound like Emma.

"Oh," she said, her voice breaking on the single syllable.

Peter turned back to Amanda. "Is Tess in there?" he asked.

Staring dully at the car, Amanda nodded slowly.

In her bathrobe, Emma climbed slowly inside the car, through the open window. Peter left Amanda and went to the car. Emma was down inside it, her head down. He couldn't see.

"Is she all right?" he asked. His heart was thundering. Emma shifted, and he could see something inside the car, pressed against the windshield. Fear filled him, panic, but he refused it: this was the wrong shape, the wrong color, to be Tess. This was crumpled, glittering with dark fluid.

"Call nine-one-one and bring me a blanket," Emma said. In the second before he could answer she said, "Go! Go!"

In the silent kitchen he turned on the sudden lights and dialed. He stood waiting, alone in the house, feeling the signal that he had sent go out through the night, across the waters. He waited. He could feel his heart inside the cavity of his chest, huge, terrified, thundering along. He would make things right by force of will.

A woman's voice said, "Nine-one-one."

"I want to report an accident," Peter said clearly, proud of himself.

"What kind?"

"A car accident," he said. He wondered suddenly if that were accurate: there was the car, the tree, the girls. But was that what you called it, a car accident?

"Anyone hurt?"

"Yes," Peter heard himself say.

"How many people are hurt?"

"Two," Peter said, "children." His throat closed on the word.

"Where are they?" Peter gave her directions, and his name.

"Hold on," she said. "Do not hang up."

The line went silent. Peter held on to the telephone tightly. He felt the seconds tick through his body. He thought of Emma out in the darkness, her bathrobe spreading around her like a cloak as she climbed down into the dark well of the car. With every second this wait became worse. He felt like shouting into the phone, Hurry. Hurry.

The woman returned. "Don't move them," she said. "Do you understand? Don't pull them from the car, don't shift their positions in any way. You could damage their spines. Don't pick them up."

"All right," Peter said. He wondered if Emma had pulled Tess out.

"Keep them warm. They're in shock. Wrap them in blankets without moving them. The police are on their way, and an ambulance. A helicopter team is on alert. The police will decide if you need the helicopter. If you do, it will arrive within thirteen minutes of the call."

"Yes," said Peter, "good." He loved this woman devoutly. He pictured her, sitting by the telephone, on her nocturnal vigil. She sat before a cluttered desk. There were phones, radio transmitters, a computer. She was in her fifties, short graying hair. Glasses. He loved her.

"Do you know the names of the victims?"

He hesitated: it was the last moment before he had to acknowledge this, name it. He told her. The sound of their names was terrible.

"And are you Peter Chatfield?"

"Yes," he said. "How did you know?"

"Your phone listing came up on my screen," she said. "What is your relationship to the victims?"

"Father," Peter said. In his mouth the word felt like a confession. He heard it resonate with guilt. It struck a vast gong, and now all the world knew. It had been his responsibility, his fault.

"I'm sorry," said the woman, but she went right on. The name of his doctor, medical insurance, addresses. Peter answered all her questions dutifully, part of his brain wondering how he would apologize, how he would explain to her, afterward, that none of this had happened, and the girls were asleep, upstairs, in their beds. He saw Tess there, vividly. She slept often on her back, her head turned sharply to one side, one palm open on the pillow. That was how she would be now, really.

After Peter hung up with the nine-one-one woman, he went upstairs for the blankets, leaping the steps three at a time. In Tess's room he turned on the light switch and looked: she might be in her bed, she might, this might easily be a mistake. Amanda could have gotten it wrong, he had misunderstood. The bed was tossed, empty. He pulled the blanket off, the quilt. He ran back downstairs, out into the terrifying night.

When he returned to the car Emma was inside it, leaning strangely from the window. He kept his eyes on her face as he gave her the blanket. He did not dare look down inside the car.

"The police and ambulance are on their way. The helicopter is on alert. Wrap them up but don't move them, don't shift them in any way, it could damage their spines."

Emma said nothing, taking the blanket with her and vanishing back inside the darkness of the Volvo. Peter took the quilt over to Amanda. She was now standing, facing the tipped car. One arm was held across her chest, the other hung limp at her side.

"Let me wrap you up," Peter said. He set the quilt carefully around her shoulders. She winced again and made a sound. He wrapped her lightly and stood behind her, feeling the solid rise of her young woman's body before him. He felt fear, a sense of waste. He thought of Byron: She walks in beauty, like the night of something climes and starry skies. He opened his mouth. He was panting with fear. This was his daughter.

"What happened?" he asked.

"I missed the turn," Amanda said.

"You were driving?" he asked, sickened.

He saw her nod.

"Is your arm all right?" he asked.

"I can't move it," she said. She sounded hopeless. Very carefully Peter kissed the top of her head, he could not hug her. At that, the touch of his mouth on her hair, he felt her sob, and she leaned slightly back, against him.

The ambulance, thrilling its nasal cry, appeared around the corner, drew up, stopped. A circling red light threw urgent beams onto the scene, alarming, disorienting. Two men in dark jackets jumped out of the ambulance and came over to Peter.

"She's inside the car," Peter said. Emma appeared in the car window and began to climb carefully out. In the lurid shifting rays of the ambulance light her hair was wild, her eyes gleamed, she looked demonic.

The man climbed carefully into the car. A police car pulled up behind the ambulance. The policeman got out and came over to Emma. He put his hand on her elbow and walked her over to Peter. It was a local man, John Garth. Peter knew him. They sometimes fished together, on the beach, in the evenings. Now, in this erratic scarlet light, Garth was a stranger, his manner stiff and official.

"Over here, please, Mrs. Chatfield," he said, herding her away from the car. His arms were raised, curved, open. "Keep back."

"No," Emma said, pulling away from him. "That's my daughter."

"I'm sorry, ma'am, I'll have to keep you away while the emergency crew is working on her." Garth had a thick brown mustache, and he wore sunglasses. Sunglasses, thought Peter, at four o'clock in the morning. Peter took Emma's arm, pulling it close to him. The policeman stood in front of them, his arms up, his body a shield from the sight of the car. He kept turning, himself, to look over his shoulder.

Emma stood by Peter's side. She did not look at Amanda.

The second man from the ambulance approached the Volvo, carrying a small stretcher, and a bag. The ambulance headlights were trained on the car, and a big lamp had been set on the ground nearby. In the frightening glare the men worked quickly. Garth asked Peter and Emma to stay where they were. His eyes sought Peter's, as the one he could trust. Peter nodded, and Garth went over to speak to the rescue workers. He stood wide legged, still blocking the view. He unhitched his walkie-talkie from his belt and spoke into it in a low voice.

Beyond Garth, around his body, they saw Tess, strapped now to a short board, lifted into the light. Wide white tapes held her tightly to the board; her nightgown was dark and brilliant. As her body rose into the light of the flares, Peter could see, like a terrible secret, that her head was dark, covered in blood.

They laid her on the larger, waiting stretcher with its open blanket. They lapped the blanket closed over her small form, so slight it vanished underneath the cloth. Peter could see her face, glistening, dark. Over her face was a mask, covering nose and mouth.

Tess, strapped down, began to struggle. In the glare they could see her head jerking, her shoulders twitching horribly. Emma started toward her, and the policeman moved back to bar her way.

"Let me by," said Emma, her eyes on Tess.

"Ma'am, I'm going to have to ask you to keep back. The rescue squad is going to take her down to the airstrip. We're waiting for the helicopter right now. They want both girls, and the helicopter will hold only one more person. If you want to go with them, now's the time to go and get ready."

But they were hypnotized by the sight of Tess. Under the blanket she thrashed fiercely, her head jerking, shoulders twisting, as though she wrestled with invisible attackers. The policeman now held his hands up, to obstruct the view. They could not take their eyes from her. His raised hands moved steadily back and forth, distracting, maddening, interrupting but not concealing the sight.

"Ma'am, the helicopter will not wait for you. Right now speed is very important. If you want to go on it, you'd better get ready."

The rescue workers carried the stretcher to the back of the ambulance. Tess, still heaving, vanished within the double doors. One of the men came for Amanda. The girls were gone. The ambulance began to pull slowly away, wallowing along the verge until it reached the pavement, its grid of red taillights horribly irradiating the road behind it.

In the bedroom, Peter and Emma moved back and forth without speaking. The room looked plundered: bed unmade, closets gaping, clothes strewn about.

"What will I need? What will I need?" Emma asked suddenly. Her eyes were wild.

"When?" Peter asked stupidly.

"Where am I going?"

"Take everything," Peter said. "You're going straight to the hospital. Take a jacket, take your pocketbook. I'll bring the car down on the first ferry." It was unnatural, dressing so early in the morning.

Outside, the police car waited for them. They had no car, Peter realized, there was no car to bring on the ferry. Emma sat in front, with Garth, Peter in back. They drove along the dark silent roads. Outside, the trees began to declare themselves against the lightening sky. The car drew up at the tiny paved strip at the western end of the island. The three of them got out and stood waiting, their faces toward the mainland. The ambulance stood beside them, its red lights on, its doors shut.

They saw the helicopter before they heard it. It was Emma who saw it first, a bright steady star, moving toward them through the night sky. She lifted her hand, pointing, and then they all saw it, passing among the other stars, shouldering them out of its way. As it neared, they heard it, a mechanical stutter, louder and louder. By the time it landed, the roar was deafening.

The landing lights shone downward, illuminating the strip. There was the worn concrete runway, the long summer grass flattened by the wind from the circling rotors. As the helicopter descended it swayed, settling like a nesting bird, making a half circle as it sank down to earth. The rescue men sprang from the ambulance and opened the rear doors. By the time the helicopter had touched lightly onto the airstrip, the men had lifted two stretchers into the noise and glare. The forms on them were swathed and motionless.

Emma stepped forward, away from Peter. She followed the men carrying Tess. She climbed lightly into the open door of the helicopter after the stretchers were lifted on. Peter came with her halfway to the helicopter, then stood still, his hand lifted to wave. Emma did not look back at him until the very end, as the door slid across the open doorway. Her eyes met his without a sign of recognition.

The door snapped shut, and without a pause the helicopter began ponderously to rise from the airstrip, drawn upward by the thundering, flickering blades. Slowly it wheeled in midair, then, responding to some mysterious internal signal, set off diagonally, rising as it moved, the cabin leaning against the slanted course, as though it were drawn magically from above. It flew steadily into the lightening sky. Peter watched it until it faded from sight. He was alone.

27

It was the fifth day.

Peter stood outside the closed door of Caroline's apartment, holding a small elegant paper bag. For a moment he wondered whether or not to open the door without ringing, and step inside, like a family member. For he was a family member; at least a member of his family lived here. It was hard to lose the habit of intimacy, the sense of natural domain. But no, of course he should ring, he knew that. He had no place here. He dreaded this visit.

He pressed the button next to the door and waited. The button was small, brass and highly polished. The door itself was black and glossy, and the floor was a black-and-white marble checkerboard. The ceiling was high, with plaster moldings. Peter had never seen this new apartment of Caroline's. Her father had died a few years ago, and she had come into some money. It had been during a dip in the real estate market, and Caroline had bought this snappy place at Seventy-third and Madison, where the doormen were tall, and wore hats and gloves.

Tall doormen were a sign of status, he supposed. Doormen were drawn from the most recent wave of immigrants, and they hadn't grown up on American vitamins. Their children would be tall, but they were not. For years, New York doormen had been Irish; then the Hispanic wave had begun. Now they were short and broad and impassive, with dark Aztec faces. Those Latino faces: Peter had seen a man, on a crowded midtown street, whose features he had seen carved over and over on the walls of a temple outside Cuernavaca. It was a stone-age emperor's face, flat and pitiless, with long narrow eyes and a broad brutal nose. The man on Fifty-fourth Street wore a white chef's jacket; he was delivering pizza.

You never saw black doormen. Peter wondered if that were racial discrimination, and if so, which race was doing the discriminating. Poor blacks wouldn't take menial jobs, nothing domestic: it was hard to understand that, hard to sympathize with it. Poor Latinos took any job they could get. Koreans kept those corner markets open twenty-four hours a day. The kids washed vegetables, swept floors, kept their grades up, went to Harvard. The blacks did nothing like that. But before civil rights and television, poor black people had worked hard: what had happened to the work ethic? Maybe all the ones who'd had it had left, and were living in the suburbs now, sending their kids to Yale. Maybe there was no one left in the ghetto except lost souls, nothing there but despair. It was America's worst problem, the trapped black underclass, impotent, enraged.

The newest wave was Russians. Peter's West Side garage was run by pale-skinned men, hawk nosed, with wild liquid black eyes. They spoke a broken and explosive English, and radiated a predatory cunning. With them it seemed that everything was negotiable, not in the mild, accommodating way of Italians but in a dangerous, threatening one. Peter was never quite sure, when he arrived at the garage, if he was going to be given his car or held up at knifepoint.

Peter pressed the bell again. There had been no audible response, and now he wondered if the bell worked. This time he held the button down for a long commanding buzz. He felt a silent sizzle under his finger. He listened for Caroline's footsteps, his heart sinking.

He had not seen Amanda since the accident. By the time he had reached New York, that awful day, she had been sent home from the hospital. She had a broken collarbone and contusions, nothing more. She was told to rest. Peter had spoken to her every day on the phone, but this was his first visit.

Behind the door he heard sudden footsteps. The door opened, and Caroline stood there in red silk and pearls. She looked sleek and impeccable, as though to remind Peter of her competence at life, even without him. Her head was high, her mouth was set.

Peter nodded. "Hello."

"Hello," Caroline said, stepping back with a militant sweep. Her perfume was new, strange to him. Inside, the front hall was dark, polished. A large gilt-framed mirror he had never seen before hung over a mahogany table. Carefully, Peter did not look around.

"How is she today?" he asked.

"She gets tired easily," Caroline said. Her voice was harsh. "She gets up in the morning and she's exhausted."

"She should rest," Peter said, nodding. "Not overdo it."

Caroline made no response. She stood, her hand still on the doorknob.

"Where is she?" Peter asked.

"In her room," Caroline answered. She still did not move.

"Can I see her?" Peter finally asked, vexed that she'd made him.

Caroline shut the door and turned without speaking. She walked down a carpeted hallway.

Peter followed. He'd known she would be rude. She had been rude to him for the last eight years, offhand, dismissive, contemptuous of his ideas. Sometimes, at the end of a conversation on the phone, she would say abruptly, "Good-bye," and hang up before Peter could reply. Each time she did this he felt a brief flush of anger, though he never responded. He mustn't rise now, he told himself. The last thing he wanted was a fight with Caroline. He had said all he had to say to Caroline. He was here to see Amanda. Caroline opened a door and went in, without looking back at him.

Amanda's room was square and good sized. Chintz curtains hung at the tall windows; a good mahogany bureau stood against one wall. There was a pretty needlepoint rug on the floor. The place was a shambles. Lying haphazardly on the carpet, as though hurled there, were shoes, clothes, magazines. The closet door stood open, and the closet light was on. The bureau top was messy. The bedside table was crammed with magazines, wadded Kleenexes, dirty glasses. A big television stood on a low bench by the window. The picture was on, but not the sound. The screen was angled to face the four-poster bed. In the bed lay Amanda, propped against a pillow. She held a magazine in one hand. Her other arm was in a white sling. She looked at Peter over the top of the magazine.

"Hi, Nanna," Peter said. His heart, crowded with anger, moved painfully at the sight of her. She looked so dreary, in this cluttered messy room, surrounded by the sad trashy debris of sickness.

Amanda waved the magazine at him, a slow flap.

Peter crossed the room and sat on the end of her bed. The bed was a hodgepodge of rumpled sheets; the blankets and bedspread were sliding off one corner.

"Can I sit here?" he asked, suddenly anxious. Perhaps she was fragile, perhaps he would upset some tenuous physical balance, sinking down on the mattress. "Is it all right?" He asked the first question of Amanda, but turned to her mother for the second: Caroline was in charge, after all.

It was disturbing, being here, so deep within Caroline's territory, seeing his daughter so stricken. And feeling such hostility from them both, such a hot sullen tide of it. Feeling hostility toward them as well: wasn't he as much the injured party as Caroline was? And how dare Amanda act angry? Hadn't he more reason for anger than she did? But he was not here to blame, he reminded himself. He was here to comfort.

At his question, Caroline nodded indifferently. She stood in the doorway, her arms folded, as though on guard there.

Peter turned back to Amanda. "How are you feeling?"

He put a tentative hand on her shin, muffled by the sheet. He wondered at once if he should: a teenage girl's body is such alarming and complicated territory. At his touch, Amanda's leg twitched, and moved reflexively away, sliding sideways.

"Sorry," Peter said.

Amanda shook her head. Her face was pale and puffy, her eyes seemed small. There were dark greenish shadows beneath them. There was a brownish patch, a healing bruise, on one cheekbone. Her hair, with the pale green streak, looked flattened and lifeless.

Peter turned to Caroline. "Is she still on painkillers?"

Caroline shook her head. "That was only the first day," she said. She sounded disapproving, as though this was something Peter should have known.

"She's not in pain now," Peter said.

Pain: he saw Tess's bruised face, the closed eyes.

"No," said Caroline. "She's recovering from shock."

"When do they think she'll be up and around?" It was easier to talk to Caroline, despite her hostility, than to Amanda, who was closed to him, distant.

"Next week, they think," said Caroline. "Doctor Kornfeld wants to see her on Friday." She used the doctor's name like a boast, an accusation: here was her ally. "He says it's important that she doesn't push herself. He doesn't want her to have a relapse. But she gets bored. She feels fine in the mornings. She gets up, then collapses."

Peter nodded. He turned back to Amanda, who lay still, as though she waited only for him to leave. She was damaged, he reminded himself. She was still suffering from shock. She had been in a car crash. At the thought of the crash he felt a choke of rage, quelled it. He was not here to blame her. He was her father, she had been hurt.

"I brought you something," Peter said. He held up the small brown bag. Amanda did not move, so he took out of it a dull gold box, tied with narrow gold twine. "Godiva."

"Thanks," Amanda answered. Her voice was a shock: so empty of energy.

Peter held out the box of chocolates and she took it without speaking. She leaned over and set it on the floor beside the bed.

A sudden gust of anger hit Peter and he leaned forward.

"If you don't want it," he said, "give it back. I'll give it to someone who does."

Amanda stared at him and did not speak.

Behind him Caroline said, "What did you say?"

Peter turned to her. "If Amanda doesn't want the chocolates, I'll give them to someone who does."

"I can't believe you said that," Caroline said, taking a step toward him. She sounded choked.

"If Amanda cares so little about what I took the trouble to bring her that she can't even bring herself to look at it—"

"She is in shock!" Caroline interrupted. "Your daughter is in shock! She's been in pain! Can you grasp that? Is that something you will ever, ever understand?"

Peter stood up, away from the disheveled bedclothes. "If she is in pain, Caroline, it's not my fault. Not everything in Amanda's life is my fault."

Caroline laughed angrily. "I see. Who do you think is responsible for the pain in Amanda's life? What do you think has made her so unhappy?"

"I think you and I are equally responsible. You're as much to blame as I am." Peter's voice rose. They shouldn't fight in front of Amanda, he thought. He moved toward the door, but Caroline did not follow him.

"I see," said Caroline. "Which of us was it that walked out on the marriage?"

"We've been through that before," Peter said, stopping. He glanced at Amanda but she lay with her face turned away from them both. "What I did was in response to what you did. We both played parts. But I also don't think it's important, now. It was almost ten years ago."

"Don't tell me it was ten years ago," said Caroline. "I don't care when it happened. It's just as true today as it was then. You walked out on us. You're still gone."

"Look," said Peter. "Time passes. Things change. You can't stay in the same place forever. I think you're stuck. And I don't think blaming is the way to live your life. That's all you do now: you blame me, and you tell Amanda to blame me. You tell her everything, *everything*, is my fault."

"I have *never* told Amanda that," Caroline said, drawing herself up in a fury of self-righteousness. She folded her arms, standing in front of the bureau.

"Not in so many words," said Peter, "but you make sure she knows it's what you think. You've made it clear that your life was poisoned when I left, and you've tried to make sure that her life is poisoned too." It was a relief to say this.

"Get out," said Caroline, smoking with anger. She set her hands on her hips. "Just get out. You despicable slime. I am not trying to poison my daughter's life."

"You teach her that your lives were ruined because I left. The despicable dad. You don't think that's poison? Children want to love their parents. You make it impossible for her to love her father. Why don't you think of her, instead of yourself, for a change?"

"*You* are telling *me* to think of Amanda instead of myself? Who were you thinking of when you ran off with Miss Teenage Atlantic City? I don't think it was Amanda."

There was a long pause.

"No," Peter said finally. "I was thinking of myself. It was selfish. I'm sorry for the pain I caused you both."

Again there was silence.

"It's not enough," Caroline declared.

"It's all I can say," Peter answered. "It's all I can offer. It happened. We're divorced. We can't let it ruin Amanda's life. She's young. We can't let her be ruined by this."

"*What do you care!*" hissed Caroline. She leaned forward, nearly spitting at Peter. "You sanctimonious shit! You're asking me to protect your daughter from your selfishness. You act as though I'm your partner in this, as though the two of us together will keep all this from our daughter. I'm not your partner. You made that clear years ago. You've betrayed and humiliated me. *I owe you nothing!* And I'm not going to cover up for you. Amanda should see you for what you really are."

"Caroline—" Peter began. He stopped.

He remembered seeing Caroline, that first day at Barney's Joy, when he could not imagine her angry. He remembered looking at her smiling face. It had been years since he had heard her voice unlaced with anger.

Caroline said challengingly, "What are you doing to make sure her life isn't ruined?"

"I love her," Peter said.

"So do I," said Caroline, "but I didn't let her sit around smoking dope all summer."

Enraged, Peter answered, "Do you think she wasn't smoking dope before? Do you think she had to come to Marten's Island to discover marijuana? She'd never seen it in New York City?"

"Stop." It was Amanda.

Peter and Caroline looked at her. Amanda's free hand covered her eyes, and her face was turned away from them both, toward the wall.

"Go away," she said.

There was a shamed silence.

"Do you want your father to leave, Nanna?" Caroline asked, stepping closer to the bed.

"Both of you," Amanda said, her voice muffled. "Go."

For a moment neither spoke.

"Nanna," began Peter slowly. He had made a mess of this.

"Just go," she said, and then she began, horribly, to cry. The sound struck at him. Amanda was breaking down, she could no longer hold out. She sounded finished; it was unbearable to hear.

"Amanda, please don't cry," he said, and bent over her. He felt his own throat close as he spoke.

"Why shouldn't I cry?" Amanda asked, sobbing. "Why shouldn't I cry?" Her voice was hoarse and racking, as though she were not sobbing but choking, as though something were preventing her from breathing.

Peter knelt beside her bed and put his arms around her. He laid his head down on the sheets next to her. He held her. He felt her shaking within his arms. He felt his own throat tighten, felt a stinging behind his eyes, felt himself begin to cry. He closed his eyes and saw at once Tess's face, battered, silent. Rage filled him again: he was furious. Amanda lay sobbing in his arms. He kept his face turned away from Caroline, he could not bear the sight of her standing, triumphant, her arms folded. He saw again Tess's face, mute, closed, perhaps forever. He could not help himself, he felt his anger at Amanda rise up in him, felt it rise into speech as he sobbed. He had never been so angry at anyone.

"How could you?" he heard himself weep against Amanda. His voice was part of his weeping. "How could you do it?" He heard his voice rise higher, louder. "How could you?" He felt himself rocking Amanda in his arms, but the rocking turned harder, more vehement. He felt himself shaking Amanda, shaking her hard against her own bed, her own pillow. He felt her limp and unresisting. He wanted to shake her more and more violently. He wanted to force her to look at him, listen to him, acknowledge who he was, accept him. He wanted to break her down and make her yield, yield to him. He wanted to shake her in some mighty and terminal way, until she gave in, stopped, ceased altogether. He heard his voice become a howl.

"*How could you do it?*" He was screaming.

Amanda lay in his arms, crying. She didn't return his embrace, didn't hold him. Peter felt Caroline tugging at him, crying out something, but he barely heard her. Close to his ear he heard Amanda speak, through sobs.

"I'm sorry," she said, crying. "I didn't mean to. I'm sorry."

28

Emma is alone in the room.

The hospital room now seems like the place where she lives. She knows every part of it, every view of it. She knows the shape of the high metal bed, its curved corners, the bulky squareness of its mattress. She knows the five perpendicular metal bars at the head and foot. The upper part of the mattress is raised, cranked up to an angle of thirty degrees, so that Tess's head and torso are elevated. This is to prevent congestion, the nurse has told her.

Emma knows also the look of the floor, with its linoleum square tiles. These are beige, and patterned with geological lines to make them look like marble, though they do not look like marble, they look like linoleum squares. Emma wonders if most people who see these tiles even know the intention of the marble pattern. Why bother with it? Why not make them a single uninflected color? Marble is no longer a part of the public's visual vocabulary, mineralogical veining carries no import. When they'd been designed, maybe in the twenties or thirties, the natural world was the standard. Nowadays, everyone assumes things are synthetic.

Emma knows the black metal window frame and the droopy beige curtains. She knows the angular metal chairs, with their brown leatherette backs and seats. She knows the molded plastic table, with its smooth white Formica top, its curved pedestal bottom. She feels as though she has known this room all her life. She feels as though she has been here for decades.

She sits now in the chair, leafing through a magazine that Peter has brought her. She cannot read books, not even one paragraph in a book, unless it is one of Tess's. She reads those, aloud or silently, without thought, her mind skimming smoothly along the narrative. Her mind touches the words lightly, lovingly, as though it is a sacred text, one so well known, so deeply absorbed, that this sort of reading is all that can be effected: at once rote, superficial, and profoundly responsive. Reading these books is like prayer for Emma. She believes that it is actively helping Tess. Or at least that it might be.

But right now she is reading a magazine. It is glossy and colorful, full of serene, light-filled houses, lush lawns, gardens overflowing with bloom. There are no people in the pictures. The people who live in these places are implied, but not stated. They are a negative pregnant, one of Emma's favorite phrases. It is a relief to her, not to have people in the pictures, not to see healthy children running across these lawns, not to see smiling parents in these kitchens. The places are all beautiful, all empty. They are soothing to look at.

Emma reads the text. "In the living room, the Middle Eastern theme is carried out with prints of Egyptian monuments by the nineteenth-century artist Robert Scott, and the pair of Anglo-Indian brass-covered side chairs, with their rams' heads which project from the chairbacks." In all these sentences there is a problem with verbs, because the articles are really only lists of objects. The problem, for the writer, is to inject some activity into the sentences, but since the subjects are all inert, it is difficult.

Emma examines the photographs. Sure enough, there is a print of the Sphinx, dim and massive, against Egyptian sands. And there, on the backs of the chairs, are rams' heads. They face away from each other, powerful, compact, with their tight spiraling curls of horns. A ram's head, thinks Emma, is one of those natural objects that's perfectly designed. Unlike a cow, for example, which is ungainly, difficult to draw. Or a big poodle, her favorite breed of dog, so graceful and elegant in reality, but impossible to render as such. Even the great Stubbs had failed: she remembers his clumsy, woolly attempt, a shapeless beige mass in a landscape. Not even a horse, with its blend of strength and delicacy, has the spare graphic perfection of a ram's head. That blunt-nosed simplicity, widening to the coiled power of the horns. Somewhere Emma has seen two rows of ancient stone rams, facing each other with silent gravity. Where was it, Luxor? Karnak? Delos? How can she not know?

There is a movement in the bed, and Emma rises at once to stand over Tess. Tess's eyelids are slightly raised, her eyes slightly open, but unseeing, unfocused. A narrow colorless tube runs into one nostril. This is now her source of nourishment. The IV was only a short-term arrangement, providing dextrose, for calories. The nasogastric tube carries more serious sustenance, the nurse told her. Emma's heart sank when she heard that. In for the long haul, she thought.

The movement that draws Emma to the bed is in Tess's foot, which jerks restlessly.

"Hello, Tessie," Emma says quietly. She takes Tess's hand. "If you can hear me, squeeze my hand," she says. She has done this hundreds of times, it seemed, hundreds and hundreds of times. But each time it is breathtakingly crucial, momentous. There is always the possibility of miraculous response, the first indication of Tess returning to them. A muscular quiver, minimal but deliberate: that's how it would happen. So quiet.

For the next second Emma is silent, motionless, holding her breath. Her whole body is listening for Tess's response. Tess's fingers in her hand are warm, living. The muscles are there, they are active, the nerves work. The hand could move, it could squeeze her fingers, right now. This was how these things happened, with a tiny gesture. One moment.

Tess's hand is soft, and Emma holds it as though she is shaking it in greeting. She squeezes it gently. Tess's narrow supple fingers collapse against each other: they are asleep. There is no resistance. There is no squeeze. The hand is inert.

Emma leans over Tess. Very carefully she smoothes the hair back from Tess's face. Peter was right, she thinks: the bruising was beginning, very slightly, to fade, the swelling beginning to lessen. Tess's own features, her own face, are now beginning to return. The rounded curve of the cheek is not quite so high, so strange. Tess's eyes are now more visible, the cheeks no longer pressed so high against them. Tess's beautiful eyes, the thick, springy lashes. The sweet line of the pale lid, folded meekly against itself. The high innocent brow, its long pure rise.

Looking at Tess's beloved face, Emma is filled unexpectedly with happiness. She feels gratitude: she doesn't know for what, but it wells powerfully up. Simply for having Tess? But this feels like prayer, blooming within her, it takes her over. She closes her eyes as it sweeps through her. She feels humble. She feels grateful for having Tess. Tess. She looks down at her daughter. Her chest fills. "Tess," she whispers. She is near tears, confused. She can't tell what she feels, but part of it, irrationally, is bliss.

Tess twitches, cocks her head suddenly sideways, then is motionless.

Emma goes to the window. The afternoon is on the wane. The sky is smoky and pale, the sun a burning white circle over the West Side. The sun is too glary, Emma thinks, glarier than it had been when she was a child. It was the vanishing ozone layer. She thinks of the ozone layer as a peaceful veil, like swathes of muffling tulle. It is soothing fog, protective, kind, necessary. And the sun had been gentle and benevolent in the past: she remembers those illustrations in old children's books, the sun's beaming face, smiling on travelers, flowers. As the ozone layer is burnt away, year by year, the sun's character is changing. Now, it's a harsh presence, flaming and malevolent. The sunlight in May is now fierce and pounding, the way it used to be in August, and the sun in August now feels deadly. When she was little it had been healthy to be outside. Children were told to run around in the sunshine. Now the sun itself, the source of life, is an enemy. Usually, thinking this, Emma feels a rising sense of terror: how could this be happening? What were they doing to the earth? It was like watching a horror movie, when the audience is unable to believe the stupidity of the characters, what they are allowing to happen. But now this fear is small and remote; the whole thing seems irrelevant. What she wants is Tess.

The park stretches out below the window, a scumbled mass of dusty green treetops. To the south is the wide light-filled expanse of the Reservoir, reflecting the colorless pallor of the sky. Around the water are the tiny figures of the runners, jogging determinedly along the dirt track. Watching them, Emma feels an unexpected tenderness for their brave, tireless, pointless efforts, jarring their spines, pounding themselves ceaselessly against the earth. What else was there to do but keep on going, circling that great flat sweep of water, drawing the harsh polluted air into their lungs, setting their feet down trustingly on the path, one in front of the other, over and over again?

Emma is looking out the window when she hears a voice behind her.

"Hello."

Emma turns. Rachel is standing in the doorway.

At the sight of her Emma feels her throat close with emotion. Rachel had loved Tess too. She had held Tess on her lap, put her arms around her. She had known Tess's tender body when it was well. Tears rise up in Emma's chest, but Emma fights to keep them down. She blinks and swallows, lifting her chin to keep from crying. It's important, not to let go, not to indulge herself. She will not cry in front of Rachel.

"Hello, Rachel," she says. "Come in. I'm so glad to see you."

"Couldn't come before," Rachel says. She looks wonderful, in a long red blazer. Her hair is no longer in braids, it's now pulled straight back, in a soft sleek helmet. She sets her bag down, her eyes on Tess.

"Come and say hello to her," Emma says. "It's good for her to hear voices she knows. I think she hears us."

Rachel bends over Tess. "Tessie," she says, her voice warm, quiet. "Tessie, it's me. Rachel. How you doing?"

Tess's foot twitches, and Emma pats it gently.

"She does that, moves," Emma says. "The doctor says it doesn't mean anything, but I think it's a good sign."

"Hello, Tessie," Rachel says again. She puts her large dark hand on Tess's brow and smooths the fine hair back, as she has done hundreds of times. She strokes Tess's cheek, gently, with her folded knuckles. Tess suddenly sighs, the sound of her breath—drawn in, expelled—a soft steamy whisper. Her eyelids flicker and still. The two women stand motionless over the bed, watching. Outside, the sun lowers. Its rays begin to redden, slanting through the window into the small room. Rachel withdraws her hand, straightens.

Emma and Rachel sit down in the chairs at the foot of the bed, and Emma begins to talk. She tells Rachel everything, the story of the crash, every detail, every moment of it. She tells her everything the doctor has said. She talks obsessively, fixedly, repeating the phrases as though, in themselves, they had some curative power.

"They had her on a respirator, at first," Emma says. "To hyperventilate her, in case there was swelling in the brain. They X-rayed her chest for pneumonia. There are risks of infection if you're in a coma."

Rachel listens to it all. She frowns responsively at the terrible things, nods understandingly when Emma describes their decisions.

"So now we wait," says Emma. "She's not in a deep coma, not the worst kind. I think she's just resting." Her voice breaks on this word and she takes a quick gasping breath, to recover. She swallows, then looks up at Rachel.

"I'm so glad you came," Emma says. "I'm so glad to see you."

She looks at Rachel's broad beautiful face with love. As Rachel smiles at her Emma remembers suddenly that time when Rachel had been so sulky, sullen. She remembers herself feeling embattled. Why had she? She can't now imagine feeling that way. Rachel had been so wonderful with Tess, she remembers that. That is all she remembers now, how Rachel would make Tess scream with laughter, how Rachel had fed her and bathed and comforted her. Emma would come into the kitchen to find the two of them speechless with laughter. Why had she been so closed to Rachel, so tense and competitive? She remembers trying to slip back into the apartment without telling Rachel that she'd been out all night: why had she done that? Why had she put poor Rachel in that position? And why had she cared what name Rachel called her? It now seemed absurd, she herself seemed absurd. She had been so anxious, so fearful, in those days, so frightened of everything. Now, in this room, all those fears are so small.

"I'm glad to see you," Rachel says, nodding. She gives Emma a warm, broad smile.

"Tell me your news. Where are you working?" Emma asks.

"An insurance company," says Rachel, laughing.

"An insurance company?" Emma laughs too, without knowing why. Rachel makes it funny.

"In Brooklyn."

"And? Do you like it?"

"I like it fine," says Rachel, shrugging her shoulders lazily. "Better than doing floors."

"Well, of course," says Emma quickly. "And how's your mother?" The famous mother, for whom Rachel had bought a goat on her birthday. Emma pictured her as large, laconic, fierce. She saw her in a small brightly painted house with banana trees around it, on a Caribbean hillside: Emma had seen the photograph of her on the porch, half-smiling, broad beamed, barefoot. The black doorway behind her.

"Mama died," Rachel says.

"I'm so sorry," says Emma. She pats Rachel's hand. It is so easy for her to say this now, it is so clear that this is the thing to do: offer your sympathy, readily. She thinks again, embarrassed, of how she had been years ago, strangled, wary, self-conscious. "I'm so sorry to hear that."

"Yeah," says Rachel, nodding primly, her accent thickening. She speaks looking straight ahead of her. "It was quick. She had a stroke. I was very sad when it happened. But now, you know, I still miss her, but I feel better that I'm not always feeling I should go home. I used to feel all the time that I should go home, go see her, go be with her. But it was her idea for me to come here in the first place! Now, I love her, but I have her here with me."

Emma nods, smiling.

The two women sit in silence. The sunset outside the window is fiery red, its rays fill the small room. Tess, on the high bed, is quiet.

"And how about your mama?" Rachel asks.

"She's fine," Emma says, her smile stiffening. "She and my father are coming down tomorrow to see Tess." She sighs, dreading it: her mother's awkward solicitude, her father's stiff judgmental presence. He will find fault with everything.

"And your sister? How's she?" asks Rachel. She had met Francie at the wedding and disapproved of her deeply.

"Francie's all right," says Emma. "She broke up with that man."

"That's good," says Rachel, nodding.

"I thought you'd say that," Emma says, and laughs. "She took up with another one."

"I thought you'd say that," Rachel says, and they both laugh.

Emma feels so comfortable with Rachel. She feels as though Rachel is her close friend. She doesn't want her to leave.

"Do you remember the time when Tess was little, when she was two or three, and you found her in her room, walking around and reciting nursery rhymes? And she had her hands on her hips, sashaying around, whispering to herself, 'Mary, Mary, quite the fairy'?"

Rachel laughs out loud at this, they both do, at the memory of Tess, so engaged, so guileless, so sure that the world was kind.

"Do you remember the time she told us she could turn all the lights out by herself? We asked her to do it, and she said, 'Watch!' and she slowly closed her eyes?"

They tell each other stories about Tess, stories from Tess's childhood. Emma finds herself laughing, rocking with laughter, a relief. She is thinking only about Rachel, and about the past, which now seems so blissfully happy, so uncomplicated. It had been heaven, she knows now. She does not let herself think about anything else, not about Tess, lying motionless against the raised bed, or about Peter, whom she hates.

As they talk, from time to time there is a movement from the bed, and then she and Rachel both rise. They both lean over Tess, murmuring to her. They both love her.

The nurse arrives: it is Cardina, a nurse Emma distrusts. She is large, black and bossy, and seldom makes eye contact with Emma. She comes in and glances sideways at Rachel, then ignores her.

"Have to ask you to step outside for a moment," she says ungraciously.

Emma takes Rachel out with her to the horrible lounge, with its thumbed and tattered magazines strewn across the low table, with its atmosphere of exhaustion and hopelessness. A blond woman sits on the plastic sofa. She is wearing running shoes and leggings, a T-shirt. Her son was hit by a car, six days ago. Her legs are folded, her arms are folded, and her head droops on her chest. She is asleep.

"Thanks for coming, Rachel," Emma says. She puts her hand on her shoulder.

Rachel looks at her and smiles. "Sure," she says.

"I really appreciate it," Emma says. She would like to go on: say, "And I'm sorry for having been so unpleasant and horrible to you, when Tess was little. I know I was unfair, and I'm sorry." She would like to say that. She nearly does. The words swirl around in her mind, but she is unable to line them up and speak them. Also, Emma is ashamed. Saying these things out loud would increase her shame, name it, make it real.

She says nothing more: also, she is afraid she would start to cry. For what if this accident, this terrible thing that has befallen Tess, is a punishment for all the times Emma has been selfish, cold, mean-spirited? There are so many of these times that she cannot think of them all, the thought overwhelms her, the number of bad things she has done, it breaks her down. She knows them very well, all of them. She could not bring herself to say anything to Rachel, she could not bear to begin.

But Rachel puts her arms around her and hugs her, slow and close. Emma begins to cry, and Rachel holds her. She rocks Emma gently in her arms.

When the nurse comes out of Tess's room, Emma pulls herself away from Rachel, and straightens up. The nurse nods grudgingly at Emma, not looking at Rachel.

"Thanks again for coming, Rachel," says Emma.

"Sure," says Rachel. "I'll be back." She strides off.

Emma watches her walk down the hall, her long pocketbook banging against her hip. Rachel is wearing clunky high heels that make her feet look huge, but she is so tall she carries it off. She looks so great, Emma thinks, with those high wide shoulders, the wrinkled scarlet blazer. Emma loves her. At the corner Rachel turns kindly to look back. Emma waves; Rachel waves back, vanishes.

Emma returns to Tess's room. She knows what Cardina has done in her absence: she has used a small suction pump to clear Tess's throat out. Tess has been turned on her side, then turned back. Cardina has lifted each limb. Emma bends over Tess: she looks no different. Her face is faintly flushed, perhaps. Emma leans closer.

"Hello, Tessie," she whispers. "I love you." She takes Tess's hand in hers. "If you can hear me, squeeze my hand." She waits.

When Peter comes in Emma is sitting in the chair again, reading the glossy magazine. He comes over to kiss her. Their lips barely touch. He goes to the bed, and Emma watches him bend over Tess. He takes Tess's hand, he whispers to her.

"She looks better," he says, coming back. "The swelling's going down."

"Rachel was here," Emma says.

"Was she," Peter says. He puts down his briefcase. "That was nice of her." Peter sits down beside her. He looks tired. "What did the doctor say?"

"He hasn't come yet. He should be here any minute."

As she speaks the door opens and Doctor Baxter sweeps in. His long white jacket is unbuttoned down the front, and billows slightly as he walks. This gives the impression that he is moving rapidly, trailing importance. He nods at both of them, unsmiling.

"Good afternoon, Mrs. Chatfield. Mr. Chatfield." He heads past them, straight for Tess. Peter and Emma stand, and move to the foot of the bed, watching. The doctor bends over Tess, lifts her eyelids, shines his narrow flashlight deep into her eyes. He checks the tube running into her nostril, he looks at her charts. He examines her face, turning it slightly from side to side. He checks for reflexes, one hand supporting her knee, the other tapping the special place on the kneecap with his hammer: there are no reflexes. Her leg hangs limp. Peter and Emma watch, mute. Doctor Baxter turns away from the bed, back to them.

"How does she look?" Peter asks.

"There hasn't been much change," says Doctor Baxter. He fits his small flashlight back into the breast pocket of his white jacket.

"And now what?" Peter asks.

"Now we have to wait," says Doctor Baxter. When he finishes a sentence he sets his lips together like a clamp, the corners of his mouth going down.

"How long?" asks Peter.

Doctor Baxter shakes his head. "We don't know," he said. He looks directly into Peter's eyes. "We just have to wait."

"But how long might it be?" Emma asks. "How long before it's, you know, too long?" There are things she will not say.

Doctor Baxter looks at her without expression. She can see the lines stacked one above the other on his forehead. "The sooner she begins to make progress, the better," he says. "But she could stay like this for a week, for two weeks, and still make a full recovery. What's important now is that there is no infection."

Two weeks. Today is only the fifth day. Emma nods at him, as though what he has said is fine, acceptable to her. As though she has some measure of control, authority. As though her nod means anything at all.

"How would she get an infection?" Peter asks. With his rumpled shirt, his unknotted tie, his hands in his pockets, he looks like a graduate student, overworked, distracted.

"Well, the human system isn't designed for immobility," Doctor Baxter says. He touches the rim of his glasses, adjusts them on the bridge of his nose. "There's a risk of blood clots, or infection from the IV, or the catheter. That's why we do the blood tests, to test for infection."

Emma and Peter nod, to show they understand. Hearing this information makes Emma feel as though she is standing in shallow water, being hit by towering waves, one after another, each enormous, killing, hitting her hard. These are all new things to worry about, terrible things. Blood clots. Infection from the IV, the nasogastric tube, the catheter. She had thought these hospital things were benign, helpful: now she realizes they are all possible enemies. Tess's sleep itself is a possible enemy. Emma stops nodding; she is stunned by all this.

Peter is still gazing at the doctor, nodding thoughtfully, looking concerned. He is frowning hard. He is also stunned.

When the doctor leaves they sit down again. Emma leans back in her chair and closes her eyes.

"Well, at least we know we have two weeks," Peter says finally. Emma does not answer.

Peter looks at her. "That's a blessing."

Emma stays still, her eyes closed.

Peter opens his briefcase noisily and takes out some papers. He spreads them on his lap and begins to read them, a pencil in his hand. He keeps thinking of Amanda. The shock of holding her in his arms, feeling her sob. Each time the thought comes to him he feels again its shock: that child, sobbing.

Finally he says, without looking up, "I saw Amanda today."

Emma's head snaps upright. She doesn't answer.

"I went to see her at Caroline's."

Emma says nothing.

"She's still in bed," Peter says. He lifts his head. "She has a sling on her arm. She looks awful." He is playing for sympathy.

He pauses. Really what he wants is to tell Emma how terrible it had been there, how furious Caroline was at him, still, after all these years, how he still felt blamed for everything, even by his daughter, even for her own behavior. How he had felt as though he'd been captured and taken inside the enemy compound, where he was reviled. How fragile he had felt, how helpless and exposed. How angry and tormented he had been, seeing Amanda lying in bed, seeing the greenish pallor of her skin, her anger, and then feeling his own rage suddenly mount, and then the bottom of it falling away, and his grief welling up, his compassion, his love for his daughter. But he won't be able to explain this to Emma, who has not even turned her head. She does not want to hear this.

"She's still in shock," he said, then pauses again.

Emma speaks without looking at him. "I don't want to hear about her."

There is a silence in the room.

Peter turns to her. "Emma, look," he begins, "Amanda—"

Emma turns to him. "I don't want to hear her name," she says, her voice terrible. "I never want to hear her name again. Never again."

They stare at each other.

Peter starts to speak.

"*Never again*," Emma repeats, louder. She sounds unbalanced, like a madwoman.

Peter looks back down at his papers, spread out across his knees. He puts his head in his hands, and spreads his fingers across his face.

Later, when it is dark, Peter goes out to get dinner. This time he has ordered a meal by phone, from Pico's, a restaurant on Madison and Ninety-first Street. He walks down Fifth Avenue through the summer evening, crossing over to Madison at Ninety-sixth Street. On Fifth there are big apartment buildings, massive, towering. Here on Madison the buildings are low and human scale. They rise only four and five stories below the purple nighttime sky. The shopfronts are cheery and gentrified: gourmet food shops, antiques, books, children's clothing. There are stars and ribbons in the windows. The people on the sidewalks are still in their day clothes; they are wrinkled, sweaty, going home. Snappy-looking young women in short black dresses, blazers, gold bangles. Young businessmen with briefcases, and those floppy Italian trousers. Madison Avenue up here, in the nineties, is mostly families.

Most of the people he passes have children, he thinks. None of them understands what is happening to Peter: he feels like a spy, an impostor. Meeting the eyes, for a second, of a passing woman, her kinky pale hair pulled back into a ponytail, her round face cool and impassive, Peter feels a sudden horrifying drop. He feels the gap between two realities, as though he is on drugs, as though he is from a different race.

He steps into the restaurant, which is small and crowded and pricey looking. The clientele is sleek, the lighting low. The front room is double height, and he walks through it to the high desk, where a young blond woman in black is standing.

"My name is Chatfield," he says. He feels again the reality dislocation. It can't be true, he thinks, everything else is normal. "I'm here to pick up two dinners I ordered."

"Okay," she says. "Let me go find them." She heads for the back. Each sentence is a shock to him: everything out here, outside, is ordinary, natural. But inside he faces chaos: the earth yawning, landslides, avalanches, the landscape of desolation. Desolation. He sees again Emma's face as she says, "Never again." He feels his teeth grind against each other. "Never again," she said. Somehow this seems the worst yet, the last straw. Is this the beginning of the end between them? He has heard that couples often split up when something happens to a child. He has thought that he and Emma would be wiser than this, that they would comfort each other, not turn against each other. But how can he stay married to a woman who will not allow him to speak the name of his daughter?

Emma is not herself, he tells himself. She's been hit by an avalanche. He can't make demands on her now.

The blond woman pushes her way out through the swinging doors. She stalks, awkwardly, on very high heels. She is smiling, but empty-handed.

"It'll be out in just a moment," she says.

"Thank you," Peter says. But when is the moment to reach conclusions?

Emma is irrational now. He should do nothing until things settle down. What if things don't settle down? He feels those chords again, those bass chords sounding, moving ominously further down in the lower register.

The blond woman hands him a heavy white paper bag. He is surprised: he doesn't remember the waiter appearing with it. Synaptic gap, is that what this is, losing moments of perception? Will he start having delusions? Lacunae in his memory? Perhaps Tess is getting better, and he has forgotten that, he thinks hopefully.

"Forty-nine seventy-eight?" the blond woman says. Her tone suggests politely that she has said this once before.

"Right," says Peter, frowning to suggest that he's been lost in thought, which he has. He pulls out his wallet and fumbles for the green plastic card. He hands it over. He feels Amanda in his arms again, sobbing. He sees Emma's face, closed. He sees Tess's face, battered.

"Here you are," says the blond woman, smiling at him. Her eyelashes are pale, nearly white. She must be naturally blond, Scandinavian, Peter thinks. He's heard that in Scandinavia women dye their hair dark, to be exotic. He thinks of Amanda's ghastly green streak: exotic. Christ, he thinks: skipping the tennis clinic. The thought is agonizing, unbearable. What did it matter? What did it matter?

"Thank you," he says to the blond girl. It is excruciatingly painful to speak.

She hands him back the credit card. Her two front teeth slant, ever so slightly, one folding in over the other. Her lips are chapped. Peter feels himself staring, and looks down. He signs the slip she hands him, then pockets his copy. He picks up the bag and starts out of the restaurant. At the corner table are two men, elbows on the table, talking intently. Business or pleasure, wonders Peter. They look in their early twenties: young to be so serious, so sober. When he was that age he had been less convinced the world was serious, dangerous. Good luck, Peter thinks wildly. Good luck. It seems crucial, right now, for him to broadcast goodwill.

He pushes through the door and sets out again, back up Madison. Each thought sweeps over him like a new blow. Skipping the tennis clinic, he thinks. He remembers Amanda's face, when they came home after the cocktail party. When he and Emma arrived, like vengeful Furies, the girls had been so happy, playing some kind of raucous tag, throwing that book across the table at each other, their faces bright, animated. It was what he and Emma had hoped for all summer: to find the two girls happy together, playing.

He remembers himself swollen with rage, bursting with it. He had felt humiliated, as though he'd been exposed before every single person at Christian Taylor's party. Everyone on the entire island had known that his daughter had been cheating and deceiving him all summer.

And so what? What difference did it make? What could possibly justify his behavior?

It was like everything else, he thinks, you learned these things by doing them wrong. When you've learned them it's too late.

He reaches the corner of Ninety-sixth and Madison, and turns west, toward Fifth. The streets are shadowy now, and Madison past Ninety-sixth is tricky. The blocks up there are poor, not gentrified. At night, the shops there do not have brightly lighted windows with ribbons in them. They have steel shutters, that rattle all the way down to the sidewalk. Up here people stand in the shadows, watching the passersby. If the passerby is white he feels uncomfortable.

A man walks slowly past Peter, pushing a shopping basket crammed with empty cans. Reagan's trickle-down economic plan had not trickled down to the streets in New York, the poor buggers. And now Reagan had Alzheimer's, and would never know what mistakes he had made. Bush thought every decision had been correct. Maybe it had been, but what about these people in the streets, in tattered clothes, who look you in the face? Even if they were lying, conning, scamming, they were still poor.

Peter turns north on Fifth. On his left the trees in the park rustle, dark and promising. On the West Side the sound of a siren rises suddenly, insistent, insane.

"Never again," Emma has said. "Never again." She has said this, declared it. He feels a rush of rage.

Peter turns in at the hospital, nodding at the black security guard. The man nods back, unfriendly. Peter walks to the elevators and pushes the slippery plastic button. It has been pushed by someone else, and is already lit from within, a ghastly glow. Beside it a man and woman are standing. The man is pale faced, and wears metal-rimmed glasses. The woman too has pale skin and bright dark eyes. They both look rumpled, and the woman dowdy in a long floppy skirt. They are silent and intent. The two stare at each other without speaking: they look like old enemies, practiced antagonists, each one waiting for the other to make a move.

Peter wonders, his own marriage so hot and hostile in his mind, what they are thinking, what holds them in that stare. Maybe all the parents with stricken children turn against each other, maybe it is unavoidable. Who else is there to turn against?

The elevator doors slide open and the three of them get in together. The man turns his back on his wife, facing the door. On the third floor they get off. The man walks away, without turning to see if his wife is following.

Peter goes on up to seven, carrying their dinner. Tonight he has ordered lamb stew, with warm rosemary bread, and a real salad. At least he is learning about take-out meals, knowledge he resents needing.

In the room Emma is bent closely over her magazine, and does not look up. Peter opens the food in silence, spreads it out. Emma takes a plate. They eat without talking.

They do not speak all evening. Once the phone rings; Emma answers it. "Hello, Mother," she says, her voice strained. "No," she says. "No. No news." There is a pause. "It's the same. No." There is another pause. "I know. Thanks. Thanks for calling." Then, "That would be great. Fine. I'll see you in the afternoon. Good. Okay, good-bye."

When she hangs up, her face closes down again. Peter waits, but she says nothing.

"That your mother?" he asks finally, angry.

Emma nods.

"Is she coming down?"

Emma nods again.

"When?"

"On Thursday."

"That's tomorrow."

"I know that."

When Emma says nothing more, Peter returns to *The Magic Mountain*. Hans Castorp was moving irrevocably toward his own doom. Every aspect of his life spoke ominously of his destruction. It troubles Peter, to have to live through this slow decline with Castorp. He feels trapped in the book, but he feels obliged to finish it. It would be somehow shameful, cowardly, of him now to give it up.

Each time there is a movement from the bed, Emma rises. She goes to Tess and speaks in a low voice. It is terrible for Peter to listen. He can hear in her voice that this is all she wants, this one thing. He remembers Amanda in his arms, the terrible ratcheting sobs. *He still has a daughter.*

At ten Peter closes his book. "It's bedtime," he says.

Emma does not look up. Her head is down, over her book, and he can see from the fixity of her chin that she does not want to hear him, does not want to respond.

"Emma," he says, "come back with me."

Without looking at him she shakes her head slowly.

"Then I'll wait for you," Peter says, and she turns to him.

He sees how grief has tightened her mouth. Her chin is pointed, her eyes narrow. Beneath her eyes there are half-moon hollows. The skin there is translucent and dark, shadowy. She looks at him steadily.

"We need to spend the night together," Peter says.

He feels no liking for her, no physical affection. He knows this is dangerous. Right now they must be careful. They must not allow this silence to go on. He holds out his hand to her. "Emma," he says.

She looks at him for a long moment, then closes her magazine and stands up. She has taken off her shoes, and he watches her fish with her bare foot for her flat ballet slipper. She shuffles into it, finds the other one, and goes again to the bed. She leans over it, takes Tess's hand, and whispers good night.

In the taxi on the way home Peter can't bring himself to touch her. The streetlights, as they pass, stripe the backseat with light, and in this erratic illumination he sees Emma's thighs set primly side by side. The thought of her body is dismal to him, her limbs are useless to his arms. He stares out the cab window as they ride through the summer night. There is a moon, and the air is clear. Insects cluster, dots of pale fire, under the high lights. The cabdriver rattles south on Fifth, then turns west, across the park, swooping around the curves and hurtling through the sudden blackness of the underpass, rising afterward to face the high cliffs of the apartment buildings along Central Park West.

Peter, swept along in this nocturnal race, wonders what he is doing. What is he attempting? He is acting as though he feels something he does not. But what else is there for him to do? He can't walk away from the marriage because Tess has been hurt. Someone must protect them from this threat, from Emma. At the thought of Emma's icy silence he feels rage, not love. He may not be able to do this.

At home they undress in separate rooms. Emma comes out of the bathroom without meeting his eyes.

"Did you take a sleeping pill?" Peter asks. Her doctor has given her a new kind, mercifully strong, fast acting, brief. She nods and gets into bed on her side. She curls into a neat roll, but not quite so far away from him as last night. Peter knows this, but he lies still, on his back, reading. He can't yet bring himself to touch her, not even to pat her shoulder. When he turns off his light she is quiet; he pretends to think she is asleep. He rolls over on his side, away from her.

In the morning the first thing he feels is his anger at Emma. Without looking at her he feels her burning presence on the far side of the bed. "Never again," she had said. He feels Amanda in his arms. He opens his eyes, his chest full of rage. He looks over at Emma, ready to talk.

She is gone. The bed is empty. He feels suddenly cheated, angrier still. It is now the sixth day. Peter lies for a moment in bed.

Never again.

29

It is not yet nine, and already it is hot. Peter can feel his shirt sticking in patches to his skin, under his jacket. He has just emerged onto the sidewalk, from the subway. It is not far from West Eighty-first Street, down and across to Rockefeller Center, but this morning the trip seems endless.

Usually Peter ignores it, his movements through it automatic, his thoughts deliberately elsewhere. This morning it seemed to him like hell: a screaming journey through the underworld, the passengers deafened, jostled, imperiled. Standing in the station, breathing in the sour damp smell of the tunnels. Standing in the cars, surrounded by mute and immobile bodies crammed, sweating, side by side. A short woman in a raincoat had stood so close to Peter that her wiry gray hair brushed the underside of his chin. Next to him, holding on casually to the greasy metal pole, was a muscular young black man in a faded red T-shirt and voluminous lowered jeans. His bulk swayed ominously against Peter on the turns, and his heavy-lidded eye, full, it seemed, of hatred, slid toward him, then away. All around Peter was the physical press of strangers, the intimate unwanted knowledge of their limbs and odors.

He dreads his conversation with Caroline. He can feel the anger she directs toward him. There is anger all around him.

Peter pushes through the heavy doors into 30 Rockefeller Center. Once inside he is part of a throng, walking across the long cathedral-like lobby, with its lofty ceilings, its deep tenebrous spaces. Its stylized chrome pseudo-Aztec details, the polished mineral surfaces, all this celebration of style is heartening, in a way more austere modern architecture is not.

Those slab-sided featureless buildings ignore humanity; this art deco ecclesiastical style condescends to it, but at least acknowledges its existence. It pays homage to human endeavor. Peter usually finds this thought comforting, but not today. Today nothing comforts him.

Streams of moving people surround Peter; he walks quickly among them, through them. The banks of elevators stand in niches, the ceilings here low, the space intimate, like confessionals. Peter pushes the elevator button with the side of his briefcase, impatient at the wait. It is unbearable to wait here, among this press of people. Everything is unbearably slow.

The doors slide open before him, the crowd presses forward and Peter moves to the back of the car. He turns to face the door; the car fills, the doors shut, the car rises in silence. Peter looks at the others and realizes that he is the oldest person there. He must be early, he thinks, to arrive with all the young thrusters. But when he looks at his watch, it is quarter of nine. Of course, he thinks, it's the end of August. Anyone with seniority is away now, on vacation. As he would have been. He sees Tess's face, the bloom of bruising. Each time the realization is new to him, bewildering, sickening.

Directly in front of Peter stands a tense young man, with a long narrow head. His tightly curled blond hair is cut very short. He seems unaware of Peter behind him, and stands too close. On the gray shoulder of his suit is a light shower of white flecks. His ear, inches from Peter's nose, flares out from the side of his long head. The curled cartilaginous flesh looks naked: pink, translucent, indecently intimate. The man smells very clean, soapy. Peter can hear the man breathing, a slow, determined tidal rhythm—in, out, in. Peter feels his teeth clench, grind slightly. He shuts his eyes, not to look at the ear.

Peter gets off on the thirtieth floor. Here it is air-conditioned, and too cold. The secretaries wear sweaters all summer. In the summer, the thermostat is set at sixty-eight, but in the winter it is seventy-two. If you reversed them you'd save billions of dollars of fossil fuel, but Americans insist on this, being too hot in the winter, too cold in the summer. A convention, a holdover from the fifties, when we were rich and oil was cheap.

His office is dim and cool, but stuffy. The closed-in air feels dead. The blinds are pulled down, the lights are off. He turns them on, revealing one wall of teak bookcases full of law books. One wall with windows behind two green leather wing chairs. Behind his desk, hanging on the wall, are his framed degrees: Harvard, Columbia Law. Peter puts his briefcase down on the desk.

He sees Emma's stubborn jutting chin, her unfriendly eyes. She will hold him off forever. This is how she is: whenever they argue, she withdraws afterwards into cold silence, and waits for Peter to make the next move. She will wait for days, mute, stubborn, implacable. When finally Peter has worn out his anger, when he does make a move, reaches out his hand, takes her in his arms, she yields at once, turning silky, remorseful. But until he speaks she will not.

In her family is the story of a nineteenth-century husband—a minister?—who announced his plan to go to New York to hear the Swedish Nightingale, Jenny Lind. "Nathaniel," said his wife—Ezekiel or Obadiah, whatever Old Testament name it was—"if you go to hear that hussy, I'll never speak to you again." And he did, and she didn't, is how the story is told. Years later, when the wife lies dying, her husband leans over and whispers something into her ear. She turns her face to the wall and, without speaking, she dies. Emma's family is proud of that story, as though it reveals integrity instead of intolerance, as though it were a victory, not a failure.

Emma's family is all like that, thinks Peter angrily. They're all censorious, stubborn, unforgiving. Worse, they are proud of it. Emma's father is the most judgmental old buzzard Peter has ever seen; Everett thinks being self-righteous makes him good. He has still never met Francie's new husband, Carlos.

Peter goes down the hall to get coffee. He needs fortifying before he calls Caroline. At the little kitchen niche carved discreetly out of the formal hallways, he fills his mug at the Mr. Coffee machine. His mug is a tan one from Starbucks, where he has never been.

In his office he closes the door and sits down at his desk. He takes a bitter black swallow and picks up his phone. He punches in the numbers of Caroline's brief atonal tune. He listens to the sound of it, those unnatural plinks. Why not real notes? Why not the regular musical scale? While the phone rings he closes his eyes. He feels himself gathering his energy to confront her, feels himself clench.

"Caroline? It's me. Amanda there?" He speaks quickly and briskly.

"She's here but I think she's still asleep," Caroline says. Her voice is cool.

"I see," Peter says, vexed at once by her response. He waits, but she says nothing more. "You're sure of that? Would you like to go and check?"

"I think she's asleep," Caroline repeats flatly.

"Well, I'd like to talk to her when she wakes up," Peter says. "Would you have her call me?"

"I'll tell her," says Caroline, not promising.

"What time do you think that will be?"

"I have no idea," says Caroline.

Peter says nothing. He is determined not to have a fight with Caroline. "Well, please ask her to call as soon as she wakes up. It's important. How's she feeling?"

"She's not up yet," repeats Caroline. "I don't know."

"Thanks," says Peter, and hangs up.

He picks up his mug. His hand, holding the thick pottery, is trembling. He looks at his fingers, concentrating, to stop the tremor. He can't. He sets down the mug and spreads his fingers in the air, the palm down. *Damn you, Caroline.*

Above the deep fustian red of his blotter floats his hand. The thickened fingers fan tautly outward. The hand itself is broad, coarse. The skin is folded and wrinkled. Dark veins trace a knotty delta of soft ridges beneath the skin. Sparse hair, pale and shining, like dune grass, drifts across the back of his hand. From the wrist upward, the hand trembles, in a steady quiver. He can't stop it.

Peter opens his briefcase. His jaw aches, and deliberately he unclenches his teeth. He will not go on like this. He will not put up with Emma's coldness, he will not permit her to turn against his daughter. He will not tolerate certain things. *Never again,* she said, and meant it. He has married a woman with a cold heart.

He takes another swallow of the bitter coffee. He feels that his life is starting to fly apart. He feels the air around him is being fractured, invisibly, constantly. Shards of his life are hurtling outward. There is something that he needs to do, some action he must take.

He sees Tess's face again, again he's washed with disbelief. He goes back to that night. He remembers the first moment of wakefulness, lying in bed, startled, listening, uncomprehending. He had not yet known: he could weep, now, for his own blissful ignorance, that moment, before the dreadful one of understanding. The mad circling red glare of the light on the police car. The weighty hovering of the helicopter. The stretcher being lifted up into its dark belly. The doors closing over it. The tennis clinic, he thinks. Christ. His own anger. His own anger. He puts his head into his hands, covering his face.

During the day, Peter usually calls Emma often. This morning he does not, working determinedly through the hours. Each time he thinks of Emma he sees her tightened mouth, the little tense twin peaks made by her lips when she is angry. Never again, she had said. She had meant it, but she is not the only one to make decisions.

Halfway through the morning, John Norman, another partner, appears. Tall, diffident, red haired, Norman stands in the doorway.

"Do you have any time today?" he asks. "I'm going to have to argue this case in front of a jury, and I'd like to discuss it with you, when you have a chance."

"Right now," Peter says, pushing his chair back from his desk. "Have a seat."

He's glad for a diversion, glad to have a physical presence to talk to. In his shirtsleeves and suspenders, Peter leans back in his chair, listening, watching Norman's long intelligent face. Norman sits down in a green leather chair and crosses his legs. He is pale skinned, with pinkish eyes and a rosy, rubbery lower lip. He has never presented a case to a jury. Jury cases have only recently become common in patent law, and Peter has more experience in them than many of his partners.

"I'll tell you how I would see it," Peter says. "I'd make it clear to the jury that there's a question about whether or not the government should properly have issued a patent. That's where I'd start."

In the middle of Peter's explanation the telephone rings.

"Excuse me," he says. Emma, he thinks, and picks it up while it is still ringing.

"Hello?" he says, eager.

"Dad?" Amanda's voice is remote.

"Hi, sweetie," he says, uncomfortable. "Can I call you back in a little while? I'm in a meeting right now."

"I'm just leaving," Amanda says. "I'll be back this afternoon. Mom's taking me out to brunch."

"No, wait a minute, I need to talk to you," Peter says. "How can you be about to go out if you just got up?"

"I got up a while ago."

"Didn't your mother ask you to call me as soon as you woke up?"

There is a pause.

"She told me to call," Amanda says carefully.

"Well, I asked her to tell you to call as soon as you got up. So please don't go out," Peter says, his temper rising. "I need to talk to you before you go."

"Dad, we're leaving right now," Amanda says. "I'll talk to you later."

Peter stands up at his desk. "Amanda, I've just asked you not to leave," he says. "I need to talk to you."

"But we have to go *now*," Amanda says, sounding anxious. "Mom has an appointment afterwards."

Norman rises tactfully and catches Peter's eye. He waves and mouthes, "I'll be back." He leaves the office, closing the door quietly behind him.

Peter sits down. "All right, let's talk now." He waits until the door is shut. "Amanda, I want you to come with me and visit Tess in the hospital."

There is a silence.

"No," Amanda says.

Instantly Peter stands up again. "Don't tell me no, Amanda," he says. He feels his chest swelling, anger pumping it up. "I know you don't want to go, but you have a responsibility here." He speaks loudly, he knows it is too loud, but he can't help it. He was unprepared for the call, distracted by Norman's presence, unsettled by Amanda threatening to go out. Angry at Caroline for sabotaging him.

"I don't want to go," Amanda says.

"I'm sure you don't," Peter says. "But you have a moral obligation, Amanda. I want you to go there."

"Dad," Amanda says, "I don't want to go."

"I don't care if you don't want to go!" Peter says, loud again. "I want you to go there! Do you hear me?"

Amanda says nothing.

"Amanda?"

She does not answer.

"Amanda," Peter says. He is now furious: she is directly disobeying him. "I want you to go. You put her there, you go there! Do you understand what you've done? You can't walk away from this. You are involved." Don't say it's your fault, he tells himself. Don't say it.

There is silence, then the muffled sounds of movement.

"Peter?" It is Caroline. "What on earth are you saying to Amanda?"

"I want her to come with me to the hospital to see Tess."

"That is out of the question," Caroline says firmly. "She's not going to. She's still in shock. She can't go trailing all over New York."

"But she can go trailing out for brunch," says Peter. "She's well enough to do that."

"That's right," Caroline says.

"Caroline, this is serious," Peter says. "Amanda can't pretend this doesn't exist. What she has done is terrible. Do you understand that? It may be irreparable."

Hearing himself say the word, Peter feels his throat thicken: *irreparable*. His eyes sting. He feels things sliding, worse, out of control. What if this were true?

"Amanda has to come in and be part of this," he says. "This is a part of her life. It's part of my life. I want her present, I want her to understand what has happened, I want her to see it. She's part of it. She can't simply walk away. And I forbid you to encourage it."

"You can't forbid me to do anything. You have no control over me whatsoever," says Caroline. "Amanda is my daughter and she's in my custody. She is not going to the hospital with you; that's a sick, morbid idea. You want to punish her for something that was an accident, something she never meant to do. You want to torment her and bully her, and I won't let you."

Peter turns to look out the window. The building across the street is covered with a skin of mirrored glass, which reflects his own building. The other building itself is weirdly invisible in the landscape, the blue sky behind it matching the blue sky in its reflections. Staring out, Peter is staring disconcertingly in at himself. His own window lies somewhere in that mirrored grid, reflected back at him, as his own rage is reflected back at him by Caroline.

He takes a deep breath and begins, talking calmly. He has prepared for this. "Caroline, if you cross me in this," he says carefully, "I will sue you for custody. I will show in court that, under your care, Amanda has been consistently smoking marijuana, which is an illegal drug. I will recount to the court the tragedy that has resulted because of her habits. I will prove you to be absent, a poor moral influence, and an unfit parent."

There is a long pause.

"I promise you I will do this," Peter says, and means it.

There is another pause.

"You despicable shit," Caroline says.

There is silence.

"Put Amanda on the phone," Peter says, keeping victory out of his voice. There is another pause, more telephone handling.

"Hello?" Amanda says miserably.

"I'm going to come and pick you up this afternoon at four," Peter says. "We're going up to the hospital."

"Dad," Amanda begins.

"Here is why I want you to go," Peter says. "I want you to think about someone else besides yourself. I want you think of Tess, and of Emma." His voice breaks on the last word. "This is something that's happened, and we all have to go through it together. I know you didn't mean to do it, but you're a part of it. You can't walk away, Amanda. *You can't walk away.*" Here he feels his chest fill again, and he cannot go on.

There is a long pause.

When Amanda answers, her voice is small and dismal. "Okay."

"Tell your mother," Peter says, and hangs up.

He looks at his watch: only twelve-fifteen. Christ. He's exhausted, wrung out. Done for the day. He feels like going home, but there is nothing for him at home. And there is nothing for him at the hospital but Emma's hostile silence. There is nothing for him anywhere, nowhere he can go for relief. There is no relief.

At exactly four o'clock Peter pushes Caroline's buzzer. The door opens almost at once.

"She's ready," Caroline says viciously.

Amanda is waiting: she looks awful. There are big dark circles under her eyes, and her skin is pale and unhealthy. The dreadful green streak in her hair is now showing dark roots. She is wearing a wrinkled T-shirt and a blue-jean skirt. On her feet are heavy black sandals. He loves her.

"Let's go," he says.

"Bye, Mom," Amanda says forlornly.

Caroline stands in the doorway, her arms folded. "Bye, Amanda," she says. She looks at Peter. "I will never forgive you for this."

"You've never forgiven me for anything," Peter says.

Caroline shuts the door, hard.

In the elevator Peter turns to Amanda. "I appreciate your coming, Amanda," he says. "I know it's hard for you." He sounds cold and formal, he thinks unhappily, like a lawyer.

Amanda watches the elevator door. "Thanks," she says.

They take a taxi up to the hospital. It is still hot, it has gotten hotter and hotter all day. Riding uptown to pick up Amanda, Peter started sweating again. The sun feels malevolent. Emma claims it's the vanishing ozone layer, but she always says this as though it is his fault, so he always denies it. Anyway, it's always hot in August. Still, the dead glare feels somehow ominous, he has to admit.

Their cab is old and cramped, without air-conditioning. Peter rolls the window down as they rattle up Park. The air feels gritty and used. He feels grubby. He still hasn't spoken to Emma, not since last night. *Never again. Never again.* Amanda's hand lies next to her on the dirty seat. Peter reaches over and takes it. It is moist and limp in his fingers. *If you can hear me squeeze my hand.* He feels his breath choke in his throat, fights it down. He carries Amanda's hand to his mouth, and kisses the back of it: the skin is smooth, and unexpectedly sweet smelling. Faintly damp with sweat.

He smiles at Amanda. "Your hand smells nice."

She looks startled, then gives him a small smile. "Thanks."

Peter kisses the hand again and puts it back on the seat. They are going up Madison now: you have to overshoot the hospital by several blocks on Madison, then go west, across to Fifth and down. Coming south along the park on Fifth, they stop at the light at 100th Street. A Latino couple is walking on the pavement along the park wall. A short dark-haired woman in a loose T-shirt, tight skirt and high heels, pushes an empty stroller. She walks with wide casual strides. Beside her is a black-haired man, carrying a child on his shoulders. His arms are folded over the child's legs, which hang down his chest. Latin men, thinks Peter, carry their kids around on the street. Italians do it, and Spaniards, South Americans. Not WASPS, not the English, not Germans: it was women who carried their babies. At least WASPS hadn't before Snuglis and women's lib, when men had started changing diapers. Peter's father would never have carried him in public. To say nothing of Emma's father, the old buzzard. He had probably made his poor wife walk one step behind him on the sidewalk.

The Hispanic woman looks up at the child and speaks. The child answers and leans over, wrapping his arms down around his father's skull, cradling his father's jaw. The father says something, his teeth bright in his dark face. The child rides trustfully above the crowd, safe from the perils of the lower regions. He rises and falls comfortably, with each step of his father's. The child's small heart, the very beating center of him, is pressed against his father's head. Peter cannot take his eyes off the family, the three of them. They seem so happy.

The cab draws up at the entrance to the hospital, behind another cab. Peter takes his wallet from his breast pocket.

Amanda, looking out the window, says, "There are Emma's parents."

Peter looks up: he had forgotten they were coming. The Kirklands are slowly climbing the steps. They are moving uncertainly: how meek they look here, Peter thinks, surprised, touched. How frail they seem, timid, even, outside their own territory. Mr. Kirkland, in a wrinkled gray suit, looks thin and stooped. Mrs. Kirkland, in a droopy skirt, clings awkwardly to his arm. They are climbing the broad shallow steps diagonally, yawing uncertainly off course, as though set by an unknown tide.

Peter pays the cabdriver and he and Amanda start up the steps behind the Kirklands.

"Hello, Everett," Peter says politely.

Everett Kirkland swivels belligerently to face him. "Oh, hello," he says, frowning.

"Hello," says Mrs. Kirkland anxiously. Neither of them looks at Amanda.

"You remember Amanda," Peter says, putting his hand on Amanda's arm and drawing her forward as they all mount the steps.

"Hello, Amanda," Mrs. Kirkland says, smiling miserably.

"Hello," says Amanda.

Mr. Kirkland stares at Amanda.

"Everett, this is my daughter, Amanda," Peter says reprovingly, reminding him.

"Hello," Mr. Kirkland says briefly, withdrawing his eyes.

They walk inside in silence.

"Over here," Peter says, leading them to the elevators. Going up, the car is crowded and silent. On the seventh floor they get out, the Kirklands straggling uncertainly behind them.

"This way," Peter says. He takes firm hold of Amanda's hand, and marshals them down the hall to Tess's room.

As Peter comes in the room he sees a white-coated shoulder. Beyond it is Emma's pale face. She is talking to the doctor.

Peter pauses. There are too many of them to come in while the doctor is there. But Peter is already inside, and he wants to see the doctor himself. He doesn't want Amanda to stay, but he doesn't want to make her wait out in the hall with someone who won't even speak her name.

Peter shoulders his way gently in, past the doctor. He sees Emma's face lift, sees her eyes seek his miserably. Then she sees who is with him: Amanda. Her eyes deepen angrily, her mouth sets tightly.

"Hello, Doctor Baxter," Peter says loudly. He hopes the Kirklands will realize that they should go and wait in the hall, but he doesn't turn around to see.

"Hello," says Doctor Baxter earnestly. He pushes his tortoiseshell glasses further up on his nose with his middle finger. The bald part of his skull is shiny.

"How are things going?" Peter asks. He wonders if Amanda is still right behind him. He can't tell, and he doesn't want to turn around, he feels he must keep his gaze on Emma and the doctor. He doesn't know if he hopes Amanda is there or not. Does he want her to hear this? He's not sure what he wants. Things are flying out of his control.

Doctor Baxter says, "I was telling your wife that I see some improvement in the pupillary response, today."

"That's good news," says Peter, nodding, though he hardly knows what it means. Amanda has moved in next to him and is standing on one side of him. Facing him, on the other side of the doctor, standing across from him, is Emma. He can feel her, like a blast furnace, sending off waves of heat and fury. She is deliberately not looking at him or Amanda, she is staring fixedly at the doctor.

"Well," says Doctor Baxter, raising one finger in a cautionary way. "It's good, but it's too soon to tell much. It's still early days yet. Early days."

Such a strange phrase, Peter thinks. *It's early days.* Ungrammatical. How had it evolved? And what is the pupillary response? He knows he knows what it is. He cannot find it. "What is the pupillary response?" he asked.

"Each day I test your daughter's pupils with a light," says the doctor.

"Tess is not his daughter," Emma says neutrally.

"I'm sorry. Your stepdaughter's eyes," says the doctor.

"It's quite all right," Peter says, furious.

Doctor Baxter pulls out the pencil-sized flashlight from his breast pocket. He turns it on, as though the light itself will reveal something. "Up to now, her pupils have been unfocused. But today I can see a shift. They have begun to draw together, toward the light, as eyes do normally."

"Good," Peter says forcefully, nodding. This is marvelous. He wonders where the Kirklands are. Are they standing tactlessly right behind him, listening? Is the consultation over? Is Doctor Baxter about to leave? Is he leaving because there are too many people here? Should Peter tell Amanda to wait outside? What if Emma tells Amanda to wait outside? He will slap her face.

Doctor Baxter nods solemnly at them both, pushing his lips outward slightly in a preoccupied pout. The front of his head gleams. Peter wonders if he does anything to make it gleam. What would you do to bald skin? Put lotion on it? Oil? Wax it, like a floor? Is it something Peter will have to learn? The doctor shifts deftly away from them, anxious to leave.

"We'll see how she is tomorrow," he says. He lifts the flashlight to put it back in the breast pocket of his white jacket but misses. He frowns slightly, pouting again. On the second try he makes it, tucking it in neatly. He nods at Peter and Emma. "Good-bye," he says, and slides past them.

Peter stands facing Emma, who still does not look at him or Amanda. She follows the doctor out to the hall, where her parents are waiting.

"Hello, Daddy, Mummy. Come on in," Peter hears her say, and they all file back into the room. They stand awkwardly.

"Hello, dear," Mrs. Kirkland is saying. "How is she? Did the doctor give you good news?"

"Yes," says Emma. "Come and see her."

Emma leads them to the bed. She has still not yet looked at Amanda.

Peter takes Amanda's hand again. He glances at her: her eyebrows are raised, aloof, her eyelids lowered, as though she is bored. As he stands next to her he catches a faint whiff from her body. Has she not bothered to shower? Damn Caroline, he thinks, damn her, damn her.

Emma leans over one side of the bed, her mother over the other. Mr. Kirkland stands stiffly beside his wife, looking at Tess, but not leaning over. Tess lies on her back, one arm flung across her stomach, the other down at her side. Today her face seems more swollen; is that possible? Maybe it's just that he's looking at her as an outsider, as these newcomers would see her for the first time. But she looks terrible. The battered nose, the cheeks. The greenish brown bruises. Christ.

"You see," Emma says, "you heard Doctor Baxter. The pupillary response is getting better. That means her eyes are beginning to focus." Tess's eyes are now closed, no one can see her pupils.

The air-conditioning is on high, and it is too cold in the room. Amanda gives a sudden shiver. Peter squeezes her hand, to comfort her, and to keep her from pulling away.

"That means," Emma begins. She stops. "That means that the

brain—" But the words are too terrible, and she cannot go on. Doctor Baxter's coolness, his caution, his deliberate flight from them all, make this tiny glimmer of hope seem suddenly pathetic in the face of the reality—Tess's battered features, her silence. Emma puts her hands to her face and hunches over, her head lowered onto her chest. Peter is at the foot of the bed, and can't reach her unless he drops Amanda's hand.

Mrs. Kirkland leans across the bed, across Tess. "Dear," she says. She touches Emma's head. "I'm so sorry," she says.

Emma turns her head away from her mother's hand, jerking as though she'd been bitten. She turns away from her parents, toward the window, and begins to cry. The others stand motionless while Emma weeps.

Peter lets go of Amanda's hand and steps around the bed to Emma. He puts his arm around her, taking hold of her shoulders, and for a moment he feels her lean against his arm, but at once she stiffens.

"Get out," Emma says, hissing.

"Emma," Peter says, warningly.

She raises her head. "Get out of here."

"Emma," Peter says, now angry.

Emma turns to Amanda. Her face is distorted with grief, tears are running down her cheeks. Her eyes are red, like an animal's. "You get out," she says. "How dare you come here."

"Emma," says Mrs. Kirkland.

"Don't say that," Peter says. "This is my daughter."

Emma stares at him. She raises her arm, pointing at the bed. "This is my daughter," she says.

"Emma," says Mrs. Kirkland again, nervous.

"Get out," Emma says.

"Don't tell me that," Peter says. "I am Tess's stepfather."

"I want you out of here," Emma says, her eyes wild. "I want you out." Her voice is rising.

"Emma, look," Peter says. He steps forward and puts his arms around her. She shakes him loose and turns away.

"Please don't touch me," she says. "Please don't ever touch me again."

"Don't say that," Mrs. Kirkland says.

Emma turns to her father. "Tell him to leave."

Peter takes Amanda's hand again. "Don't go too far, Emma," he says. "Maybe you already have."

Emma laughs terribly. "Maybe *I* already have?" she asked. "Look at my daughter." She waves her hand again at Tess. "How dare you say things like that to me. How dare you bring her here."

"Emma," Peter begins. He stops, and closes his eyes. There is nowhere left to go. "Okay, Amanda," he says. "Good-bye," he says to the Kirklands.

"Don't go," says Mrs. Kirkland uneasily.

"Go," says Emma. She has crossed her arms on her chest.

Peter leads Amanda into the hall. Outside the room he looks first left, then right. He can't remember which way the elevator is.

30

As he steps out of the elevator downstairs, into the lobby, Peter's eyes meet those of the middle-aged black woman behind the high square reception counter. Her hair is lacquered, and piled up on her head. Her heavy-lidded stare is steady and uncompromising. Under her scrutiny he realizes suddenly that he still has Amanda's hand held tightly in his.

Crossing the lobby toward the main door, he drops her hand, turning to her. "I'm not letting you go," he says. "I just don't want to be arrested for kidnapping."

Amanda looks startled, then smiles timidly. "Thanks," she says.

Her timidity strikes him, and her gratitude. I never do this, he thinks, I never explain things to her, simple things, the things I'm doing. I expect her to know things without being told, and then I'm impatient when she doesn't.

Outside on the front steps it is hot again. The lowering sun strikes powerfully at them from the sky over the West Side. The sluggish city air feels already breathed. Peter stands for a moment on the sidewalk.

"Where are we going?" Amanda asks, and again Peter feels a pang. When was she ever given a choice? Children went where they were taken. All those weekends when Amanda was taken from her own home, taken from her room, her friends, her mother, to come to their strange apartment. At his request. His command.

"Where would you like to go?" Peter asks. "What about a walk in the park? Then we could go to a movie, if you want." Now he feels timid. Here is the risk: perhaps she will reject this, him.

But Amanda says peaceably, "Okay." She walks with him to the curb. They wait for the light, to cross toward the long low stone wall bordering the park. A tangle of forsythia clamors above the coping, its foliage dark now, at the end of the summer, the leaves hanging limp, but still green, still growing. It looks cooler on the other side of the street.

Peter can feel sweat beginning at his temples. He would like to take Amanda's hand again, just for openers, just to declare himself. But it is so hot, and he doesn't want to attract stares. And she might not want him to hold her hand.

The light changes and they cross the avenue. He wonders where to begin, with Amanda. He wonders what he is going to say to her. He wonders where he is going to go that night, and what he has declared to Emma, by walking out.

"What are you going to do?" Amanda asks, looking up at him.

"Go to the club," he says. Anywhere.

"Oh," she says, and turns away.

He would have liked to reassure her. Always he has felt a responsibility to shield her from the world, to maintain a parental canopy over her, suggesting that adult behavior may be complicated and incomprehensible, but it is not something that should worry her. He has always felt his marriage to Emma, their behavior, should appear logical, orderly. That's over. He has no idea what will happen now, between himself and Emma, so he can't reassure Amanda about that. She can see for herself, she will have to make her own deductions. She can see that he is unhappy, helpless. She can see that he wouldn't let Emma turn his daughter away. She can see that he thinks Emma has gone too far.

"Is this because of me?" Amanda asks.

"Because of you, yes," says Peter. "But it's not your fault."

They walk in silence. In front of them is a short, trim woman with a yellow Lab. The woman walks languidly in the heat, the Lab, his pink tongue out, shambles lazily along beside her.

"It's not acceptable to me that Emma should treat you like that," Peter says. "I won't let her."

Amanda looks at him, then turns away.

Has he been too harsh toward Emma? He thinks again of the battered face. No. Even so, no. There are things she can't expect of him, even though Tess is hurt. And she has rejected him over and over, coldly, relentlessly. He feels again rage.

"You're my daughter," he says.

"I didn't think that mattered," Amanda says.

"What do you mean?" Peter asks.

"I mean, you always used to tell me, when I said you did everything for Tess, you always said you'd treat us the same, you'd always treat us just the same. I thought you didn't care that I was your daughter, I thought it didn't make any difference."

"Amanda—" Peter begins. Anger is the emotion he was used to feeling toward her. Amanda created havoc: she upset Tess, upset Emma, she broke rules, broke her word, broke dishes. She has been like this for years, always. What he felt when he saw her was always anger and resentment, the need to protect Emma and Tess from her. Emma and Tess stood under the shelter of one arm, and Amanda arrived with weapons, ready to attack. It was up to him to prevent Amanda from doing damage. She always managed to; she was sulky, rebellious, intractable. Willfully destructive. Now he wonders what his own part has been in all this. How had she felt, arriving to find him always protecting this other wife, this other daughter, fending her off?

"I love you," he says earnestly.

"I know you say that," Amanda answers. She sounds resigned.

"I do," says Peter, but how has he shown it?

"And you love Tess," Amanda says.

"I do, but not the way I love you."

She turns to look at him again, her face open, her eyes sorrowful. A cruel sight, sorrow in a child's face.

"You're my daughter," Peter says painfully. How can he make her understand this, know what it means? He is dependent on her, he realizes, for her life. Her life is the extension of his, he needs her to go on into the future, living on for him, better, more excitingly. She is his link, he wants her to carry on for him, to do things he had never dreamed of doing. She is his beloved connection to the world, she is his beloved daughter.

But what has it meant for her? For years he has forced her to do what he wanted. He has insisted on her obedience, demanding her presence, on his terms, against her will. Her only hope, her only liberation would come with age. What if she never wants to see him again, when she is old enough to say so? The thought smites him. What if she blames him, as he has blamed her?

In front of them, the woman stops for a moment to fix her shoe. The dog stops too, watching her. The woman takes off her shoe and shakes it out. She is wearing a loose bright shift. She is in her thirties, with short dark well-cut hair. She looks intellectual, like someone who works in a museum. Will I end up with someone like that? Peter wonders. Am I single? Is my marriage over? The thought so depresses him he puts it from him. They cross the cobbled walkway in silence.

At Ninety-second Street the sidewalk flares into a semicircular plaza, curving into the park. A neoclassical statue stands in the center of the curve, facing the street. Stone steps lead on either side of it, up into the park.

"Want to go in?" Amanda asks. "There's a really nice path that goes in here."

"Okay," Peter says, surprised by her knowledge of the park, surprised that she thinks a path is really nice, surprised to learn that she has a separate life, about which he knows nothing.

She's right. They walk along a wide beaten path, beneath high spreading branches. Above them, up a small bluff on their right, is the Reservoir. Every few moments a figure in running shorts passes, silhouetted against the sky, beating slowly forward through the sluggish air. Their footsteps form a quiet human rhythm against the harsh sounds of traffic below, on Fifth Avenue.

"When do you come here?" Peter asks. "I didn't know you knew all this about the park."

Amanda looks at him and smiles, looks away. "We used to come here after school."

And do drugs? Peter wonders. He knows nothing about her life, nothing.

"How do you like school?" he asks. "Really."

"It's okay," Amanda says, shrugging her shoulders. There is such sadness in her voice. "It's fine. I just can't wait to go away to college, that's all."

"Because of?"

She shakes her bangs away from her face, frowning. "I don't know. I just hate the way—" She stops. "You know, school is not a great experience for me."

"No," Peter agrees. "I wonder why not?"

"Was your school so great?" Amanda asks. "I mean, I just figure that everyone is miserable in school. Later it will get better, life, I mean."

"My school," says Peter, thinking about it. They have reached the bottom of the Reservoir, and the path swerves inward.

"We go this way," says Amanda, and leads him west, toward the interior of the park. "To the Great Lawn. I always like the way that sounds. The Great Lawn."

He has never heard her say anything like that before, that she likes how words sound. That she likes anything. Peter feels tremulous with pleasure, with gratitude at her trust.

"Was I happy at school?" Peter says. "I think I was, but I don't really know. There were parts of it that were fun. I liked soccer. I liked track, I liked running cross-country."

"Was that what you did?"

"Didn't you know that? I loved cross-country. I'd get up really early, in the spring and fall. The dormitory was completely quiet. I'd go outside and the whole campus was empty, green and empty. I'd run for miles before breakfast. There was a field I'd pass. In the mornings it was still covered with mist."

Amanda looks at him and smiles. "I didn't know that," she says.

"I loved running," says Peter. "I didn't have a lot of friends. A couple. There was only one teacher I liked, who taught history." But they had been chaotic, those years at boarding school. What he remembers now is a sense of wild insurrection, a constant struggle against the rules, the institution, the place. A sense of continual containment, against the students' collective wills.

"I suppose I didn't have a great time," he says. "I never really asked myself that question."

"No," says Amanda stoically. "You just wait for it to be over."

"What about drugs?" Peter asks tentatively. He wonders if he's asking too much, too quickly.

Amanda shrugs. They are walking now along the edge of the Great Lawn. It stretches, flat and tired looking, at the end of a dry summer, toward the fairy-tale spires of the West Side, rising above the trees.

"Just grass," Amanda says, uninterested. "Some kids do it all the time."

"Do you?" Peter feels anxious. Now is he going too far? But he needs to know.

Amanda nods. "I guess so," she says. "Most days."

Peter frowns: it sounds so dreary, children in these seedy furtive transactions. Hiding somewhere for the brief exhilarated high, the sad return to school, homework.

"Where do you get it?" Peter asks. "Where do you do it?"

"You can get it anywhere," Amanda answers. "Just walk along the street and they offer it. I used to get it from a guy in the park at Seventy-second Street, but now I get it from someone on Ninety-sixth. Or from a girl at school. We do it at school in our rooms at night. We used to get high at my apartment in the afternoons."

"Wasn't your mom ever around in the afternoons?" Peter asks gently.

"If she was, we went someplace else," Amanda says.

On the Great Lawn a soccer game is going on. The players are all men, shirtless, in bright shorts. Their skins are tanned and glistening. Some wear bandannas knotted at their necks. They race back and forth, shouting. The ball scoots wildly over the scuffed grass, then hurtles back. Peter glances at them for a moment.

"Nice pass," he says.

"I hate sports," Amanda says, not looking up.

"I know," Peter says. "What do you like? What do you like best?"

"I like my friends," Amanda says. "I like music. I like movies. I like museums."

"Museums?" asks Peter, surprised, impressed. He has never heard this.

"I really like museums," Amanda says.

"What kind?"

"Any kind. There's a really neat one way up on the West Side, of American Indians. We go there sometimes."

"I never knew that," Peter says humbly.

Amanda does not answer.

A siren suddenly raises its voice on Fifth Avenue, shrilling impatiently. The sound does not move, whatever the vehicle is, it is stopped, trapped. He thinks of Tess, on the stretcher. Thank God she had gone straight, swiftly. Thank God it had been four in the morning. She had been flown directly to the helipad at Sixtieth Street, and the ambulance had taken her straight to the hospital. The pupillary response: thank God it was better.

He thinks of the Knickerbocker, wonders how it will feel to stay there. Wonders what the bedrooms are like. He does not know what will happen. Perhaps this is the end of his marriage. Will he be allowed to see Tess again? When she gets well, will he be allowed to see her if he and Emma divorce? He cannot imagine it. It tears at him. Will Tess know he loved her, even if he is not permitted to see her? Does Amanda know he loves her, even though he has forced her to see him?

When they reach Sixty-second Street, he stops. "Come in with me to the Knick," he says. "I want to see if they have a room."

The entrance hall is lofty, dim, cool. The pale stone staircase rises toward the reception rooms in a great neoclassical sweep, as though the entire eighteenth century waits upstairs. It's quiet now, the big rooms are empty. Well, it's the end of August. Most of the members are somewhere else—by the sea, in the mountains. Somewhere with lawns and porches, a silent breeze.

Peter and Amanda come inside and stand at the desk by the coat check. The bedrooms are being renovated, Peter is told, but there is one available. He thanks them and says he'll be back.

Outside on the sidewalk they stand still.

"I'm going to go home and pack," Peter says. "But would you like to have dinner later? We could see a movie if you want. You choose."

Amanda hesitates. Frowning slightly, she gazes past him, down the sidewalk. He wonders if it's over, her openness, the moment of trust between them, friendship.

"I don't want to see a movie," she says. "Let's just have dinner."

Peter feels his heart lift. "Lovely," he says. "Where would you like to go? You choose."

Amanda frowns again. "Harry Cipriani," she says.

Peter laughs.

"Why are you laughing?" she asks, her eyes anxious. "Isn't that a good place?"

"It's terrific," Peter says, still laughing. He steps forward and takes her head between his hands. He kisses her carefully on both cheeks. "You're terrific. Shall I come pick you up or shall we meet there?"

"There," says Amanda. "What time?"

"Eight o'clock," says Peter. "See you there. And dress up. It's fancy."

Her face breaks into a smile, shy and charming, nearly flirtatious. "I know that," she says. She lifts her hand and gives her wrist a flick, her little finger raised. "Ta ta," she says. "Pa pa."

His elation lasts until Peter reaches the apartment. Inside it is bleak and dead. He walks swiftly back to the bedroom. From the top of his closet he takes down a suitcase. It's canvas, trimmed with leather and embossed with his initials. Emma gave it to him for Christmas years ago, one of their first Christmases together. It's fraying now along the lower seams; when he'd noticed that he'd thought he'd tell Emma, so that if she wanted to replace it for Christmas, she could. Is all that over, that business of marriage, the luxury of taking affection for granted?

He is packing for three days. By then something will be different. He will have moved back, or he will be coming back to move out for good. He moves fast, packing sloppily. He hates this. While he is setting the first layer of things in the bottom of the suitcase—running shoes, shorts, socks— the telephone rings. He stops, looking at it. He wonders if it might be Emma. She might be trying to reach him, to say she is sorry, to give him news of Tess. But she wouldn't think he was here, right now, he thinks. It would be a call for her; he will let the machine in the library take it. He can't face talking to someone else just now, pretending everything is all right, promising to carry a message from a friend, thanking someone for calling. He can't do it. It had been bad enough before, doing that while he and Emma were pretending to be a team. Though, tossing one shirt after another into a pile, he thinks back to the beginning of this. Even at the scene of the accident, from the first moment of Tess's being hurt, Emma had turned against him.

He puts in his toilet kit, its soft leather stained with shaving cream, with water from a hundred hotel bathrooms. Emma had given this to him too. She had turned against him at once, as though she had been waiting to blame him. It seems as though she has blamed him as much as she blames Amanda. She is so angry at him he wonders now if she might have turned against him even if Amanda had had nothing to do with it. She has turned away from him and toward Tess. That's how she sees them, him and Tess, as competitors in her life. He comes second. He doesn't mind coming second, after a child, but he minds being a competitor. Angry, he throws clean underwear into the suitcase, on top of the shirts.

He has married a coldhearted woman, rigid, intolerant. He looks around. What else will he need? Ties. He strides back to the closet. He wonders what they will do tonight, Emma and her parents. Wander in circles until they faint from hunger, he thinks: not one of them has ever made a restaurant reservation in their lives.

He'll go back to Marten's Island for Labor Day, he decides. He'll leave New York. Let her stay here and not speak to him. What's the point of his staying? Unless she'll let him see Tess. He doesn't want to leave Tess. But perhaps she won't let him in to see her. She would hardly look at him. Maybe he'll take Amanda away for Labor Day. They'll find a hotel somewhere in Maine, or on a lake in New Hampshire. He'll take her away, and they'll go on long walks together. They'll find a museum: carved wooden ducks, Indian birchbark canoes. Goddamn Emma. He zips the suitcase shut and sets it on the floor.

He sits on the unmade bed to call Harry Cipriani. As he dials he wonders if it had been Amanda, calling before. Was there a problem? He makes the reservation for eight o'clock, hangs up. He wonders what Amanda will do if her mother says she can't come. But this new Amanda, this young woman who likes museums, would be able to deal with this, he thinks. He can imagine Caroline's face closing and tightening at the sound of his name. Amanda cannot mention him to her mother, he supposes.

How had her life turned out this way? No wonder she has become adept at breaking rules, sneaking out, not telling the truth. Everything she feels, she has had to conceal from one of them. They have given her no choice.

He thinks of Tess, and the pupillary response. It's good news, whether or not the doctor wanted to permit them to think so. It is good news, no matter whether or not it was early days. That careful little bugger, with his polished head. Peter knows it is good news. He feels a surge of hope. He wishes he'd had more time there, he wishes he could have leaned quietly over Tessie's face and talked to her, looked deep into her eyes himself. Her brave silent eyes. That's how it will begin, the recovery. Improvement of the pupillary response. Then she will squeeze a hand.

He wonders about Emma's parents. Will they have spent the afternoon there, in awkward silence? He can't imagine Everett Kirkland sitting there hour after hour, without being the center of attention in some way. Making a fuss over something, complaining about the nurses, the doctors. And where would they stay? Emma hadn't even told him they were coming, he'd had to drag it out of her. Rage rises again in him. She wants to cut him out of her life. It's what she has been trying to do. She has done it. He will not prevent her.

Peter picks up his suitcase. He feels sick at heart. He wonders if he is really leaving. More second marriages end in divorce than first ones, maybe you see it as easier the second time. The phone rings again. He stands listening to the rings, looking around the room. He is walking out, perhaps his marriage is over. He thinks of Tess's face, he longs for her; he feels he is losing everything. He leaves as the phone is still ringing. He hears it cut off suddenly as the machine in the library picks up.

Amanda is late, but for the first time this doesn't bother him. Peter waits at the table, with a glass of white wine, watching the door. Harry Cipriani is glowing, bustling with black-jacketed waiters and tall blond Italian women. The surfaces are polished, the linen crisp. The pace here is faster, and has more flourishes, than in a French restaurant. Around Peter there is rapid Italian, flowing energetically through the air.

The door opens and a young woman comes in, wearing a black dress and a white blazer. Peter notices her because of her eyes, which are startled, anxious. Her mouth is a gash of dark red, and her eyes are heavily made up. She has short dark hair, brushed back: with a shock, he recognizes the green streak.

"Amanda," he says, standing up, waving. She looks around and sees him; her face lights up. He is surprised that she is so pretty.

"Hi there," she says, coming over.

The waiter draws her chair out with a bow. "Signorina."

Amanda sits down with a small graceful flump, smiling at the waiter to thank him. She hangs her bag over the back of the chair and puts her hands in her lap, like a little girl. She sits up very straight, and looks at her father, smiling. Her skin now glows, in the candlelight. She looks radiant. He realizes that she is wearing powder, makeup; it gives him an odd thrill, pride. Her eyes are black rimmed, the lids dark and smudged, the lashes thickened. Above her eyes stretch the long cool curves of her brows. Her black dress exposes her pale throat, surprisingly broad and handsome, a lovely column rising to the shadows beneath her jaw. At the base of her neck is the modest pearl necklace Peter gave her for Christmas. She wears big pearl earrings, rimmed with gold. Her odd spiky hair stands straight up as it always has, but now, here in the candlelight, with the earrings, the makeup, the black dress, it looks jaunty, insouciant. Chic.

She looks so different from the Amanda he knows: she looks grown-up, and—even more interesting—fun. He can't stop smiling at her, it's like falling in love. He is touched that she has taken such trouble to get ready for this. He imagines her leaning toward the mirror, marking the long line of her upper eyelid, as he has seen Emma do. Amanda looks now so elegant, or actually, almost elegant, which is even more touching. There is the faint wobble in her high-heeled step, the slight wrinkle in the black dress. Peter is so proud of her. He beams. She's so pretty: she will be a beauty. He has not seen this before, not been able to.

He's not sure what to offer her to drink. Would he be irresponsible, offering her alcohol? Would that be urging her to be an adult before she's ready? Would he be absurd not to offer her alcohol, pretending she had never had any, was still a child?

"I don't know what to order you to drink," he says candidly. It's a relief to say this. He feels he's gone as far as he can, deciding all these things by himself. He admits that he didn't know how to be a father, hasn't done much of a job. Tess's face comes into his mind. He did what he could, and most of it seems to have been wrong. He's quitting taking charge of everything. He's trying a new way. "What do you think is the right thing? What would you feel happy with?"

"I'd like one glass of white wine," Amanda says firmly, "and some mineral water. With bubbles." She has clearly thought about it.

"Waiter," Peter says, holding his hand up, pleased. Why hasn't he thought of this before, asking her? What a relief, what a lightening of the load.

"You look very elegant," he says, when they've ordered their drinks.

"Thanks," she says happily.

"I like your earrings."

She touches one with her fingertip, her eyes closing with delight. "Chanel," she reveals. "Mom gave them to me."

There she is, curdling every conversation: Caroline. She lies between them like a deadly stream, always there, divisive, malign. Chanel earrings, he thinks, automatically critical, for a fifteen-year-old. How inappropriate.

"What did you tell your mother you were doing?" he asks.

Amanda sighs, and stops smiling. "I just said I was having dinner out."

"Didn't she ask who with?"

"No. I wouldn't have told her anyway." She looks at him directly. "Every time you say that, 'your mother,' you sound mean."

Peter says nothing for a moment. He's tempted to deny it, but it's probably true. His new plan is to deny nothing. "I suppose I do," he admits. "Every time I think of her, it upsets me."

"Why still? You've been divorced for eight years."

"I don't know why," Peter says. "I suppose it's that she's still there. She's living proof of my mistake. And if she's a warm wonderful person, then how can I justify what I did? I have to make sure she's bad, and that everyone around me knows it."

Amanda looks at him, considering, her brow troubled.

"That's not really true," he says quickly. "Your mother isn't bad. Don't think I mean she is."

But Amanda says nothing, and he feels judgment in her gaze. I suppose this is what we fear the most, he thinks, being judged by our children. It's why we put it off until the last possible moment, allowing them their own thoughts, their own points of view. They can turn pitilessly upon us, having seen us at our worst.

The waiter appears, with their menus.

"Have you been here before, Nanna?" asks Peter. He wants credit for something, he wants the upper hand again. He is her father. "The food is wonderful. And look at this announcement: 'Patrons are respectfully requested not to use cellular telephones, because they interfere with the making of risotto.'" Peter looked up, smiling. "No one is more graceful than the Italians."

Amanda doesn't smile. "I've been here once," she says, and does not explain.

Chastened, Peter does not ask. When they have ordered, Amanda leans back in her chair and looks at him again.

"Did you know from the beginning that you and Mom wouldn't stay together?"

Peter thinks about it, remembering. "No, I don't think so. Or if I did, I didn't know I knew it. I didn't know how you were meant to feel, so I didn't know I didn't feel it. Why?"

"I just wondered," she says. "If you knew from the beginning you wouldn't, I wondered why you had me."

Peter leans forward and touches her cheek with the back of his hand. "We were married, and your mother got pregnant. It wouldn't have occurred to either of us not to have you. And we both loved having you. We're both glad we did." It feels strange to say "we both" and mean him and Caroline.

Amanda says nothing. She looks at him steadily.

"I hope you know that," Peter says, but he can see this is not her point. It strikes him suddenly. "Don't say you wish we hadn't," he says.

Amanda takes a sip from her white wine. "I can't imagine that," she says. "But it would have been easier, for me, if you hadn't." She speaks without self-pity; an observation. She'd have been spared misery, had they thought about it, had they been kind enough to keep her from being born.

It's insupportable. Peter sets down his glass and folds his hands on the table, looking at her. He feels that something has arrived, this is a moment after which everything will have to be different. It's up to him.

"Amanda," he begins.

He can't now imagine how he felt a month ago, two weeks ago, toward his daughter. He knows it was different, he remembers feeling distant, impatient. He can't now imagine not understanding her. How could he not have known then, as he does now, the sorrow that fills her eyes? How could he not have felt this great enfolding sympathy for her, as well as love?

But as he begins to talk, Amanda waves her hand, as though sweeping something away. "Don't tell me you love me again," she says. "I know you do. At least I know you think you do, you believe it. But you don't like me. And neither does Emma."

31

After dinner, Peter takes Amanda home in a cab. At her building he gets out with her and steps under the awning to say good night. He has said all he can say to her; he doesn't know if she believes him. He's done what he can.

He takes gentle hold of her by her upper arms, which are soft and surprisingly dense, forceful. He kisses her twice, once on each sweet cheek, and smells her perfume: flowery and warm. He strokes her funny spiky hair upright. The mad green streak is now lighthearted, charming. How could he have thought it threatening?

"Good night, Nanna," he says. "I like your hair."

"Thanks. Good night, Dad," she says. "Thanks for dinner. I love you."

He is grateful for this. "I love you," he says.

She walks inside, turns at the door to wave, and blows him a kiss. She disappears inside.

His room at the Knick is on the top floor, looking north over Sixty-second Street. There is a brass bed with round knobs; at the window are long light curtains. A battered dark-stained wooden desk with one drawer stands against the wall, across from a white upholstered armchair. The room is both comforting and strange, as though he's in the guest room of someone he doesn't know.

Peter undresses quickly. He wants to be in bed, in the dark, invisible. He wants this room invisible. He is in exile: his own apartment, his own life, is right across the park. He could nearly see it from this window, if he tried. He is not welcome there.

He wonders where Emma is, after dinner with her parents. Did she go back to the apartment with them, or to the hospital? He wonders if she will think of his being here, if she will try to find him. He wonders if this is the end of his marriage.

"Emma likes you," he had told Amanda at dinner, but as he said it he wondered. Did Emma like Amanda? Had she ever? All he could remember now were the moments Emma had been unkind. Once in the car, when Emma let Tess sit on her lap, and told Amanda she was too big. Emma scolding only Amanda for something both girls had done. Emma making critical comments about things Caroline did. Emma looking at Peter, her lips pursed, when Amanda did something wrong, waiting for his response. The year they went to Aspen, and nine-year-old Amanda asked Emma to ski with her, and Emma refused, claiming that she had to stay with Tess. All Peter can remember now are moments like this: Emma punitive, cold, intolerant. Amanda had been a small child, how could Emma have treated her like this? And how could he have let this happen? How could he have let his daughter be mistreated?

It is quarter to twelve. Peter gets into bed and turns out the lights. The air conditioner in the window makes a monotonous roar. In bed, in the dark, Peter thinks back, through the years. Even at their wedding, he remembers, something had happened. Something about the flowers: Emma had not given Amanda a bouquet. Amanda had only been given a single blossom, instead of a bouquet like Tess's. It had always been there, Emma's unkindness.

With the lights off, at first the room seems blessedly dark, a refuge, the cave of sleep. Soon his eyes adjust, and Peter sees a soft glow from the street. The night outside is leaking in. Sleep is nowhere near.

But before they were married, he remembers, Emma was kind to Amanda. Wasn't she? He's certain of it, he remembers feeling grateful for Emma's kindness. What had happened? Now he wonders if she had been shamming. The thought infuriates him. He turns on the light and sits up, puts his feet on the floor.

He sits up and looks around the room in the dim light. The curtains, flanking the metal box of the air conditioner, look stifling, their limp drapery heavy and oppressive. The brass bedstead is tarnished brown, and its row of upright bars looks like a prisoner's window. On the walls are grim black-and-white engravings, nineteenth-century life in London. The wooden desk, with its scuffed blotter and one thin drawer is meager. Peter wonders if he will be here still, a month from now.

During dinner, he had asked Amanda if she would like to go somewhere for Labor Day with him. Canada, she said at once. It surprised him, Canada seems dim to him. But it is huge, vast, its dense forests crowding the northern curve of the globe, beyond them the tundra, the real North. And there is the Gallic part along the eastern coast, all that French fuss over language, culture. He'll take Amanda there if she wants. Prince Edward Island, or is that now all condos? He's read that the Japanese go there in droves. They all read *Anne of Green Gables:* surely an odd choice for a Japanese heroine, the bold red-headed girl. The Canadian coast is all being built up, he's heard. If there is global warming, everyone should buy land in Canada, along the coast. It will be the Maine of the future. Maine would be like the Eastern Shore of Maryland, Florida like the equator. All those poor old retired geezers down there trapped by the heat, unable to leave their condos. They'd be better off staying in Queens, at least their children would visit. But even without global warming, Florida has always seemed horrible to Peter, all those grim geometric high-rises, flat highways and organ centers. Alligator farms instead of museums.

He swings his legs out of bed, sets his bare feet on the dark green rug. His toes twitch restlessly. The Kirklands will be staying in his apartment, in what is called Amanda's room, but which is, he now realizes angrily, really the guest room. Emma calls it Amanda's room, but it is decorated in chintz and roses, and the bed pulls out into an uncomfortable double. Maybe Emma went home with her parents that afternoon, after he left the hospital. Maybe she spent some time doing normal things, from her old life. Putting out towels, making up the bed, thinking of Tess, wondering each moment if there were any change. Maybe she was there just after he was, maybe he had just missed her when he was there packing. What if he had run into her? He misses Emma, wants her.

The bruised face. He remembers the pupils, beginning their mysterious movement toward synchronicity like the shifting of a tide, dark water starting to turn without a sound. He feels a tiny blossom of gladness. What if he were to go up to the hospital right now? He is free to do anything, now, anything. He could put on his clothes and stand out on Fifth Avenue, hailing a slow-moving cab in the fresh night air, the city silent around him. They would let him in, at the hospital, that surly guard knows he is a member of the family. They don't know that he is only the stepfather, that he and his wife are no longer speaking. Estranged. He could go into the room and bend over the sleeping child. He could stand in the silent nighttime room and murmur to her the things he wants her to hear, the things that he had not been able to tell her today. *I love you, Tess. If you can hear me, squeeze my hand.*

Dear God, he thinks, let her get well.

His toes twist against one another. He can smell his armpits, the rich sweaty smell of himself. The air conditioner is set on high, but it seems to do nothing but pump heat into the room. Would Emma think of calling here? He misses her. He's still angry at her, but this is separate. Apart from his anger, he misses her. He wants her presence, wants her back. He wants all this not to have happened.

He remembers his last weekend at Marten's, the ferry coming into the harbor. He remembers standing with the other husbands on the deck, watching, looking for his wife. Seeing her among the other wives, looking so cool and pretty. She stood with her feet set neatly together, her curving bowlegs in white pants, her hands tucked into her pockets. She had been talking to someone, smiling. He had felt so proud of her, the way she looked, so calm, with her crisp white pants and shirt, her soft dark hair. Her narrow crinkling eyes, so warm. She saw him too, he saw her searching the faces until she found his, their eyes met. He remembers the last, final twist of relief he had felt at that moment: now I'm home, he had thought, meeting her eyes.

He had always felt that she was his partner. He had felt then it was he and Emma together who were taking on Amanda, life. At night, they slept close, connected, during the perilous journey through the darkness, one touching the other always. Sometimes Emma lay with her back tight against his stomach, setting herself deep into his enfolding curve. And when he put his arm around her and over her shoulder, tucking his hand beneath her pillow, she turned her head and kissed his arm, his hand, whatever she could reach. When he rolled over, away from her, she rolled over, toward him. She slid her foot against his ankle, his leg, whatever she could reach. Through the night he could feel her loving him. He felt her presence as love. He misses it now. He wonders where she is right now. Alone in their bed? At the hospital, curled up in the uncomfortable chair?

If she were at the hospital, if he called her there now, could they have a secret, private conversation, outside their fight? They could fight later, in the daytime. Now, he misses her. He lowers his head and sets his fists onto the sheets on either side of him. He had hoped someday they would get a dog, that had been part of his plan for the house on Marten's. He had grown up with Labs. Now he can't see how this might happen.

He looks at his small traveling clock. It's only one. How long would

Emma wait? She would never call him. He did, and she didn't, he thinks, remembering her family story, disgusted. His toes torment one another, struggling. One o'clock. He can feel the sleeplessness in his eyes. He can't imagine sleep. He wonders if Tess's eyes are drifting into rightness at night, as she sleeps, or if it's only during the day, when she's closer to waking. Is there any difference for her, between day and night? Is one part of her sleep different from another? He hates the word *coma.*

He feels suddenly that she will get well.

"She will get well," he says, out loud. His voice, in the small room, is startling. He looks around. The words stay with him. He lifts his chin, stretching his neck. He closes his eyes. But where is she? Where is Emma?

He gets up and goes into the bathroom. He has brought some of Emma's sleeping pills. In the white-tiled room, with its old porcelain fixtures, he stands by the big square sink. He takes two of the oblong pills. He drinks a full glass of New York water. This is said to be the best city water in America, but it reeks of chlorine, and he holds his breath while he drinks it.

He goes back into the bedroom. He looks at the engravings of London: carriages drawn by snake-necked horses, elegant men in top hats and tailcoats, women in long skirts and crinolines. The scene is airless and sterile. He feels he has lived here in this room for years. He is trapped in here, like the poor old geezers in their condos in Florida.

Where is she? Why does she not call him? She must know he is awake. How could she have been unkind, year after year, to his daughter? He sees Amanda's hopeful face as she entered the restaurant, her anxious gaze as she searched the tables for her father. Her eyes, so touchingly made up, the black lashes clumped together, the lids smudged. Her skin is dense and smooth, beautiful, he has never noticed that before. His daughter is lovely. And the way she walked in her high heels, there was something Minnie Mouseish about her step. Endearing. But all children are endearing, if they're yours. If they aren't, they're a nuisance. Emma finds his daughter a nuisance, though she expects him to find hers endearing.

The thought infuriates him, and he throws himself onto the bed, ramming his feet down under the sheets. He lies on his back, his hands clasped together behind his head.

Emma has always done that, he thinks severely. She's always taken for granted the fact that I loved Tess. He thinks back, he remembers the night at Marten's, when Tess came into their bed. Emma knew he opposed it, she paid no attention to him. His rules for her daughter meant nothing, but her rules for his daughter were sacred. He had heard Tess come in: Emma spoiled her. He had heard Emma lift the sheet for Tess to climb in with them. Tess was too old to come into their bed at night. Emma spoiled her and ignored him. He lies thinking of this, fuming, reciting his reasons for anger.

He had been angry the next day, too, he had let her know how he felt. Emma, though, had not responded, had not defied him. In fact she had been meek, placatory. She accepted his anger, bowing her head as though she were in disgrace. She had been in disgrace. He had left for the day without speaking to her.

He thinks now of Emma's hushed and stealthy movements, raising the sheet for Tess. He thinks of her, lying anxiously between the two loved bodies, fearful that one will erupt at the presence of the other. In fact, she did not expect anything of him then, not sympathy, not affection. She was taking nothing for granted.

He remembers the next morning, how angry he had been, how intolerant. And why had he been so angry? Why did it matter, he wonders now. Why had he been so sure that was important, keeping their bed empty of children? Why did he care, if Tess were frightened, if she came into their bed for comfort? It had been Amanda's book, he knew, that had frightened her. The thought, now, of denying Tess anything was intolerable. The thought of Tess, standing in the dark, frightened, asking to climb into bed.

The fact is he cannot remember times when Emma has taken his love of Tess for granted. She didn't expect him to love her. She has acted as though she must protect Tess from him.

Above the air conditioner in the window he can see the dim infernal glow of the New York night. In the country, looking toward the city at night, you could see a great purple radiance, as though it were a gigantic amusement park. It was never dark in New York, at night it was only darker.

Peter remembers spending a summer night out camping with his dog. He was twelve or thirteen. He had gone down in the orchard with Achilles and his sleeping bag. The night had been absolutely black, he had felt it close down on his eyelids and press against him. But his father had bet him fifty cents that he wouldn't stay out the whole night, and Peter was determined. He had ended up trying to pull Achilles entirely into the sleeping bag with him. In the morning he found his nose next to Achilles' fat black tail, with the dog stretched out toward his feet. It was early, and when he opened his eyes he saw the long grass of the orchard, the air blue with mist. Silence. The birds had not yet begun. Silence, and the freshness of orchard air in the summer dawn, and that blue light.

Peter punches his pillow. He loves Emma's daughter, but she does not love his. This is unfair. He has lived with her daughter for years, but Emma finds it hard to live with his daughter for one month at a time. Though it's true that Tess loves him, and Amanda does not love Emma, and this makes a difference.

"She'll get well," he says out loud again. This time it frightens him: what if this is bad luck, hubris? "Thank you, God," he adds.

He remembers the camping out again, the long warm spine of the dog pressed against him. As he was going to sleep that night he heard the branches overhead moving slightly, barely, in the night air. The black dog was invisible, only a warm presence, richly scented, in his arms. He wonders if the dog has ever been to Marten's Island, then realizes his mind is drifting into sleep. It's the pills, he understands, grateful for a moment, before they draw him into that other place, soft, luxurious, full of rolling darkness.

In the morning the air conditioner sounds different. It's humming a new, more plangent, note. It must be harder work, during the daytime, Peter thinks, groping into wakefulness. Now it's hotter outside. He opens his eyes onto the white ceiling. Where is Emma? When will she call? She must have thought of him being here, she must have figured it out. He thinks of calling Tess's room. There's no machine, and if Emma isn't there, no one would answer. But he doesn't want the sudden sound to disturb Tess, in this early dawn. He believes Tess is still occupied, now, absorbed. Behind the closed lids her eyes are shifting slowly. Peter looks at the clock: it's ten past six. The seventh day.

Peter lies still but his eyes are open, dry. He blinks. He has a slight headache, from the pills, but he's awake for the day. The sheets are twisted, they've tangled around his limbs like ropes. He kicks at them, freeing his feet. He squeezes his eyes shut.

Sleep is gone. He sits up decisively: he'll go running. He's brought his gear. He feels aflame with energy, restlessness.

Where is Emma? When will she call him?

He imagines the evening with her parents: Emma cold, frozen, silent, sitting through their talk, her father's self-absorbed monologue, her mother's bright comments. He knows she will feel that he has let her down, by walking out and leaving her with them. And so he has.

He no longer feels the bright pulse of anger when he thinks of Emma and Amanda. Now he feels only that Emma was wrong. As he has been. And he misses her.

He puts on his running shorts, a T-shirt, his running shoes. He jogs down the broad staircase. The great public rooms, with their tall curtained windows, are silent and shadowy as he passes. He pushes through the heavy front door and steps out into the street. He sets out straight up Fifth Avenue, running on the pavement along the park. The air is fresh against his face. The streets are nearly empty. On the sidewalk are a few other runners, on their solitary ways, pounding along the cobblestones in the early city morning. The paving stones are slick and glittery with moisture.

Peter runs straight up alongside Fifth Avenue. Twenty blocks to a mile, it's a little over a mile up to the Reservoir from here, a mile and a quarter around it, and another mile back. He usually runs four miles. This morning he feels full of suppressed energy, as though he could easily do ten. He has read that you can always run double your normal distance, if you need to. The thought is comforting to him. He can't imagine what the need would be—a natural disaster? What natural disaster would be slow enough for you to outjog it? But still he likes knowing that he has this secret reserve, the steady eight miles, ready when he needs them. To save someone's life, if that were what it took. He sees Tess's face.

The dog owners are out. Some are standing around looking furtive, obviously wearing raincoats over nightgowns or pajamas. Their faces are grim, still set in the lines of sleep, unprepared for human exchanges.

Ahead stands a white brick apartment building, among all the heavy rusticated stone ones. The early sun makes it dazzle, brilliant. Emma had told him once that Edward Hopper said the only thing that interested him was "the way sunlight hits a white wall." It's pretty good. He thinks of Hopper's desolate landscapes, the white bare walls.

He thinks of Emma, imperious, hateful: *never again*. But it no longer angers him. Now he feels compassion for her. As he runs he feels himself becoming lighter, fuller of energy. His strides lift him above the damp rounded cobblestones. He is more powerful, now, more certain of what he can do.

He turns into the park on a path at Seventy-sixth Street, following the winding pavement north. He doesn't know the paths on this side of the park. This one twists and dips, ducking beneath a heavy black stone bridge, wide, sinister, reeking of urine. He comes out on the other side, up a small hill. The lumbering Metropolitan Museum is on his right now; he snakes along behind the Temple of Dendur. Absurd, he thinks, to take up Central Park space to put a building inside the museum. Why not a whole village? Museums are for objects, not buildings. American arrogance, putting their buildings inside our museums.

He crosses the park drive behind the museum, empty, right now, peaceful and silent. To the north he can see the high bluff rising to the Reservoir. He runs along the drive; from behind, a sudden rush of taxis surges fanatically past in a tight cluster, gunning their engines like racers, and then they're gone. Now the drive is empty again, flat and silent, like a country road. The city hums, waking, outside the park, but here the air is calm, balmy, quiet.

He runs across a short wooden bridge, unpainted and oddly rustic, beneath the trees. Beyond it are concrete steps, and at the top of them is a majestic stone pumping station, standing serenely at the water's edge, the southern shore of the Reservoir. The Italianate silhouette stands guard over the stream of joggers that moves steadily past; Peter is no longer alone. He steps out onto the soft earth track among the others, legs pumping, hearts pounding, heads down, chins out, hands loosely clenched, doggedly pursuing this silent goal.

Peter moves in among them, finding himself a niche, adjusting his strides in the group. He finds himself just behind an older man, and runs politely in back of him until the track turns north again, lying parallel to Fifth. Peter makes his move, passing the man, who looks at him sideways, with an outraged glance.

At this moment Peter could pass anyone. He feels wonderfully light, filled with power. He feels he could run the Reservoir over and over, all morning. He is in an empty space among the joggers, right alongside the high mesh fence, with the calm sweep of light-filled water beyond it. A breeze moves across the surface, making a faint choppy grid. Along the shoreline is a dense forest of blue-green reeds. Among them is a pair of mallards, male and female, their colors bold, their outlines trim against the reeds. Mallards mate for life, he remembers.

Peter passes the squat Guggenheim, with its spiralling shout up toward the sky.

He will call Emma. He will not wait. He can feel his heart pounding exultantly: he is stronger than she is, it doesn't matter who makes the first move. She isn't capable of this, and he is. He doesn't hold it against her. They share their strengths, that's how it should be. He finishes the long stretch, the long east side of the Reservoir, and turns the corner along the north side, holding the sweet pale shimmering stretch of the water at his side. His heart is thundering in his chest. He loves Emma. He knows she's not capable of certain things. Why should he expect her to do everything? There were things that he couldn't do, that she could. He sees Amanda's face as it has always been in the past—sullen, closed, awful. He has forced that on Emma for years. He has insisted, he has never asked either Amanda or Emma how she felt.

He hears another runner behind him, going much faster. He pounds alongside, a lean hungry man about twenty, gulping air. He wears a headband, and a runner's gaping undershirt. He thuds on past Peter, snaking in and out among the runners, and is lost among them. On the black cindery path dark puddles appear; Peter jumps them, feeling his legs stretch and widen. He could take hurdles. He feels powerful, and kind. He wishes the twenty-year-old Godspeed. He himself is no longer lean and hungry: Peter is in his forties, and at last he is beginning to learn things. He feels grateful for that.

He passes the small stone pumping station on the north side, like a tiny castle in a European forest. He loves these fanciful park buildings, the castellated pumping stations, the wonderful Belvedere, with its stone tower and ramparts, tucked deep into the woods.

Peter turns the next corner, and begins the run along the west side of the Reservoir. He feels perilously close to his apartment, he feels the pull of its gravity. He wonders if Emma can tell he's nearby. He has a sudden image of Tess's face. He feels somehow surreptitious, as though he's deliberately hiding from Emma. But he is not: he's registered at the Knick, she could easily have thought of that. He'll call her as soon as he gets back. He'll call her at once. First he'll call the hospital, in case she went back last night, in case she's gone there early, then he'll call her at home. Even if he wakes her up. He doesn't care if he wakes her up. He especially doesn't care if he wakes up her father.

Though now, this morning, the sky turning clearer and bluer over his head, the wide water gleaming and open beside him, Peter finds himself feeling compassion even for Everett Kirkland. Trapped inside yourself, how could you get out? You might sense there was something else, something you were missing that other people had, but you could not reach it.

Everett was trapped inside his own self-regard, caged, helpless. And he loved his children, loved his wife, in his crabbed, ungenerous way. The poor beast, Peter thinks. Emma is stubborn and self-righteous too, like her father, but Peter, with this power sweeping through him, is going to take care of that. His steps pound along the cinder path, like the beating of a drum, thoughtful, steady.

Coming into the turn onto the southern edge of the Reservoir, he sees again the turreted pumping station where he started. But he's hardly winded, he can run for miles more. He doesn't want to stop here, and without thinking further he runs on past the station, making the turn again onto the eastern side, setting himself north once more. The mallards are further along now, out in the open water. The male's glossy head, greenly iridescent, dabs swiftly at something in the waves. The female, brown, subdued, one paddle behind her mate, dabs eagerly at it as well. Once you're mated you can't discard someone because she isn't perfect: she isn't. You aren't. You go on. He wonders if he could have gone on with Caroline. What if he had insisted on friendship, intimacy, a real alliance? This is the key. This is what he is going to insist on from Emma, no matter what she wanted, what she said. He sees that he has asked too much of her.

At the northern end of that side he realizes why he is there: he's going on to the hospital. At once he ducks off the soft cindery path and down the slope, running full tilt through the bushes and shrubs, his arms pinwheeling as he hurtles through the August-limp foliage. He hears his footsteps, thundering on the bare ground: he's running toward Tess.

He runs to the edge of the park, and straight up the sidewalk along Fifth. At the hospital they'll let him in, even in his running clothes. This will be his moment alone with Tess, no matter what happens later with Emma. At Ninety-sixth Street he waits at the light, jogging in place: he has more energy than he can use. His back is drenched in sweat, his legs are slick with it. He feel weightless, triumphant.

The light changes; a gang of cars rushes by. A bus lumbers past, stinking, rocking heavily down the avenue. Peter crosses the street, still going north, heading for the hospital. When he reaches its street he waits again for the light, to cross Fifth. The hospital towers over him, a concrete grid. If he counted the floors he could find Tess's room. He puts his hands on his hips, looking upward, counting. He feels sweat on his neck, running down his back, as he cranes upward. He hears his name.

Emma is on the steps of the hospital. She comes down them stiffly, her arms folded tightly. Her face looks drawn, and he feels a sudden clench of fear. What has happened? She reaches the sidewalk; the light changes and she hurries across the avenue, toward him. By the time she reaches him she's crying.

Peter steps back, away from the street and cars, and opens his arms for her. She steps into them, weeping.

Oh God, he thinks, it's happened. It's happened. He thinks of the terrible bruising inside her brain, the places he did not dare imagine, the blood seeping horribly into places that could not absorb it. The brain, the brain. He puts his arms tightly around Emma and rocks her. He pulls her further back, toward the trees, toward the park.

"I'm so glad I found you," Emma says, crying. "Where were you?"

"I was at the Knick," Peter says.

"I wanted you," Emma says, into his sweaty shirt.

He pats her back. He will not ask what has happened, he doesn't want to hear the words.

"I missed you," he says. He holds her while she cries against him.

She pulls back and looks up at him. "I thought about you all night. I have to tell you something," she says, crying. "I know I'm not a good person. I know you hoped I was, but I'm not. I'm not a good person. I know it."

Peter pushes the hair off her forehead. "You are a good person," he says.

Emma shakes her head. "I'm not." She puts her head against his chest again. "I know how I was meant to behave toward Amanda. I wanted to be that way, but I couldn't. I'm sorry."

Peter pats her back, holding her. "It's all right," he says. "It was too much for you. I asked too much from you. You did the best you could."

Emma pulls away from him. "Let's sit down," she says, looking around. "We look like something out of the movies."

A wooden bench, damp with dew, stands by the stone wall. They sit side by side on the soaking planks. Peter puts his arm around her and takes her hand. Emma begins to talk, gazing straight ahead.

"I didn't know how to do it," she says. "I did everything wrong. But she was mean to Tess. And she hated everything I said, everything I asked her to do, everything that was me. Everything I thought would be fun, she hated."

"I know she did," Peter says remorsefully. Now he remembers Emma trying. He remembers Emma singing to Amanda, reading to her, taking her on walks. Amanda sulking, shrugging her shoulders, scowling. He squeezes Emma's hand.

"But I know that's no excuse," says Emma. "I know I'm the grown-up and she's the child. I tried to be like her mother, but she was so angry," says Emma. "And I didn't love her." She looks at Peter. The sound of it is painful. "I'm so sorry, but I didn't. I know I should have, and I know you love Tess, and I felt so guilty because I didn't love Amanda. At first I was ready to, but she was so angry, and she just got more and more horrible to me. She was so hostile."

Peter squeezes her hand.

"And I could never tell you anything," Emma says. "I was always afraid to tell you. I was afraid you'd be angry. I was afraid you wouldn't love me anymore." She looks at him. Her eyes are pink and swollen, her cheeks smeared with tears. "I still am. I suppose you won't love me now. How could you? I've let you down, I've failed you so badly." She looks away again. "But I didn't know what to do. Everything I wanted to do with Tess, Amanda would ruin." She shakes her head. "I sound sorry for myself, I know. I should have been a bigger person than I am, but I'm not. It was partly because of Tess. If I hadn't had Tess I'd have concentrated on Amanda. I'd have let her have her own rules, the ones she had at home, but how could I let Amanda break all Tess's rules and make Tess keep them? Watch TV and not let Tess? How could I let Amanda eat junk food and not let Tess? How could I let Amanda be rude and sloppy and not let Tess?" Emma let out a long breath. "But I know how I should have done it. I was meant to act like a mother, and I didn't. I acted like a stepmother, the worst. I'm sorry. I just couldn't do it better. I wish I'd been able to but I couldn't, I didn't, and I'm sorry." She bows her head, gazing straight ahead.

Peter reaches up and touches her chin. He turns her head him and looks into her eyes. "Even so," he says, "I love you."

"But why?" asks Emma, starting to cry again.

"Because you're part of me," Peter says. He puts his arms around her. "Because we both made mistakes. I shouldn't have forced her on you. You didn't force Tess on me. You let me love her on my own. I'm grateful for that."

Emma says nothing. She's warm and damp in his arms. The traffic, alongside them, is growing heavier. Three buses in a row rock precariously past, blowing out clouds of exhaust.

Peter draws his head back and looks at her. He will not ask her about

Tess. He will hold that off. He will believe that Emma would have told him by now if there were bad news. "I had dinner last night with Amanda."

Emma closes her eyes and puts her hands over her ears. "Don't tell me what she said about me."

"No," says Peter. "She didn't say anything mean about you. But she wanted to go somewhere fancy, and she got all dressed up for it. She wore earrings and makeup, it was so sweet. I'd never seen her look like that, and I thought how seldom I'd taken her out alone. How little attention I pay to her alone. I was so determined to make us into a family that I wouldn't see her unless she was with you and Tess."

"Tess," says Emma.

Peter hugs her again. She still hasn't told him. It might be all right. He closes his eyes, preparing himself.

"Did you spend the night there?" he asks.

"Yes," she says, and draws away from him. "I haven't told you."

"What?" He holds his breath. This moment, before he hears, may be the last one in which he holds out hope, the last one in which he can think of Tess without pain.

"She's better," says Emma; she smiles. "This morning I was awake when it got light. It was around five-fifteen. I got up and I was standing over her bed. She twitched, her knee jerked, her foot. I took her hand, and I felt her fingers twitch. I said, 'Tess, if you can hear me, squeeze my hand.' I was so sad, I was so unhappy about you and so miserable, I just said it as a sort of mantra, something to say, like a prayer, and her fingers moved again in my hand. I thought it was just another twitch, I couldn't believe it. I waited for a moment, and then I said it again. 'If you can hear me, Tessie, squeeze my hand.' And she squeezed my hand. And I looked down at her, and she was looking up at me."

Now Emma starts to cry again, and Peter feels the rush of his own tears, feels himself open upward in gratitude, feels such a final silence inside him, of thanks, thanks, thanks, for this child's return.

THIS IS MY DAUGHTER

Set on the Upper East Side of Manhattan and in a summer retreat in New England, Roxana Robinson's second novel, *This Is My Daughter,* is the gripping, emotional story of two divorced parents trying to forge a new family. Still contending with the guilt and anger that accompanied the dissolution of their first marriages, Emma and Peter marry with the best intentions. They embark on a new life together, confident that their love and commitment will help their daughters Tess and Amanda heal after the tragedy of divorce. But the obstacles prove more challenging than either Peter or Emma had imagined. As their daughters' resentments and rebellions intensify, deceit, split loyalties, and a tragic accident threaten to tear the family apart. *This Is My Daughter* is an insightful and heartbreaking examination of the dynamics of divorce, the sorrows of childhood, the nature of familial love, and the possibility for redemption and new beginnings.

DISCUSSION QUESTIONS

1. Are Peter and Emma both justified in ending their first marriages? When Peter tells Amanda that he and Caroline are separating, he says: "It's not your fault, and it's not your mother's fault. It's no one's fault." Emma says: "When you get divorced you never feel it's your fault. . . . Everyone feels they've been driven to it." Is Emma "driven" to divorce? Is Peter? To what degree can blame be assigned to one partner when a marriage ends? Do you feel sympathy for Caroline and/or Warren? Why or why not?

2. How does Emma's relationship to her father—and her parents' relationship to each other—affect Emma's choices and influence her marriages? Everett Kirkland blames his daughter for the failure of her first marriage. "You have surrendered the right to take a moral position on things," he tells Emma. "You have broken your promise, destroyed your marriage, and deprived your child of a father." Do you find his criticism harsh and naive, or principled? Is divorce always selfish when children are involved? Is it nobler to sacrifice individual happiness to keep a family intact at all costs? Or would the emotional strain of such an arrangement be as damaging to a child as divorce?

3. Early in the novel both Amanda and Tess have nannies who help

care for them. Compare and contrast the nature of Tess's relationship with Rachel and Amanda's relationship with Maeve. How do these relationships reflect the girls' personalities and their family lives? How do they influence the girls' reactions to divorce?

4. As a young girl, Amanda feels comforted by the boundaries Maeve establishes—her "little rules about everything in life." Yet when Emma later tries to impose rules on Amanda at Marten's Island, Amanda is resentful and hostile. Why? Discuss the theme of rule-breaking throughout the book. Does the book as a whole suggest that rules are necessary, or made to be broken? Or both?

5. Amanda is portrayed as a troubled child even before Peter and Caroline separate. Why is Amanda so uncommunicative as a young girl? Are her rebellious teen years solely attributable to her parents' divorce? How do you view Amanda? Do you find her to be neglected or spoiled? Deprived or undisciplined? Victimized or abusive? How would Amanda's life have been different had Peter and Caroline stayed together? Or had Peter left, but not remarried?

6. "Children have no choice: they are at our mercy," Emma thinks to herself early in the novel. Do the events of the book support this statement? Or are Peter and Emma equally at the mercy of their children?

7. Over the years, Amanda continually thwarts Emma's attempts at closeness. Do you think Emma's efforts are sincere? Would a different approach have been more successful, or would Amanda have been implacable regardless? How would you try to get through to Amanda if you were in Emma's shoes? Compare Emma's strained relationship with her sister Francie to her difficulties with Amanda. Are there parallels between the two relationships?

8. Emma admits that she doesn't love Amanda but wishes that she could. "It was so baffling, being a stepmother, so difficult to figure out," Emma thinks. Discuss the proper role of a stepparent. Should a stepparent be a friend? A disciplinarian? A parent? All three? Does the role depend upon each child's age and temperament? Do you think it is harder to be a stepmother than a stepfather? Does the book portray stepparenting as a no-win situation? After reading this novel, would you argue that it is better for a child to be raised by a single parent or by a parent and stepparent?

9. Ironically, Tess displays the most tolerance for Amanda, despite her stepsister's cruelty and indifference toward her. On numerous occasions, Tess defends Amanda and tries to befriend her. Why does Tess have sympathy for Amanda? Why isn't she more threatened by Amanda? Why does Tess have an easier time adjusting to the remarriage?

10. In Tess's hospital room after the car accident, Peter walks in on Emma and Warren in an embrace. Emma then harshly rebukes

Peter when he touches Tess. "The complicity was gone, Peter and Emma were no longer allies," Robinson writes. What major themes of the book does this scene illustrate? How did you feel about Emma's rejection of Peter after the accident? Did you think it was fair or unfair, or simply inevitable? For which character did you feel the most sympathy after the accident? Before the accident?

11. The book ends on a hopeful note. Amanda reaches out to her father, Tess shows signs of recovery, and Peter and Emma renew their commitment to one another. To what degree does the accident serve as a catalyst for growth and communication? Do you think the accident—though tragic—strengthens Peter and Emma's marriage? Do you think reconciliation would have been possible had Tess died in the accident? If Amanda, rather than Tess, had been gravely injured, how would Peter and Emma have reacted?

12. What kind of relationship do you think Emma will have with Amanda ten years after the book ends? How do you predict their relationship will evolve? When Tess emerges from her coma and understands what has happened, how do you think she will respond to Amanda? Do you think Peter and Emma's marriage will last? Why or why not?

ABOUT THE AUTHOR

ROXANA BARRY ROBINSON *is the author of the novel* Summer Light, *the biography* Georgia O'Keeffe: A Life, *and the short-story collections* A Glimpse of Scarlet *and* Asking for Love. *Her writing has appeared in* The Atlantic Monthly, Harper's, The New Yorker, *and* Vogue, *as well as in* Best American Short Stories, *and has been read on National Public Radio. Three of her books have been selected as* New York Times *Notable Books of the Year. She is the recipient of a Creative Writing Fellowship from the National Endowment for the Arts. She lives in Westchester County and New York City.*